LIMITS AND RENEWALS

Also available in Papermac

LIMITS
AND
RENEWALS

BY

RUDYARD KIPLING

PAPERMAC

ISBN 0 333 52201 X

MACMILLAN LONDON LIMITED
London and Basingstoke

Associated companies in Auckland, Delhi, Dublin, Gaborone,
Hamburg, Harare, Hong Kong, Johannesburg, Kuala Lumpur,
Lagos, Manzini, Melbourne, Mexico City, Nairobi, New York,
Singapore and Tokyo

First edition 1932
Uniform edition 1932
Pocket edition 1932
Sussex edition 1937
Edition de Luxe 1938
Bombay edition 1938
Library edition 1949
Centenary edition 1968
Centenary edition (n.s.) 1982
Paperback edition 1983

Papermac edition 1990

Printed in Hong Kong

CONTENTS

Dayspring Mishandled

Dayspring Mishandled

C'est moi, c'est moi, c'est moi !
  Je suis la Mandragore !
La fille des beaux jours qui s'éveille à l'aurore—
  Et qui chante pour toi !

C. Nodier.

In the days beyond compare and before the Judgments, a genius called Graydon foresaw that the advance of education and the standard of living would submerge all mind-marks in one mudrush of standardised reading-matter, and so created the Fictional Supply Syndicate to meet the demand.

Since a few days' work for him brought them more money than a week's elsewhere, he drew many young men—some now eminent—into his employ. He bade them keep their eyes on the Sixpenny Dream Book, the Army and Navy Stores Catalogue (this for backgrounds and furniture as they changed), and *The Hearthstone Friend*, a weekly publication which specialised unrivalledly in the domestic emotions. Yet, even so, youth would not be denied, and some of the collaborated love-talk in 'Passion Hath Peril,' and ' Ena's Lost Lovers,' and the account of the murder of the Earl in ' The Wickwire Tragedies ' —to name but a few masterpieces now never mentioned for fear of blackmail—was as good as anything to which their authors signed their real names in more distinguished years.

Among the young ravens driven to roost awhile on Graydon's ark was James Andrew Manallace —a darkish, slow northerner of the type that does not ignite, but must be detonated. Given written or verbal outlines of a plot, he was useless; but, with a half-dozen pictures round which to write his tale, he could astonish.

And he adored that woman who afterwards became the mother of Vidal Benzaquen,[1] and who suffered and died because she loved one unworthy. There was, also, among the company a mannered, bellied person called Alured Castorley, who talked and wrote about ' Bohemia,' but was always afraid of being ' compromised ' by the weekly suppers at Neminaka's Café in Hestern Square, where the Syndicate work was apportioned, and where everyone looked out for himself. He, too, for a time, had loved Vidal's mother, in his own way.

Now, one Saturday at Neminaka's, Graydon, who had given Manallace a sheaf of prints—torn from an extinct children's book called *Philippa's Queen*—on which to improvise, asked for results. Manallace went down into his ulster-pocket, hesitated a moment, and said the stuff had turned into poetry on his hands.

' Bosh ! '

' That's what it isn't,' the boy retorted. ' It's rather good.'

---

[1] ' The Village that voted the Earth was Flat.' *A Diversity of Creatures.*

'Then it's no use to us.' Graydon laughed. 'Have you brought back the cuts?'

Manallace handed them over. There was a castle in the series; a knight or so in armour; an old lady in a horned head-dress; a young ditto; a very obvious Hebrew; a clerk, with pen and inkhorn, checking wine-barrels on a wharf; and a Crusader. On the back of one of the prints was a note, 'If he doesn't want to go, why can't he be captured and held to ransom?' Graydon asked what it all meant.

'I don't know yet. A comic opera, perhaps,' said Manallace.

Graydon, who seldom wasted time, passed the cuts on to someone else, and advanced Manallace a couple of sovereigns to carry on with, as usual; at which Castorley was angry and would have said something unpleasant but was suppressed. Half-way through supper, Castorley told the company that a relative had died and left him an independence; and that he now withdrew from 'hackwork' to follow 'Literature.' Generally, the Syndicate rejoiced in a comrade's good fortune, but Castorley had gifts of waking dislike. So the news was received with a vote of thanks, and he went out before the end, and, it was said, proposed to 'Dal Benzaquen's mother, who refused him. He did not come back. Manallace, who had arrived a little exalted, got so drunk before midnight that a man had to stay and see him home. But liquor never touched him above the belt, and when he had slept awhile, he recited to the gas-chandelier the poetry he had made out of the pictures; said that, on second thoughts, he would convert it into comic opera; deplored the Upas-tree influence of Gilbert and Sullivan; sang somewhat to illustrate his point; and—after words, by the way, with a negress in yellow satin—was steered to his rooms.

In the course of a few years, Graydon's foresight and genius were rewarded. The public began to read and reason upon higher planes, and the Syndicate grew rich. Later still, people demanded of their printed matter what they expected in their clothing and furniture. So, precisely as the three guinea hand-bag is followed in three weeks by its thirteen and sevenpence ha'penny, indistinguishable sister, they enjoyed perfect synthetic substitutes for Plot, Sentiment, and Emotion. Graydon died before the Cinema-caption school came in, but he left his widow twenty-seven thousand pounds.

Manallace made a reputation, and, more important, money for Vidal's mother when her husband ran away and the first symptoms of her paralysis showed. His line was the jocundly-sentimental Wardour Street brand of adventure, told in a style that exactly met, but never exceeded, every expectation.

As he once said when urged to 'write a real book': 'I've got my label, and I'm not going to chew it off. If you save people thinking, you can do anything with 'em.' His output apart, he was genuinely a man of letters. He rented a small cottage in the country and economised on everything, except the care and charges of Vidal's mother.

Castorley flew higher. When his legacy freed him from 'hackwork,' he became first a critic—in which calling he loyally scalped all his old associates as they came up—and then looked for some speciality. Having found it (Chaucer was the prey), he consolidated his position before he occupied it, by his careful speech, his cultivated bearing, and the whispered words of his friends whom he, too, had saved the trouble of thinking. It followed that, when he published his first serious articles on Chaucer, all the world which is interested in Chaucer said: 'This is an authority.' But he was no impostor. He learned and knew his poet and his age; and in a month-long dog-fight in an austere literary weekly, met and mangled a recognised Chaucer expert of the day. He also, 'for old sake's sake,' as he wrote to a friend, went out of his way to review one of Manallace's books with an intimacy of unclean deduction (this was before the days of Freud) which long stood as a record. Some member of the extinct Syndicate took occasion to ask him if he would—for old sake's sake—help Vidal's mother to a new treatment. He answered that he had 'known the lady very slightly and the calls on his purse were so heavy that,' etc. The writer showed the letter to Manallace, who said he was glad Castorley hadn't interfered. Vidal's mother was then wholly paralysed. Only her eyes could move, and those always looked for the husband who had left her. She died thus in Manallace's arms in April of the first year of the War.

During the War he and Castorley worked

as some sort of departmental dishwashers in the Office of Co-ordinated Supervisals. Here Manallace came to know Castorley again. Castorley, having a sweet tooth, cadged lumps of sugar for his tea from a typist, and when she took to giving them to a younger man, arranged that she should be reported for smoking in unauthorised apartments. Manallace possessed himself of every detail of the affair, as compensation for the review of his book. Then there came a night when, waiting for a big air-raid, the two men had talked humanly, and Manallace spoke of Vidal's mother. Castorley said something in reply, and from that hour—as was learned several years later—Manallace's real life-work and interests began.

The War over, Castorley set about to make himself Supreme Pontiff on Chaucer by methods not far removed from the employment of poison-gas. The English Pope was silent, through private griefs, and influenza had carried off the learned Hun who claimed continental allegiance. Thus Castorley crowed unchallenged from Upsala to Seville, while Manallace went back to his cottage with the photo of Vidal's mother over the mantel-piece. She seemed to have emptied out his life, and left him only fleeting interests in trifles. His private diversions were experiments of uncertain outcome, which, he said, rested him after a day's gadzooking and vitalstapping. I found him, for instance, one week-end, in his toolshed-scullery, boiling a brew of slimy barks which were, if mixed with oak-galls, vitriol and wine, to become an

ink-powder.   We boiled it till the Monday, and
it turned into an adhesive stronger than birdlime,
and entangled us both.

At other times, he would carry me off, once
in a few weeks, to sit at Castorley's feet, and hear
him talk about Chaucer.   Castorley's voice, bad
enough in youth, when it could be shouted down,
had, with culture and tact, grown almost insup-
portable.   His mannerisms, too, had multiplied
and set.   He minced and mouthed, postured and
chewed his words throughout those terrible
evenings ; and poisoned not only Chaucer, but
every shred of English literature which he used to
embellish him.   He was shameless, too, as regarded self-advertisement and ' recognition '—
weaving elaborate intrigues ; forming petty friend-
ships and confederacies, to be dissolved next week
in favour of more promising alliances ; fawning,
snubbing, lecturing, organising and lying as un-
restingly as a politician, in chase of the Knighthood due not to him (he always called on his
Maker to forbid such a thought) but as tribute
to Chaucer.   Yet, sometimes, he could break
from his obsession and prove how a man's work
will try to save the soul of him.   He would tell
us charmingly of copyists of the fifteenth century
in England and the Low Countries, who had
multiplied the Chaucer MSS., of which there
remained—he gave us the exact number—and
how each scribe could by him (and, he implied,
by him alone) be distinguished from every other
by some peculiarity of letter-formation, spacing
or like trick of pen-work; and how he could fix

the dates of their work within five years.   Sometimes he would give us an hour of really interesting stuff and then return to his overdue 'recognition.' The changes sickened me, but Manallace defended him, as a master in his own line who had revealed Chaucer to at least one grateful soul.

This, as far as I remembered, was the autumn when Manallace holidayed in the Shetlands or the Faroes, and came back with a stone 'quern'— a hand corn-grinder.   He said it interested him from the ethnological standpoint.   His whim lasted till next harvest, and was followed by a religious spasm which, naturally, translated itself into literature.   He showed me a battered and mutilated Vulgate of 1485, patched up the back with bits of legal parchments, which he had bought for thirty-five shillings.   Some monk's attempt to rubricate chapter-initials had caught, it seemed, his forlorn fancy, and he dabbled in shells of gold and silver paint for weeks.

That also faded out, and he went to the Continent to get local colour for a love-story, about Alva and the Dutch, and the next year I saw practically nothing of him.   This released me from seeing much of Castorley, but, at intervals, I would go there to dine with him, when his wife— an unappetising, ash-coloured woman—made no secret that his friends wearied her almost as much as he did.   But at a later meeting, not long after Manallace had finished his Low Countries' novel, I found Castorley charged to bursting-point with triumph and high information hardly withheld. He confided to me that a time was at hand when great matters would be made plain, and 'recognition' would be inevitable. I assumed, naturally, that there was fresh scandal or heresy afoot in Chaucer circles, and kept my curiosity within bounds.

In time, New York cabled that a fragment of a hitherto unknown Canterbury Tale lay safe in the steel-walled vaults of the seven-million-dollar Sunnapia Collection. It was news on an international scale—the New World exultant—the Old deploring the 'burden of British taxation which drove such treasures, etc.,' and the lighter-minded journals disporting themselves according to their publics; for 'our Dan,' as one earnest Sunday editor observed, 'lies closer to the national heart than we wot of.' Common decency made me call on Castorley, who, to my surprise, had not yet descended into the arena. I found him, made young again by joy, deep in just-passed proofs.

Yes, he said, it was all true. He had, of course, been in it from the first. There had been found one hundred and seven new lines of Chaucer tacked on to an abridged end of *The Persone's Tale*, the whole the work of Abraham Mentzius, better known as Mentzel of Antwerp (1388–1438/9)—I might remember he had talked about him—whose distinguishing peculiarities were a certain Byzantine formation of his *g*'s, the use of a 'sickle-slanted' reed-pen, which cut into the vellum at certain letters; and, above all, a tendency to spell English words on Dutch lines, whereof the manuscript carried one convincing proof.

For instance (he wrote it out for me), a girl praying against an undesired marriage, says :—

> 'Ah Jesu-Moder, pitie my oe peyne.
> Daiespringe mishandeelt cometh nat agayne.'

Would I, please, note the spelling of ' mis-handeelt '? Stark Dutch and Mentzel's besetting sin! But in *his* position one took nothing for granted. The page had been part of the stiffen-ing of the side of an old Bible, bought in a parcel by Dredd, the big dealer, because it had some rubricated chapter-initials, and by Dredd shipped, with a consignment of similar odds and ends, to the Sunnapia Collection, where they were making a glass-cased exhibit of the whole history of illumination and did not care how many books they gutted for that purpose. There, someone who noticed a crack in the back of the volume had unearthed it. He went on : ' They didn't know what to make of the thing at first. But they knew about *me* ! They kept quiet till I'd been consulted. You might have noticed I was out of England for three months.

' I was over there, of course. It was what is called a " spoil "—a page Mentzel had spoiled with his Dutch spelling—I expect he had had the English dictated to him—then had evidently used the vellum for trying out his reeds ; and then, I suppose, had put it away. The " spoil " had been doubled, pasted together, and slipped in as stiffen-ing to the old book-cover. I had it steamed open, and analysed the wash. It gave the flour-grains in the paste—coarse, because of the old millstone

—and there were traces of the grit itself. What? Oh, possibly a handmill of Mentzel's own time. He may have doubled the spoilt page and used it for part of a pad to steady wood-cuts on. It may have knocked about his workshop for years. That, indeed, is practically certain because a beginner from the Low Countries has tried his reed on a few lines of some monkish hymn—not a bad lilt tho'—which must have been common form. Oh yes, the page may have been used in other books before it was used for the Vulgate. That doesn't matter, but *this* does. Listen! I took a wash, for analysis, from a blot in one corner—that would be after Mentzel had given up trying to make a possible page of it, and had grown careless—and I got the actual *ink* of the period! It's a practically eternal stuff compounded on—I've forgotten his name for the minute—the scribe at Bury St. Edmunds, of course—hawthorn bark and wine. Anyhow, on *his* formula. *That* wouldn't interest you either, but, taken with all the other testimony, it clinches the thing. (You'll see it all in my Statement to the Press on Monday.) Overwhelming, isn't it?'

' Overwhelming,' I said, with sincerity. ' Tell me what the tale was about, though. That's more in my line.'

' I know it; but *I* have to be equipped on all sides. The verses are relatively easy for one to pronounce on. The freshness, the fun, the humanity, the fragrance of it all, cries—no, shouts —itself as Dan's work. Why " Daiespringe mishandled " alone stamps it from Dan's mint.

Plangent as doom, my dear boy—plangent as doom! It's all in my Statement. Well, substantially, the fragment deals with a girl whose parents wish her to marry an elderly suitor. The mother isn't so keen on it, but the father, an old Knight, is. The girl, of course, is in love with a younger and a poorer man. Common form? Granted. Then the father, who doesn't in the least want to, is ordered off to a Crusade and, by way of passing on the kick, as we used to say during the War, orders the girl to be kept in duresse till his return or her consent to the old suitor. Common form, again? Quite so. That's too much for her mother. She reminds the old Knight of his age and infirmities, and the discomforts of Crusading. Are you sure I'm not boring you?'

'Not at all,' I said, though time had begun to whirl backward through my brain to a red-velvet, pomatum-scented side-room at Neminaka's and Manallace's set face intoning to the gas.

'You'll read it all in my Statement next week. The sum is that the old lady tells him of a certain Knight-adventurer on the French coast, who, for a consideration, waylays Knights who don't relish crusading and holds them to impossible ransoms till the trooping-season is over, or they are returned sick. He keeps a ship in the Channel to pick 'em up and transfers his birds to his castle ashore, where he has a reputation for doing 'em well. As the old lady points out:

> 'And if perchance thou fall into his honde
> By God how canstow ride to Holilonde?'

'You see? Modern in essence as Gilbert and Sullivan, but handled as only Dan could! And she reminds him that " Honour and olde bones " parted company long ago. He makes one splendid appeal for the spirit of chivalry:

> Lat all men change as Fortune may send,
> But Knighthood beareth service to the end,

and *then*, of course, he gives in:

> For what his woman willeth to be don
> Her manne must or wauken Hell anon.

'Then she hints that the daughter's young lover, who is in the Bordeaux wine-trade, could open negotiations for a kidnapping without compromising him. And *then* that careless brute Mentzel spoils his page and chucks it! But there's enough to show what's going to happen. You'll see it all in my Statement. Was there ever anything in literary finds to hold a candle to it? ... And they give grocers Knighthoods for selling cheese!'

I went away before he could get into his stride on that course. I wanted to think, and to see Manallace. But I waited till Castorley's Statement came out. He had left himself no loophole. And when, a little later, his (nominally the Sunnapia people's) 'scientific' account of their analyses and tests appeared, criticism ceased, and some journals began to demand 'public recognition.' Manallace wrote me on this subject, and I went down to his cottage, where he at once asked me to sign a Memorial on Castorley's behalf. With luck, he said, we might get him a K.B.E. in the next Honours List.   Had I read the Statement?

' I have,' I replied.   ' But I want to ask you something first.   Do you remember the night you got drunk at Neminaka's, and I stayed behind to look after you? '

' Oh, *that* time,' said he, pondering.   ' Wait a minute! I remember Graydon advancing me two quid.   He was a generous paymaster.   And I remember—now, who the devil rolled me under the sofa—and what for? '

' We all did,' I replied.   ' You wanted to read us what you'd written to those Chaucer cuts.'

' I don't remember that.   No!   I don't remember anything after the sofa-episode. . . . *You* always said that you took me home—didn't you? '

' I did, and you told Kentucky Kate outside the old Empire that you had been faithful, Cynara, in your fashion.'

' Did I? ' said he.   ' My God!   Well, I suppose I have.'   He stared into the fire.   ' What else? '

' Before we left Neminaka's you recited me what you had made out of the cuts—the whole tale!   So—you see? '

' Ye-es.'   He nodded.   ' What are you going to do about it? '

' What are *you*? '

' I'm going to help him get his Knighthood—first.'

' Why? '

' I'll tell you what he said about 'Dal's mother —the night there was that air-raid on the offices.'

He told it.

' That's why,' he said. ' Am I justified? '

He seemed to me entirely so.

' But after he gets his Knighthood? ' I went on.

' That depends. There are several things I can think of. It interests me.'

' Good Heavens! I've always imagined you a man without interests.'

' So I was. I owe my interests to Castorley. He gave me every one of 'em except the tale itself.'

' How did *that* come? '

' Something in those ghastly cuts touched off something in me—a sort of possession, I suppose. I was in love too. No wonder I got drunk that night. I'd *been* Chaucer for a week! Then I thought the notion might make a comic opera. But Gilbert and Sullivan were too strong.'

' So I remember you told me at the time.'

' I kept it by me, and it made me interested in Chaucer—philologically and so on. I worked on it on those lines for years. There wasn't a flaw in the wording even in '14. I hardly had to touch it after that.'

' Did you ever tell it to anyone except me? '

' No, only 'Dal's mother—when she could listen to anything—to put her to sleep. But when Castorley said—what he did about her, I thought I might use it. 'Twasn't difficult. *He* taught me. D'you remember my birdlime experiments, and the stuff on our hands? I'd been trying to get that ink for more than a year. Castorley told me where I'd find the formula. And your falling over the quern, too? '

'That accounted for the stone-dust under the microscope?'

'Yes. I grew the wheat in the garden here, and ground it myself. Castorley gave me Mentzel complete. He put me on to an MS. in the British Museum which he said was the finest sample of his work. I copied his "Byzantine *g*'s" for months.'

'And what's a "sickle-slanted" pen?' I asked.

'You nick one edge of your reed till it drags and scratches on the curves of the letters. Castorley told me about Mentzel's spacing and margining. I only had to get the hang of his script.'

'How long did that take you?'

'On and off—some years. I was too ambitious at first—I wanted to give the whole poem. That would have been risky. Then Castorley told me about spoiled pages and I took the hint. I spelt "Dayspring mishandeelt" Mentzel's way—to make sure of him. It's not a bad couplet in itself. Did you see how he admires the "plangency" of it?'

'Never mind him. Go on!' I said.

He did. Castorley had been his unfailing guide throughout, specifying in minutest detail every trap to be set later for his own feet. The actual vellum was an Antwerp find, and its introduction into the cover of the Vulgate was begun after a long course of amateur bookbinding. At last, he bedded it under pieces of an old deed, and a printed page (1686) of Horace's *Odes*, legitimately used for repairs by different owners in the seventeenth and eighteenth centuries; and at the

last moment, to meet Castorley's theory that
spoiled pages were used in workshops by beginners,
he had written a few Latin words in fifteenth century script—the Statement gave the exact date—
across an open part of the fragment.   The thing
ran : ' *Illa alma Mater ecca, secum afferens me
acceptum. Nicolaus Atrib.*'   The disposal of the
thing was easiest of all.   He had merely hung
about Dredd's dark bookshop of fifteen rooms,
where he was well known, occasionally buying
but generally browsing, till, one day, Dredd Senior
showed him a case of cheap black-letter stuff,
English and Continental—being packed for the
Sunnapia people—into which Manallace tucked
his contribution, taking care to wrench the back
enough to give a lead to an earnest seeker.

' And then ? ' I demanded.

' After six months or so Castorley sent for me.
Sunnapia had found it, and as Dredd had missed it,
and there was no money-motive sticking out, they
were half convinced it was genuine from the start.
But they invited him over.   He conferred with their
experts, and suggested the scientific tests.   *I* put
that into his head, before he sailed.   That's all.
And now, will you sign our Memorial ? '

I signed.   Before we had finished hawking it
round there was a host of influential names to help
us, as well as the impetus of all the literary discussion which arose over every detail of the glorious
trove.   The upshot was a K.B.E.[1] for Castorley

---

[1] Officially it was on account of his good work in the Departmental of Co-ordinated Supervisals, but all true lovers of literature
knew the real reason, and told the papers so.

in the next Honours List; and Lady Castorley, her cards duly printed, called on friends that same afternoon.

Manallace invited me to come with him, a day or so later, to convey our pleasure and satisfaction to them both. We were rewarded by the sight of a man relaxed and ungirt—not to say wallowing naked—on the crest of Success. He assured us that ' The Title ' should not make any difference to our future relations, seeing it was in no sense personal, but, as he had often said, a tribute to Chaucer; ' and, after all,' he pointed out, with a glance at the mirror over the mantelpiece, ' Chaucer was the prototype of the " veray parfit gentil Knight " of the British Empire so far as that then existed.'

On the way back, Manallace told me he was considering either an unheralded revelation in the baser Press which should bring Castorley's reputation about his own ears some breakfast-time, or a private conversation, when he would make clear to Castorley that he must now back the forgery as long as he lived, under threat of Manallace's betraying it if he flinched.

He favoured the second plan. ' If I pull the string of the shower-bath in the papers,' he said, ' Castorley might go off his veray parfit gentil nut. I want to keep his intellect.'

' What about your own position ? The forgery doesn't matter so much. But if you tell this you'll kill him,' I said.

' I intend that. Oh—my position ? I've been dead since—April, Fourteen, it was. But there's

no hurry. What was it *she* was saying to you just
as we left? '

' She told me how much your sympathy and
understanding had meant to him. She said she
thought that even Sir Alured did not realise the
full extent of his obligations to you.'

' She's right, but I don't like her putting it
that way.'

' It's only common form—as Castorley's always saying.'

' Not with *her*. She can hear a man think.'

' She never struck me in that light.'

' *You* aren't playing against her.'

' 'Guilty conscience, Manallace? '

' H'm! I wonder. Mine or hers? I *wish* she
hadn't said that. " More even than *he* realises
it." I won't call again for awhile.'

He kept away till we read that Sir Alured,
owing to slight indisposition, had been unable to
attend a dinner given in his honour.

Inquiries brought word that it was but natural
reaction, after strain, which, for the moment, took
the form of nervous dyspepsia, and he would be
glad to see Manallace at any time. Manallace
reported him as rather pulled and drawn, but full
of his new life and position, and proud that his
efforts should have martyred him so much. He
was going to collect, collate, and expand all his
pronouncements and inferences into one authoritative volume.

' I must make an effort of my own,' said Manallace. ' I've collected nearly all his stuff about
the Find that has appeared in the papers, and

he's promised me everything that's missing. I'm going to help him. It will be a new interest.'

' How will you treat it?' I asked.

' I expect I shall quote his deductions on the evidence, and parallel 'em with my experiments—the ink and the paste and the rest of it. It ought to be rather interesting.'

' But even then there will only be your word. It's hard to catch up with an established lie,' I said. ' Especially when you've started it yourself.'

He laughed. ' I've arranged for *that*—in case anything happens to me. Do you remember the " Monkish Hymn "?'

' Oh yes! There's quite a literature about it already.'

' Well, you write those ten words above each other, and read down the first and second letters of 'em; and see what you get.'[1] My Bank has the formula.'

He wrapped himself lovingly and leisurely round his new task, and Castorley was as good as his word in giving him help. The two practically collaborated, for Manallace suggested that all Castorley's strictly scientific evidence should

[1] *Illa
alma
Mater
ecca
secum
afferens
me
acceptum
Nicolaus
Atrib.*

be in one place, with his deductions and dithy-
rambs as appendices. He assured him that the
public would prefer this arrangement, and, after
grave consideration, Castorley agreed.

' That's better,' said Manallace to me. ' Now
I sha'n't have so many hiatuses in my extracts.
Dots always give the reader the idea you aren't
dealing fairly with your man. I shall merely
quote him solid, and rip him up, proof for proof,
and date for date, in parallel columns. His book's
taking more out of him than I like, though. He's
been doubled up twice with tummy attacks since
I've worked with him. And he's just the sort
of flatulent beast who may go down with ap-
pendicitis.'

We learned before long that the attacks were
due to gall-stones, which would necessitate an
operation. Castorley bore the blow very well.
He had full confidence in his surgeon, an old
friend of theirs ; great faith in his own constitu-
tion ; a strong conviction that nothing would
happen to him till the book was finished, and,
above all, the Will to Live.

He dwelt on these assets with a voice at times
a little out of pitch and eyes brighter than usual
beside a slightly-sharpening nose.

I had only met Gleeag, the surgeon, once or
twice at Castorley's house, but had always heard
him spoken of as a most capable man. He told
Castorley that his trouble was the price exacted,
in some shape or other, from all who had served
their country ; and that, measured in units of
strain, Castorley had practically been at the front

through those three years he had served in the
Office of Co-ordinated Supervisals. However,
the thing had been taken betimes, and in a few
weeks he would worry no more about it.

'But suppose he dies?' I suggested to Manallace.

'He won't. I've been talking to Gleeag. He
says he's all right.'

'Wouldn't Gleeag's talk be common form?'

'I *wish* you hadn't said that. But, surely,
Gleeag wouldn't have the face to play with me—
or her.'

'Why not? I expect it's been done before.'

But Manallace insisted that, in this case, it
would be impossible.

The operation was a success and, some weeks
later, Castorley began to recast the arrangement
and most of the material of his book. 'Let me
have my way,' he said, when Manallace protested.
'They are making too much of a baby of me. I
really don't need Gleeag looking in every day
now.' But Lady Castorley told us that he required careful watching. His heart had felt the
strain, and fret or disappointment of any kind
must be avoided. 'Even,' she turned to Manallace, 'though you know ever so much better how
his book should be arranged than he does himself.'

'But really,' Manallace began. 'I'm very
careful not to fuss——'

She shook her finger at him playfully. 'You
don't think you do; but, remember, he tells me
everything that you tell him, just the same as he

told me everything that he used to tell *you*. Oh,
I don't mean the things that men talk about. I
mean about his Chaucer.'

' I didn't realise that,' said Manallace, weakly.

' I thought you didn't. He never spares me
anything; but *I* don't mind,' she replied with a
laugh, and went off to Gleeag, who was paying his
daily visit. Gleeag said he had no objection to
Manallace working with Castorley on the book for
a given time—say, twice a week—but supported
Lady Castorley's demand that he should not be
over-taxed in what she called ' the sacred hours.'
The man grew more and more difficult to work
with, and the little check he had heretofore set on
his self-praise went altogether.

' He says there has never been anything in the
History of Letters to compare with it,' Manallace
groaned. ' He wants now to inscribe—he never
dedicates, you know—inscribe it to me, as his
" most valued assistant." The devil of it is that
she backs him up in getting it out soon. Why?
How much do you think she knows?'

' Why should she know anything at all?'

' You heard her say he had told her everything
that he had told me about Chaucer? (I *wish* she
hadn't said that!) If she puts two and two together, she can't help seeing that every one of his
notions and theories has been played up to. But
then—but then . . . Why is she trying to hurry
publication? She talks about me fretting him.
She's at him, all the time, to be quick.'

Castorley must have over-worked, for, after a
couple of months, he complained of a stitch in his

right side, which Gleeag said was a slight sequel, a little incident of the operation. It threw him back awhile, but he returned to his work undefeated.

The book was due in the autumn. Summer was passing, and his publisher urgent, and—he said to me, when after a longish interval I called—Manallace had chosen this time, of all, to take a holiday. He was not pleased with Manallace, once his indefatigable *aide*, but now dilatory, and full of time-wasting objections. Lady Castorley had noticed it, too.

Meantime, with Lady Castorley's help, he himself was doing the best he could to expedite the book; but Manallace had mislaid (did I think through jealousy?) some essential stuff which had been dictated to him. And Lady Castorley wrote Manallace, who had been delayed by a slight motor accident abroad, that the fret of waiting was prejudicial to her husband's health. Manallace, on his return from the Continent, showed me that letter.

'He has fretted a little, I believe,' I said.

Manallace shuddered. 'If I stay abroad, I'm helping to kill him. If I help him to hurry up the book, I'm expected to kill him. *She* knows,' he said.

'You're mad. You've got this thing on the brain.'

'I have not! Look here! You remember that Gleeag gave me from four to six, twice a week, to work with him. She called them the " sacred hours." You heard her? Well, they *are*! They are Gleeag's and hers. But she's so infernally plain, and I'm such a fool, it took me weeks to find it out.'

'That's their affair,' I answered. 'It doesn't prove she knows anything about the Chaucer.'

'She *does*! He told her everything that he had told me when I was pumping him, all those years. She put two and two together when the thing came out. She saw exactly how I had set my traps. I know it! She's been trying to make me admit it.'

'What did you do?'

''Didn't understand what she was driving at, of course. And then she asked Gleeag, before me, if he didn't think the delay over the book was fretting Sir Alured. He didn't think so. He said getting it out might deprive him of an interest. He had that much decency. *She's* the devil!'

'What do you suppose is her game, then?'

'If Castorley knows he's been had, it'll kill him. She's at me all the time, indirectly, to let it out. I've told you she wants to make it a sort of joke between us. Gleeag's willing to wait. He knows Castorley's a dead man. It slips out when they talk. They say "He was," not "He is." Both of 'em know it. But *she* wants him finished sooner.'

'I don't believe it. What are you going to do?'

'What can I? I'm not going to have him killed, though.'

Manlike, he invented compromises whereby Castorley might be lured up by-paths of interest, to delay publication. This was not a success. As autumn advanced Castorley fretted more, and suffered from returns of his distressing colics. At last, Gleeag told him that he thought they might be due to an overlooked gallstone working down. A second comparatively trivial operation would eliminate the bother once and for all. If Castorley cared for another opinion, Gleeag named a surgeon of eminence. 'And then,' said he, cheerily, 'the two of us can talk you over.' Castorley did not want to be talked over. He was oppressed by pains in his side, which, at first, had yielded to the liver-tonics Gleeag prescribed; but now they stayed—like a toothache—behind everything. He felt most at ease in his bedroom-study, with his proofs round him. If he had more pain than he could stand, he would consider the second operation. Meantime Manallace—'the meticulous Manallace,' he called him—agreed with him in thinking that the Mentzel page-facsimile, done by the Sunnapia Library, was not quite good enough for the great book, and the Sunnapia people were, very decently, having it re-processed. This would hold things back till early spring, which had its advantages, for he could run a fresh eye over all in the interval.

One gathered these news in the course of stray visits as the days shortened. He insisted on Manallace keeping to the 'sacred hours,' and Manallace insisted on my accompanying him when possible. On these occasions he and Castorley would confer apart for half an hour or so, while I listened to an unendurable clock in the drawing-room. Then I would join them and help wear out the rest of the time, while Castorley rambled. His speech, now, was often clouded and uncertain—the result of the 'liver-tonics'; and his face came to look like old vellum.

It was a few days after Christmas—the operation had been postponed till the following Friday—that we called together. She met us with word that Sir Alured had picked up an irritating little winter cough, due to a cold wave, but we were not, therefore, to abridge our visit. We found him in steam perfumed with Friar's Balsam. He waved the old Sunnapia facsimile at us. We agreed that it ought to have been more worthy. He took a dose of his mixture, lay back and asked us to lock the door. There was, he whispered, something wrong somewhere. He could not lay his finger on it, but it was in the air. He felt he was being played with. He did not like it. There was something wrong all round him. Had we noticed it? Manallace and I severally and slowly denied that we had noticed anything of the sort.

With no longer break than a light fit of coughing, he fell into the hideous, helpless panic of the sick—those worse than captives who lie at the judgment and mercy of the hale for every office and hope. He wanted to go away. Would we help him to pack his Gladstone? Or, if that would attract too much attention in certain quarters, help him to dress and go out? There was an urgent matter to be set right, and now that he had The Title and knew his own mind it would all end happily and he would be well again. *Please* would we let him go out, just to

speak to—he named her; he named her by her
'little' name out of the old Neminaka days?
Manallace quite agreed, and recommended a pull
at the 'liver-tonic' to brace him after so long
in the house. He took it, and Manallace suggested that it would be better if, after his walk,
he came down to the cottage for a week-end and
brought the revise with him. They could then
re-touch the last chapter. He answered to that
drug and to some praise of his work, and presently
simpered drowsily. Yes, it *was* good—though he
said it who should not. He praised himself
awhile till, with a puzzled forehead and shut eyes,
he told us that *she* had been saying lately that it
was too good—the whole thing, if we understood,
was *too* good. He wished us to get the exact
shade of her meaning. She had suggested, or
rather implied, this doubt. She had said—he
would let us draw our own inferences—that the
Chaucer find had 'anticipated the wants of
humanity.' Johnson, of course. No need to
tell *him* that. But what the hell was her implica-
tion? Oh God! Life had always been one long
innuendo! *And* she had said that a man could
do anything with anyone if he saved him the
trouble of thinking. What did she mean by that?
He had never shirked thought. He had thought
sustainedly all his life. It *wasn't* too good, was
it? Manallace didn't think it was too good—did
he? But this pick-pick-picking at a man's brain
and work was too bad, wasn't it? *What* did she
mean? Why did she always bring in Manallace,
who was only a friend—no scholar, but a lover of

the game—Eh?—Manallace could confirm this
if he were here, instead of loafing on the Continent
just when he was most needed.

'I've come back,' Manallace interrupted, un-
steadily. 'I can confirm every word you've said.
You've nothing to worry about. It's *your* find—
your credit—*your* glory and—all the rest of it.'

'Swear you'll tell her so then,' said Castorley.
'She doesn't believe a word I say. She told me
she never has since before we were married.
Promise!'

Manallace promised, and Castorley added that
he had named him his literary executor, the pro-
ceeds of the book to go to his wife. 'All profits
without deduction,' he gasped. 'Big sales if it's
properly handled. *You* don't need money. . . .
Graydon'll trust *you* to any extent. It 'ud be a
long . . .'

He coughed, and, as he caught breath, his
pain broke through all the drugs, and the outcry
filled the room. Manallace rose to fetch Gleeag,
when a full, high, affected voice, unheard for a
generation, accompanied, as it seemed, the clamour
of a beast in agony, saying: 'I wish to God someone would stop that old swine howling down
there! *I* can't . . . I was going to tell you
fellows that it would be a dam' long time before
Graydon advanced *me* two quid.'

We escaped together, and found Gleeag waiting, with Lady Castorley, on the landing. He
telephoned me, next morning, that Castorley had
died of bronchitis, which his weak state made it
impossible for him to throw off. 'Perhaps it's

just as well,' he added, in reply to the condolences I asked him to convey to the widow. ' We might have come across something we couldn't have coped with.'

Distance from that house made me bold.

' You knew all along, I suppose? What was it, really?'

' Malignant kidney-trouble—generalised at the end. 'No use worrying him about it. We let him through as easily as possible. Yes! A happy release. . . . What? . . . Oh! Cremation. Friday, at eleven.'

There, then, Manallace and I met. He told me that she had asked him whether the book need now be published; and he had told her this was more than ever necessary, in her interests as well as Castorley's.

' She is going to be known as his widow—for a while, at any rate. Did I perjure myself much with him?'

' Not explicitly,' I answered.

' Well, I have now—with *her*—explicitly,' said he, and took out his black gloves. . . .

As, on the appointed words, the coffin crawled sideways through the noiselessly-closing door-flaps, I saw Lady Castorley's eyes turn towards Gleeag.

GERTRUDE'S PRAYER

(Modernised from the ' Chaucer ' of Manallace.)

That which is marred at birth Time shall not mend,
  Nor water out of bitter well make clean ;
All evil thing returneth at the end,
  Or elseway walketh in our blood unseen.
Whereby the more is sorrow in certaine—
Dayspring mishandled cometh not againe.

To-bruizéd be that slender, sterting spray
  Out of the oake's rind that should betide
A branch of girt and goodliness, straightway
  Her spring is turnèd on herself, and wried
And knotted like some gall or veiney wen.—
Dayspring mishandled cometh not agen.

Noontide repayeth never morning-bliss—
  Sith noon to morn is incomparable ;
And, so it be our dawning goth amiss,
  None other after-hour serveth well.
Ah ! Jesu-Moder, pitie my oe paine—
Dayspring mishandled cometh not againe!

The Woman in His Life

DINAH IN HEAVEN

She did not know that she was dead,
　　But, when the pang was o'er,
Sat down to wait her Master's tread
　　Upon the Golden Floor

With ears full-cock and anxious eyes,
　　Impatiently resigned ;
But ignorant that Paradise
　　Did not admit her kind.

Persons with Haloes, Harps, and Wings
　　Assembled and reproved ;
Or talked to her of Heavenly things,
　　But Dinah never moved.

There was one step along the Stair
　　That led to Heaven's Gate ;
And, till she heard it, her affair
　　Was—she explained—to wait.

And she explained with flattened ear,
　　Bared lip and milky tooth—
Storming against Ithuriel's Spear
　　That only proved her truth!

Sudden—far down, the Bridge of Ghosts
  That anxious spirits clomb—
She caught that step in all the hosts,
  And knew that he had come.

She left them wondering what to do,
  But not a doubt had she.
Swifter than her own squeals she flew
  Across the Glassy Sea ;

Flushing the Cherubs everywhere,
  And skidding as she ran,
She refuged under Peter's Chair
  And waited for her man.

. . . . .

There spoke a Spirit out of the press
  'Said :—' Have you any here
That saved a fool from drunkenness,
  And a coward from his fear ?

' That turned a soul from dark to day
  When other help was vain.
That snatched it from wanhope and made
  A cur a man again ? '

' Enter and look,' said Peter then,
  And set The Gate ajar.
' If I know aught of women and men
  I trow she is not far.'

' Neither by virtue, speech nor art
  Nor hope of grace to win ;

But godless innocence of heart
  That never heard of sin:

' *Neither by beauty nor belief*
  Nor white example shown.
Something a wanton—more a thief ;
  But—most of all—mine own.'

' *Enter and look,' said Peter then,*
  ' *And send you well to speed ;*
But, for all that I know of women and men
  Your riddle is hard to read.'

Then flew Dinah from under the Chair,
  Into his arms she flew—
And licked his face from chin to hair
  And Peter passed them through !

The Woman in His Life

Fairest of darkie daughters
Was Dinah Doe!

Negro Melody.

FROM his boyhood John Marden had a genius
for improvising or improving small labour-saving
gadgets about his father's house and premises.
So, when the War came, shortly after he had been
apprenticed to a tool-making firm in the Midlands,
he chose the Engineers, and eventually found
himself at a place called Messines, where he
worked underground, many months, among interesting devices. There he met a Cockney named
Burnea, who diagnosed sick machinery by touch
—with his eyes shut. Between them, and a few
fellow-workers, Messines Ridge went up.

After the War, the two men joined forces on
four thousand pounds capital; a dozen young
veterans of Messines; a lease of some sheds in
a London suburb, and a collection of second-hand
lathes and stampers. They gave out that they were
ready to make anything for anybody.

A South African mine-manager asked about a
detachable arrangement on a drill-head, which he
could not buy in open market for less than four
shillings and sevenpence wholesale. Marden con-

sidered the drawings, cut down the moving parts
a half. Burnea made an astonished machine undertake strange duties, and by the time he had
racked it to bits, they were delivering the article
at one shilling and tenpence. A newly opened
mine on a crest of the Andes, where llamas were,
for the moment, cheaper than lorries, needed metal
stiffenings and clips for pack-saddles (drawing
enclosed). The first model went back in a month.
In another fortnight the order was filled, with
improvements. At the end of their first year, an
Orinoco dredging concern, worried over some
barges which did not handle auriferous sludge as
they ought; and a wild-cat proposition on a New
Guinea beach where natives treated detonating
capsules with contempt; were writing their friends
that you could send Burnea and Marden the
roughest sketches of what you wanted, because
they understood them.

So the firm flourished. The young veterans
drove the shifts ten hours a day; the versatile
but demoralised machinery was displaced by
sterner stuff; and their third year's profits ran into
five figures. Then Burnea, who had the financial
head, died of pulmonary trouble, a by-product of
gas-poison, and left Marden his share of the Works,
plus thirty-six thousand pounds all on fixed deposit
in a Bank, because the head of one of its branches
had once been friendly with him in a trench.
The Works were promptly enlarged, and Marden
worked fourteen hours a day instead of twelve,
and, to save time, followed Burnea's habit of pushing money which he did not need into the same

Bank at the same meek rate of interest. But, for
the look of the thing, he hired a genuine financial
secretary, who was violently affected when John
explained the firm's theory of investments, and
recommended some alterations which Marden was
too busy to attend to. Six months later, there
fell on him three big contracts, which surpassed
his dreams of avarice. At this point he took what
sleep was forced on him in a cot in Burnea's old
office. At this point, too, Jerry Floyd, ex-Sergeant
of Sappers at Messines, and drawing eighteen
pounds a week with irregular bonuses, struck
loudly.

'What's the matter with your job, Jerry?'
John asked.

''Tain't a job—that's all. My machines do
everything for me except strike. *I've* got to do
that,' said Jerry with reproach.

'Soft job. Stick to it,' John counselled.

'Stick to bloomin' what? Turnin' two taps
and fiddlin' three levers? Get a girl to do it for
you. Repetition-work! I'm fed up!'

'Take ten days' leave, you fool,' said John;
which Jerry did, and was arrested for exceeding
the speed-limit through angry gipsies at Brough
horse-fair. John Marden went to bed behind his
office as usual, and—without warning—suffered a
night so memorable that he looked up the nearest
doctor in the Directory, and went to see him.
Being inarticulate, except where the Works were
concerned, he explained that he felt as though he
had got the hump—was stale, fed-up, and so
forth. He thought, perhaps, he might have been

working a bit too hard; but he said not a word of the horror, the blackness, the loss of the meaning of things, the collapses at the end, the recovery and retraversing of the circle of that night's Inferno; nor how it had waked up a certain secret dread which he had held off him since demobilisation.

'Can't you rest a bit?' asked the doctor, whose real interests were renal calculi.

'I've never tried.'

'Haven't you any hobbies or—friends, then?'

'Except the Works, none.'

'Nothing—more important in your life?'

John's face was answer enough. 'No! No! But what'll I do? What'll I *do*?' he asked wildly. 'I—I have never been like this before!'

'I'll give you a sedative, but you must slack off, and divert your mind. Yes! That's it. Divert your mind.'

John went back to the Works, and strove to tell his secretary something about the verdict. The man was perfunctorily sympathetic, but what he wanted John to understand (he seemed at the other end of the world as he spoke) was that, owing to John's ignorance of finance, the whole of the Works stood as John's personal property. So that, if John died, they would be valued and taxed thirty or forty per cent for death-duties, and that would cripple things badly. Not a minute should be lost before turning the concern into a chain of companies. He had the scheme drafted. It would need but a couple of days' study. John looked at the papers, listened to the explanation, stared at a calendar on the wall, and heard himself speaking as from the bottom of a black, cold crater :

' It don't mean anything—half a million or three quarters or—or—or anything.   Oh sorry ! It's gone up like the Ridge, and I'm a dud, you know.'

Then he returned to his expensive flat, which the same secretary had taken for him a year before, and prepared to do nothing for a month except to think upon the night he had passed in Burnea's old office, and to expect, and get, others like it. A few men came—once each—grinned at him, told him to buck up, and went on to their own concerns.   He was ministered to by his ex-batman, Corporal Vincent Shingle, systematically a peculator, intermittently a drunkard, and emphatically a liar.   Twice—once underground, where he had penetrated with a thermos full of hot coffee, and a piece of gallery had sat down on him; and once at Bailleul, when the lunatics of the local asylum were let out, and he was chased by a homicidal maniac with a thigh-bone— Marden had saved Shingle's life.   Twice—once out of the crumbling rim of a crater; and once by the slack of his breeches, when a whiff of gas dropped him over the mouth of a shaft—he had saved Marden's.   Therefore, he came along with the rest of the Messines' veterans to the Works, whence Jerry Floyd kicked him into space at the end of the first month.   Upon this, he returned to John Marden's personal service and the study of John's private correspondence and most intimate possessions. As he explained to Probert, the janitor of the flats, the night after the doctor had spoken :

' The 'ole game of gettin'-on is to save your bloke trouble. 'E don't know it, but I do 'is 'ome work for 'im while 'e makes money for me at 'is office. Na-o ! 'E don't spend it on me. *That* I 'ave to do meself. But I don't grudge the labour.'

' Then what's 'e been seein' the doctor *about* ? ' said Probert, who had an impure mind.

' 'Cause 'e's got what Jerry Floyd 'ad. 'E's fed up with repetition-work and richness. I've watched it comin' on. It's the same as we used to 'ave it in the War—but t'other way round. You can't mistake.'

' What's goin' to 'appen ? '

' Gawd knows ! I'm standin' to. The doctor 'as told 'im to lie off everythin' for a month—in one motion. If you stop runnin' machinery without slowin' 'er down, she'll lift 'erself off the bedplate. I've seen so with pumps.'

But machinery suddenly arrested has no resources in itself. Human mechanism under strain finds comfort in a drink or two. Running about in cars with no definite object bored John Marden as much as drumming under the clouds in aeroplanes ; theatres made him think impotently of new gadgets for handling the scenery, or extracting opera-glasses from their clips ; cards and golf ended in his counting the pips in his hand, or the paces between shot and shot ; whereas drinks softened the outlines of things, if not at once, then after a little repetition-work.

The result came when a Fear leaped out of the goose-fleshed streets of London between the icy shop-fronts, and drove John to his flat. He argued that it must have been a chill, and fortified himself against it so resolutely that an advertisement, which had caught the tail-end of his eye, stood up before him in the shape of a full-sized red and white bullock, dancing in a tea-cup. It was succeeded a few days later by a small dog, pressed against the skirting-board of his room—an inky, fat horror with a pink tongue, crouched in the attitude of a little beast he had often watched at Mr. Wilham's fashionable West End pet-shop, where dogs lived in excelsior-floored cubicles, appealing to the passers-by. It began as a spreading blurr, which morning after morning became more definite. It was better than the ox in the tea-cup, till it was borne in on John Marden one dawn that, if It crawled out into the centre of the room, the Universe would crash down on him. He wondered till he sweated, dried and broke out again, what would happen to him then, and how suicides were judged. After a drink or two, he became cunning and diplomatic with—of all experts in the world—his batman, to whom he told the tale of a friend who ' saw things.' The result was tabulated that afternoon in the basement, where Shingle and Probert were drinking his whisky.

' Well,—*now* we're arrivin' at objective A,' said Shingle. ' I knew last week 'e'd begun seein' 'em, 'cause 'e couldn't turn 'is eyes out o' corners. O' course, 'e says it's overtook a friend of 'is.'

' Reasonable enough,' said Probert. ' We all keep that friend.'

' Let's get down to figures,' Shingle went on. ' Two bottles is 'is week's whack. *An*' we know 'e don't use cocktails. Well; that don't make much more'n four drinks a day. You can't get nothin' special on that issue—not in nature.'

' Women *al*so?', Probert suggested.

' Be-e damned! I know there ain't. No. It's a black dawg. That's neither 'ere nor there. *But*, if it comes out into the room, 'is pore friend 'll go off 'is rocker. That is objective B.'

' Ye-es,' said Probert. ' I've 'ad 'em too. What about it?'

' I'm askin' you if reel dawgs are allowed in the flats. Are they?' said Shingle.

Probert dismissed the matter loftily.

' As between *us*!' he began. ' Don't stay awake for it! I've sanctioned kittens in two flats this spring. What's the game?'

' 'Air o' the dog that bit 'im,' Shingle answered. ' I mean 'is pore friend!'

' What about small-arms in 'is possession,' said Probert. ' *You* know.'

' On'y 'is pistol, an' 'e'll 'ave a proper 'unt for that. Now mind you don't go back on what you said about keepin' dawgs 'ere.'

Shingle went off, dressed in most items out of his master's wardrobe, with the pawnticket for his master's revolver in his pocket.

John's state was less gracious. He was walking till he should tire himself out and his brain would cease to flinch at every face that looked so closely

at him because he was going mad. If he walked
for two hours and a half without halt, round
and round the Parks, he might drug his mind by
counting his paces till the rush of numbers would
carry on awhile after he finished. At seven o'clock
he re-entered the flat, and stared at his feet, while
he raced through numbers from eleven thousand
up. When he lifted his eyes, the black Thing he
expected was pressed against the skirting-board.
The tonic the doctor had prescribed stood on a
table. He drew the cork with his teeth, and
gulped down to the first mark on the glass. He
fancied he heard small, thumping sounds. Turning, it seemed to him that the Thing by the wall
was working outwards.

Then there were two John Mardens—one dissolved by terror ; the other, a long way off, detached, but as much in charge of him as he used
to be of his underground shift at Messines.

'It's coming out into the room,' roared the
first. 'Now you've *got* to go mad ! Your pistol—
before you make an exhibition of yourself ! '

'Call it, you fool ! Call it ! ' the other commanded.

'Come along ! Good dog ! Come along !'
John whispered.

Slowly, ears pressed to head, the inky blurr
crawled across the parquet on to the rug.

'Go-ood doggie. Come along, then ! ' John
held out a clenched fist and felt, he thought, a
touch of hell-fire that would have sent him through
the window, except for the second John, who
said :—

'Right! All right! A cold nose is the sign of a well dog. It's all right! It's alive!'

'No. It's *come* alive!' shouted the first. 'It'll grow like the bullock in the cup! Pistol, you!'

'No—no—alive! Quite alive!' the other interrupted. 'It's licking your fist, and—nff!—it's made a mess in the corner—on the polished three-eighth-inch oak-parquet, set on cement with brick archings. Shovel!—*Not* pistol! Get the shovel, you ass!'

Then, John Marden repeated aloud:—

'Yes. It's made a mess. I'll get the shovel—shovel—steel—nickel-handled—one. Oh, you filthy little beast!'

He reached among the fire-irons and did what was necessary. The small thing, flat, almost, as a postage-stamp, crawled after him. It was sorry, it whimpered. Indeed, it had been properly brought up, but circumstances had been too much for it, and it apologised—on its back. John stirred it with a toe. Feeling its amends had been accepted, it first licked and then rapturously bit his shoe.

'It's a dog right enough,' said John. He lifted a cracked voice and called aloud:—

'There *is* a dog here! I mean there's a dog here.'

As he remembered himself and leaned towards the bell-push, Shingle entered from the bedroom, where he had been laying out dinner-kit, with a story of some badly washed shirts that seemed on his mind.

' But there's a dog—' said John.

Oh, yes! Now that John mentioned it, a pup had arrived at 5.15 P.M.—brought over from the dog-shop by Mr. Wilham himself who, having observed Captain Marden's interest in his windows, had taken the liberty of sending on approval—price fifteen guineas—one Dinah, jet black Aberdeen of the dwarf type, aged five months and a fortnight, with pedigree attached to Mr. Wilham's letter (on the mantelpiece, left when Mr. Wilham found Captain Marden was not at home, sir) and which would confirm all the above statements. Shingle took his time to make everything clear, speaking in a tone that no man of his acquaintance had ever heard. He broke back often to the badly washed shirts, which somehow John found comforting. The pup ceased to grovel.

' Wilham was right about 'er breedin'. Not a white 'air on 'er! An' look at 'er boo-som frills!' said Shingle voluptuously.

Dinah, ears just prickable, sat on the floor between them, looking like a bandy-legged bat.

' But one can't keep dogs in these flats. It's forbidden, isn't it? ' John asked.

' Me an' the janitor 'll arrange that. Probert 'll come in 'andy to take 'er walks, too.' Shingle mused aloud.

' But I don't know anything about dogs.'

' *She'll* look after all that. She's a bitch, you see, sir. An' so that 'll be all right.'

Shingle went back to the evening-kit.

John and Dinah faced each other before the

fire. His feet, as he sat, were crossed at the ankles. Dinah moved forward to the crotch thus presented, jammed her boat-nosed head into it up to the gullet, pressed down her chin till she found the exact angle that suited her, tucked her forelegs beneath her, grunted, and went to sleep, warm and alive. When John moved, she rebuked him, and Shingle, ten minutes later, found him thus immobilised.

' H'sh ! ' said John.

But Dinah was awake and said so.

' Oh ! That's it, is it ? ' Shingle grinned. ' She knows 'oo's what already.'

' How d'you mean ? ' John asked.

' She knows where I come in. She's yours. *I've* got to look after 'er. That's all. 'Tisn't as if she was a dog-pup.'

' Yes, but what am I to do about her ? '

' We-ell, o' course, you must be careful you don't mix up with others. She's just the right age for distemper. She'll 'ave to be took out on the lead. An' then there'll be 'er basket an' sundries.'

John Marden did not attend, because in the corner, close to the skirting-board, lay That Other, who had borne him company for the past few days.

' She—looks like a good ratter,' he stammered.

' I'd forgot that. 'Ere ! Young lady !' said Shingle, following the line of John's eye. ' 'Ave you ever 'eard anything about rats ? '

Dinah rose at once and signified that she had —lots.

' That's it, then ! Rrrats ! Rrats, ducky ! Rrrout 'em out ! '

She in turn followed the hint of Shingle's hand, scuttled to the corner indicated, and said what she would have done had enemies been present. When she trotted back, That Other took shape again behind her, but John felt relieved.

'Now about dinner, sir!' said Shingle. 'It's 'er first night at 'ome. 'Twouldn't do to disappoint 'er, would it?'

'Bring something up here then,' said John. 'I'll dress now.'

On Shingle's departure he rose and, followed by an interested Dinah, trod, not for the first time, firmly in the corners of his room. Then he went to dress. Dinah backed against the bath, the wisdom of centuries in her little solemn mask, till John's fluttering shirt-tails broke it all up. She leaped, grabbed them, and swung into John's calves. John kicked back. She retired under the bulge of the porcelain and told him what she thought of him. He sat down and laughed. She scolded till he dropped a stud, and the two hunted for it round the cork mat, and he was just able to retrieve it from between her teeth. Both sat down to meat, a little warm and dishevelled. That Other watched them, but did not insist, though Dinah backed into him twice.

'I've made a temp'ry collar and lead off Probert. I'll take 'er for 'er last walk,' Shingle announced when he had cleared away.

'You will not,' said John. 'Give 'em to me.'

The upshot was some strenuous exercise in the Mall, when Dinah, to whom night and London were new, lassoed John twice and a stranger once, besides nearly choking when she was snatched from under the wheels of a car. This so saddened her that she sat down, and had to be brought home, languidly affectionate, in a taxi. As John said, the adventure showed she would not be afraid of cars.

' There's nothin' that young woman's afraid of, 'cept not bein' made much of,' Shingle replied. ' Green 'ud suit 'er better than red in collars. But I expect you'll do your own buyin', sir.'

' I will. You get the dog-biscuit,' said John.

' Puppy - biscuit ! ' said Shingle, deeply shocked, and he mentioned the only brand. ' A pup's like a child—all stummick.'

Going to bed was a riot. Dinah had no intention of being left out, and when John moved a foot, tried to chew down to it through the blankets till she was admitted. Shingle, with the shaving-water, would have given her her walk before breakfast next morning; but John took the duty, and she got muddy and had to be cleaned and dried on her return. Then, at Shingle's reminder, came the shopping expedition. John bought a green collar for Sunday, and a red for weekdays ; two ditto leads; one wicker basket with green baize squab; two brushes; one toothed comb and one curry; and—Shingle sent him out again for these—pills, alterative, tonic, and antithelmintic. Ungrateful Dinah chewed the basket's varnished rim, ripped the bowels out of the squab, nipped Marden's inexperienced fingers as he gave her her first pill, and utterly refused to be brushed.

'Gawd!' said the agile Shingle, who was helping. 'Mother used to say a child was a noosance. Twins ain't in it with you, Dinah. An' now I suppose you'll 'ave to show 'em all off in your car.'

John's idea had been a walk down the Mall, but Shingle dwelt on the dangers of distemper and advised Richmond Park in, since rain was likely, the limousine. Dinah condescended a little when it came round, but hopped up into the right-hand seat, and gave leave to get under way. When they reached the Park she was so delighted that she clean forgot her name, and John chivvied her, shouting till she remembered. Shingle had put up a lunch, for fear, he explained, of hotels where ladies brought infectious Pekes, flown over for them by reprobate lovers in the Air Service; and after a couple of hours bounding through bracken, John appreciated the half-bottle of Burgundy that went with it. On their return, all Dinah's wordly pose dropped. 'I am,' she sniffed, 'but a small pup with a large nose. Let me rest it on your breast and don't you stop loving me for one minute.' So John slept too, and the chauffeur trundled them back at five o'clock.

'Pubs?' Probert demanded out of a corner of his mouth when John had gone indoors.

'Not in *ther* least,' said Shingle. 'Accordin' to our taxi-man '—(Shingle did not love John's chauffeur)—' Women and Song was 'is game. 'E says you ought to 'ave 'eard 'im 'owling after 'er. 'E'll be out in his own Hizzer-Swizzer in a week.'

' That's *your* business. But what about my
commission on the price? You don't expect me
to sanction dawgs 'ere for nothin'? Come *on*! It's
all found money for you.'

John went drowsily up in the lift and finished
his doze. When he waked, That Other was in
his corner, but Shingle had found two tennis balls,
with which Dinah was playing the Eton Wall
Game by herself up and down the skirting-board
—pushing one with her nose, patting the other
along with her paws, right through That Other's
profiles.

' That shows she's been kitten-trained,' said
Shingle. ' I'll bring up the janitor's and make
sure.'

But the janitor's kitten had not been pup-
trained and leaped on the table, to make sure.
Dinah followed. It took all hands ten minutes
to clear up the smashed glass of siphon, tumbler,
and decanter, in case she cut her feet. The
aftermath was reaped by a palpitating vacuum-
cleaner, which Dinah insisted was hostile.

When she and John and That Other in the
corner sat it out after dinner, she discovered gifts
of conversation. In the intervals of gossip she
would seek and nose both balls about the room,
then return to John's foot, lay her chin over it,
and pick up where she had left off, in eloquent
whimperings.

' Does she want anything?' he asked Shingle.

' Nothin', excep' not to be out of your mind
for a minute. 'Ow about a bone now, Dinah?'

Out came her little pink tongue, sideways,

there was a grunt and a sneeze, and she pirouetted gaily before the serving-man.

' Come downstairs, then,' he said.

' Bring it up here ! ' said John, sweeping aside Shingle's views on Bokhara rugs. This was messy—till Dinah understood that bones must be attended to on newspapers spread for that purpose.

These things were prelude to a month of revelations, in which Dinah showed herself all that she was, and more, since she developed senses and moods for John only. She was by turns, and in places, arrogant, imbecile, coy, forthcoming, jealous, exacting, abject, humourous, or, apparently, stone-cold, but in every manifestation adorable, and to be attended to before drinks. Shingle, as necessary to her comfort, stood on the fringe of her favours, but John was her Universe. And for her, after four weeks, he found himself doing what he had never done since Messines. He sang sentimental ditties—on his awful top-notes Dinah would join in—such as :—

> ' Oh, show me a liddle where to find a rose
>   To give to ma honey chi-ile !
> Oh, show me a liddle where my love goes
>   An' I'll follow her all de while ! '

At which she would caper, one ear up and one a quarter down. Then :—

> ' Ma love she gave me a kiss on de mouf,
>   An' how can I let her go-o?
> And I'll follow her norf, and I'll follow her souf
>   Because I love her so ! '

' 'Oo-ooo! Oooo!' Dinah would wail to the ceiling.

And then came calamity, after a walk in the Green Park, and Shingle said :—' I told you so.' Dinah went off her feed, shivered, stared, ran at the nose, grew gummy round the eyes, and coughed.

' Ye-es,' said Shingle, rubbing his chin above her. ' The better the breed, the worse they cop it. Oh, damn the 'ole Air Force! It'll be a day-and-night job, I'm thinkin'. Look up a Vet in the Directory? Gawd! *No!* This is distemper. I know a Canine Specialist and——'

He went to the telephone without asking leave.

The Canine Specialist was duly impressed by John and his wealth, and more effectively by Shingle. He laid down rules of nursing and diet which the two noted in duplicate, and split into watches round the clock.

' She 'as worked like a charm 'itherto,' Shingle confided to Probert, whose wife cooked for Dinah's poor appetite. ' She's jerked 'im out of 'isself proper. But if anythin' 'appens to 'er *now*, it'll be all Messines over again for 'im.'

' Did 'e cop it bad there, then?'

' Once, to my knowledge. I 'eard 'im before 'e went underground prayin' that 'is cup might parse. It 'ad come over 'im in an 'eap. Ye-es! It 'appens—it 'appens, as mother used to say when we was young.'

' Then it's up to you to see nothing happens this time.'

' 'Looks it! But she's as jealous as a schoolteacher over 'im. Pore little bitch! Ain't it odd, though? She knows 'ow to play Weepin' Agnes with 'im as well as a woman! But she's cured 'im of lookin' in corners, an' 'e's been damnin' me something like 'olesome.'

John, indeed, was unendurably irritable while Dinah's trouble was increasing. He slept badly at first, then too heavily, between watches, and fussed so much that Shingle suggested Turkish baths to recover his tone. But Dinah grew steadily worse, till there was one double watch which Shingle reported to Probert as a 'fair curiosity.' 'I 'eard 'im Our Fatherin' in the bath-room when 'e come off watch and she 'adn't conked out.'

Presently there was improvement, followed by relapse, and grave talk of possible pneumonia. That passed, too, but left a dreadful whimpering weakness, till one day she chose to patter back to life with her scimitar tail going like an egg-whisk. During her convalescence she had discovered that her sole concern was to love John Marden unlimitedly; to follow him pace by pace when he moved; to sit still and worship him when he stopped; to flee to his foot when he took a chair; to defend him loudly against enemies, such as cats and callers; to confide in, cherish, pet, cuddle, and deify without cease; and, failing that, to mount guard over his belongings. Shingle bore it very well.

'Yes, I know *you*!' he observed to her one morning when she was daring him to displace John's pyjamas from their bed. 'I'd be no good to you unless I was a puppy-biscuit. An' yet I *did* 'ave an' 'and in pullin' you through, you *pukka* little bitch, you.'

For some while she preferred cars to her own feet, and her wishes were gratified, especially in the Hizzer-Swizzer which, with John at the wheel—you do not drink when you drive Hizzer-Swizzers—suited her. Her place was at his left elbow, nose touching his sleeve, until the needle reached fifty, when she had to throw it up and sing aloud. Thus, she saw much of summer England, but somehow did not recover her old form, in spite of Shingle's little doses of black coffee and sherry.

John felt the drag of the dull, warm days too; and went back to the Works for half a week, where he sincerely tried to find out what his secretary meant by plans for reorganisation. It sounded exactly like words, but conveyed nothing. Then he spent a night like that first one after Jerry Floyd had struck, and tried to deal with it by the same means; but found himself dizzily drunk almost before he began.

'The fuse was advanced,' Shingle chuckled to Probert. ''E was like a boy with 'is first pipe. *An'* a virgin's 'ead in the mornin'! That shows the success of me treatment. But a man 'as to think of 'is own interests once-awhile. It's time for me Bank 'Oliday.'

'You an' your 'olidays. Ain't your bloke got any will of 'is own?'

'Not yet. 'E's still on the dole. 'Urry your Mrs. P. up with our medical comforts.'

That was Dinah's beef-tea, and very good.
But if you mix with it a few grains of a certain
stuff, little dogs won't touch it.

'She's off 'er feed again,' said Shingle de-
spairingly to John, whose coaxings were of no
avail.

'Change is what you want,' said Shingle to
her under his breath. ''Tain't fair to keep a
dawg in town in summer. I ain't sayin' anythin' against the flat.'

'What's all that?' said John. Shingle's back
was towards him.

'I said I wasn't sayin' anythin' against the
flat, sir. A man can doss down anywhere———'

'Doss? I pay eight hundred a year for the
thing!'

'But it's different with dawgs, sir, was all I was
going to remark. Furniture's no treat to *them*.'

'She stays with me,' John snapped, while
Dinah tried to explain how she had been defrauded
of her soup.

'Of course she stays—till she conks out.'
Shingle removed the bowl funereally. . . .

'No, I 'ave *not* pulled it off at one go,' he said
to Probert. 'If you 'ad jest finished with seein'
dawgs in corners, *you* wouldn't want to crash into
society at a minute's notice, either. You'd think
a bit before'and an' look round for a dry dug-out.
That's what we're doin'.'

Two days later, he dropped a word that he had
a sister in the country, married to a cowkeeper,
who took in approved lodgers. If anyone doubted
the merits of the establishment, the Hizzer-

Swizzer could get there in two hours, and make sure. It did so, and orders were given for the caravan to start next day, that not a moment might be lost in restoring Dinah.

She hopped out into a world of fields full of red and white bullocks, who made her (and John) flinch a little; and rabbits always on the edge of being run down. There was, too, a cat called Ginger, evidently used to dogs; and a dusty old collie, Jock, whom she snapped into line after five abject minutes.

'It suits 'er,' Shingle pronounced. 'The worst she'll catch off Jock is fleas. *Fairy Anne!* I've brought the Keatings.'

Dinah left Jock alone. Ginger, who knew all about rats and rabbits, was more to her mind, and those two ladies would work together along the brookside on fine, and through the barns on wet, mornings, chaperoned by John and a nobby stick. She was bitten through the nose at her first attempt, but said nothing about it at the time, nor when she laid out the disinterred corpse in his bedroom—till she was introduced to iodine.

The afternoons were given to walks which began with a mighty huntress before her lord, standing on hind legs at every third bound to overlook the tall September grass, and ended with a trailing pup, who talked to John till he picked her up, laid her across his neck, a pair of small feet in each hand, and carried her drowsily licking his right cheek.

For evenings, there were great games. Dinah

had invented a form of 'footer' with her tennis ball. John would roll it to her, and she returned it with her nose, as straight as a die, till she thought she had lulled him into confidence. Then angle and pace would change, and John had to scramble across the room to recover and shoot it back, if possible past her guard. Or she would hide (cheating like a child, the while) till he threw it into a corner, and she stormed after it, slipped, fetched up against the skirting-board and swore. Last of all came the battle for the centre of the bed; the ferocious growling onsets; the kisses on the nose; the grunt of affectionate defeat and the soft jowl stretched out on his shoulder.

With all these preoccupations and demands, John's days slipped away like blanks beneath a stamping-machine. But, somehow, he picked up a slight cold one Sunday, and Shingle, who had been given the evening off with a friend, had reduced the neglected whisky to a quarter bottle. John eked it out with hot water, sugar, and three aspirins, and told Dinah that she might play with Ginger while he kept himself housed.

He was comfortably perspiring at 7 P.M., when he dozed on the sofa, and only woke for Sunday cold supper at eight. Dinah did not enter with it, and Shingle's sister, who had small time-sense, said that she had seen her with Ginger mousing in the wash-house 'just now.' So he did not draw the house for her till past nine; nor finish his search of the barns, flashing his torch in all corners, till later. Then he hurried to the kitchen and told his tale.

' She've been wired,' said the cowman. ' She've been poaching along with Ginger, an' she've been caught in a rabbit-wire. Ginger wouldn't never be caught—twice. It's different with dogs *as* cats. That's it. Wired.'

' Where, think you? '

' All about the woods somewhere—same's Jock did when 'e were young. But 'e give tongue, so I dug 'im out.'

At the sound of his name, the old ruffian pushed his head knee-high into the talk.

' She'd answer *me* from anywhere,' said John.

' Then you'd best look for her. I'd go with 'e, but it's foot-washin's for me to-night. An' take you a graf' along. I'll tell Shingle to sit up till you come back. 'E ain't 'ome yet.'

Shingle's sister passed him a rabbiting-spade out of the wash-house, and John went forth with three aspirins and some whisky inside him, and all the woods and fields under the stars to make choice of. He felt Jock's nose in his hand and appealed to him desperately.

' It's Dinah! Go seek, boy! It's Dinah! Seek ! '

Jock seemed unconcerned, but he slouched towards the brook, and turned through wet grasses while John, calling and calling, followed him towards a line of hanging woods that clothed one side of the valley. Stumps presently tripped him, and John fell several times but Jock waited. Last, for a long while, they quartered a full-grown wood, with the spotlight of his torch making the fallen stuff look like coils of half-buried wire between the Lines. He heard a church clock strike eleven as he drew breath under the top of the rise, and wondered a little why a spire should still be standing. Then he remembered that this was England, and strained his ears to make sure that his calls were not answered. The collie nosed ground and moved on, evidently interested. John thought he heard a reply at last; plunged forward without using his torch, fell, and rolled down a steep bank, breathless and battered, into a darkness deeper than that of the woods. Jock followed him whimpering. He called. He heard Dinah's smothered whine—switched on the light and discovered a small cliff of sandstone ribbed with tree-roots. He moved along the cliff towards the sound, till his light showed him a miniature cañon in its face, which he entered. In a few yards the cleft became a tunnel, but—he was calling softly now—there was no doubt that Dinah lay somewhere at the end. He held on till the lowering roof forced him to knees and elbows and, presently, stomach. Dinah's whimper continued. He wriggled forward again, and his shoulders brushed either side of the downward-sloping way. Then every forgotten or hardly-held-back horror of his two years' underground-work returned on him with the imagined weight of all earth overhead.

A handful of sand dropped from the roof and crumbled between his neck and coat-collar. He had but to retire an inch or two and the pressure would be relieved, and he could widen the bottle-necked passage with his spade; but terror beyond all terrors froze him, even though Dinah was appealing somewhere a little ahead. Release came in a spasm and a wrench that drove him backward six feet like a prawn. Then he realised that it would be all to do again, and shook as with fever.

At last his jerking hand steadied on the handle of the spade. He poked it ahead of him, at half-arm's length, and gingerly pared the sides of the tunnel, raking the sand out with his hands, and passing it under his body in the old way of the old work, till he estimated, by torchlight, that he might move up a little without being pinned again. By some special mercy the tunnel beyond the section he had enlarged grew wider. He followed on, flashed once more, and saw Dinah, her head pressed close to the right-hand side of it, her white-rimmed eyes green and set.

He pushed himself forward over a last pit of terror, and touched her. There was no wire, but a tough, thumb-shaped root, sticking out of the sand-wall, had hooked itself into her collar, sprung backwards and upwards, and locked her helplessly by the neck. His fingers trembled so at first that he could not follow the kinks of it. He shut his eyes, and humoured it out by touch, as he had done with wires and cables deep down under the Ridge; grabbed Dinah, and pushed himself back to the free air outside.

There he was sick as never he had been in all his days or nights. When he was faintly restored, he saw Dinah sitting beside Jock, wondering why her Lover—King—and God did all these noisy things.

On his feet at last, he crawled out of the sand-pit that had been a warren, badger's holt, and foxes' larder for generations, and wavered home-ward, empty as a drum, cut, bruised, bleeding, streaked with dirt and raffle that had caked where the sweat had dried on him, knees bending both ways, and eyes unable to judge distance. Nothing in his working past had searched him to these depths. But Dinah was in his arms, and it was she who announced their return to the still-lighted farm at the hour of 1 A.M.

Shingle opened the door, and without a word steered him into the wash-house, where the copper was lit. He began to explain, but was pushed into a tub of very hot water, with a blanket that came to his chin, and a drink of something or other at his lips. Afterwards he was helped upstairs to a bed with hot bricks in it, and there all the world, and Dinah licking his nose, passed from him for the rest of the night and well into the next day again. But Shingle's sister was shocked when she saw his torn and filthy clothing thrown down in the wash-house.

' 'Looks as if 'e'd been spending a night be-tween the Lines, don't it?' her brother com-mented. ''Asn't 'alf sweated either. Three hours of it, Marg'ret, an' rainin' on an' off. Must 'ave been all Messines with 'im till 'e found 'er.'

' An' 'e done it for 'is dog! What wouldn't 'e do for 'is woman!' said she.

' Yes. You *would* take it that way. I'm thinkin' about *'im*.'

'Ooh! Look at the blood. 'E must 'ave cut 'isself proper.'

'I went over 'im for scratches before breakfast. Even the iodine didn't wake 'im. 'Got 'is tray ready?'

Shingle bore it up, and Dinah's impenitent greeting of him roused her master.

'She wasn't wired. She knew too much for that,' were John's first words. 'She was hung up by her collar in an old bury. Jock showed me, an' I got her out. I fell about a bit, though. It was pitch-black; quite like old times.'

He went into details between mouthfuls, and Dinah between mouthfuls corroborated.

'So, you see, it wasn't her fault,' John concluded.

'That's what they all say,' Shingle broke in unguardedly.

'Do they? That shows they know Ginger. Dinah, you aren't to play with Ginger any more. Do you hear me?'

She knew it was reproof, as she flattened beneath the hand that caressed it away.

'Oh, and look here, Shingle,' John sat up and stretched himself. 'It's about time we went to work again. Perhaps you've noticed I have not been quite fit lately?'

'What with Dinah and all?—ye-es, sir—a bit,' Shingle assented.

'Anyhow, I've got it off the books now. It's behind me.'

'Very glad to 'ear it. Shall I fill the bath?'

'No. We'll make our last night's boil do

for to-day.   Lay out some sort of town-kit while
I shave.   I expect my last night's rig is pretty
well expended, isn't it?'

'There ain't one complete scarecrow in the
'ole entire aggregate.'

''Don't wonder.   Look here, Shingle, I was
underground a full half-hour before I could get
at her.   I should have said there wasn't enough
money 'top of earth to make me do *that* over again.
But I did.   Damn it—I did!   Didn't I, Dinah?
"*Oh, show me a liddle where to find a rose.*"   Get
off the bed and fetch my slippers, young woman!
"*To give to ma honey chi-ile.*"   No; put 'em down;
don't play with 'em!'

He began to strop his razor, always a mystery
to Dinah.   'Shingle, this is the most damnable
Government that was ever pupped.   Look here!
If I die to-morrow, they take about a third of the
cash out of the Works for Death-duties, counting
four per cent. interest on the money from the
time I begin to set.   That means one-third of
our working capital, which *is* doing something,
will be dug out from under us, so's these dam'
politicians can buy more dole-votes with it.   An'
I've got to waste my thinkin' time, which means
making more employment—(I say, this razor
pulls like a road-scraper)—I've got to knock off
my payin' work and spend Heaven knows how
many days reorganising into companies, so that
we shan't have our business knocked out if I go
under.   It's the *time* I grudge, Shingle.   And
we've got to make *that* up too, Dinah!'

The rasp of the blade on the chin set her tail

thumping as usual. When he was dressed, she went out to patronise Jock and Ginger by the barn, where Shingle picked her up later, with orders to jump into the Hizzer-Swizzer at once and return to duty. She made her regulation walk round him, one foot crossing the other, and her tongue out sideways.

'Yes, *that's* all right, Dinah! You're a bitch! You're all the bitch that ever was, but you're a useful bitch. That's where you ain't like some of 'em. Now come and say good-bye to your friends.'

He took her to the kitchen to bid farewell to the cowman and his wife. The woman looked at her coldly as she coquetted with the man.

'She'll get 'er come-uppance one of these days,' she said when the car was reported.

'What for? She's as good a little thing as ever was. 'Twas Ginger's fault,' said the cowman.

'I ain't thinkin' of *her*,' she replied. 'I'm thinkin' she may 'ave started a fire that someone else'll warm at some fine day. It 'appens—it 'appens—as mother used to say when we was all young.'

FOUR-FEET

I have done mostly what most men do,
And pushed it out of my mind;
But I can't forget, if I wanted to,
Four-Feet trotting behind.

Day after day, the whole day through—
Wherever my road inclined—
Four-Feet said, ' I am coming with you! '
And trotted along behind.

Now I must go by some other round,—
Which I shall never find—
Somewhere that does not carry the sound
Of Four-Feet trotting behind.

The Tie

THE TOTEM

Ere the mother's milk had dried
   On my lips, the Brethren came—
Tore me from my nurse's side,
   And bestowed on me a name

Infamously overtrue—
   Such as ' Bunny,' ' Stinker,' ' Podge ';—
But, whatever I should do,
   Mine for ever in the Lodge.

Then they taught with palm and toe—
   Then I learned with yelps and tears—
All the Armoured Man should know
   Through his Seven Secret Years . . .

Last, oppressing as oppressed,
   I was loosed to go my ways
With a Totem on my breast
   Governing my nights and days—

Ancient and unbribeabie,
   By the virtue of its Name—
Which, however oft I fell
   Lashed me back into The Game.

And the World, that never knew,
  Saw no more beneath my chin
Than a patch of rainbow-hue,
  Mixed as Life and crude as Sin.

The Tie

This tale was written so long ago that I have honestly forgotten how much of it, if any, may be my own and how much is in Christopher Mervyn's own words. But it is certain that Mervyn is dead, with Blore and Warrender. Macworth died ten years ago of tubercle after gas. Morrison Haylock's father is a Peer of the Realm, and every trace of the 26th Battalion (Birdfanciers), Welland and Withan Rifles, has vanished. Nothing, unless some sort of useless moral, remains of a tale of 1915.

MEN, in war, will instinctively act as they have been taught to do in peace—for a certain time. The wise man is he who knows when that time is up. Mr. Morrison Haylock (Vertue and Pavey, Contractors, E.C.) did not know. But I give the tale, with a few omissions for decency's sake, from the pen of Christopher Mervyn, anciently a schoolmaster of an ancient foundation, and later Lieutenant in the 26th (Birdfanciers) Battalion, Welland and Withan Rifles, quartered at Blagstowe. He wrote, being then second Lieutenant :—

. . . We older men have learned most. It is hard for anyone over thirty, with what he was used to think the rudiments of a mind, to absorb the mechanics of militarism. My Lieutenant, aged twenty-two, says to me :—' The more civilian rot a man has in his head, the less use he is as a subaltern.' He is quite right. I make mistakes which, a year ago, I should have called a child of sixteen a congenital idiot for perpetrating. I am told so with oaths and curses and that sort of sarcasm (I recognise it now) which I used to launch at the heads of junior forms. So I die daily, but, I believe, am being slowly reborn. . . .

Macworth tells me he has told you of our little affair with Haylock, the unjust caterer, and that you propose to dress it up in the public interest. Don't! The undraped facts, as I shall give them to you, are far beyond anything in the range of your art. I suppose I ought to be ashamed of my share in the row, but I have dug up the remnant of my civilian conscience. It is quite impenitent.

. . . The awful food for which the officers' mess pays six shillings a head! You say things are as bad in other messes under other contractors, but that is Satan's own argument—the arch-excuse for inefficiency. You are wise enough never to break bread with us, so I can't make you realise the extraordinary and composite vileness of our meals nor the ' knotted horrors of the Anglo-Parisienne' menus—*Jambons à la Grecque*, for instance, which are clods of rancid bacon on pats of green dirt, supposed to be spinach ; or our deep yellow blancmange, daubed with pink sauce that tastes of cat. Food is *the* vital necessity to men in hard work. One comes to lunch and dinner—

breakfast is always a farce—with the primitive
emotions, and when, week after week, the food is
not only uneatable but actively poisonous, as our
sardine savouries are, one's emotions become more
than primitive. I'm prepared to suffer for my
country, but ptomaine poisoning isn't cricket!

As you know, our battalion is quartered in
Blagstowe Gaol, a vast improvement on huts. We
should have been quite content had they only given
us prisoners' food. We tried every remedy our
civilian minds could suggest. We threatened our
mess-steward, who was merely insolent. We
pleaded and implored. We tried to write to the
papers, but here the law of libel interfered. My
platoon sergeant (he's a partner in Healey and
Butts, solicitors) expounded it to us. The C.O.
wrote officially to the directors of that infernal
tripeshop, Haylock, Vertue, and Pavey. The rest
of us weighed in with a round-robin. I composed
it. Not half a bad bit of English either. We
begged to have our army rations given us, ' simple
of themselves,' but by some devilish chicane they
were all mixed up, we were told, in the *Jambons à
la Grecque* and the catty blancmange and couldn't
be dissected out. . . .

If a man is not properly fed, he automatically
takes to drink. I didn't know this till I did. I
steadily overdrank for a fortnight out of pure
hunger. *I* can hold my liquor, but it isn't fair on
the youngsters, my seniors. . . .

On account of some scare or other, we had to
furnish pickets to hold up all cars on the London
road, take owners' names and addresses, and check

drivers' licences. My picket was at the south entrance to the town, close to the main gate of the Gaol, and out of pure zeal and bad temper, I had put up a barricade made of a scaffold-pole resting on a baker's cart at one end and on a cement barrel at the other. About nine o'clock a natty little grey and black self-driven coupé came from Brighton way at the rate of knots. It didn't brake soon enough after the outlying sentry had warned it of my barricade, and so knocked my scaffolding-pole down. Very good dependence for a quarrel, even before the driver gave me his name, which he did at the top of his voice. He sat in the glare of his own electrics with an Old E.H.W. School tie on his false bosom, bawling : ' I'm Haylock. Carry on, you men ! I tell you, I'm Haylock.' He is one of the push-and-go type—with a lot of rib-fat—*not* semitic, but the flower of the Higher Counterjumpery, by Transatlantic out of Top-Hat. He was in a hurry ; ' hustling ' I presume. I was monolithically military and—glory be!—he hadn't his licence on him. My duty as second Lieuten-ant was clear. No licence, no passage, and—· ' Come to the guard-room for examination.' Then, to put it coarsely, he broke loose. In his pauses, Private Gillock, who poses as a wit, was stage-whispering me for leave to ' put a shot into his radiator.' (The New Armies are horrid quick on the trigger.) I dismounted him from his wheel, detailed Gillock to drive—he mangled the gears consumedly—and ran the whole confection into the guard-room, which, when the Gaol we inhabit is at work, is the condemned cell. I was perfectly

sober at the time—no thanks to Haylock and his
minions. I was savage, though not murderous,
from semi-starvation and indigestion. I was glad
to have some means of honourably annoying him,
but I assure you that not till the lock of the condemned cell clicked, and I realised that this pur-
veyor of filthy delicatessen was at my mercy, did
my real self wake up and sing. I went to the
anteroom and told them that God had delivered
to us Morrison Haylock. We all ran out to the
condemned cell. No one spoke a word. *That* is
how revolutions are made. I unlocked the door
and—condemned cells are remorselessly lighted—
there sat Haylock on the cot behind his flaming
O.E.H.W. tie. At least, that was our united impression afterwards. As you know, it's the deuce
and all of a tie, invented to match that school's
attitude towards life and taste and the Eternal
Verities.

Anyhow, it fetched us up dead. We all
looked at Mackworth, who's an O.E.H.W.,
though a very junior lieutenant. The door was
shut; and it's sound-tight for reasons connected
with the last nights of the condemned. Mackworth took charge. He began : ' What was your
House at school? ' Haylock gave it with a smile.
He thought—but he couldn't have really—that
he'd fallen among friends. ' What's your name? '
Mackworth went on in the prefectorial, which is
the orderly-room, voice. Haylock gave that too,
quite perkily. I expect his suborned press would
call him ' breezy ' and ' genial.'

' *Is* it? ' said Mackworth. ' Then take that! '

and he smacked the brute's head—a full open-handed smite, just as one smacks a chap who isn't big enough to beat. It was sudden, I admit, but as inevitable as the highest art, and it carried conviction and atmosphere at once, for Haylock yapped and his hand went up to the hurt place absolutely on the old school lines. Then Norgate, who is a corn-factor in a solid way and my very rude Company Captain, pulled the hand down, and gave him another slap on the chops. Warrender and Blore, boys under twenty-two, but my seniors, followed, and I finished up with a judicial stinger. Someone said, 'There!' in the very tone of virtuous youth (forgive the alliteration), and everyone felt that justice had been done. Even Haylock did, for all the grown-man dropped from him too, and he snuffled: 'What's that *for?*' Fat Norgate, who is forty if a day, stood in front of him with a ready hand and shouted: 'You jolly well know what it's for.'

To him, Haylock trying to put his tie and collar straight (how well one remembers the attitude!) 'No, I don't. And, anyhow, I can't be supposed to look after 'em all.'

Norgate (*triumphantly to the rest of us*): 'That proves him a liar. He said he doesn't know what it's for.' Not one of us by the way had uttered a word about our grievance till then.

Me (*ferociously clutching my sword in lieu of a cane*): 'Haylock, you're a dirty little thief.' I wasn't a second Lieutenant. I wasn't even a beak any more. I was just starving, outraged Boy.

Haylock (*with equal directness*): 'Ugh! That's

what *you* think, you big brute! *I* don't get much out of it. I wish to God I had never touched the rotten contracts.'

'That's confession and avoidance,' said my platoon sergeant, of Healey and Butts. He'd slipped in with us, professionally and gratuitously as he explained, to give legal colour to the proceedings. But we weren't legal for the moment. Then Mackworth, whom we all regarded as head prefect in the matter, went on: 'Nobody *asked* you to touch 'em. You did it for your own beastly profits, and you've got to look after our grub properly or you'll be toed all round the parade-ground.'

I give the exact words. Then we all began to talk at once, each man recalling fragments of dreadful menus and what followed on 'em. Silence is the Mother of Revolution, but Speech is the Father of Atrocities. The more we dwelt on our wrongs, the redder we saw, but—I stick to it—that flaming Old E.H.W. tie saved and steadied us.

Haylock, who was blue-scared, backed into a corner. His knuckles weren't in his eyes, but that was the effect he produced. He still had enough rags of speech left to assure us that he was on his way down to investigate our complaints when I arrested him. I said—I mean, I roared—'What a deliberate lie! You were bunking up to town as hard as you could go when I collared you.'

Omnes (*diverted for the moment from murder*): 'Oh, you damned liar!'

Haylock: 'I'm not, I tell you.'

Omnes: 'Shut up. You are.'

Another pause. Then Norgate: 'Well, hurry up! What are you going to do about it?'

Haylock: 'I'll speak to my agents.'

Mackworth: 'Swear you will. At once.'

Haylock: 'I swear I will. Right now.'

Me (and it's not my fault that I love English): 'None of your Transatlantic slang here. Say "at once".'

Haylock: 'At once. At once! I'll do it the minute I get to town. I swear I will.'

That seemed enough for us seniors (I speak of age, not rank), but we hadn't allowed for the necessary cruelty (a wise provision of nature) of the young. Warrender, my lieutenant, and Blore, another angry child, said that Haylock must have supper with us before he left. They indicated mess cake, what (and it was much) was left over of the eternal blancmange, a sardine savoury, and the mess sherry. We protested. They said he deserved to be poisoned, and that they didn't value their commissions a tinker's curse. A vindictive lot! But Haylock slipped the noose round his own neck when he assured us that he 'wouldn't report anyone' for the recent proceedings. We groaned with disgust, and escorted him from the condemned cell to the anteroom, as our guest. It was twenty minutes before we could dig up the mess-steward, who, when he saw Haylock, came near to swooning. Haylock re-established himself in his own esteem by telling him off in the tradesmen's style, which I had never heard before. It justifies the Teuton's hatred of England. Warrender and Blore added cold meat from the sideboard—the greener slices for choice—to our guest's simple fare. Lastly, Mackworth, whose mind, except on parade, when mine doesn't function, moves slowly, lectured—'jawed'—Haylock on the disgrace he had brought on their school. He ended with the classical tag : 'I've a great mind to give you a special licking on my own account for the House's sake. You've got off very cheap with only your head smacked.'

'Thank you,' said Haylock, mouthing through our ossuary. 'You see my partners were educated privately.'

Debased as the dog was, he couldn't keep the proper note of scorn out of his voice. We are of all nations the most incomprehensibly marvellous!

He left at midnight, fulfilled with garbage— we looking at him as the islanders looked at St. Paul. But he took no hurt—*dura ilia messorum* —the indurated intestines of the mess-caterer : and the reforms began next day. We had clean, well-cooked gammon of bacon with pease pudding, followed by excellent treacle-roll and an anchovy toast that was toast and anchovy, not to mention twentieth century eggs. The mess-steward drops on all fours and wags his tail when we whistle now. The C.O. pretends officially to believe that it was the outcome of his letter. One learns to lie in the Army quicker even than on the land.

I don't know what Mackworth may have told you, but these are the bald facts. Use them as I furnish them. There are volumes, social, political, and military in them, but for this occasion, *do* abstain from dotting your *i*'s and crossing your *t*'s.   Circumstances, not scribes, are making the public to think.

After which, it is only fair to tell you that I tied up my platoon on parade this morning owing to an exalted mentality which for the moment (I was thinking over the moral significance of Old School ties and the British social fabric) prevented me from distinguishing between my left hand and my right.   Nineveh was saved because there were six hundred thousand inhabitants in just my case, as I told Norgate afterwards.   I won't tell you what he told me on the parade-ground!

The Church that was at Antioch

The Church that was at Antioch

'But when Peter was come to Antioch, I withstood him to the face, because he was to be blamed.'—St. Paul's Epistle to the Galatians, ii. 11.

His mother, a devout and well-born Roman widow, decided that he was doing himself no good in an Eastern Legion so near to free-thinking Constantinople, and got him seconded for civil duty in Antioch, where his uncle, Lucius Sergius, was head of the urban Police. Valens obeyed as a son and as a young man keen to see life, and, presently, cast up at his uncle's door.

'That sister-in-law of mine,' said the elder, 'never remembers me till she wants something. What have you been doing?'

'Nothing, Uncle.'

'Meaning everything?'

'That's what mother thinks. But I haven't.'

'We shall see. Your quarters are across the inner courtyard. Your—er—baggage is there already. . . . Oh, I shan't interfere with your private arrangements! I'm not the uncle with the rough tongue. Get your bath. We'll talk at supper.'

But before that hour 'Father Serga,' as the

Prefect of Police was called, learned from the Treasury that his nephew had marched overland from Constantinople in charge of a treasure-convoy which, after a brush with brigands in the pass outside Tarsus, he had duly delivered.

' Why didn't you tell me about it? ' his uncle asked at the meal.

' I had to report to the Treasury first,' was the answer.

Serga looked at him. ' Gods! You *are* like your father,' said he. ' Cilicia is scandalously policed.'

' So I noticed. They ambushed us not five miles from Tarsus town. Are we given to that sort of thing here? '

' You make yourself at home early. No. *We* are not, but Syria is a Non-regulation Province—under the Emperor—not the Senate. We've the entire unaccountable East to one side ; the scum of the Mediterranean on the other ; and all hellicat Judaea southward. Anything can happen in Syria. D'you like the prospect? '

' I shall—under you.'

' It's in the blood. The same with men as horses. Now what have you done that distresses your mother so? '

' She's a little behind the times, sir. She follows the old school, of course—the home-worships, and the strict Latin Trinity. I don't think she recognises any Gods outside Jupiter, Juno, and Minerva.'

' I don't either—officially.'

' Nor I, as an officer, sir. But one wants more

than that, and—and—what I learned in Byzant
squared with what I saw with the Fifteenth.'

'You needn't go on. All Eastern Legions
are alike. You mean you follow Mithras—eh?'

The young man bowed his head slightly.

'No harm, boy. It's a soldier's religion, even
if it comes from outside.'

'So I thought. But Mother heard of it. She
didn't approve and—I suppose that's why I'm
here.'

'Off the trident and into the net! Just like a
woman! All Syria is stuffed with Mithraism.
My objection to fancy religions is that they mostly
meet after dark, and that means more work for the
Police. We've a College here of stiff-necked
Hebrews who call themselves Christians.'

'I've heard of them,' said Valens. 'There
isn't a ceremony or symbol they haven't stolen
from the Mithras ritual.'

''No news to *me*! Religions are part of my
office-work; and they'll be part of yours. Our
Synagogue Jews are fighting like Scythians over
this new faith.'

'Does that matter much?'

'So long as they fight each other, we've only
to keep the ring. Divide and rule—especially
with Hebrews. Even these Christians are divided
now. You see—one part of their worship is to
eat together.'

'Another theft! The Supper is the essential
Symbol with us,' Valens interrupted.

'With *us*, it's the essential symbol of trouble
for your uncle, my dear. Anyone can become a

Christian. A Jew may; but he still lives by his
Law of Moses (I've had to master that cursed
code, too), and it regulates all his doings. Then
he sits down at a Christian love-feast beside a
Greek or Westerner, who doesn't kill mutton or
pig—No! No! Jews don't touch pork—as the
Jewish Law lays down. Then the tables are
broken up—but not by laughter—No! No!
Riot!'

'That's childish,' said Valens.

''Wish it were. But my lictors are called in
to keep order, and I have to take the depositions of
Synagogue Jews, denouncing Christians as traitors
to Caesar. If I chose to act on half the stuff their
Rabbis swear to, I'd have respectable little Jew
shop-keepers up every week for conspiracy. *Never*
decide on the evidence, when you're dealing with
Hebrews! Oh, you'll get your bellyful of it!
You're for Market-duty to-morrow in the Little
Circus ward, all among 'em. And now, sleep you
well! I've been on this frontier as far back as
anyone remembers—that's why they call me the
Father of Syria—and oh—it's good to see a sample
of the old stock again!'

Next morning, and for many weeks after,
Valens found himself on Market-inspection duty
with a fat Aedile, who flew into rages because the
stalls were not flushed down at the proper hour.
A couple of his uncle's men were told off to him,
and, of course, introduced him to the thieves' and
prostitutes' quarters, to the leading gladiators, and
so forth.

One day, behind the Little Circus, near Singon

Street, he ran into a mob, where a race-course gang were trying to collect, or evade, some bets on recent chariot-races. The Aedile said it was none of his affair and turned back. The lictors closed up behind Valens, but left the situation in his charge. Then a small hard man with eyebrows was punted on to his chest, amid howls from all around that he was the ringleader of a conspiracy. 'Yes,' said Valens, 'that was an old trick in Byzant; but I think we'll take *you*, my friend.' Turning the small man loose, he gathered in the loudest of his accusers to appear before his uncle.

'You were quite right,' said Serga next day. 'That gentleman was put up to the job—by some-one else. I ordered him one Roman dozen. Did you get the name of the man they were trying to push off on you?'

'Yes. Gaius Julius Paulus. Why?'

'I guessed as much. He's an old acquaint-ance of mine, a Cilician from Tarsus. Well-born —a citizen by descent, and well-educated, but his people have disowned him. So he works for his living.'

'He spoke like a well-born. He's in splendid training, too. 'Felt him. All muscle.'

'Small wonder. He can outmarch a camel. He is really the Prefect of this new sect. He travels all over our Eastern Provinces starting their Colleges and keeping them up to the mark. That's why the Synagogue Jews are hunting him. If they could run him in on the political charge, it would finish him.'

'Is he seditious, then?'

'Not in the least. Even if he were, I wouldn't feed him to the Jews just because they wanted it. One of our Governors tried that game down-coast —for the sake of peace—some years ago. He didn't get it. Do you like your Market-work, my boy?'

'It's interesting. D'you know, uncle, I think the Synagogue Jews are better at their slaughter-house arrangements than we.'

'They are. That's what makes 'em so tough. A dozen stripes are nothing to Apella, though he'll howl the yard down while he's getting 'em. You've the Christians' College in your quarter. How do they strike you?'

''Quiet enough. They're worrying a bit over what they ought to eat at their love-feasts.'

'I know it. Oh, I meant to tell you—we mustn't try 'em too high just now, Valens. My office reports that Paulus, your small friend, is going down-country for a few days to meet another priest of the College, and bring him back to help smooth over their difficulties about their victuals. That means their congregation will be at loose ends till they return. Mass without mind always comes a cropper. So, *now* is when the Synagogue Jews will try to compromise them. I don't want the poor devils stampeded into what can be made to look like political crime. ''Understand?'

Valens nodded. Between his uncle's discursive evening talks, studded with kitchen-Greek and out-of-date Roman society-verses; his morning tours with the puffing Aedile; and the confidences of his lictors at all hours; he fancied he understood Antioch.

So he kept an eye on the rooms in the colonnade behind the Little Circus, where the new faith gathered. One of the many Jew butchers told him that Paulus had left affairs in the hands of some man called Barnabas, but that he would come back with one, Petrus—evidently a well-known character—who would settle all the food-differences between Greek and Hebrew Christians. The butcher had no spite against Greek Christians as such, if they would only kill their meat like decent Jews.

Serga laughed at this talk, but lent Valens an extra man or two, and said that this lion would be his to tackle, before long.

The boy found himself rushed into the arena one hot dusk, when word had come that this was to be a night of trouble. He posted his lictors in an alley within signal, and entered the common-room of the College, where the love-feasts were held. Everyone seemed as friendly as a Christian—to use the slang of the quarter—and Barnabas, a smiling, stately man by the door, specially so.

'I am glad to meet you,' he said. 'You helped our Paulus in that scuffle the other day. We can't afford to lose *him*. I wish he were back!'

He looked nervously down the hall, as it filled with people, of middle and low degree, setting out their evening meal on the bare tables, and greeting each other with a special gesture.

'I assure you,' he went on, his eyes still astray, '*we've* no intention of offending any of the brethren. Our differences can be settled if only——'

As though on a signal, clamour rose from half a dozen tables at once, with cries of 'Pollution! Defilement! Heathen! The Law! The Law! Let Caesar know!' As Valens backed against the wall, the crowd pelted each other with broken meats and crockery, till at last stones appeared from nowhere.

'It's a put-up affair,' said Valens to Barnabas.

'Yes. They come in with stones in their breasts. Be careful! They're throwing your way,' Barnabas replied. The crowd was well-embroiled now. A section of it bore down to where they stood, yelling for the Justice of Rome. His two lictors slid in behind Valens, and a man leaped at him with a knife.

Valens struck up the hand, and the lictors had the man helpless as the weapon fell on the floor. The clash of it stilled the tumult a little. Valens caught the lull, speaking slowly: 'Oh, citizens,' he called, '*must* you begin your love-feasts with battle? Our tripe-sellers' burial-club has better manners.'

A little laughter relieved the tension.

'The Synagogue has arranged this,' Barnabas muttered. 'The responsibility will be laid on me.'

'Who is the Head of your College?' Valens called to the crowd.

The cries rose against each other.

'Paulus! Saul! *He* knows the world——
No! No! Petrus! Our Rock! *He* won't betray
us. Petrus, the Living Rock.'

'When do they come back?' Valens asked.
Several dates were given, sworn to, and denied.

'Wait to fight till they return. I'm not a
priest; but if you don't tidy up these rooms, our
Aedile (Valens gave him his gross nick-name in
the quarter) will fine the sandals off your feet.
And you mustn't trample good food either. When
you've finished, I'll lock up after you. Be quick.
I know our Prefect if you don't.'

They toiled, like children rebuked. As they
passed out with baskets of rubbish, Valens smiled.
The matter would not be pressed further.

'Here is our key,' said Barnabas at the end.
'The Synagogue will swear I hired this man to
kill you.'

'Will they? Let's look at him.'

The lictors pushed their prisoner forward.

'Ill-fortune!' said the man. 'I owed you
for my brother's death in Tarsus Pass.'

'Your brother tried to kill me,' Valens retorted.

The fellow nodded.

'Then we'll call it even-throws,' Valens signed
to the lictors, who loosed hold. 'Unless you
really want to see my uncle?'

The man vanished like a trout in the dusk.
Valens returned the key to Barnabas, and said:

'If I were you, I shouldn't let your people
in again till your leaders come back. You don't
know Antioch as I do.

He went home, the grinning lictors behind him, and they told his uncle, who grinned also, but said that he had done the right thing—even to patronising Barnabas.

'Of course, *I* don't know Antioch as you do; but, seriously, my dear, I think you've saved their Church for the Christians this time. I've had three depositions already that your Cilician friend was a Christian hired by Barnabas. 'Just as well for Barnabas that you let the brute go.'

'You told me you didn't want them stampeded into trouble. Besides, it was fair-throws. I may have killed his brother after all. We had to kill two of 'em.'

'Good! You keep a level head in a tight corner. You'll need it. There's no lying about in secluded parks for *us*! I've got to see Paulus and Petrus when they come back, and find out what they've decided about their infernal feasts. Why can't they all get decently drunk and be done with it?'

'They talk of them both down-town as though they were Gods. By the way, uncle, all the riot was worked up by Synagogue Jews sent from Jerusalem—not by our lot at all.'

'You *don't* say so? Now, perhaps, you understand why I put you on market-duty with old Sow-Belly! You'll make a Police-officer yet.'

Valens met the scared, mixed congregation round the fountains and stalls as he went about his quarter. They were rather relieved at being locked out of their rooms for the time; as well as by the news that Paulus and Petrus would report to the Prefect of Police before addressing them on the great food-question.

Valens was not present at the first part of that interview, which was official. The second, in the cool, awning-covered courtyard, with drinks and *hors-d'œuvre*, all set out beneath the vast lemon and lavender sunset, was much less formal.

'You have met, I think,' said Serga to the little lean Paulus as Valens entered.

'Indeed, yes. Under God, we are twice your debtors,' was the quick reply.

'Oh, that was part of my duty. I hope you found our roads good on your journey,' said Valens.

'Why, yes. I think they were.' Paulus spoke as if he had not noticed them.

'We should have done better to come by boat,' said his companion, Petrus, a large fleshy man, with eyes that seemed to see nothing, and a half-palsied right hand that lay idle in his lap.

'Valens came overland from Byzant,' said his uncle. 'He rather fancies his legs.'

'He ought to at his age. What was your best day's march on the Via Sebaste?' Paulus asked interestedly, and, before he knew, Valens was reeling off his mileage on mountain-roads every step of which Paulus seemed to have trod.

'That's good,' was the comment. 'And I expect you march in heavier order than I.'

'What would you call your best day's work?' Valens asked in turn.

'I have covered . . .' Paulus checked him-

self. ' And yet not I but the God,' he muttered.
' It's hard to cure oneself of boasting.'

A spasm wrenched Petrus' face.

' Hard indeed,' said he.   Then he addressed
himself to Paulus as though none other were
present.   ' It is true I have eaten with Gentiles
and as the Gentiles ate.   Yet, at the time, I
doubted if it were wise.'

' That is behind us now,' said Paulus gently.
' The decision has been taken for the Church—
that little Church which you saved, my son.'   He
turned on Valens with a smile that half-captured
the boy's heart.   ' Now—as a Roman and a
Police-officer—what think you of us Christians? '

' That I have to keep order in my own
ward.'

' Good!   Caesar must be served.   But—as
a servant of Mithras, shall we say—how think
you about our food-disputes? '

Valens hesitated.   His uncle encouraged him
with a nod.   ' As a servant of Mithras I eat with
any initiate, so long as the food is clean,' said
Valens.

' But,' said Petrus, ' *that* is the crux.'

' Mithras also tells us,' Valens went on, ' to
share a bone covered with dirt, if better cannot be
found.'

' You observe no difference, then, between
peoples at your feasts? '   Paulus demanded.

' How dare we?   We are all His children.
Men make laws.   Not Gods,' Valens quoted
from the old Ritual.

' Say that again, child! '

'Gods do not make laws. They change men's hearts. The rest is the Spirit.'

'You heard it, Petrus? You heard that? It is the utter Doctrine itself!' Paulus insisted to his dumb companion.

Valens, a little ashamed of having spoken of his faith, went on:

'They tell me the Jew butchers here want the monopoly of killing for your people. Trade feeling's at the bottom of most of it.'

'A little more than that perhaps,' said Paulus. 'Listen a minute.' He threw himself into a curious tale about the God of the Christians, Who, he said, had taken the shape of a Man, and Whom the Jerusalem Jews, years ago, had got the authorities to deal with as a conspirator. He said that he himself, at that time a right Jew, quite agreed with the sentence, and had denounced all who followed the new God. But one day the Light and the Voice of the God broke over him, and he experienced a rending change of heart—precisely as in the Mithras creed. Then he met, and had been initiated by, some men who had walked and talked and, more particularly, had eaten, with the new God before He was killed, and who had seen Him after, like Mithras, He had risen from His grave. Paulus and those others—Petrus was one of them—had next tried to preach Him to the Jews, but that was no success; and, one thing leading to another, Paulus had gone back to his home at Tarsus, where his people disowned him for a renegade. There he had broken down with overwork and despair.

Till then, he said, it had never occurred to any of them to show the new religion to any except right Jews; for their God had been born in the shape of a Jew. Paulus himself only came to realise the possibilities of outside work, little by little. He said he had all the foreign preaching in his charge now, and was going to change the whole world by it.

Then he made Petrus finish the tale, who explained, speaking very slowly, that he had, some years ago, received orders from the God to preach to a Roman officer of Irregulars down-country; after which that officer and most of his people wanted to become Christians. So Petrus had initiated them the same night, although none of them were Hebrews. 'And,' Petrus ended, 'I saw there is nothing under heaven that we dare call unclean.'

Paulus turned on him like a flash and cried:

'You admit it! Out of your own mouth it is evident.' Petrus shook like a leaf and his right hand almost lifted.

'Do *you* too twit me with my accent?' he began, but his face worked and he choked.

'Nay! God forbid! And God once more forgive *me*!' Paulus seemed as distressed as he, while Valens stared at the extraordinary outbreak.

'Talking of clean and unclean,' his uncle said tactfully, 'there's that ugly song come up again in the City. They were singing it on the city-front yesterday, Valens. Did you notice?'

He looked at his nephew, who took the hint.

'If it was "Pickled Fish," sir, they were. Will it make trouble?'

' As surely as these fish '—a jar of them stood
on the table—' make one thirsty. How does it
go? Oh yes.' Serga hummed:

> Oie-eaah!
> 'From the Shark and the Sardine—the clean and the unclean—
> To the Pickled Fish of Galilee, said Petrus, shall be mine.

He twanged it off to the proper gutter-drawl.

> (Ha-ow?)
> In the nets or on the line,
> Till the Gods Themselves decline.
> (Whe-en?)
> When the Pickled Fish of Galilee ascend the Esquiline!

That'll be something of a flood—worse than live
fish in trees! Hey?'

' It will happen one day,' said Paulus.

He turned from Petrus, whom he had been
soothing tenderly, and resumed in his natural,
hardish voice:

' Yes. We owe a good deal to that Centurion
being converted when he was. It taught us that
the whole world could receive the God; and it
showed *me* my next work. I came over from
Tarsus to teach here for a while. And I shan't
forget how good the Prefect of Police was to us
then.'

' For one thing, Cornelius was an early colleague,' Serga smiled largely above his strong cup.
' " Prime companion "—how does it go?—" we
drank the long, long Eastern day out together,"
and so on. For another, I know a good work-
man when I see him. That camel-kit you made
for my desert-tours, Paul, is as sound as ever.

And for a third—which to a man of my habits is most important—that Greek doctor you recommended me is the only one who understands my tumid liver.'

He passed a cup of all but unmixed wine, which Paulus handed to Petrus, whose lips were flaky white at the corners.

'But your trouble,' the Prefect went on, 'will come from your own people. Jerusalem never forgives. They'll get you run in on the charge of *laesa majestatis* soon or late.'

'Who knows better than I?' said Petrus. 'And the decision we *all* have taken about our love-feasts may unite Hebrew and Greek against us. As I told you, Prefect, we are asking Christian Greeks not to make the feasts difficult for Christian Hebrews by eating meat that has not been lawfully killed. (Our way is much more wholesome, anyhow.) Still, we may get round that. But there's *one* vital point. Some of our Greek Christians bring food to the love-feasts that they've bought from your priests, after your sacrifices have been offered. That we can't allow.'

Paulus turned to Valens imperiously.

'You mean they buy Altar-scraps,' the boy said. 'But only the very poor do it; and it's chiefly block-trimmings. The sale's a perquisite of the Altar-butchers. They wouldn't like its being stopped.'

'Permit separate tables for Hebrew and Greek, as I once said,' Petrus spoke suddenly.

'That would end in separate churches. There

shall be but *one* Church,' Paulus spoke over his shoulder, and the words fell like rods. 'You think there may be trouble, Valens?'

'My uncle——' Valens began.

'No, no!' the Prefect laughed. 'Singon Street Markets are your Syria. Let's hear what our Legate thinks of his Province.'

Valens flushed and tried to pull his wits together.

'Primarily,' he said, 'it's pig, I suppose. Hebrews hate pork.'

'Quite right, too. Catch *me* eating pig east the Adriatic! *I* don't want to die of worms. Give me a young Sabine tush-ripe boar! I have spoken!'

Serga mixed himself another raw cup and took some pickled Lake fish to bring out the flavour.

'But, still,' Petrus leaned forward like a deaf man, 'if we admitted Hebrew and Greek Christians to separate tables we should escape——'

'Nothing, except salvation,' said Paulus. 'We have broken with the whole Law of Moses. We live in and through and by our God only. Else we are nothing. What is the sense of harking back to the Law at meal-times? Whom do we deceive? Jerusalem? Rome? The God? You yourself have eaten with Gentiles! You yourself have said——'

'One says more than one means when one is carried away,' Petrus answered, and his face worked again.

'This time you will say precisely what is **meant**,' Paulus spoke between his teeth. 'We

will keep the Churches *one*—in and through the
Lord.   You dare not deny this?'

'I dare nothing—the God knows!   But I
have denied Him. . . .   I denied Him. . . .
And He said—He said I was the Rock on which
His Church should stand.'

'*I* will see that it stands, and yet not I——'
Paulus' voice dropped again.   'To-morrow you
will speak to the one Church of the one Table the
world over.'

'That's *your* business,' said the Prefect.   'But
I warn you again, it's your own people who will
make you trouble.'

Paulus rose to say farewell, but in the act he
staggered, put his hand to his forehead and, as
Valens steered him to a divan, collapsed in the
grip of that deadly Syrian malaria which strikes
like a snake.   Valens, having suffered, called to
his rooms for his heavy travelling-fur.   His girl,
whom he had bought in Constantinople a few
months before, fetched it.   Petrus tucked it
awkwardly round the shivering little figure; the
Prefect ordered lime-juice and hot water, and
Paulus thanked them and apologised, while his
teeth rattled on the cup.

'Better to-day than to-morrow,' said the
Prefect.   'Drink—sweat—and sleep here the
night.   Shall I send for my doctor?'

But Paulus said that the fit would pass naturally, and as soon as he could stand he insisted
on going away with Petrus, late though it was, to
prepare their announcement to the Church.

'Who was that big, clumsy man?' his girl

asked Valens as she took up the fur. 'He made more noise than the small one, who was really suffering.'

'He's a priest of the new College by the Little Circus, dear. He believes, uncle told me, that he once denied his God, Who, he says, died for him.'

She halted in the moonlight, the glossy jackal skins over her arm.

'Does he? *My* God bought me from the dealers like a horse. Too much, too, he paid. Didn't he? 'Fess, thou?'

'No, thee!' emphatically.

'But I wouldn't deny *my* God—living or dead!... Oh—but *not* dead! My God's going to live—for me. Live—live Thou, my heart's blood, for ever!'

It would have been better had Paulus and Petrus not left the Prefect's house so late; for the rumour in the city, as the Prefect knew, and as the long conference seemed to confirm, was that Caesar's own Secretary of State in Rome was, through Paulus, arranging for a general defilement of the Hebrew with the Greek Christians, and that after this had been effected, by promiscuous eating of unlawful foods, all Jews would be lumped together as Christians—members, that is, of a mere free-thinking sect instead of the very particular and troublesome 'Nation of Jews within the Empire.' Eventually, the story went, they would lose their rights as Roman citizens, and could then be sold on any slave-stand.

'Of course,' Serga explained to Valens next

day, ' that has been put about by the Jerusalem Synagogue. Our Antioch Jews aren't clever enough. Do you see their game? Petrus is a defiler of the Hebrew nation. If he is cut down to-night by some properly primed young zealot so much the better.'

' He won't be,' said Valens. ' I'm looking after him.'

' 'Hope so. But, if he isn't knifed,' Serga went on, ' they'll try to work up city riots on the grounds that, when all the Jews have lost their civil rights, he'll set up as a sort of King of the Christians.'

' At Antioch? In the present year of Rome? That's crazy, Uncle.'

' *Every* crowd is crazy. What else do we draw pay for? But, listen. Post a Mounted Police patrol at the back of the Little Circus. Use 'em to keep the people moving when the congregation comes out. Post two of your men in the Porch of their College itself. Tell Paulus and Petrus to wait there with them, till the streets are clear. Then fetch 'em both over here. Don't hit till you have to. Hit hard *before* the stones fly. Don't get my little horses knocked about more than you can help, and—look out for " Pickled Fish " ! '

Knowing his own quarter, it seemed to Valens as he went on duty that evening, that his uncle's precautions had been excessive. The Christian Church, of course, was full, and a large crowd waited outside for word of the decision about the feasts. Most of them seemed to be Christians of sorts, but there was an element of gesticulating Antiochene loafers, and like all crowds they amused themselves with popular songs while they waited. Things went smoothly, till a group of Christians raised a rather explosive hymn, which ran:

> ' Enthroned above Caesar and Judge of the Earth!
>   We wait on Thy coming—oh tarry not long!
>   As the Kings of the Sunrise
>   Drew sword at Thy Birth,
>   So we arm in this midnight of insult and wrong!'

' Yes—and if one of their fish-stalls is bumped over by a camel—it's *my* fault!' said Valens. ' Now they've started it!'

Sure enough, voices on the outskirts broke into ' Pickled Fish,' but before Valens could speak, they were suppressed by someone crying:

' Quiet there, or you'll get your pickle before your fish.'

It was close on twilight when a cry rose from within the packed Church, and its congregation breasted out into the crowd. They all talked about the new orders for their love-feasts, most of them agreeing that they were sensible and easy. They agreed, too, that Petrus (Paulus did not seem to have taken much part in the debate) had spoken like one inspired, and they were all extremely proud of being Christians. Some of them began to link arms across the alley, and strike into the ' Enthroned above Caesar ' chorus.

' And this, I *think*,' Valens called to the young Commandant of the Mounted Patrol, ' is where we'll begin to steer 'em home. Oh! And " Let night also have her well-earned hymn," as Uncle 'ud say.'

There filed out from behind the Little Circus four blaring trumpets, a standard, and a dozen Mounted Police. Their wise little grey Arabs sidled, passaged, shouldered, and nosed softly into the mob, as though they wanted petting, while the trumpets deafened the narrow street. An open square, near by, eased the pressure before long. Here the Patrol broke into fours, and gridironed it, saluting the images of the Gods at each corner and in the centre. People stopped, as usual, to watch how cleverly the incense was cast down over the withers into the spouting cressets; children reached up to pat horses which they said they knew; family groups re-found each other in the smoky dusk; hawkers offered cooked suppers; and soon the crowd melted into the main traffic avenues. Valens went over to the Church porch, where Petrus and Paulus waited between his lictors.

'That was well done,' Paulus began.

'How's the fever?' Valens asked.

'I was spared for to-day. I think, too, that by The Blessing we have carried our point.'

'Good hearing! My uncle bids me say you are welcome at his house.'

'That is always a command,' said Paulus, with a quick down-country gesture. 'Now that this day's burden is lifted, it will be a delight.'

Petrus joined up like a weary ox. Valens greeted him, but he did not answer.

'Leave him alone,' Paulus whispered. 'The

virtue has gone out of me—him—for the while.'
His own face looked pale and drawn.

The street was empty, and Valens took a short
cut through an alley, where light ladies leaned out
of windows and laughed. The three strolled
easily together, the lictors behind them, and far
off they heard the trumpets of the Night Horse
saluting some statue of a Caesar, which marked
the end of their round. Paulus was telling Valens
how the whole Roman Empire would be changed
by what the Christians had agreed to about their
love-feasts, when an impudent little Jew boy stole
up behind them, playing ' Pickled Fish ' on some
sort of desert bag-pipe.

' Can't you stop that young pest, one of you? '
Valens asked laughing. ' You shan't be mocked
on this great night of yours, Paulus.'

The lictors turned back a few paces, and shook
a torch at the brat, but he retreated and drew them
on. Then they heard Paulus shout, and when
they hurried back, found Valens prostrate and
coughing—his blood on the fringe of the kneeling
Paul's robe. Petrus stooped, waving a helpless
hand above them.

' Someone ran out from behind that well-head.
He stabbed him as he ran, and ran on. Listen ! '
said Paulus.

But there was not even the echo of a footfall
for clue, and the Jew boy had vanished like a bat.
Said Valens from the ground :

' Home ! Quick ! I have it ! '

They tore a shutter out of a shop-front, lifted
and carried him, while Paulus walked beside.

They set him down in the lighted inner courtyard of the Prefect's house, and a lictor hurried for the Prefect's physician.

Paulus watched the boy's face, and, as Valens shivered a little, called to the girl to fetch last night's fur rug. She brought it, laid the head on her breast, and cast herself beside Valens.

'It isn't bad. It doesn't bleed much. So it *can't* be bad—can it?' she repeated. Valens' smile reassured her, till the Prefect came and recognised the deadly upward thrust under the ribs. He turned on the Hebrews.

'To-morrow you will look for where your Church stood,' said he.

Valens lifted the hand that the girl was not kissing.

'No—no!' he gasped. 'The Cilician did it! For his brother! He said it.'

'The Cilician you let go to save these Christians because I——?' Valens signed to his uncle that it was so, while the girl begged him to steal strength from her till the doctor should come.

'Forgive me,' said Serga to Paulus. 'None the less I wish your God in Hades once for all. . . . But what am I to write his mother? Can't either of you two talking creatures tell me what I'm to tell his mother?'

'What has *she* to do with him?' the slave-girl cried. 'He is mine—mine! I testify before all Gods that he bought me! I am his. He is mine.'

'We can deal with the Cilician and his friends later,' said one of the lictors. 'But what now?'

For some reason, the man, though used to butcher-work, looked at Petrus.

'Give him drink and wait,' said Petrus. 'I have—seen such a wound.' Valens drank and a shade of colour came to him. He motioned the Prefect to stoop.

'What is it? Dearest of lives, what troubles?'

'The Cilician and his friends. . . . Don't be hard on them. . . . They get worked up. . . . They don't know what they are doing. . . . Promise!'

'This is not I, child. It is the Law.'

''No odds. You're Father's brother. . . . Men make laws—not Gods. . . . Promise! . . . It's finished with me.'

Valens' head eased back on its yearning pillow.

Petrus stood like one in a trance. The tremor left his face as he repeated:

'"Forgive them, for they know not what they do." Heard you *that*, Paulus? He, a heathen and an idolator, said it!'

'I heard. What hinders now that we should baptize him?' Paulus answered promptly.

Petrus stared at him as though he had come up out of the sea.

'Yes,' he said at last. 'It is the little maker of tents. . . . And what does he *now*—command?'

Paulus repeated the suggestion.

Painfully, that other raised the palsied hand that he had once held up in a hall to deny a charge.

'Quiet!' said he. 'Think you that one who has spoken Those Words needs such as *we* are to certify him to any God?'

Paulus cowered before the unknown colleague,

vast and commanding, revealed after all these years.

'As you please—as you please,' he stammered, overlooking the blasphemy. 'Moreover there is the concubine.'

The girl did not heed, for the brow beneath her lips was chilling, even as she called on her God who had bought her at a price that he should not die but live.

THE DISCIPLE

He that hath a Gospel,
  To loose upon Mankind,
Though he serve it utterly—
  Body, soul, and mind—
Though he go to Calvary
  Daily for its gain—
It is His Disciple
  Shall make his labour vain.

He that hath a Gospel,
  For all earth to own—
Though he etch it on the steel,
  Or carve it on the stone—
Not to be misdoubted
  Through the after-days—
It is His Disciple
  Shall read it many ways.

It is His Disciple
  (Ere Those Bones are dust)
Who shall change the Charter
  Who shall split the Trust—
Amplify distinctions,
  Rationalise the Claim,
Preaching that the Master
  Would have done the same.

It is His Disciple
  Who shall tell us how
Much the Master would have scrapped
  Had he lived till now—
What he would have modified
  Of what he said before—
It is His Disciple
  Shall do this and more. . . .

He that hath a Gospel
  Whereby Heaven is won
(Carpenter, or Cameleer,
  Or Maya's dreaming son),
Many swords shall pierce Him,
  Mingling blood with gall;
But His Own Disciple
  Shall wound Him worst of all!

Aunt Ellen

THE PLAYMATE

She is not Folly—that I know.
Her steadfast eyelids tell me so
When, at the hour the lights divide,
She steals as summonsed to my side.

When, finger on the pursèd lip ;
In secret, mirthful fellowship
She, heralding new-framed delights,
Breathes, ' This shall be a Night of Nights ! '

Then out of Time and out of Space,
Is built an Hour and a Place
Where all an earnest, baffled Earth
Blunders and trips to make us mirth ;

Where, from the trivial flux of Things,
Rise unconceived miscarryings
Outrageous but immortal, shown,
Of Her great love, to me alone. . . .

She is not Wisdom but, may be,
Wiser than all the Norns is She :
And more than Wisdom I prefer
To wait on Her,—to wait on Her !

Aunt Ellen

A PRUDENT man, working from the North to London, along the Eastern Counties, provides himself with friends from whom he can get food and lodging.

Miss Gillon, whom all her world calls 'Aunt Ellen,' gave me lunch at her house near Grantham. She wished to send an eiderdown quilt to an old family servant at Hammersmith. Surely I remembered Prescott from past ages? To-morrow would be Prescott's birthday. The quilt had been delayed for repairs. A man would not know, of course, how tender eiderdown quilts were. Should I be in London that evening? Then, in the morning, would I take the quilt round to Prescott's address? Prescott would be so pleased! And surprised, too; for there were some little birthday remembrances from herself and from Saunders wrapped up in the quilt.

Saunders, Prescott's successor, went upstairs and returned, her mouth full of knotted strings, clasping an outsized pasteboard coffin. The eiderdown, a loudly-patterned affair, was rolled into bolster form, bound in two places with broad puce ribbons, and coaxed into it. Saunders wove lashings over all and I carried it out and up-ended it beside my steering-wheel.

Going down the drive I could scarcely squint round the corner of the thing, and at the turn into the road, it lurched into my eye. So I declutched it, and tied it to the back of the two-seater. True, I made most of the knots with my gloves on, but, to compensate, I wove Saunders' reef-points into the rear of the car as carefully as the pendulous oriole stays her nest.

Then I went on to dine at a seat of learning where I was due to pick up a friend—Henry Brankes Lettcombe, O.B.E.—once a Colonel of Territorials—whose mission, in peace, was the regeneration of our native cinema industry. He was a man of many hopes, which translated themselves into prospectuses that faded beneath the acid breath of finance. Sometimes I wrote the prospectuses, because he promised me that, when his ship came in, he would produce the supreme film of the world—the ' Life of St. Paul.' He said it would be easier than falling off a log, once he had launched his Pan-Imperial Life-Visions' Association.

He had said I should find him at St. Martin's College, which lies in a rather congested quarter of a University town. I always look on my mud-guards as hostages to Fortune ; yet even I was a little piqued at the waywardness of the traffic. It was composed of the hatless young, in flannel trousers and vivid blazers, who came and went and stopped without warning, in every manner of machine. They were as genial as those should be whose fathers pay all their bills. Only one, a thick-set youth in a canoe-ended natural wood sporting machine, rammed me on the starboard quarter and declared it was my fault.

His companion—slim, spotless, and urbane—smiled disarmingly. ' I shouldn't chide with him if I were you, sir,' he said. ' He's been tuning-in.'

I disengaged, and passed on to St. Martin's where I found Lettcombe also tuning-in. He was returned lately from a place called Hollywood, and he told us of energies unparalleled, and inventions beyond our imaginings, controlled by super-men who, having no racial prepossessions, could satisfy the ' mass-appetence ' of all the races who attend ' Sinnymus.' He spoke, further, of ' injuncted psychoses ' and ' endyoclinics '—unsafe words to throw at the Learned who do not attend ' Ki-*ne*-mas.' They retaliated with abracadabras of their own, and demanded definitions of his. Lettcombe, always nebulous, except in action, drank a little College Madeira to help him define, and when we left, at last, for London, was quite definite.

While driving, I listened to the creation, on improved lines, of the Pan-Imperial Life-Visions' Association. It was now, he said, to be run in conjunction with Hollywood. (He had abandoned my scheme of vast studios at the top of Helvellyn ; with marine annexes on the Wash and Holy Island!) I led back tactfully to the St. Paul, pointing out that it would be silly to have the Apostle sunstruck among Californian cacti which, in the nature of things, could not have been discovered till fifteen hundred years after his martyrdom. Lettcombe retorted that the spirit, not the letter, gave life, and offered a semi-annually divorced Film Star for the part of the Elect Lady.

I was beginning to formulate some preliminary objections, when I heard behind us one single smart, drum-like tap. Lettcombe had just unpacked from his imported vocabulary the compelling word, ' crypto-psychic-apperceptiveness.' I braked, being cryptically aware that Saunders' coffin had come adrift, and was lying in the fairway, at the same time as I psychically apperceived the scented loveliness of the early summer night, and the stillness that emphasises percipience when one's car has stopped. Lettcombe was so full of the shortcomings of all the divorced husbands of the Lady to be elected, that he kept on taking her part to the abandoned steering-wheel long after I had descended and gone back afoot (the reverse not suiting my car's temperament) to recover the lost packet.

The road behind us ran straight, a few hundred yards, to a small wood and there turned. It was wholly void when I started. First I found the coffin, void also; hacked it into the ditch that it had nearly reached, and held on, looking for a bed-quilt tied in two places. A large head-light illuminated the wood. A small car pelted round the curve. A horn squawked. There was a sound of ironmongery in revolt; the car bounded marsupially to its right, and, with its head-light, disappeared. But before it did this, I fancied I had seen my bundle lying in its path. I went to look.

Obviously no one had been hurt, for an even voice out of the dark pronounced that someone had done it now. A second voice, gruff and heated, asked if he had seen why he had done it. 'For Women and Wine,' said the first voice dreamily. 'Unless that's how you always change gears.'

They continued talking, like spirits who had encountered by chance in pure space.

The car, meanwhile, knelt on its forehead, presenting a canoe-shaped stern of elaborate carpenter's work to the chill road. Beneath its hindwheels lay a longish lump, that stopped three of my heart-beats, so humanly dead did it show, till I saw that I should have to find Prescott another eiderdown; and I grew hot against those infants growling and cooing together by the bows of their meretricious craft. Let them enjoy my sensations unwarned, and all the better, if they should imagine they had done murder. Thus I argued in my lower soul; but, on the higher planes of it, where thought merges into Intuition and Prophecy, my Demon of Irresponsibility sang :—' I am with you once more! Stand back and let Me take charge. This night shall be also One of the Nights.' So I stood back and waited, as I have before, on Chance and Circumstance which, accepted humbly, betray not the True Believer.

A shadow in a tight-waisted waterproof, with a dress-suit beneath it, came out of the ditch ; saw what I had seen ; drew its breath sharply, and, after a pause, laid hands slowly on the horror beneath the rear wheels. Suddenly it raised one of its own hands to its mouth and sucked it. I caught a hissing expulsion of relief and saw its outline relax. It then tugged, drew things free, and hauled and hauled at—shall we say Aunt Ellen?—till she was clear. The end of her that came out last was, so to speak, burst. The shadow coiled her up, embraced her with both arms, and partly decanted, partly stuffed, her into the dicky of the car, which it closed silently. I heard a very low chuckle, and I too laughed. The shadow tiptoed over to me. 'Yours?' it breathed. 'Yes,' I whispered. 'Do you need it, sir?' 'I leave it to you, partner,' I replied. It chuckled again and patted me on the shoulder with what seemed a mixture of appreciation and almost filial reverence, or even—but this might have been senile vanity—camaraderie. Then it turned and spoke towards the ditch: 'Phil! She's as dead as a classic.'

The reply, delivered apparently through herbage, was that 'Phil' had ruined his shirt-front.

The shadow sighed, resignedly, 'Never mind. We'll break it to him later, sir,' and patted my shoulder once more. In the silence that followed I heard Lettcombe who, by now, had come to miss me, in search along the road. He chanted his desire that the glow-worm should lend me her eyes, and that shooting-stars, which are as rare as glow-worms in early summer, should chaperone me through all the Eastern Counties.

A London-bound lorry came round the bend, and asked him how much of the road he needed. Lettcombe replied in the terms of the front-line of '16; the lorry hurled them back with additions from the same gory lexicon, laughed pleasantly, and went on.

'Well,' said the voice called Phil, 'are you going to stick here all night? I've *got* to get—'

'Hush,' replied the shadow. 'I've disposed of her now, thank goodness. Back out, if you can.'

'"Thus—thus to come unto thee!"' carolled Lettcombe. '*Did* you see that lorry? 'Nearly ran me down! What's the matter? Has there been an accident? I'm looking for a friend.'

'Was she a woman?' the shadow asked him.

The two had barely time to skip aside, when the car, with unnecessary power, belched its indecent little self back on to the tar. Phil, a thick-set youth, confused among levers, put pieces of questions to the shadow, which at a vast leisure answered to the name of 'Bunny.'

'What's happened? What's *really* happened? What were you saying about women?' Phil repeated.

'I seldom say anything about women. Not even when they are dead,' Bunny replied.

'Have you seen a dead woman, then?' Phil turned on Lettcombe.

'Nothing but that dam' lorry. 'Nearly ran me down, too. Didn't you see?'

'Look here, Bunny,' Phil went on. 'I've *got* to be at Cadogan Gardens by midnight and—I—I'm here and—Haman's head-light's wonky. Something *must* have happened. *What's* happened?'

'And I haven't seen my friend, either,'

Lettcombe struck in. ' I wouldn't worry about him, only I don't drive much.' He described me with the lewd facility which pavement and cinema artists are given in place of love of beauty or reverence for intellect.

' Never mind him ! ' said Bunny. ' Here's the Regius Professor of Medicine of ——— ' he named the opposition seat of learning, and by a certain exquisite expansion of bearing included me in the circle. Phil did not.

' Then what the devil's he doing up *our* street? Home ! Go home, sir ! ' he said to me. There was no reverence in this address, but Bunny apologised for him very prettily.

' You see, he's in love,' he began. ' He's using this car to—er thus—thus—to come unto her. That makes him nervous and jealous. And he has run over an old lady, though he doesn't realise it. When I get *that* into his head he'll react quite differently. By the way, sir, did *you* observe any sign of life after we released her ? '

' I did not.' The actual Regius Professor of Medicine could not have spoken more authoritatively.

' Oh, Lord ! Someone dead ? ' Phil gasped. ' Where ? '

' I slipped her into that lorry just now—to give her a chance. She looked rather bitten about the back, but she may be alive. We must catch up with her and find out,' said Bunny.

' You can't mistake the lorry either,' Lettcombe added. ' It stinks of hens. 'Nearly ran me down. You saw it, didn't you ? '

'In that case we had better get a move on,' Bunny suggested.

The ditching had not improved the car, but she was still far from contemptible. Her left fore-wheel inclined, on its stub-axle, towards (technically speaking) the Plane of the Ecliptic; her radiator sweated like Samson at Gaza; her steering-gear played like all Wordsworth's own daffodils; her swivelling head-light glared fixedly at the ground beneath it like a Trappist monk under penance; but her cranking-handle was beyond comparison, because it was not there. She answered, however, to the self-starter, with promising kicks. There may have been a few spare odds and ends left behind us, but, as Bunny said, that was Haman's fault for not having provided a torch. I understood that Mr. Haman was seldom permitted to use his own car in term-time, because he had once volunteered that he was a 'thorough-goin' sport,' and was now being educated; and as soon as Lettcombe understood why I had accepted a Regius Professorship of Medicine, and what and where the old lady was, he dropped a good deal of his morbid hate against his lorry, and, for a man of his unimaginative trade, did good work.

Our labours were rather interrupted by Phil's officious attempts to find out whether his victim were dead or like to live. Bunny was as patient with him as any nurse, even when he began once more to hope to reach Cadogan Gardens by 'a little after midnight'; it being then eleven forty-seven and a clear night.

We all, except Phil, felt we knew each other well when Mr. Haman's car was assembled and controllable, and, like the travellers of old, ' decided henceforth to journey in company.' Mr. Haman's car led, with mine in support to light it should any of its electric fittings fail.

Owing to her brutalised fore-wheel, which gave her the look and gait of a dachshund, she carried, as mariners say, a strong port helm ; and if let off the wind for an instant, slid towards the ditch. This reduced her speed, but, on the other hand, there was not so much overtaking, at which manoeuvre her infirmities made her deadlier than Boadicea's chariots.

Thus, then, we laboured London-ward for a while, deep in the heart of the night and all its unpredictable allures. (The caption is Lettcombe's.) Presently we smelt a smell out of the dear dead days when horses drew carts, and blacksmiths shod them—but not at midnight. Lettcombe was outlining ' The Shaving of Shagpat ' for film purposes, when our squadron-leader stopped ; and Bunny, sniffing, walked back to us. ' Do you happen to remember,' he asked, ' if she wore a feather bonnet—or a boa ? '

Lettcombe and I remembered both these articles distinctly.

' Then *that*'s all right.' He called back : ' She *did*, Phil. See if it's anywhere on the dumb-iron.'

Phil got out and grovelled, as we walked towards the smell. He rose with a piece of loudly-patterned silk in his hand.

' I've found this ! ' said he hoarsely, ' Low down on the radiator.'

' Petticoat ! ' said Bunny. ' Torn off ! Tck ! Tck ! I *am* sorry, old top.'

' It don't prove anything,' said Lettcombe, ' except that you may have grazed her. What we've got to do is to catch up with that lorry. Perhaps she's only stunned.'

' She's pretty well red-hot,' said Bunny, beside the crackling car.

He opened the bonnet, and the smell let itself out. It was complex, but with no trace of inferiority.

I remembered then that at least a quarter of ' Aunt Ellen's ' figure had been missing after the collision. We recovered a good deal of it, loose and blackening inside the bonnet ; yet I did not at first see why there should be greasy, fluffy deposits over the exhaust and the mechanism, any more than I could get abreast of the smell. There were motives in it of fats, butyric acid, alcohols, mineral oils, heated rubber, and singed leather, to a broadly-handled accompaniment of charred feathers, lightened by suggestions of crisped flesh.

I began to work out the birthday presents which Miss Gillon and the kindly Saunders must have packed inside ' Aunt Ellen.' Butter and hair-oil I could identify; gloves, perhaps ; a horn or tortoiseshell comb certainly. The alcohol might have begun the journey as eau-de-Cologne ; and there were traces of kidney. On digital exploration, it appeared to be the hair-oil that had really stopped so many of the radiator-holes with pledgets of oiled down. The fan must have sucked the mixture from the piece of quilt that had adhered to the radiator until the whole had impacted, whereby Mr. Haman's machine had naturally choked and her works turned plum-colour.

'Those holes ought to be cleared while she cools,' I said.

'Your tie-pin's the thing.' Bunny turned to Lettcombe, who, being of a decorative breed, detached a cameo head of Eros from his green made-up tie and handed it to Phil, who fell to work. A winkle-vendor could not have excelled him.

As Regius Professor of Medicine, my diagnosis of his condition was that the jolt into the ditch, combined with previous 'tunings-in,' had passed Phil into a waking trance, in which he reacted mechanically to stimuli, but felt no real pain.

'Now, we've got to fill the radiator,' said Bunny, while Phil blew at each hole after it was cleared.

In democratic England, if you make noise enough in public, someone, official or unofficial, will attend to your wants. While our twin Klaxons were developing this theme, a man came out of a gate in a hedge, and told us reproachfully that he had been sitting up solely in order to catch 'W.E.A.F.' on the midnight hush. Lettcombe said that at the present conjunction of the planets there was no chance of this till crack of dawn. Instantly all arguments dissolved into the babble of fellow-imbeciles. Bunny and I left them (the man tossed his head at us sideways, saying ' Oh, *that's* all right. Ask Ma.') and went up a path to a new, dampish bungalow where there was a room with a water-tap and a jug. An old lady in a kimono came out of another room, and at once fell a victim to Bunny in his partially revealed dress-suit, who explained our position at the same time as he filled the jug, which I bore out to the car. On my first trip I passed the bungalow-man and Lettcombe still at the gate wrangling over the Alphabet. On my next, they had run into the bungalow to decide whether the amours of an ill-conducted cattery or the single note of a dismal flageolet represented all that the Western Hemisphere could give of uplift. But I continued to serve the radiator, and, before I had done, got to know something of Phil. He had, he told me, devoted himself to rowing, but that afternoon they had discarded him from his College boat on account of a slipped cartilage ; since when, he had been ' tuning in a little.' He was, he said, the son of an Archdeacon, and would enter the Church if forced, but much preferred an unembarrassed life in one of our Dominions. He wanted to kill Mr. Haman, because Haman's car had prevented him getting to Cadogan Gardens to keep an appointment on which a great deal depended. And throughout, he perspired inordinately. When the man and Lettcombe, followed by the old lady of the kimono and Bunny, came out, each bearing one large bottle of Bass, he accepted his with gratitude. The man told us he had been in the service of a Malayan Rubber Company at Kalang-Alang, which is eighty-three miles from the nearest white man, and that his mother had kept house for him there. His mother told Bunny that, as between leeches and tigers,—she advised him to take tigers every time, because leeches got up your legs. Then, with appropriate farewells, we resumed our journey.

Barring the front wheel, which was an accident, the late Mr. Haman's car behaved very well. We were going to compliment Phil on his work, but as soon as he got in beside Bunny, who took the wheel, he fell asleep.

Thanks to my iron nerve, and my refusal to be drawn from my orbit by the performances of the car ahead, I reached the outer suburbs of London, and steered among the heavy traffic that halts for refreshment at the wayside coffee-stalls which are so quiet by day.

Only the speed of my reactions saved me from bumping into Bunny when he pulled up without warning beside a lorry.

'We've found her,' he cried. 'Wake up, Phil, and ask for what I told you.'

I heard Phil crash out of his sleep like a buffalo from a juicy wallow, and shout :—' Have you got an old lady inside there?'

The reply, in a pleasant, though uncultivated, voice, was :—' Show yourself, Maria. There's a man after ye at last.'

And that which Phil had been told to ask for he got. Only the shadow of a profile, next the driver, showed in the lorry, so everything was as

impersonal as Erebus. The allocution supposed
Phil to be several things, and set them out in
order and under heads. It imputed to him
motives, as it proved that he had manners, of a
revolting sort, and yet, by art beyond imitation,
it implied all its profounder obscenities. The
shallower ones, as Lettcombe said, were pelted
in like maxim-belts between the descents of
barrages. The pitch scarcely varied, and the
temperature of the whole was that of liquefied air.
When there was a pause, Bunny, who is ahead of
his years in comprehension and pity, got out,
went to the lorry and, uncovering, asked with
reverence of the driver, 'Are you married to her,
sir?'

'I am,' said the pleasant voice proudly. 'So
it isn't often I can 'ear it from the gallery, as you
might say. Go on, Maria.'

Maria took breath between her teeth and went
on. She defined Phil's business as running up
and down the world, murdering people better
than himself. That was the grey canvas she
embroidered idly, at first, as with flowers; then
illuminated with ever-soaring fireworks; and
lastly rent asunder from wing to wing with forked-
lightning-like yells of:—'*Mur*derer! *Mur*derer!'

All England seemed to be relieved by the
silence when it came. Phil, alone in the car,
emitted (the caption, again, is Lettcombe's) a low
wolf-like howl, shifted into the driving-seat, and
fled up the London road.

'Better keep him in sight.' Bunny had already
established himself beside me. 'Better let *me*

drive, sir '; and he was at the wheel, hustling my astounded two-seater out of all her respectable past. Phil, however, took insane risks among the lorries that were bringing vegetables for London to boil, and kept in front.

' I can't make out what's the matter with him.' (Bunny seemed to find talking and driving at high speeds quite normal.) ' He was all right till the woman came.'

' They mostly are,' said Lettcombe cheaply.

' Perhaps he's worrying about the accident,' I suggested.

' Oh, I had forgotten about that. I've told him about it, for ever so long, but he didn't seem to take it in at the time. I expect it's realised remorse.'

' It ain't hydrophobia, at any rate,' said Lettcombe, who was keeping a look-out ahead.

We had reached the opening of one of our much-advertised but usually incomplete by-passes. It by-passed what had been a village where men used to water horses and wash carriages in a paved ' flash ' or pond close to a public-house. Phil had turned into the pond and was churning it up a good deal.

' What's the matter, old thing?' Bunny asked affectionately as we drew up on the edge. ' Won't she swim?'

' I'm getting rid of the proofs,' Phil cried. ' You heard what that woman said? She's right. This wheel's stiff with blood. So are the cushions.' He flung them overboard, and continued his circular tour.

'I don't suppose Haman will miss 'em much more than the rest,' said Bunny to me. 'I cut my hand on a bit of a bottle in your quilt, sir. It was port wine, I think. It must have splashed up through the floor. It splashed a lot.—Row ashore, Phil, and we'll search her properly.'

But Phil went astern. He said he was washing the underbody clear of the head on the dumb-iron, because no decent girl could be expected to put up with that sort of thing at a dance.

'That is very strange,' Bunny mused to himself. 'I thought he'd forgotten about that too. I only said "bonnet." He must have evolved "head" out of his subliminal mind.—She's looking beautiful now, Phil.'

'Do you really think so? Do you really think a girl 'ud *like* to see me in it?' Phil roared above the waters he troubled.

We all said she would, and he swashed out of his pool, damp but prepared to do his duty. Bunny took the wheel at once and said they would show it to her before the dance ended.

'But then,' said Phil, 'would that be fair on the woman I've killed? No decent girl could put up with *that*, you know. Doris least of all.'

'Oh, you can always explain,' Lettcombe suggested. 'Just a simple explanation taken in the spirit in which it was offered.'

Phil thought upon it, while he crammed hand-fuls of wet dress-shirt-front back into position.

'You're right,' he assented. 'I'll explain. . . . Bunny, drive like hell to Haman's diggings. I've got to kill him.'

'Quite right, old thing,' said Bunny, and headed for London.

Once again we followed, and for some absurd reason Lettcombe was laid low by laughter. But I saw the zenith beginning to soften towards dawn, and the dim shoulders of the world taking shape against the first filtrations of light. It was the hour I knew of old—the one in which my Demon wrought his mightiest. Therefore, I never insult him by mirth till he has released the last foot of it.

(But what should a man who visits Hollywood for instruction know of any God?)

Dawn breathed upon that immense width of barren arterial tar, with its breadth of tintless stuff at either side. A red light marked a distant crossing. Bunny was letting the dachshund range rather generously all over the unoccupied area, and I suppose he hypnotised me. At any rate both cars seemed to be abreast at the moment that one lonely young Policeman stopped us and wanted to know what we were doing all that for.

I speculated, while he partially undressed himself to get at his notebook, what words my Demon would put into my mouth. They came—weighted —gigantesque—of themselves.

'Robert William Peel,' they ran, 'it is necessary in the pursuit of Art that these things should be. Amen!'

He answered that quoting Scripture had nothing to do with driving to the common danger.

I pitied him—and that he might not go uncomforted to whatever doom awaited, I told him so; merely adding that the other car had been stolen from a Mr. Mordecai, Senior Acolyte of Old Bailey, and that I was observing it on behalf of the Midland Motors' Recoveries Company. This last convincing cadenza prevented him from trying to smell my breath any longer. Then Phil said he had run over an old lady up the road, but wished to explain and to hang like a gentleman. He continued in this frame of mind and habit of speech for the rest of the conference; but— thanks to the sublime instincts of an ancient people broken to alcohol for a thousand years—the Bobby stuck to the civil charge. *Why* were we driving to the common danger?

I repeated my firm's well-chosen name. To prevent theft, not murder, were my instructions; and what was the Policeman going to do about it? Bunny saved him trouble by owning that it was a fair cop, but, given half a chance, he would reform. The Policeman said he didn't know, and he couldn't say, but there was something wrong *some*where.

Then, of course, we all had to help him.

He pointed out that he had stopped us. We admitted it. Then would we kindly wait where we were till he went and fetched his Sergeant? He put it to us as gentlemen who wished to save trouble—would we? What else could we do? He went off. We wished to save him trouble, so we waited where we were. Phil sat down on the running-board of Mr. Haman's car, whimpering ' Doris ! ' at intervals. Lettcombe, who does not markedly click with Aurora, rubbed his chin and said he could do with a shave. Bunny lit a cigarette and joined me. The night had left no trace on him—not even a feather's weight on anything that he wore; and his young face, insolent as the morning that hurried towards it, had no fear of her revelations.

'By the way,' I asked, 'have you a plan or a policy, or anything of that sort?'

'Plan?' said he. 'When one is alive? What for?'

''Sorry,' said I. 'But I *should* like to know who your father is.'

'Speaking as an—er—Uncle, would you advise me to tell, sir, if you were in my position?' the child replied.

'Certainly not,' I answered. '*I* never did.'

Whereupon he told me and went on: 'If Police Sergeants have been up all night on duty they appreciate a run in the fresh air before turning in. If they've been hoicked out of bed, *ad hoc*, they're apt to be anfractuous. It's the Sergeant Complex.'

A lorry came along, and asked Lettcombe if any particular complaint caused him to wave his hands in that way. Lettcombe said that the Policeman had warned him and his friends not to go on till he came back with the Borough Surveyor to see if the road was safe. Mass-psychology being much the same in machines as in men, we presently accumulated three lorries, who debated together with the crispness of the coming morning's self. A north-bound vehicle approached, was halted, and said that, so far as it knew, nothing was wrong with the road into

London. This had to be discussed all over again, and then we saw, far off, the Policeman and his Sergeant advancing at the quickstep. Lettcombe, to encourage them, started a song with the refrain ' *Inky-pinky parlez-vous*,' which the first and third lorries took up in perfect time. The second hissed it conscientiously.

The Sergeant, however, did not attend to us all together. The lorries wanted their cases considered first. Lettcombe said that the Bobby had said that the road wasn't safe. The Bobby said that he had said, that the way in which those two cars were driven on *that* road would make *any* road unsafe. His remarks were meant to be general—not particular. He would have explained further, but the lorries said that they were poor working-men. The Sergeant demurred at ' poor,' but, before any protest could be organised, a voice from the second lorry said : ' A word with you, Master Sergeant Stinking Inspector General of Police, *if* you please.'

The Sergeant at once changed manner, and answered, like a shop-walker : ' Oh, *good* morning, Mrs. Shemahen.' ' *No* good morning for you *this* morning, thank *you*,' was the reply, and Mrs. Shemahen spoke, as she had spoken to Phil not so long ago. Her discourse this time had more of personal knowledge to relish it, and—which spurs every artist—all her points were taken by her audience. (They seemed to be a neighbourly lot along that stretch of road.) When she drew breath, the Bobby would cry hopefully : ' Pass along ! *Pass* along, there, please ! ' but without the least effect on the enraptured lorries. When the Sergeant tried to interrupt (as to an alleged bigamous marriage) they all cried : ' Hush up ! ' and when Mrs. Shemahen said she had done with such as him, they demanded an encore.

They then drove on, and the Sergeant, morally more naked than at birth, turned to us as the loyal and zealous Policeman began : ' At or about two-ten this morning, being on point duty——'

' I wish to hell you hadn't,' said the Sergeant.

' By the way,' said Bunny, in a tone that will work woe in his world before long, 'who was the woman who was speaking just now ? She told *us* off a little while ago—much better than she did *you*. Her husband called her Maria, didn't he ? '

' Oh yes. She's quite a local character ! ' (the seduced Sergeant returned to ease of manner, and natural bearing, as, some day, a girl or two will drop her guard with Bunny and—) 'She runs a chicken-farm a bit along hereabouts. They give out she's crazy. What do *you* think, sir ? '

' With a little training she'd be a revelation in *our* business,' Lettcombe broke in. 'Speaking as one who knows something about it, *I* can guarantee that.'

I started ! Was my Demon going to lay the hot coal of inspiration on Lettcombe's unshorn lips—not on mine ? But I would allow him the count fairly, and I began, ' One—Two—Three ' —while the Bobby made a second shot at his catechism—(' Six—Seven ')—After all, it was more in Lettcombe's line than mine, yet—Lett-

combe drew himself up, took breath, and—I saw
the end, coming with the day.

'Well, boys,' he began on what I feel sure is
the standardised Hollywood screech of a Pro-
ducer. 'The light's about good enough now for
a trial-shot. Jimmy,' he pointed to Phil, 'you've
got to register guilt and remorse for the murder
much stronger than you've done up to now.'

'Here!' I broke in, on the off-chance that my
Demon might relent, 'let me help too.'

'Not much,' Lettcombe replied. 'This is *my*
St. Paul!'

'Ah! I think I see . . .' the Sergeant began.

'You're right, Sergeant.' Lettcombe swept
on. 'It's called "Love among the Leeches"—
the English end of it. Doug!' (This was black-
guardly of Lettcombe. I do not resemble Mr.
Fairbanks in the least.) You're out of this.
You've given up trying to blackmail Jimmy and
you've doped him.'

'You needn't have given Jimmy all our whisky,
though,' said Bunny aggrievedly. 'He'd have
registered just as well on half of it.'

'Exactly,' Lettcombe resumed. 'That's what
Mr. Fairbanks meant, Sergeant, when he told
your man about doing things for Art's sake.
You'll find it in his notebook. I saw him write it
down. And, Jimmy, register that you're quite
convinced it was Clara you ran over in your car,
and that she had committed suicide through grief
after the tigers had killed her mother at Kalang-
Alang. 'Got that? Say it, then.'

'Kalang-alang-alang-alang,' said Phil, like a

level-crossing gong. ' Look here! When do I
kill Haman? '

' In the second reel,' Lettcombe commanded.
' We must shoot the accident to the car all over
again. Oh, we use up cars in our job as easy as
lyin', Sergeant. Now! 'Tention! Charlie! '—
(Bunny took this serve)—' You're going to show
poor Jimmy what he thought was Clara's corpse.
That comes *after* Jimmy's arrest. Sergeant, do
you mind telling your man to stand beside Jimmy?
He has only got to look as if he didn't know what's
coming next. Ready? '

And down the fully revealed road moved the
wind that comes with morning-turn—a point or
two south of sou-west, ever fortunate to me.
Bunny moved to the dicky of Mr. Haman's car
and opened it.

' Stand closer to the Bobby, Phil,' he called,
' and, Bobby darling, put your hand on his
shoulder as though you were arresting him. Keep
out of the picture, Sergeant, and you'll be able to
see exactly how it's done.'

At the same time that Lettcombe levelled a
light valise, in lieu of camera, Bunny took out
from the dicky what he had put there less than
two hours ago. And, as he had then hauled
' Aunt Ellen ' out backwards, so now he shook
her and he shook her and he kept on shaking her,
forward from where her skirt was to where her
head had been. Bits of paper, buttered; bits of
bottle-glass; pieces of pomatum-pot (I must have
been wrong about the hair-oil) and pieces of
groceries came out; but what came out most

and seemed as if it would never stop, was the
down of the eider-duck (*Somateria mollissima*).
Such is the ingenuity of man, who, from a few
square feet of bed-gear, can evoke earth-envelop-
ing smoke-screens of ' change, alarm, surprise '—
but, above all, surprise!

The Policeman disappeared. When we saw
him again—Lo! he was older than Abraham, and
whiter than Lot's wife. He blew a good deal
through his Father Christmas moustache, but no
words came. Then he took off his Esquimaux
gloves, and picked feebly at his Polar Bear belly.

Phil lurched towards us like a penguin through
a blizzard. He was whiter than the Policeman,
for he had been hatless, and his hair had been
oiled, and he was damp all over. Bunny motioned
him daintily to the open dicky.

The Sergeant, as advised, had kept out of the
picture, and so had been able to see exactly how
it was done. He sat at the base of the lamp-post
at the crossing of the arterial by-pass, and hugged
its standard with both arms. After repeated inquiries, none of which he was able to answer,
because he could not speak, we left him there,
while the Policeman persisted in trying to moult.

* * * * *

I do not laugh when I drive, which is why I
was as nearly as possible dead when we followed
the dachshund into Cadogan Gardens, where the
numbers are ill-arranged, and drove round and
round till some young people, who had been
dancing, came out from beneath a striped awning

into the first of the pure morning sunlight.   One
of them was called Doris.   Phil called her, so that
all Cadogan Gardens were aware.   Yet it was an
appreciable time before she connected the cry with
the plumage of that mating bird.

NAAMAN'S SONG

' Go, wash thyself in Jordan—go, wash thee and be
    clean ! '
Nay, not for any Prophet will I plunge a toe therein !
For the banks of curious Jordan are parcelled into sites,
Commanded and embellished and patrolled by
    Israelites.

There rise her timeless capitals of Empires daily born,
Whose plinths are laid at midnight, and whose streets
    are packed at morn ;
And here come hired youths and maids that feign to
    love or sin
In tones like rusty razor-blades to tunes like smitten tin.

And here be merry murtherings, and steeds with fiery
    hooves ;
And furious hordes with guns and swords, and
    clamberings over rooves ;
And horrid tumblings down from Heaven, and flights
    with wheels and wings ;
And always one weak virgin who is chased through
    all these things.

And here is mock of faith and truth, for children to
    behold ;
And every door of ancient dirt reopened to the old ;

With every word that taints the speech, and show that
        weakens thought;
And Israel watcheth over each, and—doth not watch
        for nought. . . .

But Pharphar—but Abana—which Hermon launch-
        eth down—
They perish fighting desert-sands beyond Damascus-
        town.
But yet their pulse is of the snows—their strength is
        from on high,
And, if they cannot cure my woes, a leper will I die!

Fairy-Kist

THE MOTHER'S SON

I have a dream—a dreadful dream—
   A dream that is never done,
I watch a man go out of his mind,
   And he is My Mother's Son.

They pushed him into a Mental Home,
   And that is like the grave :
For they do not let you sleep upstairs,
   And you're not allowed to shave.

And it was not disease or crime
   Which got him landed there,
But because They laid on My Mother's Son
   More than a man could bear.

What with noise, and fear of death,
   Waking, and wounds and cold,
They filled the Cup for My Mother's Son
   Fuller than it could hold.

They broke his body and his mind
   And yet They made him live,
And They asked more of My Mother's Son
   Than any man could give.

For, just because he had not died
    Nor been discharged nor sick :
They dragged it out with My Mother's Son
    Longer than he could stick. . . .

And no one knows when he'll get well—
    So, there he'll have to be :
And, 'spite of the beard in the looking-glass,
    I know that man is me !

Fairy-Kist

THE only important society in existence to-day is
the E.C.F.—the Eclectic *but* Comprehensive Fra-
ternity for the Perpetuation of Gratitude towards
Lesser Lights. Its founders were William Lemming, of Lemming and Orton, print-sellers;
Alexander Hay McKnight, of Ellis and McKnight,
provision-merchants; Robert Keede, M.R.C.P.,
physician, surgeon, and accoucheur; Lewis Hol-
royd Burges, tobacconist and cigar importer—all
of the South Eastern postal districts—and its
zealous, hard-working, but unappreciated Secretary. The meetings are usually at Mr. Lemming's little place in Berkshire, where he raises
pigs.

I had been out of England for awhile, missing
several dinners, but was able to attend a summer
one with none present but ourselves; several red
mullets in paper; a few green peas and ducklings;
an arrangement of cockscombs with olives, and
capers as large as cherries; strawberries and cream;
some 1903 Chateau la Tour; and that locked
cabinet of cigars to which only Burges has the key.

It was at the hour when men most grace-
fully curvet abroad on their hobbies, and after

McKnight had been complaining of systematic pilfering in his three big shops, that Burges told us how an illustrious English astrologer called Lily had once erected a horoscope to discover the whereabouts of a parcel of stolen fish. The stars led him straight to it and the thief and, incidentally, into a breeze with a lady over 'seven Portugal onions' also gone adrift, but not included in the periscope. Then we wondered why detective-story writers so seldom use astrology to help out the local Sherlock Holmes; how many illegitimate children that great original had begotten in magazine form; and so drifted on to murder at large. Keede, whose profession gives him advantages, illustrated the subject.

'I wish I could do a decent detective story,' I said at last. 'I never get further than the corpse.'

'Corpses are foul things,' Lemming mused aloud. 'I wonder what sort of a corpse I shall make.'

'You'll never know,' the gentle, silver-haired Burges replied. 'You won't even know you're dead till you look in the glass and see no reflection. An old woman told me that once at Barnet Horse Fair—and I couldn't have been more than seven at the time.'

We were quiet for a few minutes, while the Altar of the Lesser Lights, which is also our cigar-lighter, came into use. The single burner atop, representing gratitude towards Lesser Lights in general, was of course lit. Whenever gratitude towards a named Lesser Light is put forward and proven, one or more of the nine burners round

the base can be thrown into action by pulling its
pretty silver draw-chain.

' What will you do for me,' said Keede, puffing,
' if I give you an absolutely true detective yarn? '

' If I can make anything of it,' I replied, ' I'll
finish the Millar Gift.'

This meant the cataloguing of a mass of
Masonic pamphlets (1831–59), bequeathed by a
Brother to Lodge Faith and Works 5836 E.C.—
a job which Keede and I, being on the Library
Committee, had together shirked for months.

' Promise you won't doctor it if you use it? '
said Keede.

' And for goodness' sake don't bring *me* in any
more than you can help,' said Lemming.

No practitioner ever comprehends another
practitioner's methods ; but a promise was given,
a bargain struck ; and the tale runs here substantially as it was told.

That past autumn, Lemming's pig-man (who
had been sitting up with a delicate lady-Berkshire)
discovered, on a wet Sunday dawn in October,
the body of a village girl called Ellen Marsh lying
on the bank of a deep cutting where the road from
the village runs into the London Road. Ellen, it
seemed, had many friends with whom she used
to make evening appointments, and Channet's
Ash, as the cross-roads were called, from the big
ash that overhung them, was one of her well-
known trysting-places. The body lay face down
at the highest point of a sloping footpath which
the village children had trodden out up the bank,
and just where that path turned the corner under

Channet's Ash and dropped into the London
Road. The pig-man roused the village constable,
an ex-soldier called Nicol, who picked up, close
to the corpse, a narrow-bladed fern-trowel, its
handle wrapped with twine. There were no signs
of a struggle, but it had been raining all night.
The pig-man then went off to wake up Keede,
who was spending the week-end with Lemming.
Keede did not disturb his host, Mrs. Lemming
being ill at the time, but he and the policeman
commandeered a builder's handcart from some
half-built shops down the London Road; wheeled
the body to the nearest inn—the Cup o' Grapes—
pushed a car out of a lock-up; took the shove-
halfpenny board from the Oddfellows' Room, and
laid the body on it till the regular doctor should
arrive.

'He was out,' Keede said, 'so I made an
examination on my own. There was no question of
assault. She had been dropped by one scientific
little jab, just at the base of the skull, by someone
who knew his anatomy. That was all. Then
Nicol, the Bobby, asked me if I'd care to walk
over with him to Jimmy Tigner's house.'

'Who was Jimmy Tigner?' I asked.

'Ellen's latest young man—a believing soul.
He was assistant at the local tinsmith's, living
with his mother in a cottage down the street. It
was seven o'clock then, and not a soul about.
Jimmy had to be waked up. He stuck his head
out of the window, and Nicol stood in the garden
among the cabbages—friendly as all sin—and
asked him what he'd been doing the night before,

because someone had been knocking Ellen about.
Well, there wasn't much doubt what Jimmy had
been up to. He was altogether "the morning
after." He began dressing and talking out of the
window at the same time, and said he'd kill any
man who touched Ellen.'

'Hadn't the policeman cautioned him?'
McKnight demanded.

'What for? They're all friends in this
village. Then Jimmy said that, on general
principles, Ellen deserved anything she might
have got. He'd done with her. He told us a
few details (some girl must have given her away),
but the point he kept coming back to was that
they had parted in "high dungeon." He repeated that a dozen times. Nicol let him run
on, and when the boy was quite dressed, he said:
"Well, you may as well come on up-street an'
look at her. She don't bear you any malice now."
(Oh, I tell you the War has put an edge on things
all round!) Jimmy came down, jumpy as a cat,
and, when we were going through the Cup o'
Grapes yard, Nicol unlocked the garage and
pushed him in. The face hadn't been covered
either.'

'Drastic,' said Burges, shivering.

'It was. Jimmy went off the handle at once;
and Nicol kept patting him on the back and
saying: "That's all right! I'll go bail *you* didn't
do it." Then Jimmy wanted to know why the
deuce he'd been dragged into it. Nicol said:
"Oh, that's what the French call a confrontation.
But you're all right." Then Jimmy went for

Nicol. So we got him out of the garage, and gave him a drink, and took him back to his mother. But at the inquest he accounted for every minute of his time. He'd left Ellen under Channet's Ash, telling her what he thought of her over his shoulder for a quarter of a mile down the lane (that's what "high dungeon" meant in their language). Luckily two or three of the girls and the bloods of the village had heard 'em. After that, he'd gone to the Cup o' Grapes, filled himself up, and told everybody his grievances against Ellen till closing-time. The interestin' thing was that he seemed to be about the only decent boy of the lot.'

'Then,' Lemming interrupted, 'the reporters began looking for clues. They—they behaved like nothing *I*'ve ever imagined! I was afraid *we*'d be dragged into it. You see, that wretched Ellen had been our scullery-maid a few months before, and—my wife—as ill as she was. . . . But mercifully that didn't come out at the inquest.'

'No,' Keede went on. 'Nicol steered the thing. He's related to Ellen. And by the time Jimmy had broken down and wept, and the reporters had got their sensation, it was brought in " person or persons unknown." '

' What about the trowel ?' said McKnight, who is a notable gardener.

' It was a most valuable clue, of course, because it explained the *modus operandi*. The punch—with the handle, the local doctor said— had been delivered through her back hair, with just enough strength to do the job and no more.

I couldn't have operated more neatly myself. The Police took the trowel, but they couldn't trace it to anyone, somehow. The main point in the village was that no one who knew her wanted to go into Ellen's character. She was rather popular, you see. Of course the village was a bit disappointed about Jimmy's getting off; and when he broke down again at her funeral, it revived suspicion. Then the Huish poisoning case happened up in the North; and the reporters had to run off and take charge of it. What did your pig-man say about 'em, Will?'

'Oh, Griffiths said: "'Twas Gawd's own Mercy those young gen'elmen didn't 'ave 'alf of us 'ung before they left. They were that energetic!"'

'They were,' said Keede. 'That's why I kept back my evidence.'

'There was the wife to be considered too,' said Lemming. 'She'd never have stood being connected with the thing, even remotely.'

'I took it upon myself to act upon that belief,' Keede replied gravely. 'Well—now for *my* little bit. I'd come down that Saturday night to spend the week-end with Will here; and I couldn't get here till late. It was raining hard, and the car skidded badly. Just as I turned off the London Road into the lane under Channet's Ash, my lights picked up a motor-bike lying against the bank where they found Ellen; and I saw a man bending over a woman up the bank. Naturally one don't interfere with these little things as a rule; but it occurred to me there might have been a smash. So I called out:

"Anything wrong? Can I help?" The man said: "No, thanks. We're all right," or words to that effect, and I went on. *But* the bike's letters happened to be my own initials, and its number was the year I was born in. I wasn't likely to forget 'em, you see.'

'You told the Police?' said McKnight severely.

''Took 'em into my confidence at once, Sandy,' Keede replied. 'There was a Sergeant, Sydenham way, that I'd been treating for Salonika fever. I told him I was afraid I'd brushed a motor-bike at night coming up into West Wickham, on one of those blind bends up the hill, and I'd be glad to know I hadn't hurt him. He gave me what I wanted in twenty-four hours. The bike belonged to one Henry Wollin—of independent means—livin' near Mitcham.'

'But West Wickham isn't in Berkshire—nor is Mitcham,' McKnight began.

'Here's a funny thing,' Keede went on, without noticing. 'Most men and nearly all women commit murder single-handed; but no man likes to go man-hunting alone. Primitive instinct, I suppose. That's why I lugged Will into the Sherlock Holmes business. You hated too.'

'I hadn't recovered from those reporters,' said Lemming.

'They *were* rather energetic. But I persuaded Will that we'd call upon Master Wollin and apologise—as penitent motorists—and we went off to Mitcham in my two-seater. Wollin had a very nice little detached villa down there.

The old woman—his housekeeper—who let us
in, was West Country, talkin' as broad as a
pat o' butter. She took us through the hall
to Wollin, planting things in his back-garden.'

' A wonderful little garden for that soil,' said
Lemming, who considers himself an even greater
gardener than McKnight, although he keeps two
men less.

' He was a big, strong, darkish chap—middle-
aged—wide as a bull between the eyes—no
beauty, and evidently had been a very sick man.
Will and I apologised to him, and he began to
lie at once. He said he'd been at West Wickham at the time (on the night of the murder, you
know), and he remembered dodging out of the
way of a car. He didn't seem pleased that we
should have picked up his number so promptly.
Seeing we were helping him to establish an *alibi*,
he ought to have been, oughtn't he?'

' Ye mean,' said McKnight, suddenly en-
lightened, ' that he was committing the murder
here in Berkshire on the night that he told you he
was in West Wickham, which is in Kent.'

' Which is in Kent. Thank you. It is.
And we went on talking about that West Wickham
hill till he mentioned he'd been in the War, and
that gave me *my* chance to talk. And he was an
enthusiastic gardener, he said, and that let Will
in. It struck us both that he was nervous in a
carneying way that didn't match his build and
voice at all. Then we had a drink in his study.
Then the fun began. There were four pictures
on the wall.'

' Prints—prints,' Lemming corrected professionally.

' 'Same thing, aren't they, Will? Anyhow, *you* got excited enough over them. At first I thought Will was only playing up. But he was genuine.'

' So were they,' Lemming said. ' Sandy, you remember those four " Apostles " I sold you last Christmas ? '

' I have my counterfoil yet,' was the dry answer.

' What sort of prints were they ? ' Burges demanded.

The moonlike face of Alexander McKnight, who collects prints along certain lines, lit with devout rapture. He began checking off on his fingers.

' The firrst,' said he, ' was the draped one of Ray—the greatest o' them all. Next, yon French print o' Morrison, when he was with the Duke of Orleans at Blois ; third, the Leyden print of Grew in his youth ; and, fourth, that wreathed Oxford print of Hales. The whole aapostolic succession of them.'

' I never knew Morrison laid out links in France,' I said.

' Morrison? Links? Links? Did you think those four were gowfers then ? '

' Wasn't old Tom Morrison a great golfer ? ' I ventured.

McKnight turned on me with utter scorn. ' Those prints—' he began. ' But ye'd not understand. They were—we'll say they were just pictures of some garrdeners I happened to be interested in.'

This was rude of McKnight, but I forgave him because of the excellence of his imported groceries. Keede went on.

' After Will had talked the usual buyer's talk, Wollin seemed willin' to part with 'em, and we arranged we'd call again and complete the deal. Will 'ud do business with a criminal on the drop o' course. He gave Wollin his card, and we left; Wollin carneying and suckin' up to us right to the front door. We hadn't gone a couple of miles when Will found he'd given Wollin his personal card—*not* his business one—with his private address in Berkshire ! The murder about ten days old, and the papers still stinkin' with it ! I think I told you at the time you were a fool, Will ? '

' You did. I never saw how I came to make the mistake. These cards are different sizes too,' poor Lemming said.

' No, we were not a success as man-hunters,' Keede laughed. ' But Will and I had to call again, of course, to settle the sale. That was a week after. And this time, of course, Wollin— not being as big a fool as Will—had hopped it and left no address. The old lady said he was given to going off for weeks at a time. That hung us up ; but to do Will justice, which I don't often, he saved the situation by his damned commercial instincts. He said he wanted to look at the prints again. The old lady was agreeable—rather forth- comin' in fact. She let us into the study, had the prints down, and asked if we'd like some tea. While she was getting it, and Will was hanging over the prints, I looked round the room. There was a cupboard, half opened, full of tools, and on top of 'em a new—what did you say it was, Will?—fern-trowel. 'Same pattern as the one Nicol found by Ellen's head. That gave me a bit of a turn. I'd never done any Sherlockin' outside my own profession. Then the old lady came back and I made up to her. When I was a sixpenny doctor at Lambeth, half my great success——'

'Ye can hold that over,' McKnight observed. 'The murrder's what's interestin' me.'

'Wait till your next go of gout. *I'll* interest you, Sandy. Well, she expanded (they all do with me), and, like patients, she wanted advice gratis. So I gave it. Then she began talking about Wollin. She'd been his nurse, I fancy. Anyhow, she'd known him all his life, and she said he was full of virtue and sickness She said he'd been wounded and gassed and gangrened in the War, and after that—oh, she worked up to it beautifully—he'd been practically off his head. She called it " fairy-kist." '

'That's pretty—very pretty,' said Burges.

'Meanin' he'd been kissed by the fairies?' McKnight inquired.

'It would appear so, Sandy. I'd never heard the word before. 'West Country, I suppose. And she had one of those slow, hypnotic voices, like cream from a jug. Everything she said squared with my own theories up to date. Wollin was on the break of life, and, given wounds, gas,

and gangrene just at that crisis, why anything—
Jack the Ripperism or religious mania—might
come uppermost. I knew that, and the old lady
was as good as telling it me over again, and
putting up a defence for him in advance. 'Wonderful bit of work. Patients' relatives *are* like
that sometimes—specially wives.'

'Yes, but what about Wollin?' I said.

'Wait a bit. Will and I went away, and we
talked over the fern-trowel and so forth, and we
both agreed we ought to release our evidence.
There, somehow, we stuck. Man-hunting's a
dirty job. So we compromised. I knew a fellow
in the C.I.D., who thought he had a floating
kidney, and we decided to put the matter before
him and let him take charge. He had to go
North, however, and he wrote he could not see us
before the Tuesday of next week. This would be
four or five weeks after the murder. I came
down here again that week-end to stay with Will,
and on Saturday night Will and I went to his study
to put the finishing touches to our evidence. I
was trying to keep my own theory out of it as
much as I could. Yes, if you want to know, Jack
the Ripper *was* my notion, and my theory was
that my car had frightened the brute off before
he could do anything in that line. And *then*,
Will's housemaid shot into the study with Nicol
after her, and Jimmy Tigner after him!'

'Luckily my wife was up in town at the time,'
said Lemming. 'They all shouted at once too.'

'They did!' said Keede. 'Nicol shouted
loudest, though. He was plastered with mud,

waving what was left of his helmet, and Jimmy was in hysterics. Nicol yelled :—" Look at me! Look at this! It's all right! Look at me! I've got it ! " He *had* got it too ! It came out, when they quieted down, that he had been walking with Jimmy in the lane by Channet's Ash. Hearing a lorry behind 'em—you know what a narrow lane it is—they stepped up on to that path on the bank (I told you about it) that the school-children had made. It was a contractor's lorry—Higbee and Norton, a local firm—with two girders for some new shops on the London Road. They were deliverin' late on Saturday evening, so's the men could start on Monday. Well, these girders had been chucked in anyhow on to a brick lorry with a tail-board. Instead of slopin' forward they cocked up backwards like a pheasant's tail, sticking up high and overhanging. They were tied together with a few turns of rope at the far ends. Do you see.'

So far we could see nothing. Keede made it plainer.

'Nicol said he went up the bank first—Jimmy behind him—and after a few steps he found his helmet knocked off. If he'd been a foot higher up the bank his head 'ud have gone. The lorry had skidded on the tar of the London Road, as it turned into it left-handed—her tail swung to the right, and the girders swung with it, just missing braining Nicol up on the bank. The lorry was well in the left-hand gutter when he got his breath again. He went for the driver at once. The man said all the lorries always skidded under

Channet's Ash, when it was wet, because of the camber of the road, and they allowed for it as a regular stunt. And he damned the road authorities, and Nicol for being in the light. Then Jimmy Tigner, Nicol told us, caught on to what it meant, and he climbed into the lorry shouting :—" *You* killed Ellen !" It was all Nicol could do to prevent him choking the fellow there and then ; but Nicol didn't pull him off till Jimmy got it out of the driver that he had been delivering girders the night Ellen was killed. Of course, he hadn't noticed anything.

' Then Nicol came over to Lemming and me to talk it over. I gave Jimmy a bromide and sent him off to his mother. He wasn't any particular use, except as a witness—and no good after. Then Nicol went over the whole thing again several times, to fix it in our minds. Next morning he and I and Will called on old Higbee before he could get to church. We made him take out the particular lorry implicated, with the same driver, and a duplicate load packed the same way, and demonstrate for us. We kept her stunting half Sunday morning in the rain, and the skid delivered her into the left-hand gutter of the London Road every time she took that corner ; and *every* time her tail with the girders swiped along the bank of that lane like a man topping a golf-ball. And when she did that, there were half-a-dozen paces—not more—along that school-children's path, that meant sure death to anyone on it at the time. Nicol was just climbing into the danger-zone when he stepped up, but he was a foot too low.   The girders only brushed through his hair.   We got some laths and stuck 'em in along the path (Jimmy Tigner told us Ellen was five foot three) to test our theory.   The last lath was as near as could be to where the pig-man had found the body; and that happened to be the extreme end of the lorry's skid.   'See what happened?   *We* did.   At the end of her skid the lorry's rear wheels 'ud fetch up every time with a bit of a jar against the bank, and the girders 'ud quiver and lash out a few inches—like a golf-club wigglin'.   Ellen must have caught just enough of that little sideway flick, at the base of her skull, to drop her like a pithed ox.   We worked it all out on the last lath.   The rope wrappings on the end of the damned things saved the skin being broken.   Hellish, isn't it?   And then Jimmy Tigner realised that if she had only gone two paces further she'd have been round the corner of the bank and safe.   Then it came back to him that she'd stopped talkin' " in dungeon " rather suddenly, and he hadn't gone back to see! I spent most of the afternoon sitting with him. He'd been tried too high—too high.   I had to sign his certificate a few weeks later.   No!   He won't get better.'

We commented according to our natures, and then McKnight said :—' But—if so—why did Wollin disappear? '

' That comes next on the agenda, Worshipful Sir.   Brother Lemming has *not* the instincts of the real man-hunter.   He felt shy.   I had to remind him of the prints before he'd call on

Wollin again. We'd allowed our prey ten days to get the news, while the papers were busy explainin' Ellen's death, and people were writin' to 'em and saying they'd nearly been killed by lorries in the same way in other places. Then old Higbee gave Ellen's people a couple of hundred without prejudice (he wanted to get a higher seat in the Synagogue—the Squire's pew, I think), and everyone felt that her character had been cleared.'

'But Wollin?' McKnight insisted.

'When Will and I went to call on him he'd come home again. I hadn't seen him for—let's see, it must have been going on for a month— but I hardly recognised him. He was burned out—all his wrinkles gashes, and his eyes readjustin' 'emselves after looking into Hell. One gets to know that kind of glare nowadays. But he was immensely relieved to see us. So was the old lady. If he'd been a dog, he'd have been wagging his tail from the nose down. That was rather embarrassing too, because it wasn't our fault we hadn't had him tried for his life. And while we were talking over the prints, he said, quite suddenly: "*I* don't blame you! I'd have believed it against myself on the evidence!" That broke the ice with a brick. He told us he'd almost stepped on Ellen's body that night—dead and stiffening. Then I'd come round the corner and hailed him, and that panicked him. He jumped on his bike and fled, forgetting the trowel. So he'd bought another with some crazy notion of putting the Law off the track. That's what hangs **murderers.**

' When Will and I first called on him, with our
fairy-tales about West Wickham, he had fancied
he might be under observation, and Will's mixing
up the cards clinched it. . . . So he disappeared.
He went down into his own cellar, he said, and
waited there, with his revolver, ready to blow his
brains out when the warrant came. What a
month! Think of it! A cellar and a candle, a
file of gardening papers, and a loaded revolver
for company! Then I asked why. He said no
jury on earth would have believed his explanation
of his movements. '' Look at it from the prose-
cution's point of view," he said. " Here's a
middle-aged man with a medical record that 'ud
account for any loss of controls—and that would
mean Broadmoor—fifty or sixty miles from his
home in a rainstorm, on the top of a fifteen foot
cutting, at night. He leaves behind him, with
the girl's body, the very sort of weapon that might
have caused her death. I read about the trowel
in the papers. Can't you see how the thing 'ud
be handled? " he said.

' I asked him then what in the world he really
was doing that had to be covered up by suicide.
He said he was planting things. I asked if he
meant stolen goods. After the trouble we'd
given him, Will and I wouldn't have peached on
him for that, would we, Will? '

' No,' said Lemming. ' His face was enough.
It was like——' and he named a picture by an
artist called Goya.

' " Stolen goods be damned," Wollin said to
me. " If you *must* have it, I was planting out

plants from my garden." What did you say to
him then, Will?'

'I asked him what the plants were, of course,'
said Lemming, and turned to McKnight. 'They
were daffodils, and a sort of red honeysuckle,
and a special loosestrife—a hybrid.' McKnight
nodded judicially while Lemming talked incom-
prehensible horticulture for a minute or two.

'Gardening isn't my line,' Keede broke in,
'but Will's questions acted on Master Wollin
like a charm. He dropped his suicide talk, and
began on gardening. After that it was Will's
operation. I hadn't a look-in for ten minutes.
Then I said : "What's there to make a fuss about
in all this?" Then he turned away from Will
and spoke to me, carneying again—like patients
do. He began with his medical record—one
shrapnel peppering, and one gassing, with gangrene. He had put in about fourteen months
in various hospitals, and he was full of medical
talkee-talkee. Just like *you*, Sandy, when you've
been seeing your damned specialists. And he'd
been doped for pain and pinched nerves, till the
wonder was he'd ever pulled straight again. He
told us that the only thing that had helped him
through the War was his love of gardening.
He'd been mad keen on it all his life—and even
in the worst of the Somme he used to get comfort out of plants and bot'ny, and that sort of
stuff. *I* never did. Well, I saw he was speaking the truth ; but next minute he began to
hedge. I noticed it, and said something, and
then he sweated in rivers. He hadn't turned a

hair over his proposed suicide, but now he sweated till he had to wipe it off his forehead.

'Then I told him I was something else besides a G.P., and Will was too, if that 'ud make things easier for him. And it did. From then on he told the tale on the Square, in grave distress, you know. At his last hospital he'd been particularly doped, and he fancied that that was where his mind had gone. He told me that he was insane, and had been for more than a year. I asked him not to start on his theories till he'd finished with his symptoms. (You patients are all the same.) He said there were Gotha raids round his hospital, which used to upset the wards. And there was a V.A.D.—she must have been something of a woman, too—who used to read to him and tell him stories to keep him quiet. He liked 'em because, as far as he remembered, they were all about gardening. *But*, when he grew better, he began to hear Voices—little whispers at first, growing louder and ending in regular uproars— ordering him to do certain things. He used to lie there shaking with horror, because he funked going mad. He wanted to live and be happy again, in his garden—like the rest of us.

'When he was discharged, he said, he left hospital with a whole Army Corps shouting into his ears. The sum and substance of their orders was that he must go out and plant roots and things at large up and down the country-side. Naturally, he suffered a bit, but, after a while, he went back to his house at Mitcham and obeyed orders, because, he said, as long as he was carry-

ing 'em out the Voices stopped. If he knocked
off even for a week, he said, they helled him on
again. Being a methodical bird, he'd bought a
motor-bike and a basket lined with oil-cloth, and
he used to skirmish out planting his silly stuff by
the wayside, and in coppices and on commons.
He'd spy out likely spots by day and attend to
'em after dark. He was working round Channet's
Ash that night, and he'd come out of the meadow,
and down the school-children's path, right on
to Ellen's body. That upset him. I wasn't
worryin' about Ellen for the moment. I headed
him back to his own symptoms. The devil of
it was that, left to himself, there was nothing he'd
have liked better than this planting job; but the
Voices ordering him to do it, scared the soul out
of him. Then I asked him if the Voices had
worried him much when he was in the cellar
with his revolver. He said, comin' to think of it,
that they had not; and I reminded him that there
was very little seasickness in the boats when submarines were around.'

'You've forgotten,' said Lemming, 'that he
stopped fawning as soon as he found out we were
on the Square.'

'He did so,' Keede assented. '*And* he insisted on our staying to supper, so's he could
tell his symptoms properly. ('Might have been
you again, Sandy.) The old lady backed him up.
She was clinging to us too, as though we'd done
her a favour. And Wollin told us that if he'd
been in the dock, he *knew* he'd have come out
with his tale of his Voices and night-plantings,

just like the Ancient Mariner; and that would
have sent him to Broadmoor. It was Broadmoor,
not hanging, that he funked. And so he went
on and on about his Voices, and I cross-examined.
He said they used to begin with noises in his
head like rotten walnuts being smashed; but he
fancied that must have been due to the bombs in
the raid. I reminded him again that I didn't
want his theories. The Voices were sometimes
like his V.A.D.'s, but louder, and they were all
mixed up with horrible dope-dreams. For instance, he said, there was a smiling dog that ran
after him and licked his face, and the dog had
something to do with being able to read gardening books, and that gave him the notion, as he
lay abed in hospital, that he had water on the
brain, and that that 'ud prevent him from root-
gatherin' an' obeying his orders.'

'He used the words "root-gathering." It's
an unusual combination nowadays,' said Lemming suddenly. 'That made me take notice,
Sandy.'

Keede held up his hand. 'No, you don't,
Will! I tell this tale much better than you.
Well, then Will cut in, and asked Wollin if he
could remember exactly what sort of stuff his
V.A.D. had read to him during the raids. He
couldn't; except that it was all about gardening,
and it made him feel as if he were in Paradise.
Yes, Sandy, he used the word "Paradise." Then
Will asked him if he could give us the precise
wording of his orders to plant things. He
couldn't do that either. Then Will said, like a

barrister: " I put it to you, that the Voices ordered you to plant things by the wayside *for such as have no gardens*." And Will went over it slowly twice. " My God!" said Wollin. " That's the *ipsissima verba*." " Good," said Will. " Now for your dog. I put it to you that the smiling dog was really a secret friend of yours. What was his colour?" " Dunno," said Wollin. " It was yellow," says Will. " A big yellow bull-terrier." Wollin thought a bit and agreed. " When he ran after you," says Will, " did you ever hear anyone trying to call him off, in a very loud voice?" " Sometimes," said Wollin. " Better still," says Will. " Now, I put it to you that that yellow bull-terrier came into a library with a Scotch gardener who said it was a great privilege to be able to consult botanical books." Wollin thought a bit, and said that those were some of the exact words that were mixed up with his Voices, and his trouble about not being able to read. I shan't forget his face when he said it, either. My word, he sweated.'

Here Sandy McKnight smiled and nodded across to Lemming, who nodded back as mysteriously as a Freemason or a gardener.

' All this time,' Keede continued, ' Will looked more important than ever I've seen him outside of his shop ; and he said to Wollin : " Now I'll tell you the story, Mr. Wollin, that your V.A.D. read or told you. Check me where your memory fails, and I'll refresh it." That's what you said, wasn't it, Will? And Will began to spin him a long nursery-yarn about some children who planted flowers out in a meadow that wasn't theirs, so that such as had no gardens might enjoy them; and one of the children called himself an Honest Root-gatherer, and one of 'em had something like water on the brain; and there was an old Squire who owned a smiling yellow bull-terrier that was fond of the children, and he kept his walnuts till they were rotten, and then he smashed 'em all. You ought to have heard Will! He can talk—even when there isn't money in it.'

'*Mary's Meadow*!' Sandy's hand banged the table.

'Hsh!' said Burges, enthralled. 'Go on, Robin.'

'And Wollin checked it all, with the sweat drying on him—remember, Will?—and he put in his own reminiscences—one about a lilac sun-bonnet, I remember.'

'Not lilac—marigold. One string of it was canary-colour and one was white.' McKnight corrected as though this were a matter of life and death.

'Maybe. And there was a nightingale singing to the Man in the Moon, and an old Herbal—not Gerard's, or I'd have known it—"Paradise" something. Wollin contributed that sort of stuff all the time, with ten years knocked off his shoulders and a voice like the Town Crier's. Yes, Sandy, the story *was* called *Mary's Meadow*. It all came back to him—*via* Will.'

'And that helped?' I asked.

'Well,' Keede said slowly, 'a General Practi-tioner can't much believe in the remission of sins,

can he? But if that's possible, I know how a
redeemed soul looks. The old lady had pretended
to get supper, but she stopped when Will began
his yarn, and listened all through. Then Wollin
put up his hand, as though he were hearing his
dam' Voices. Then he brushed 'em away, and he
dropped his head on the table and wept. My God,
how he wept! And then she kissed him, *and* me.
Did she kiss you, Will?'

'She certainly did not,' said the scandalised
Lemming, who has been completely married for a
long while.

'You missed something. She has a seductive
old mouth still. And Wollin wouldn't let us go—
hung on to us like a child. So, after supper, we
went over the affair in detail, till all hours. The
pain and the dope had made that nursery story
stick in one corner of his mind till it took charge—
it does sometimes—but all mixed up with bomb-
ings and nightmares. As soon as he got the
explanation it evaporated like ether and didn't
leave a stink. I sent him to bed full of his own
beer, and growing a shade dictatorial. He was a
not uncommon cross between a brave bully and
an old maid; but a man, right enough, when the
pressures were off. The old lady let us out—she
didn't kiss me again, worse luck! She was
primitive Stone Age—bless her! She looked on
us as a couple of magicians who's broken the spell
on him, she said.'

'Well, you had,' said Burges. 'What did he
do afterwards?'

'Bought a side-car to his bike, to hold more

vegetables—he'll be had up for poaching or tres-
passing, some day—and he cuts about the Home
Counties planting his stuff as happy as—Oh my
soul! *What* wouldn't I give to be even one
fraction as happy as he is! *But*, mind you, he'd
have committed suicide on the nod if Will and I
had had him arrested. We aren't exactly first-
class Sherlocks.'

McKnight was grumbling to himself. ' Juli-
aana Horratia Ewing,' said he. ' The best, the
kindest, the sweetest, the most eenocent tale ever
the soul of a woman gied birth to. I may sell
tapioca for a living in the suburbs, but I know
that. An' as for those prints o' mine,' he turned
to me, ' they were not garrdeners. They were the
Four Great British Botanists, an'—an'—I ask
your pardon.'

He pulled the draw-chains of all the nine
burners round the Altar of the Lesser Lights before we had time to put it to the vote.

A Naval Mutiny

THE COINER

(*circa* 1611)

(To be sung by the unlearned to the tune of 'King John and the Abbot of Canterbury,' and by the learned to 'Tempest-a-brewing.')

Against the Bermudas we foundered, whereby
This Master, that Swabber, yon Bo'sun, and I
(Our pinnace and crew being drowned in the main)
Must beg for our bread through old England again.

For a bite and a sup, and a bed of clean straw
We'll tell you such marvels as man never saw,
On a Magical Island which no one did spy
Save this Master, that Swabber, yon Bo'sun, and I.

Seven months among Mermaids and Devils and
Sprites,
And Voices that howl in the cedars o' nights,
With further enchantments we underwent there.
Good Sirs, 'tis a tale to draw guts from a bear!

'Twixt Dover and Southwark it paid us our way,
Where we found some poor players were labouring a
play;
And, willing to search what such business might be,
We entered the yard, both to hear and to see.

One hailed us for seamen and courteous-ly
Did take us apart to a tavern near by
Where we told him our tale (as to many of late),
And he gave us good cheer, so we gave him good
*   weight.*

Mulled sack and strong waters on bellies well lined
With beef and black pudding do strengthen the mind;
And seeing him greedy for marvels, at last
From plain salted truth to flat leasing we passed.

But he, when on midnight our reckoning he paid,
Says, ' Never match coins with a Coiner by trade,
Or he'll turn your lead pieces to metal as rare
As shall fill him this globe, and leave something to
*   spare. . . .'*

We slept where they laid us, and when we awoke
'Was a crown or five shillings in every man's poke.
We bit them and rang them, and, finding them good,
We drank to that Coiner as honest men should!

For a cup and a crust, and a truss, etc.

A Naval Mutiny

WHAT bronchitis had spared of him came, by medical advice, to Stephano's Island, that gem of sub-tropical seas, set at a height above the Line where parrots do not breed.

Yet there were undoubtedly three of them, squawking through the cedars. He asked a young lady, who knew the Island by descent, how this came. 'Two are ours,' she replied. 'We used to feed them in the veranda, but they got away, and set up housekeeping and had a baby.'

'What does a baby parrot look like?'

'Oh, just like a little Jew baby. I expect there will be some more soon.' She smiled prophetically.

. . . .

He watched H.M.S. *Florealia* work her way into the harbour. She moored, and sent a gig ashore. The bull-terrier, who is *de facto* Chief Superintendent of the Island Police, was explaining Port Regulations to the dog in charge of a Florida lumber schooner at the quay. His Policeman stood beside him. The gig, after landing her officer, lay off. The Policeman said in a clear voice to the dog: 'Come on, then, Polly! Pretty Polly! Come on, Polly, Polly, Polly!' The gig's crew seemed to grind their teeth a little as man and dog moved off. The invalid exchanged a few sentences with the Policeman and limped along the front street to the far and shallow end of the harbour, where Randolph's boat-repairing yard stands, just off the main road, near the mangrove clump by the poinsettias. A small mongrel fox-terrier pup, recovering from distemper, lay in the path of two men, who wanted to haul in a forty-foot craft, known to have been in the West India trade for a century, and now needing a new barrel to her steering-wheel.

'Let Lil lay,' Mr. Randolph called. 'Bring the boat in broadside, and run a plank to her.' Then he greeted the visitor. 'Mornin', Mr. Heatleigh. How's the cough? Our climate suitin' you? That's fine. Lil's fine too. The milk's helpin' her. You ain't the only one of her admirers. Winter Vergil's fetchin' her milk now. He ought to be here.'

'Winter Vergil! What the—who's he?'

'He hasn't been around the last week. He's had trouble.' Mr. Randolph laughed softly. 'He's a Navy Bo'sun—any age you please. He took his pension on the Island when I was a boy. 'Married on the Island too—a widow out of Cornwall Parish. That 'ud make her a Gallop or a Mewett. Hold a minute! It *was* Mewett. Her first man was a Gallop. He left her five acres of good onion-ground, that a Hotel wanted for golf-development. So-o, *that* way, an' Vergil havin' saved, he has his house an' garden handy to the Dockyard. 'No more keepin' Daddy away from

there than land-crabs off a dead nigger. I'm
expectin' him any time now.'

Mr. Heatleigh unbuttoned his light coat, for
the sun was beginning to work deliciously. Behind the old boat lay a scarlet hydroplane crowded
with nickel fitments and reeking of new enamels.

' That's Rembrandt Casalis's latest,' Mr. Randolph explained. ' He's Glucose Utilities—wuth
fifteen million they say. But no boatman. He
took her alongside a wharf last week. That don't
worry me. His estate can pay my repair-bills.
I'm doo to deliver her back this morning. . . .
Now! Now! Don't get movin' jest as you're
come. Set in the shed awhile. Vergil's bound
to be along with Lil's milk. Lay-to an' meet
him. I'd not go, 'lest I had to. But Lil 'll keep
you company.'

He splashed out to the hydroplane, which he
woke to outrageous howlings, and departed in one
splitting crack. The dead-water-rubbish swirled
in under the mangrove-stems as the sound of her
flight up-harbour faded. Mr. Heatleigh watched
the two hands on the West Indiaman. They laid
a gang-plank up to her counter, bore away the
rusty scarred wheel-barrel, and went elsewhere.
Lil slept, and along the white coral road behind
passed a procession of horse-drawn vehicles; for
another tripper-steamer had arrived, and her
passengers were being dealt out to the various
hotels. An old, spare, clean-shaven man, in spotless tussore silk, stepped off the road into the yard.
He bore left-handedly (his right was bandaged)
a sealed bottle of sterilised milk. Lil ran to him,

and he asked where her master might be. Mr. Heatleigh told him, and they exchanged names. Mr. Vergil rummaged a clean saucer out of the shed, but found he could not pour single-handed. Mr. Heatleigh helped him.

' She may be worth seventy-five cents,' Mr. Vergil observed as Lil lapped. ' She's cost more'n four dollars a week the last six weeks. Well, she's Randolph's dam' dog, anyhow.'

' 'Not fond of dogs ? ' Mr. Heatleigh asked.

' Not of any pets you might say, just now.'

Mr. Heatleigh glanced at the neatly-bandaged hand and nodded.

' No—not dogs,' said Mr. Vergil. ' Parrots. The medical officer at the Dockyard said it was more like the works of vulshures.'

' I don't know much about parrots.'

' You get to know about most things in the Navy—sooner or later. Burst-a-Frog, you do ! '

' Mr. Randolph told me you had been in the Ser—Navy.'

' Boy and man—forty odd years. I took my pension here in Nineteen Ten when Jacky's dam' first silly *Dreadnought* came in. All this so-called noo Navy has hove up since my time. I was boy, for example, in the old Black Fleet—*Warrior*, *Minotaur*, *Hercules*, an' those. In the Hungry Six too, if that means anything. . . . Are ye going away ? ' Mr. Heatleigh had moved out from the shed.

' Oh no ! I was only thinking of bringing my —sitting up there for a bit.' Mr. Heatleigh turned towards the boat, but seemed to wait for

Mr. Vergil to precede him up the gang-plank. The old man ran up it and dropped inboard little less nimbly than Mr. Heatleigh, who followed. They settled themselves at the stern, by the wheel. All forward of her mast was the naked hold of black rock-hard timbers. Mr. Vergil's glance, under frosty eyebrows, swept his companion's long visage as a searchlight sweeps a half-guessed fore-shore. ' 'Tourist?' he demanded suddenly.

' Yes, for a bit. I've got a motor-boat at Southampton.'

' 'Don't believe in 'em—never did. This beats 'em all ! '

He pointed to the bleached and cracked mast. There was silence while the two sunned them-selves. Mr. Heatleigh joined hands across one knee to help lift a rather stiff leg, as he lolled against the low stern-rail. The action drew his coat-cuff more than half-way up his wrist, which was tattooed. Mr. Vergil, backed against the sun, dug out his pipe-bowl. A breath of warmed cedar came across a patch of gladioli. ' Think o' Southampton Water now ! ' said Mr. Vergil. ' Thick—*an*' cold ! '

The three parrots screamed and whirled across the tip of the harbour. Mr. Vergil shook his bandaged hand at them.

' How did it happen?' Mr. Heatleigh asked.

' 'Obligin' a friend. 'No surer way.'

' How?—If you don't mind.' But there was command in the voice.

Once more Mr. Vergil's eyes raked the lean figure. ' It's due,' he said, ' to the Navy keepin' pets. Battleships an' armoured cruisers carry bears till they start huggin' senior ranks. Smaller craft, monkeys and parrots where allowed. There was a man in the old *Audacious*—Go-ood Lord, an' how she steered !—kep' chameleons in the engine-room, but they interfered with the movin' parts. Parrots are best. People pay high for well-spoken parrots.'

'Who teaches 'em?'

'Parrots are like women. They pick up where they shouldn't. I've heard it's the tone that attracts 'em. Now we've two cruisers—sloops *I* call 'em—on the Station. One's *Bulleana*, and t'other's the *Florealia*. Both of 'em stinkin' with parrots. Every dam' kind o' green—an' those pink-tailed greys like we used to get on the West Coast. Go-ood Lord! Burst-a-Frog! When was I in the Bight last? An' what in? *Theseus*—*St. George*, was it? Benin Expedition, was it? When we found those four hundred sovereigns and the four dozen champagne left in the King's Royal Canoe? An' no one noticed the cash till after ! . . . But parrots. There's a man called Mowlsey, a sort of Dockyard makee-do on the Stores side. He came to see me, knowin' Mrs. Vergil had a parrot. My house is handy to the Dockyard, because that way I can gratify my tastes. What I mean is what I've worked at forty years is good enough for me to stay by. That bein' so, I am often asked to bear a hand at delicate jobs.'

'Quite so,' said Mr. Heatleigh, still further extending himself to toast his lizard-like stomach. His coat-cuff was well above the wrist now.

'An'—that evenin' I'm speakin' of—this Mowlsey wanted me for special dooties. Owin' to approachin' target-practice for both ships, all Squadron parrots was to be handed in to the Riggin' Loft. There would be an O.C. Parrots, authorised to charge per diem for food an' maintenance. On return of Squadron, parrots would be returned to respective owners. He showed me the Orders—typed; an' Mrs. Vergil havin' a parrot, an' Mowlsey saying I had the requisite prestige, made me take on. The Riggin' Loft ain't a bad place, too, to sit in. Go-ood Lord! I remember when it used to be chock-a-block with spars, an' now—who'd know a stuns'le-boom from a wash-pole if they was crucified on 'em?'

'Why do they send parrots ashore for target-practice?'

'On account of the concussion strikin' 'em dumb. They don't like it themselves either. We had a big dog-baboon in the old *Penelope* (she with that stern) never could stummick big gun-practice even with black powder. He used to betake himself to the Head an' gnash his teeth against all an' sundry. Now that was a noosance —because the Head——'

Mr. Heatleigh coughed. 'Bronchitis,' he explained swiftly. 'Car—go ahead.'

'My instructions was to prepare to receive parrots at five bells. I daresay they told you in your passenger-steamer comin' out what time *that* is aboardship.'

'It's on the back of the passenger-list, I think,' Mr. Heatleigh answered meekly.

Mr. Vergil drew an impatient breath and went on.

'There was a bin full of parrot-rations inside. I put it down to Dockyard waste as usual. I had no notion what it 'ud mean for me. Now a Riggin' Loft, I may tell you, is mostly windows, an' along beneath 'em was spare awnin'-stretchers and sailin'-boat spars stacked on booms. I shifted some to make a shelving for the cages. I didn't see myself squattin' on the deck to attend to 'em. 'Takes too long to get up again, these days. (Go-ood Lord! Burst-a-Frog! An' I was an upper-yard-man for six years—leadin' hand, fore cross-trees, in the *Resistance*.) While I was busy, it sounded like our Marines landing in Crete—an' how long ago was *that*, now? They marched up from the boat-steps, *Bulleanas* leadin', *Florealias* in the rear, each man swingin' a cage to keep his bird quiet. When they halted an' the motion ceased they all began to rejoice—the birds, I mean—at findin' themselves together. A Petty Officer wraps his hands round my ear an' megaphones :— " Look sharp, Daddy. 'Tain't a cargo that'll keep."

' Nor was it. I could only walk backwards, semaphorin' *Bulleanas* to stack cages to port, an' *Florealias* to starboard o' the Loft. They marched in an' stacked accordin'—forty-three *Bulleana* birds, an' twenty-nine *Florealias*, makin' seventy-two in all.'

' Why didn't you say a hundred? ' Mr. Heatleigh asked.

' Because there weren't that many. The

landin' parties then proceeded to the far doors,
an', turnin' port or starboard, accordin' to their
ships, navigated back again along outside the
premises to say good-bye. Seventy-two birds,
and seventy-two lower-deck ratin's leanin' through
the windows, tellin' 'em to be good an' true till
they returned. An' *that* had to be done in dumb-
crambo too! A Petty Officer towed me into the
offing before we could communicate. But he
only said:—" Gawd help you, Daddy!" an'
marched 'em aboard again. That broke the
birds' hearts . . . *Do?* If you can't do anything, don't make yourself a laughing-stock. I
hung on an' off outside waitin' for a lull in the
typhoon. Go-ood Lord-Burst-a-Frog! How
many have I seen of 'em? But, look you—'wasn't
any typhoon scuppered the *Serpent*! She was
overgunned forrard, an' couldn't shake her head
clear of a ripple. Sister-ship to *Viper* an' *Cobra*,
was she? No! No! They were destroyers.
But all unlucky sampans! . . . An' about my
parrots. I went into the Loft an' said:—" Hush!"
like Mrs. Vergil. They detailed a coverin'-party
to keep up the fire, but most of 'em slued their
heads round, and took stock of me—sizin' me up,
the same as the watches do their Warrants and
Bo'suns before the ship's shaken down. I took
stock o' them, to spot the funny-men an' trouble-
makers for the ensuin' commission. Burst-a-
Frog! How often have I done that! The
screechers didn't worry me. Most men can't
live, let alone work, unless they're chewin' the
rag. It was the noocleus — the on-the-knee

parties—that I wanted to identify. Why? If a man knows one job properly, don't matter what it is, he ought to know 'em all. For example. I had spent twenty odd years headin' off bad hats layin' to aggravate me ; *and* liars and sea-lawyers tryin' to trip me on Admiralty Regulations ; not to mention the usual cheap muckin's, eatin' into the wind. An' there they was—every man I'd ever logged or got twisted at seven bells—*all* there, metamorfused into those dam' birds, an' o' course, havin' been Navy trained, talkin' lower-deck.'

As Mr. Vergil paused, Mr. Heatleigh nodded with apparent understanding.

' There was a pink-tail grey—a West Coast ju-ju-wallah—squatting on the floor of his cage. I'd ha' put *him* in the bowse on his general tally if he'd been a regular ratin'. He waited till me eye travelled past him, as I was lookin' 'em over. Then he called me It out of his belly, ventriloquial. Now there was an upper-yard-man in—now which one of those old bitch-cruisers was it? No! No! *Resistance*—five masts. Yes,—who had the very same gift, and other men got the blame. Jemmy Reader was his name—a sour dog with a broken mouth. I said to him, the bird I mean :— " The anchor ain't fairly stowed yet; so I didn't hear you. But I won't forget it, Jemmy." And Burst-a-Frog! I hadn't thought of Jemmy Reader in thirty odd years.

' An' there was a sulphur-crested cockatoo, swearin' like poison. He reminded me o' some-one I couldn't fit, but I saw he was good for trouble. One way an' another, I spotted half-a-dozen proper jokers, an' a dozen, maybe, that 'ud follow 'em if things went well. The rest was ord'nary seamen, ready to haul with any crowd that promised a kick-up. (I'd seen it *all* before, when I had to know seven hundred men by name and station within the first week. 'Never allowed meself or anyone else any longer.)

'Then Mrs. Vergil came down with me luncheon. We had to go a long way outside the Loft to talk. They weren't ladies' birds. But she said, quick as cordite:—" Our Polly's cage-cover's the thing." And I said:—" The heart of her husband shall safely trust in her. Send it down now. One of 'em's overdue for it already." She sent it, an' my Presentation Whistle which they had presented to me on leaving the *Raleigh*. Burst-a-Frog! She *was* a ship. Ten knots on a bowline, comin' out o' Simonstown, draggin' her blasted screw.'

'What did you want your Call for?' Once more Mr. Vergil's eyes pierced Mr. Heatleigh through at the question.

'If the game was workin' out on lower-deck lines, how could I do without it? Next time that cockatoo-bird began cursin' me, I piped down. It fetched him up with a round turn. He squatted an' said, " Lord love a Duck!" He hadn't Jemmy's guts. An' just *that*, mark you, hove him up in my mind for the man which he'd been. It was Number Three at the port six-pounder—she hadn't much else—in the old *Polyphemus*-ram, that broke the boom at Berehaven—how long back? He was a beefy beggar, with a greasy lollopin' lovelock on his forehead—but I can't remember his tally. There were some other duplicates o' men I had known, but Jemmy and the Polyphemus bird were the ringleaders. Bye and bye those green screechers cooled off a bit—creakin' an' mutterin' like hens on a hot day; an' I did a caulk by the open door, where the boat-rollers are. Then Jemmy sprung it on me, an' I heard what I haven't in a long day! "Hand-of-a-Mess for biscuits!" They feed 'em on French rolls in the so-called New Navy; but it used to be, when a boy heard that, he sculled off an' drew what was on issue for his mess, or got kicked. An' just then I *was* a boy bringin' a boat alongside the old *Squirrel* training-brig in slow time. (Dreamin' I mean.) So I was half-way down the Loft 'fore I woke, an' they all scoffed at me! Jemmy leadin'. But there was somethin' at the back o' the noise (you can always tell), an' while I was rubbin' my eyes open, I saw the bin o' parrot-food. Seven bells in the after-noon-watch, it was, an' what they wanted, an' what by Admiralty Regulations, d'ye see, they were entitled to, was their food-pans refillin'. *That's* where Jemmy showed his cunnin'! Lots o' food was still unexpended, but they were within their rights; an' he had disrated me to Hand-of-a-Mess in his birdshop!'

'What did you do?'

'Nothin'. It was a lower-deck try-on. 'Question was should I treat 'em as birds or blue-jackets. I gave 'em the benefit o' the doubt. Navy-

pattern they was, an' Navy tack they should get.
I filled pans and renewed water where requisite,
an' they mocked me. They mocked me all the
time. That took me through the first dog-watch.
Jemmy waited till I had finished, an' then he
called me It again. (Jemmy Reader out on a
weather-earrin' to the life !) An' that started Polyphemus. I dowsed Jemmy's glim with our
Polly's cage-cover. That short-circuited the quiff-
bird too ; provin' they was workin' off the same
lead. I carried on cleanin' their cages, with a
putty-knife. It gratified 'em highly to see me
Captain of the Head as well as Mess Boy.
Jemmy o' course couldn't see, but Polyphemus
told him, an' he said what he shouldn't in the
dark. He had guts. I give him that. I then
locked up the Loft and went home.

' Mrs. Vergil said that I had done well, but I
knew that, so far, it had only been ranging on the
target. Mut'ny an' conspiracy was their game,
an' the question was how they'd work it. Go-ood
Lord-Burst-a-Frog ! I've seen three years' con-
tinuous mut'ny, slave-dhowing in the Red Sea,
under single awnin's, with "Looney Dick" in
the old *Petruchio* corvette—the one that dropped
her bottom out off The Minicoys. By the end of
the commission, all Officers not under open arrest
was demandin' court-martials, an' the lower-deck
was prowlin' murder.'

' How did it finish ? ' Mr. Heatleigh asked.

' Navy-fashion. We came home. When our
cockroaches had died—off Gozo that would be—
Dick piped all hands to look at a kit-bag full of

evidence, in the waist, under the Ensign. "There's enough bile an' spite an' perjury there," he says, " to scupper all hands—an' me first. If you want it taken home, say so." We didn't. " Then we'll give it Christian burial," he says. We did ; our Doctor actin' Chaplain. . . . But about my parrots. I went back to 'em at sunrise—you could have heard 'em off the Bahamas since dawn—but that was the bird in 'em. I gave them room to swing till it crossed my mind they were mockin' me again. (The nastiest rux I ever saw, when a boy, began with " All hands to sky-lark." *I* don't hold with it.) When I took our Polly's cage-cover off Jemmy, he didn't call me anything. He sat an' scoffed at me. I couldn't tell what traverse he was workin' till he cocked one eye up—Jemmy Reader workin' some dirty game to the life !—an' there, in the roof, was a little green beggar skimmin' up an' down. He'd broke out of his cage. Next minute, there was another promenadin' along a spar, looking back at me like a Gosport lady to see how I took it. I shut doors an' windows before they had made up their minds to run. Then I inspected cages. They'd been busy since light unpickin' the wire granny-knots this so-called Noo Navy had tied 'em in with. At sea, o' course, there was nowhere to break out to, an' they knew it. Ashore, they had me pawled as responsible for 'em if run or dead. An' *that* was why Jemmy had scoffed. They'd been actin' under his orders.'

' But couldn't it have been Polyphemus ? ' Mr. Heatleigh suggested.

' He may have passed on Jemmy's orders, but he hadn't Jemmy's mind. All I heard out of *him* was mockin's an' curses. Any way, I couldn't round up those common greens, hoppin' out their cages by dozens, an' when you can't exercise authority—don't. So I slipped out o' the door, and listened outside. 'Reg'lar lower-deck palaver. Jemmy damned 'em all for bitchin' the evolution. The first deserters ought to ha' run as units, d'ye see, instead o' waitin' to make up a boatload. Polyphemus damned back at Jemmy like a Chatham matey, an' the rest made noises because they liked listenin'-in to themselves. If it wasn't for chin-wagging, there'd be serious trouble in lots of families. But I thought it was time this was being put a stop to. So I went to the house for a pair o' scissors.'

' I don't quite see what——'

' I told you that that gunner in the *Polyphemus* had a quiff an' fancied himself the whole watch an' a half till—Go-ood Lord, how it all came back watchin' those poultry—he was run round to the barber an' Dartmoor-clipped for wearin' oily and indecent appendages. It tamed him. Only I *can't* remember his name.'

Mr. Vergil wrinkled his brows, and it seemed as though Mr. Heatleigh did the like. But there was no result.

' When I went to 'em again, there must ha' been twenty small greens loose. But they couldn't break out o' the ship, so I disregarded 'em, an' struck at the root o' the matter. I tried to get Polyphemus to let me scratch his head—the sweep! He bit like a bloodhound on the snap of the scissors.' Mr. Vergil waved his right hand. 'I had to drag an' scrag him 'fore I offed it—his quiff—crest, I mean. An' then—Go-ood Lord-Burst-a-Frog!—he keeled over on his side in a dead faint like a Christian! The barberin' had worked livin' wonders with—with the man he was, but, even so, I *was* surprised at that pore bald fowl! "That's for you, you yellow dog," I said. "The rest's for Jemmy Reader." Jemmy hadn't missed a stroke of my operations. He knew what was comin'. He turned on his back like a shark, an' began to fight tooth an' nail. It must ha' meant as much to him as pig-tails used to—his tail, I mean.

'I said:—"Jemmy, there's never been more than one Bo'sun in any ship I've served in. Dead or alive, you're for disratin', so you can say what you please. It won't go in the report."'

'And did he?'

'Yes—oh yes! But I didn't log it against him, the charge being strictly mut'ny. I got him at last—torn to ribbons twice over—an' I sheared off his red tail-feathers level with his bare behind. He'd been askin' for it the whole Commission.'

'And what did he do?'

'He stopped. I've never heard anyone chat much after disratin'. They can't manage the voice, d'ye see? He tried to squat, but his back-stays were carried away. Then he climbed up the wires to his ring, like an old, old man; an' there he sat bobbin' an' balancin', all down by the head like a collier-brig. Pore beggar!'

Mr. Heatleigh echoed him. ' And that finished the business?' he said.

' I had struck at the root of the matter,' Mr. Vergil replied simply. ' There was only those common greens flyin' loose. When they found I didn't notice 'em, they began going back to their cages, two an' three together for company's sake, an' arguin' about it. I hurried 'em up by throwin' my cap (the Loft was gettin' warmish through bein' shut up), an' 'fore sundown they were all back, an' I fastened up behind 'em with the same spun-yarn tricks as their silly owners had. Don't *anyone* teach *anything* in this Noo Navy nowadays?'

' What about Jemmy and Polyphemus?' Mr. Heatleigh asked.

' Jemmy was busy gettin' used to his new trim, an' Polyphemus squatted, croakin' like a frog an' sayin', " Lord love a Duck ! " No guts ! That's how it was till the Squadron returned.'

' But wasn't there some sort of fuss then between ships? A Policeman on the wharf told me —and the *Florealia's* gig——'

' They've been rubbin' it in to 'em on the Island; that's why. Yes. The *banzai*-parties came ashore, all hats and hosannas like a tax-payers' treat. The Petty Officer checked my seventy-two cages—one bird per cage—an' that finished my watch. But, *then* he gave the party time to talk to their sweethearts instead o' marchin' off at once. Some oily-wad of a *Bulleana* struck up about not having got his proper bird. I heard a P.O. say :—" Settle it among yourselves." (Democratic, I suppose he thought it.) The man naturally started across the Loft to do so. He met a *Florealia* with the same complaint. They began settlin' it. That let everything go by the run. They were holdin' up their cages, and lookin' at 'em in the light like glasses o' port. Wonderful thing—the eye o' Love! Yes, they began settlin' in pairs.'

' But what about Jemmy Reader and Polyphemus?'

' There was a good deal o' talk over them too. A torpedo-midwife, or some such ratin', sculled about lookin' for the beggar who had cut off his poor Josie's tail. (It never hit me till then that Jemmy might have been a lady.) He fell foul of Polyphemus (the owner, I mean) moaning over his quiff; an', not bein' shipmates, they began settlin' too. Then such as had drawn their proper true-loves naturally cut in for their ship or mess. I've seen worse ruxes in my time, but a quicker breeze-up—never! *As* usual there was something behind it. I heard one of the ships had been dished out pre-war cordite for target practice, and so her shooting was like the old *Superb's* at Alexandria, till we touched off the magazine. The other ship had stood by condoling with five-flag hoists. So both parties landed more or less horstile. When the noise was gettin' noticeable outside, a P.O. says to me :—" They won't listen to us, Daddy. They say we ain't impartial!" I said :—" God knows what you *ain't*. But I know what you *are*! You're less use than ten mines in a Portuguee pig-knot. Close doors an' windows, an' let me take charge." So they did, an' what

with the noise bein' bottled up inside, an' the
Loft gettin' red-hot, an' no one interferin', which
was what I recommended, the lower-deck broke
away from the clinch, and began to pick up
bashed cage-work an' argue.

'Then I piped "Clear Lower Deck," an' I told
'em how I'd disrated Jemmy an' Polyphemus for
doin' what they did. (Jemmy *was* a lady, after
all. He laid an egg next day aboard ship, an' his
owner sent me a kodak picture.) That took their
minds off. I told 'em how I'd sweated in the
Loft, guardin' their treasures for 'em, an' they
had no right to complain if the poor little lonely
beggars had mixed hammicks in their absence.
When I had 'em laughing, I told 'em they was all
gas an' gaspers an' hair-oil, like the rest of the
so-called Noo Navy, an' they were marched off.
Otherwise—even if some fool wouldn't ha' sent
for the Marines, and spilled some silly mess into
the papers—those two ships 'ud ha' been sortin'
parrots out of each other the rest of the commission. You know what *that* means in the way of
ruxes ashore! As it is, they are actin' as a unit
when they're chipped about " pretty Pollies " all
over the Island. The worse they'll do now is to
kill a Policeman or two. An', if I may say so, my
handlin' of 'em—birds *an*' lower-deck—shows
what comes of a man knowing his profession, Sir
Richard.'

Mr. Heatleigh's countenance and bearing
changed as they expanded. He held out his hand.
Mr. Vergil rose to his feet and shook it. The
two beamed on each other.

' I can testify to that, Vergil, since my first commission. You knew me all along?'

' I thought it was you, sir, when you signalled me to go into this boat ahead of you. But I wasn't certain till I saw that bit of work I put on you.' Mr. Vergil pointed to the bared wrist, where the still deep blue foul-anchor showed under red hairs.

' In the foretop of the *Resistance*, off Port Royal,' Mr. Heatleigh said.

Mr. Vergil nodded and smiled. ' It's held,' said he. ' But—what's happened to your proper tally, Sir Richard?'

' That was because better men than me died in the War. I inherited, you see.'

' Meanin' you're a Lord now?'

The other nodded. Then he slapped his knee. ' 'Got it at last,' he cried. ' That *Polyphemus* gunner! It was Harris—Chatty, *not* Bugs. He was with me in the *Comus* and *Euryalus* after. 'Used to lend money.'

' That's him,' Mr. Vergil cried. ' I always thought he was a bit of a Jew. Who commanded the *Comus* then? I mean that time in the Adriatic, when she was pooped an' dam-near drowned the owner in his cabin.'

Mr. Heatleigh fished up that name also from his memory; and backwards and forwards through time they roved, recovering ships and men of ancient and forgotten ages. For, as the old know, the dead draw the dead, as iron does iron. The Admiral sat in the curve of the stern-timbers, his hands clenched on his knees,

as though tiller-lines might still be there. Mr.
Vergil, erect for the honour of great days and
names, faced him across the battered disconnected wheel, swaying a shade in the rush of the
memories that flooded past him. Victorias and
phaetons began to come back from the filled hotels.
One of them held a perspiring officer of the
Bulleana, who had been instructed to find by all
means Admiral (Retired) Lord Heatleigh, somehow mis-registered in some boarding-house, and
to convey to him his Captain's invitation to do
them the honour of lunching with them. And it
was already perilously near cocktail time ! . . .

Later, over those same cocktails, Lord Heat-
leigh gathered that the opinion of His Majesty's
Squadron on the station was that 'Daddy'
Vergil merited hanging at the yard-arm.

' 'Glad you haven't got one between you,'
was the answer. 'He taught me most of my
seamanship when I was a Snotty. The best
Bo'sun and—off duty—*the* biggest liar in the
Service.'

The Debt

The Debt

THE Doctor of the Gaol and his wife had gone to tennis in the Gardens, leaving their six-year-old son, William, in nominal care of his ayah, but actually to One Three Two and old Mahmud Ali, his mother's *dharzi*, or sewing-man, who had made frocks for her mother since the day when skirts were skirts.

One Three Two was a ' lifer,' who had unluckily shot a kinsman a little the wrong side of the British frontier. The killing was a matter he could no more have shirked than a decent Englishman his Club dues. The error in geography came from a head-wound picked up at Festubert, which had affected his co-ordinations. But the judge who tried the case made no allowance, and One Three Two only escaped the gallows on an appeal engineered and financed by the Colonel and officers of his old regiment, which he had left after twenty years of spotless service with a pension and—as was pointed out at the trial—urgent private affairs to settle.

His prison duties—he had been a non-commissioned officer—were to oversee the convicts working in the Doctor's garden, where, bit by bit, he took it upon his battered and dishonoured head to be William's bodyguard or, as he called it, 'sacrifice.' Few people are more faithful to such trusts than the man of one fair killing, and William made him chief of all his court, with honorary title of Busi-bandah, which means much the same as 'Goosey-gander.'

So, when William came out with his scooter into the afternoon smell of newly watered paths, which attracts little snakes, One Three Two, with a long-handled hoe, kept within striking distance of him at every turn, till the child wearied of the play.

'Put away, Busi-bandah,' he commanded, and climbed up the veranda steps to old Mahmud, cross-legged on the carpet, surrounded by beautiful coloured stuffs. It was a dinner dress, and Mahmud held a seam of it between his toes.

'Drink tobacco,' said William spaciously. '*They* will not return till dark.'

'But this stuff will tell,' said Mahmud above the frock, 'for the smell of *hukah* tobacco clings.'

'Take of my father's cigarettes.' William pointed indoors with his chin.

One Three Two went into the drawing-room and came back with a couple of cigarettes from the store beside the wireless cabinet.

'What word of the Padishah's sickness?' he asked.

William swelled importantly. It was one of his prerogatives to announce what the Man in the Box said about the sick Padishah.

'He slept little last night, because of the fever.

He does not desire to eat. None the less his strength holds. Five doctors have taken oath to this. There will be no more talk out of the Bokkus till after I am asleep.'

'What does thy father say?' Mahmud asked.

'My father says that it is in the balance—thus!' William picked up Mahmud's embroidery-scissors and tried to make them ride on his forefinger.

'Have a care! They may cut. Give me.' Mahmud took them back again.

'But my mother says that, now all people everywhere are praying for the Padishah's health, their prayers will turn the balance, and he will be well.'

'If Allah please,' said Mahmud, who in private life was Imam or leader of the little mud mosque of the village by the Gaol gates, where he preached on Fridays.

'I also pray every night,' William confided cheerily. 'After "Make me a good boy," I stand to 'tenshin, and I say: "God save the King." Is that good namaz (prayer)?'

'There is neither hem nor border nor fringe to the Mercy of Allah,' Mahmud quoted.

'Well spoken, tailor-man.' One Three Two laughed. He was a hard-bitten Afridi from the Khaiber hills, who, except among infidels, rode his faith with a light hand.

'Good talk,' William echoed. 'For when I had the fever last year, and my father said it was tach-an-go—that is, in the balance—my mother prayed for me, and I became well. Oh, here is my blue buttony-bokkus!' He reached out for

Mahmud's lovely, old, lacquered Kashmiri pen-case, where oddments were kept, and busied himself with the beads and sequins. One Three Two rolled a deep-set eye towards Mahmud.

'That news of the Padishah is bad,' said he. 'Hast thou inquired of the Names, Imam, since his sickness came?'

The Koran discourages magic, but it is lawful to consult the Names of Allah according to a system called the Abjad, in which each letter of the Arabic alphabet carries one of the Nine-and-ninety Names of God beginning with that letter. Each Name has its arbitrary Number, Quality, Element, Zodiacal sign, Planet, and so forth. These tables are often written out and used as amulets. Even William, who thought he knew everything, did not know that Mahmud had sewn an Abjad into the collar of his cold-weather dressing-gown.

'All the world has questioned,' Mahmud began.

'Doubtless. But I do not know much of the world from here. How came it with thee?'

'I took the age of the Padishah, which is sixty-and-three. Now the Number Sixty carries for its attribute the Hearer. This may be good or bad, for Allah hears all things. Its star is Saturn, the outermost of the Seven. That is good and commanding. But its sign is the Archer, which is also the sign of the month (November) in which his sickness first struck the Padishah. Twice, then, must the Archer afflict the Padishah.'

One Three Two nodded. That seemed reasonable enough.

'As for the Number Three, its attribute is the Assembler, which again may be good or bad. For who knows to what judgment Allah calls men together? Its sign is the Crab, which, being female, is in friendship with the Archer. It may be, then, that if the Archer spare the Padishah both now and later—for he will surely smite twice—the Padishah will be clear of his malady in the month of the Crab (late June or early July).'

'And what is the Planet of the Number Three?' said the other.

'Mars assuredly. He is King. The Abjad does not lie. Hast thou used it?'

'There was a priest of ours cast it for me, when I would learn how my affairs would go. The dog said, truly enough, that I should punish my cousin, but he said nothing of my punishment here.'

'Did he reckon by thy name-letters or by thy age?'

'By my name, I think. I am no great scholar.'

' 'Be merciful!' said Mahmud. 'No wonder thou art afflicted, O Zuhan Khan. Thy letter is Zad, which carries for its Name the Punisher. Its attribute is Terrible, and its quality Hate.'

'All true,' One Three Two returned. 'Am I not here till I die? I submit myself to the fixed decree. And, certainly, were I free'—he chuckled impiously—'my kin on the hills would kill me. But I live. Why? Because a man may draw back-pay, as it were, for his good deeds. I dug my Captain, who is now Colonel, out of some ground that fell upon him in Frangistan (France). It was part of our work. He said nothing—nor I. But seven years after—when I was condemned for that affair of my burnt cousin—he spent money like water on lawyers and lying witnesses for my sake. Otherwise——' One Three Two jerked his beard towards a little black shed on a roof outside the high garden wall. No one had ever told William what it was for.

' It may be thy good deed in saving that Captain's life was permitted to count in thy balance,' Mahmud volunteered.

' And *I* am no more than a convict. . . . What is the order, Baba? I am here.'

William had suddenly shut the pencase. ' Enough,' he said. ' Bring again my *eskootah*, Busi-bandah. I will be a horseman. I will play polo.'

Now little snakes, who have a habit of coming out on damp garden-paths, cast no warning shadow when a low sun is blinded by thick mango-trees.

' It is brought,' said One Three Two ; but in place of getting it he said to Mahmud : ' While he rides, I will tell thee a tale of the Padishah which my Colonel told me.'

' No! Let be my *eskootah*. I will listen to that tale. Make me my place ! ' said William.

It was not five steps to the man's side, but by the time William had taken them, an inviting lap awaited him, into which he dropped, his left cheek on the right shoulder in its prison blanket, his right hand twined in the beard, and the rest of him relaxed along the curve of the right arm.

' Begin, Busi-bandah,' he commanded from off his throne.

' By thy permission,' One Three Two began. ' Early in the year when thou wast born, which was the year I came to be with thee, Baba, my Colonel told me this tale to comfort my heart. It was when I—when I——'

' Was to be hanged for thy bad cousin,' said William, screwing up his eyes as he pointed with his left third finger to the hut on the roof. ' *I* know.'

' " Keep a thing from women and children, and sieves will hold water," ' Mahmud chuckled in his big, silver-black beard.

' Yes, Baba, that was the time,' said One Three Two, recovering himself. ' My Colonel told me that after the war in Frangistan was ended, the Padishah commanded that every man who had died in his service—and there were multitudes upon multitudes—should be buried according to his faith.'

William nodded. When he went out, he always met funeral processions on their way to the Moslem cemetery near the race-course ; and, being a child below the age of personality, there were few details of wedding or burial that he had not known since he could ask questions.

' This was done as commanded, and to each man was his tomb, with his name, rank, and service cut in white stone, all one pattern, whether he had been General or Sweeper—Sahib—Mussulman—Yahudi—Hubashi—or heathen. My Colonel told me that the burial-places resembled walled towns, divided by paths, and planted with trees and flowers, where all the world might come and walk.'

'On Fridays,' murmured William. Friday is the day when Muhammedan families visit their dead. He had often begged afternoons off for the servants to go there.

'And every day. And when all was done, and the People of the Graves were laid at ease and in honour, it pleased the Padishah to cross the little water between Belait and Frangistan, and look upon them. He give order for his going in this way. He said: "Let there be neither music nor elephants nor princes about my way, nor at my stirrup. For it is a pilgrimage. I go to salute the People of the Graves." Then he went over. And where he saw his dead laid in their multitudes, there he drew rein; there he saluted; there he laid flowers upon great stones after the custom of his people: And for *that* matter,' One Three Two addressed Mahmud, 'so do our women on Fridays. Yes, and the old women and the little staring children of Frangistan pressed him close, as he halted among the bricks and the ashes and the broken wood of the towns which had been killed in the War.'

'Killed in the War,' William answered vaguely.

'But the People of the Graves waited behind their white walls, among the grass and flowers—orderly in their lines—as it were an inspection with all gear set out on the cots.'

One Three Two gathered the child closer as he grew heavier.

'My Colonel told me this. And my Colonel said—and Allah be my witness *I* know!—it was killing cold weather. Frangistan is colder than all my own hills in winter—cold that cuts off a man's toes. Yes! That is why I lack two toes, Baba. And bitter it was when the Padishah came in spring. The sun shone, but the winds cut. And, at the last, and the last, was a narrow cemetery, walled with high walls, entered by one door in a corner. Yes—like this Gaol-Khana. It was filled with our own people for the most part— Mussulmans who had served. It lay outside a city, among fields where the winds blew. Now, in the order of the Padishah's pilgrimage, it was commanded that wheresoever he chose to draw rein, there should wait on him some General-sahib, who had fought near that place in the long War. Not princes, priests, nor elephants, but a General of his service. And so to this narrow, high-walled burial-place of the one gate came a General-sahib, sworded and spurred, with many medals, to wait the Padishah's coming. And while he waited he clothed himself—for he had been sick—in his big coat, his *Baritish warrum*.'

'I know,' said William, rousing himself. 'Mahmud made me a little one out of the old one of my father, when he came back. But Mahmud would not sew me any crowns or stars on the shoulder.'

Mahmud drew a quick breath (he had been putting away his hand sewing-machine) and went

softly into the house.   The sun was setting, and
there was a change in the air.

' Yes, all the world knows *Baritish warrum.*
So the General waited, sheltering himself from the
wind that blew through that gate till the feet of the
Padishah were heard walking across the waste
ground without.'

One Three Two reached up his left hand, took
the cold-weather dressing-gown that Mahmud
fetched from the nursery, and laid it lightly over
William.

His voice went on in a soothing purr. ' And
when the feet of the Padishah were heard without
the gate, that General stripped off his heavy coat
and stood forth in his medalled uniform, as the
order is.   Then the Padishah entered.   The
General saluted, but the Padishah did not heed.
He signed with his open hand thus, from right to
left—my Colonel showed me—and he cried out :
" By Allah, O man, I conjure thee put on that
coat on one breath !   This is no season to catch
sickness."   And he named the very sickness that
was to fall upon himself five years after.   So the
General cast himself into that big coat again with
speed, and in one breath the Padishah became in
all respects again the Padishah.   His equerries
rehearsed the General's name and honours, and the
General saluted and put forward his sword-hilt to
be touched, and he did the Padishah duty and
attendance in that place through the appointed
hour.   And on the out-going the Padishah said to
him : " Take heed that never again, O man, do I
find thee at such seasons without thy thick coat

upon thee. For the good are scarce." And he
went down to the sea, and they cast off in the
silence of ten thousand bare-headed. (He had
forbidden music because it was a *haj* [pilgrimage].)
And thus it was accomplished; and this, my Colonel
told me, was his last act in his *haj* to the People of
the Graves. . . . Wait thy prayer awhile, Mahmud.
The child sleeps. When the Padishah was gone
the General said to my Colonel, who was on leave
in Frangistan, " By Allah, to the Padishah do I
owe my life, for an hour coatless in that chill would
have slain me ! " '

' The Padishah forenamed the sickness that
fell upon himself ? ' Mahmud asked.

William breathed evenly.

' That very sickness—five full years before it
fell.'

' It may be a sign,' Mahmud conceded, ' even
though it is a little one.'

' A man's life is not a little thing. See what a
tamasha (circus) that fat Hindu pig of a judge
made over the one I spilled.'

' A little thing beside the great things which
the Padishah does daily, in his power.'

' What do *we* know of them ? He is Padishah.
The more part of his rule is worked by his head-
men—as, but for my Colonel, my hanging would
have been. Nay ! Nay ! We say, in the Regiment : " How does a man bear himself *off* parade ? " And we say in our Hills, of those cursed
crooked Kabul-made rifles : " A gun does not
throw true unless it has been bored true." But
thou art no soldier.'

'True! And yet in my trade we say: "As the silk, so the least shred of it. As the heart, so the hand."'

'And it is truth! This deed that the Padishah did among the People of the Graves declared the quality and nature of the Padishah himself. It was a fair blood-debt between a man and a man. The life of that General is owing to the Padishah. I hold it will be paid to him, and that the Padishah will live.'

'If God please,' said Mahmud, and laid out his mat. The sun had set, and it was time for the fourth prayer of the day. Mahmud, as Imam of a mosque, was strict in ritual, but One Three Two only prayed at dawn and full dark. So he sat till he heard the Doctor's car challenged at the Gaol gate before he carried William in to the nursery.

'What did the Man in the Bokkus tell about the King?' William asked his mother when she kissed him good-night in his cot. He was all but asleep.

'Only the same as this morning. Shall I hear your prayers, little man?'

'No need!' muttered William. Then he sat bolt upright, intensely awake, and speaking in chosen English: 'Because Busi-bandah says the King will get well, anyhow. He says it is his back-pay for making the cold General put on his *Baritish warrum*.'

He flopped back, burrowed in his pillow, grunted, and dived far beneath the floods of sleep.

AKBAR'S BRIDGE

Jelaludin Muhammed Akbar, Guardian of Mankind,
Moved his standards out of Delhi to Jaunpore of lower
*   Hind,*
Where a mosque was to be builded, and a lovelier
*   ne'er was planned;*
And Munim Khan, his Viceroy, slid the drawings
*   'neath his hand.*

(High as Hope upsheered her towers to the promised
*   Heavens above.*
Deep as Faith and dark as Judgment her unplumbed
*   foundations dove.*
Wide as Mercy, white as moonlight, stretched her fore-
*   courts to the dawn;*
And Akbar gave commandment, ' Let it rise as it is
*   drawn.')*

Then he wearied—the mood moving—of the men and
*   things he ruled,*
And he walked beside the Goomti while the flaming
*   sunset cooled,*
Simply, without mark or ensign—singly, without
*   guard or guide,*
And he heard an angry woman screeching by the river-
*   side.*

'Twas the *Widow of the Potter*, a virago feared and
    known,
In haste to cross the ferry, but the ferry-man had gone.
So she cursed him and his office, and hearing *Akbar's*
    tread,
(She was very old and darkling) turned her wrath
    upon his head.

But he answered—being *Akbar*—'Suffer me to scull
    you o'er.'
Called her ' Mother,' stowed her bundles, worked the
    clumsy scow from shore,
Till they grounded on a sand-bank, and the *Widow*
    loosed her mind ;
And the stars stole out and chuckled at the *Guardian
    of Mankind*.

' Oh, most impotent of bunglers ! Oh, my daughter's
    daughter's brood,
Waiting hungry on the threshold ; for I cannot bring
    their food,
Till a fool has learned his business at their virtuous
    grandam's cost,
And a greater fool, our *Viceroy*, trifles while her name
    is lost !

' *Munim Khan*, that Sire of Asses, sees me daily come
    and go
As it suits a drunken boatman, or this ox who cannot
    row.
Munim Khan, the Owl's Own Uncle—*Munim Khan*,
    the Capon's seed,
Must build a mosque to *Allah* when a bridge is all we
    need !

'*Eighty years I eat oppression and extortion and delays—*
Snake and crocodile and fever—flood and drouth, be-set my ways.
But Munim Khan must tax us for his mosque what-e'er befall;
Allah knowing (May He hear me!) that a bridge would save us all!'

While she stormed that other laboured and, when they touched the shore,
Laughing brought her on his shoulder to her hovel's very door.
But his mirth renewed her anger, for she thought he mocked the weak;
So she scored him with her talons, drawing blood on either cheek. . . .

Jelaludin Muhammed Akbar, Guardian of Mankind,
Spoke with Munim Khan his Viceroy, ere the midnight stars declined—
Girt and sworded, robed and jewelled, but, on either cheek appeared
Four shameless scratches running from the turban to the beard.

'*Allah burn all Potters' Widows! Yet, since this same night was young,*
One has shown me by sure token, there was wisdom on her tongue.
Yes, I ferried her for hire. Yes,' he pointed, ' I was paid.'
And he told the tale rehearsing all the Widow did and said.

And he ended, ' Sire of Asses—Capon—Owl's Own
    Uncle—know
I—most impotent of bunglers—I—this ox who cannot
    row—
I—Jelaludin Muhammed Akbar, Guardian of Man-
    kind—
Bid thee build the hag her bridge and put our mosque
    from out thy mind.'

So 'twas built, and Allah blessed it ; and, through
    earthquake, flood, and sword,
Still the bridge his Viceroy builded throws her arch
    o'er Akbar's Ford !

The Manner of Men

The Manner of Men

'If after the manner of men I have fought with beasts.'—
1 Cor. xv. 32.

HER cinnabar-tinted topsail, nicking the hot
blue horizon, showed she was a Spanish wheat-
boat hours before she reached Marseilles mole.
There, her mainsail brailed itself, a spritsail broke
out forward, and a handy driver aft; and she
threaded her way through the shipping to her
berth at the quay as quietly as a veiled woman
slips through a bazaar.

The blare of her horns told her name to the
port. An elderly hook-nosed Inspector came
aboard to see if her cargo had suffered in the run
from the South, and the senior ship-cat purred
round her captain's legs as the after-hatch was
opened.

'If the rest is like this—' the Inspector sniffed
—'you had better run out again to the mole and
dump it.'

'That's nothing,' the captain replied. 'All
Spanish wheat heats a little. They reap it very
dry.'

''Pity you don't keep it so, then. What
would you call *that*—crop or pasture?'

225

The Inspector pointed downwards. The grain was in bulk, and deck-leakage, combined with warm weather, had sprouted it here and there in sickly green films.

' So much the better,' said the captain brazenly. ' That makes it waterproof. Pare off the top two inches, and the rest is as sweet as a nut.'

' *I* told that lie, too, when I was your age. And how does she happen to be loaded?'

The young Spaniard flushed, but kept his temper.

' She happens to be ballasted, under my eye, on lead-pigs and bagged copper-ores.'

' I don't know that they much care for verdigris in their dole-bread at Rome. But—you were saying?'

' I was trying to tell you that the bins happen to be grain-tight, two-inch chestnut, floored and sided with hides.'

' Meaning dressed African leathers on your private account?'

' What has that got to do with you? We discharge at Port of Rome, not here.'

' So your papers show. And what might you have stowed in the wings of her?'

' Oh, apes! Circumcised apes—just like you!'

' Young monkey! Well, if you are not above taking an old ape's advice, next time you happen to top off with wool and screw in more bales than are good for her, get your ship undergirt before you sail. I know it doesn't look smart coming into Port of Rome, but it 'll save your decks from lifting worse than they are.'

There was no denying that the planking and waterways round the after-hatch had lifted a little. The captain lost his temper.

'I know your breed!' he stormed. 'You promenade the quays all summer at Caesar's expense, jamming your Jew-bow into everybody's business; and when the norther blows, you squat over your brazier and let us skippers hang in the wind for a week!'

'You have it! Just that sort of a man am I now,' the other answered. 'That'll do, the quarter-hatch!'

As he lifted his hand the falling sleeve showed the broad gold armlet with the triple vertical gouges which is only worn by master mariners who have used all three seas—Middle, Western, and Eastern.

'Gods!' the captain saluted. 'I thought you were——'

'A Jew, of course. Haven't you used Eastern ports long enough to know a Red Sidonian when you see one?'

'Mine the fault—yours be the pardon, my father!' said the Spaniard impetuously. 'Her topsides *are* a trifle strained. There was a three days' blow coming up. I meant to have had her undergirt off the Islands, but hawsers slow a ship so—and one hates to spoil a good run.'

'To whom do you say it?' The Inspector looked the young man over between horny sun and salt creased eyelids like a brooding pelican. 'But if you care to get up your girt-hawsers to-morrow, I can find men to put 'em overside.

It's no work for open sea. Now! Main-hatch,
there! . . . I thought so. She'll need another
girt abaft the foremast.' He motioned to one of
his staff, who hurried up the quay to where the
port Guard-boat basked at her mooring-ring. She
was a stoutly-built, single-banker, eleven a side,
with a short punching ram; her duty being to
stop riots in harbour and piracy along the coast.

'Who commands her?' the captain asked.

'An old shipmate of mine, Sulinus—a River
man. We'll get his opinion.'

In the Mediterranean (Nile keeping always
her name) there is but one river—that shifty-
mouthed Danube, where she works through her
deltas into the Black Sea. Up went the young
man's eyebrows.

'Is he any kin to a Sulinor of Tomi, who used
to be in the flesh-traffic—and a Free Trader? My
uncle has told me of him. He calls him Mango.'

'That man. He was my second in the wheat-
trade my last five voyages, after the Euxine grew
too hot to hold him. But he's in the Fleet now.
. . . You know your ship best. Where do you
think the after-girts ought to come?'

The captain was explaining, when a huge dish-
faced Dacian, in short naval cuirass, rolled up the
gangplank, carefully saluting the bust of Caesar
on the poop, and asked the captain's name.

'Baeticus, for choice,' was the answer.

They all laughed, for the sea, which Rome mans
with foreigners, washes out many shore-names.

'My trouble is this——' Baeticus began, and
they went into committee, which lasted a full hour.

At the end, he led them to the poop, where an awning had been stretched, and wines set out with fruits and sweet shore water.

They drank to the Gods of the Sea, Trade, and Good Fortune, spilling those small cups overside, and then settled at ease.

'Girting's an all-day job, if it's done properly,' said the Inspector. 'Can you spare a real working-party by dawn to-morrow, Mango?'

'But surely—for you, Red.'

'I'm thinking of the wheat,' said Quabil curtly. He did not like nicknames so early.

'Full meals *and* drinks,' the Spanish captain put in.

'Good! Don't return 'em too full. By the way'—Sulinor lifted a level cup—'where do you get this liquor, Spaniard?'

'From our Islands (the Balearics). Is it to your taste?'

'It is.' The big man unclasped his gorget in solemn preparation.

Their talk ran professionally, for though each end of the Mediterranean scoffs at the other, both unite to mock landward, wooden-headed Rome and her stiff-jointed officials.

Sulinor told a tale of taking the Prefect of the Port, on a breezy day, to Forum Julii, to see a lady, and of his lamentable condition when landed.

'Yes,' Quabil sneered. 'Rome's mistress of the world—as far as the foreshore.'

'If Caesar ever came on patrol with me,' said Sulinor, 'he might understand there was such a thing as the Fleet.'

'Then he'd officer it with well-born young Romans,' said Quabil. 'Be grateful you are left alone. *You* are the last man in the world to want to see Caesar.'

'Except one,' said Sulinor, and he and Quabil laughed.

'What's the joke?' the Spaniard asked.

Sulinor explained.

'We had a passenger, our last trip together, who wanted to see Caesar. It cost us our ship and freight. That's all.'

'Was he a warlock—a wind-raiser?'

'Only a Jew philosopher. But he *had* to see Caesar. He said he had; and he piled up the *Eirene* on his way.'

'Be fair,' said Quabil. 'I don't like the Jews—they lie too close to my own hold—but it was Caesar lost me my ship.' He turned to Baeticus. 'There was a proclamation, our end of the world, two seasons back, that Caesar wished the Eastern wheat-boats to run through the winter, and he'd guarantee all loss. Did *you* get it, youngster?'

'No. Our stuff is all in by September. I wager Caesar never paid you! How late did you start?'

'I left Alexandria across the bows of the Equinox—well down in the pickle, with Egyptian wheat—half pigeon's dung—and the usual load of Greek sutlers and their women. The second day out the sou'-wester caught me. I made across it north for the Lycian coast, and slipped into Myra till the wind should let me get back into the regular grain-track again.'

Sailor-fashion, Quabil began to illustrate his voyage with date and olive stones from the table.

'The wind went into the north, as I knew it would, and I got under way. You remember, Mango? My anchors were apeak when a Lycian patrol threshed in with Rome's order to us to wait on a Sidon packet with prisoners and officers. Mother of Carthage, I cursed him!'

''Shouldn't swear at Rome's Fleet. 'Weatherly craft, those Lycian racers! Fast, too. I've been hunted by them! 'Never thought I'd command one,' said Sulinor, half aloud.

'And now I'm coming to the leak in *my* decks, young man,' Quabil eyed Baeticus sternly. 'Our slant north had strained her, and I should have undergirt her at Myra. Gods know why I didn't! I set up the chain-staples in the cable-tier for the prisoners. I even had the girt-hawsers on deck —which saved time later; but the thing I should have done, that I did *not*.'

'Luck of the Gods!' Sulinor laughed. 'It was because our little philosopher wanted to see Caesar in his own way at our expense.'

'Why did he want to see him?' said Baeticus.

'As far as I ever made out from him and the centurion, he wanted to argue with Caesar—about philosophy.'

'He was a prisoner, then?'

'A political suspect—with a Jew's taste for going to law,' Quabil interrupted. 'No orders for irons. Oh, a little shrimp of a man, but—but he seemed to take it for granted that he led everywhere. He messed with us.'

'And he was worth talking to, Red,' said Sulinor.

'*You* thought so; but he had the woman's trick of taking the tone and colour of whoever he talked to. Now—as I was saying . . .'

There followed another illustrated lecture on the difficulties that beset them after leaving Myra. There was always too much west in the autumn winds, and the *Eirene* tacked against it as far as Cnidus. Then there came a northerly slant, on which she ran through the Aegean Islands, for the tail of Crete; rounded that, and began tacking up the south coast.

'Just darning the water again, as we had done from Myra to Cnidus,' said Quabil ruefully. 'I daren't stand out. There was the bone-yard of all the Gulf of Africa under my lee. But at last we worked into Fairhaven—by that cork yonder. Late as it was, *I* should have taken her on, but I had to call a ship-council as to lying up for the winter. That Rhodian law may have suited open boats and cock-crow coasters,[1] but it's childish for ocean-traffic.'

'*I* never allow it in any command of mine,' Baeticus spoke quietly. 'The cowards give the order, and the captain bears the blame.'

Quabil looked at him keenly. Sulinor took advantage of the pause.

'We were in harbour, you see. So our Greeks tumbled out and voted to stay where we were. It

---

[1] Quabil meant the coasters who worked their way by listening to the cocks crowing on the beaches they passed. The insult is nearly as old as sail.

was my business to show them that the place was
open to many winds, and that if it came on to blow
we should drive ashore.'

'Then I,' broke in Quabil, with a large and
formidable smile, ' advised pushing on to Phenike,
round the cape, only forty miles across the bay.
My mind was that, if I could get her undergirt
there, I might later—er—coax them out again on
a fair wind, and hit Sicily. But the undergirting
came first. She was beginning to talk too much
—like me now.'

Sulinor chafed a wrist with his hand.

' She was a hard-mouthed old water-bruiser in
any sea,' he murmured.

' She could lie within six points of any wind,'
Quabil retorted, and hurried on. ' What made
Paul vote with those Greeks? He said we'd be
sorry if we left harbour.'

' Every passenger says that, if a bucketful
comes aboard,' Baeticus observed.

Sulinor refilled his cup, and looked at them
over the brim, under brows as candid as a child's,
ere he set it down.

' Not Paul. He did not know fear. He gave
me a dose of my own medicine once. It was a
morning watch coming down through the Islands.
We had been talking about the cut of our topsail
—he was right—it held too much lee wind—
and then he went to wash before he prayed.
I said to him : " You seem to have both ends and
the bight of most things coiled down in your
little head, Paul. If it's a fair question, what *is*
your trade ashore?" And he said : " I've been

a man-hunter—Gods forgive me; and now that I think The God has forgiven me, I am man-hunting again." Then he pulled his shirt over his head, and I saw his back. Did *you* ever see his back, Quabil?'

' I expect I did—that last morning, when we all stripped; but I don't remember.'

' *I* shan't forget it! There was good, sound lictor's work and criss-cross Jew scourgings like gratings; and a stab or two; and, besides those, old dry bites—when they get good hold and rugg you. That showed he must have dealt with the Beasts. So, whatever he'd done, he'd paid for. I was just wondering what he *had* done, when he said: " No; not your sort of man-hunting." " It's your own affair," I said: " but *I* shouldn't care to see Caesar with a back like that. I should hear the Beasts asking for me." " I may that, too, some day," he said, and began sluicing himself, and—then—— What's brought the girls out so early? Oh, I remember ! '

There was music up the quay, and a wreathed shore-boat put forth full of Arlesian women. A long-snouted three-banker was hauling from a slip till her trumpets warned the benches to take hold. As they gave way, the *hrmph-hrmph* of the oars in the oar-ports reminded Sulinor, he said, of an elephant choosing his man in the Circus.

' She has been here re-masting. They've no good rough-tree at Forum Julii,' Quabil explained to Baeticus. ' The girls are singing her out.'

The shallop ranged alongside her, and the

banks held water, while a girl's voice came across the clock-calm harbour-face :

'Ah, would swift ships had never been about the seas to rove!
For then these eyes had never seen nor ever wept their love.
Over the ocean-rim he came—beyond that verge he passed,
And I who never knew his name must mourn him to the last !'

'And you'd think they meant it,' said Baeticus, half to himself.

'That's a pretty stick,' was Quabil's comment as the man-of-war opened the island athwart the harbour. 'But she's overmasted by ten foot. A trireme's only a bird-cage.'

''Luck of the Gods I'm not singing in one now,' Sulinor muttered. They heard the yelp of a bank being speeded up to the short sea-stroke.

'I wish there was some way to save mainmasts from racking.' Baeticus looked up at his own, bangled with copper wire.

'The more reason to undergirt, my son,' said Quabil. '*I* was going to undergirt that morning at Fairhaven. You remember, Sulinor? I'd given orders to overhaul the hawsers the night before. My fault! Never say "To-morrow." The Gods hear you. And then the wind came out of the south, mild as milk. All we had to do was to slip round the headland to Phenike—and be safe.'

Baeticus made some small motion, which Quabil noticed, for he stopped.

'My father,' the young man spread apologetic palms, 'is not that lying wind the in-draught of Mount Ida? It comes up with the sun, but later——'

'You need not tell *me*! We rounded the cape, our decks like a fair (it was only half a day's sail), and then, out of Ida's bosom the full north-easter stamped on us! Run? What else? I needed a lee to clean up in. Clauda was a few miles down wind; but whether the old lady would bear up when she got there, I was not so sure.'

'She did.' Sulinor rubbed his wrists again. 'We were towing our longboat half-full. I steered somewhat that day.'

'What sail were you showing?' Baeticus demanded.

'Nothing—and twice too much at that. But she came round when Sulinor asked her, and we kept her jogging in the lee of the island. I said, didn't I, that my girt-hawsers were on deck?'

Baeticus nodded. Quabil plunged into his campaign at long and large, telling every shift and device he had employed. 'It was scanting daylight,' he wound up, 'but I daren't slur the job. Then we streamed our boat alongside, baled her, sweated her up, and secured. You ought to have seen our decks!'

''Panic?' said Baeticus.

'A little. But the whips were out early. The centurion—Julius—lent us his soldiers.'

'How did your prisoners behave?' the young man went on.

Sulinor answered him. 'Even when a man is being shipped to the Beasts, he does not like drowning in irons. They tried to rive the chain-staples out of her timbers.'

'I got the main-yard on deck'—this was

Quabil. 'That eased her a little. They stopped yelling after a while, didn't they?'

'They did,' Sulinor replied. 'Paul went down and told them there was no danger. And they believed him! Those scoundrels believed him! He asked me for the keys of the leg-bars to make them easier. "*I've* been through this sort of thing before," he said, "but they are new to it down below. Give me the keys." I told him there was no order for him to have any keys; and I recommended him to line his hold for a week in advance, because we were in the hands of the Gods. "And when are we ever out of them?" he asked. He looked at me like an old gull lounging just astern of one's taffrail in a full gale. *You* know that eye, Spaniard?'

'Well do I!'

'By that time'—Quabil took the story again— 'we had drifted out of the lee of Clauda, and our one hope was to run for it and pray we weren't pooped. None the less, I could have made Sicily with luck. As a gale I have known worse, but the wind never shifted a point, d'ye see? We were flogged along like a tired ox.'

'Any sights?' Baeticus asked.

'For ten days not a blink.'

'Nearer two weeks,' Sulinor corrected. 'We cleared the decks of everything except our ground-tackle, and put six hands at the tillers. She seemed to answer her helm—sometimes. Well, it kept *me* warm for one.'

'How did your philosopher take it?'

'Like the gull I spoke of. He was there,

but outside it all. *You* never got on with him, Quabil?'

'Confessed! I came to be afraid at last. It was not my office to show fear, but I was. *He* was fearless, although I knew that he knew the peril as well as I. When he saw that trying to—er—cheer me made me angry, he dropped it. 'Like a woman, again. You saw more of him, Mango?'

'Much. When I was at the rudders he would hop up to the steerage, with the lower-deck ladders lifting and lunging a foot at a time, and the timbers groaning like men beneath the Beasts. We used to talk, hanging on till the roll jerked us into the scuppers. Then we'd begin again. What about? Oh! Kings and Cities and Gods and Caesar. He was sure he'd see Caesar. I told him I had noticed that people who worried Those Up Above'—Sulinor jerked his thumb towards the awning—'were mostly sent for in a hurry.'

'Hadn't you wit to see he never wanted you for yourself, but to get something out of you?' Quabil snapped.

'Most Jews are like that—and all Sidonians!' Sulinor grinned. 'But what *could* he have hoped to get from anyone? We were doomed men all. You said it, Red.'

'Only when I was at my emptiest. Otherwise I *knew* that with any luck I could have fetched Sicily! But I broke—we broke. Yes, we got ready—you too—for the Wet Prayer.'

'How does that run with you?' Baeticus

asked, for all men are curious concerning the bride-bed of Death.

'With us of the River,' Sulinor volunteered, 'we say: "I sleep; presently I row again."'

'Ah! At our end of the world we cry: "Gods, judge me not as a God, but a man whom the Ocean has broken."' Baeticus looked at Quabil, who answered, raising his cup: 'We Sidonians say, "Mother of Carthage, I return my oar!" But it all comes to the one in the end.' He wiped his beard, which gave Sulinor his chance to cut in.

'Yes, we were on the edge of the Prayer when —do you remember, Quabil?—*he* clawed his way up the ladders and said: "No need to call on what isn't there. My God sends me sure word that I shall see Caesar. *And* he has pledged me all your lives to boot. Listen! No man will be lost." And Quabil said: "But what about my ship?"' Sulinor grinned again.

'That's true. I had forgotten the cursed passengers,' Quabil confirmed. 'But he spoke as though my *Eirene* were a fig-basket. "Oh, she's bound to go ashore, somewhere," he said, "but not a life will be lost. Take this from me, the Servant of the One God." Mad! Mad as a magician on market-day!'

'No,' said Sulinor. 'Madmen see smooth harbours and full meals. I have had to—soothe that sort.'

'After all,' said Quabil, 'he was only saying what had been in my head for a long time. I had no way to judge our drift, but we likely might hit something somewhere. Then he went away to spread his cook-house yarn among the crew. It did no harm, or I should have stopped him.'

Sulinor coughed, and drawled :

' I don't see anyone stopping Paul from what he fancied he ought to do. But it was curious that, on the change of watch, I——'

' No—I ! ' said Quabil.

' Make it so, then, Red. Between us, at any rate, we felt that the sea had changed. There was a trip and a kick to her dance. *You* know, Spaniard. And then—I *will* say that, for a man half-dead, Quabil here did well.'

' I'm a bosun-captain, and not ashamed of it. I went to get a cast of the lead. (Black dark and raining marlinspikes !) The first cast warned me, and I told Sulinor to clear all aft for anchoring by the stern. The next—shoaling like a slip-way— sent me back with all hands, and we dropped both bowers and spare and the stream.'

' He'd have taken the kedge as well, but I stopped him,' said Sulinor.

' I had to stop *her* ! They nearly jerked her stern out, but they held. And everywhere I could peer or hear were breakers, or the noise of tall seas against cliffs. We were trapped ! But our people had been starved, soaked, and half-stunned for ten days, and now they were close to a beach. That was enough ! They must land on the instant ; and was I going to let them drown within reach of safety ? *Was* there panic ? I spoke to Julius, and his soldiers (give Rome her due !) schooled them till I could hear my orders again.

But on the kiss-of-dawn some of the crew said that Sulinor had told them to lay out the kedge in the long-boat.'

' I let 'em swing her out,' Sulinor confessed. ' I wanted 'em for warnings. But Paul told me his God had promised their lives to him along with ours, and any private sacrifice would spoil the luck. So, as soon as she touched water, I cut the rope before a man could get in. She was ashore—stove—in ten minutes.'

' Could you make out where you were by then ?' Baeticus asked Quabil.

' As soon as I saw the people on the beach—yes. They are my sort—a little removed. Phoenicians by blood. It was Malta—*one* day's run from Syracuse, where I would have been safe ! Yes, Malta and my wheat gruel. Good port-of-discharge, eh ? '

They smiled, for Melita may mean ' mash ' as well as ' Malta.'

' It puddled the sea all round us, while I was trying to get my bearings. But my lids were salt-gummed, and I hiccoughed like a drunkard.'

' And drunk you most gloriously were, Red, half an hour later ! '

' Praise the Gods—and for once your pet Paul ! That little man came to me on the fore-bitts, puffed like a pigeon, and pulled out a breastful of bread, and salt fish, and the wine—the good new wine. " Eat," he said, " and make all your people eat, too. Nothing will come to them except another wetting. They won't notice that, after they're full. Don't worry about *your* work either," he said.

" You *can't* go wrong to-day. You are promised
to me." And then he went off to Sulinor.'

' He did. He came to me with bread and
wine and bacon—good they were! But first he
said words over them, and then rubbed his hands
with his wet sleeves. I asked him if he were a
magician. " Gods forbid ! " he said. " I am so
poor a soul that I flinch from touching dead pig."
As a Jew, he wouldn't like pork, naturally. Was
that before or after our people broke into the
store-room, Red ? '

' Had *I* time to wait on them ? ' Quabil snorted.
' I know they gutted my stores full-hand, and a
double blessing of wine atop. But we all took
that—deep. Now this is how we lay.' Quabil
smeared a ragged loop on the table with a wine-wet
finger. ' Reefs—see, my son—and overfalls to
leeward here ; something that loomed like a point
of land on our right there ; and, ahead, the blind
gut of a bay with a Cyclops surf hammering it.
How we had got in was a miracle. Beaching was
our only chance, and meantime she was settling
like a tired camel. Every foot I could lighten
her meant that she'd take ground closer in at the
last. I told Julius. He understood. " I'll keep
order," he said. " Get the passengers to shift the
wheat as long as you judge it's safe." '

' Did those Alexandrian achators really work ? '
said Baeticus.

' *I*'ve never seen cargo discharged quicker. It
was time. The wind was taking off in gusts, and
the rain was putting down the swells. I made out
a patch of beach that looked less like death than

the rest of the arena, and I decided to drive in on a gust under the spitfire-sprit—and, if she answered her helm before she died on us, to humour her a shade to starboard, where the water looked better. I stayed the foremast; set the spritsail fore and aft, as though we were boarding; told Sulinor to have the rudders down directly he cut the cables; waited till a gust came; squared away the sprit, and drove.'

Sulinor carried on promptly:—

' I had two hands with axes on each cable, and one on each rudder-lift; and, believe me, when Quabil's pipe went, both blades were down and turned before the cable-ends had fizzed under! She jumped like a stung cow! She drove. She sheared. I think the swell lifted her, and over-ran. She came down, and struck aft. Her stern broke off under my toes, and all the guts of her at that end slid out like a man's paunched by a lion. I jumped forward, and told Quabil there was nothing but small kindlings abaft the quarter-hatch, and he shouted: " Never mind! Look how beautifully I've laid her ! " '

' I had. What I took for a point of land to starboard, y'see, turned out to be almost a bridge-islet, with a swell of sea 'twixt it and the main. And that meeting-swill, d'you see, surging in as she drove, gave her four or five foot more to cushion on. I'd hit the exact instant.'

' Luck of the Gods, *I* think! Then we began to bustle our people over the bows before she went to pieces. You'll admit Paul was a help there, Red?'

' I dare say he herded the old judies well enough ; but he should have lined up with his own gang.'

' He did that, too,' said Sulinor. ' Some fool of an under-officer had discovered that prisoners must be killed if they look like escaping ; and he chose that time and place to put it to Julius— sword drawn. Think of hunting a hundred prisoners to death on those decks ! It would have been worse than the Beasts ! '

' But Julius saw—Julius saw it,' Quabil spoke testily. ' I heard him tell the man not to be a fool. They couldn't escape further than the beach.'

' And how did your philosopher take *that*?' said Baeticus.

' As usual,' said Sulinor. ' But, you see, we two had dipped our hands in the same dish for weeks ; and, on the River, that makes an obligation between man and man.'

' In my country also,' said Baeticus, rather stiffly.

' So I cleared my dirk—in case I had to argue. Iron always draws iron with me. But *he* said : " Put it back. They are a little scared." I said : " Aren't *you*? " " What? " he said; " of being killed, you mean? No. Nothing can touch me till I've seen Caesar." Then he carried on steadying the ironed men (some were slavering-mad) till it was time to unshackle them by fives, and give 'em their chance. The natives made a chain through the surf, and snatched them out breast-high.'

'Not a life lost! 'Like stepping off a jetty,'
Quabil proclaimed.

'Not quite. But he had promised no one
should drown.'

'How *could* they—the way I had laid her—
gust and swell and swill together?'

'And was there any salvage?'

'Neither stick nor string, my son. We had
time to look, too. We stayed on the island till the
first spring ship sailed for Port of Rome. They
hadn't finished Ostia breakwater that year.'

'And, of course, Caesar paid you for your ship?'

'I made no claim. I saw it would be hopeless ;
and Julius, who knew Rome, was against any appeal
to the authorities. He said that was the mistake
Paul was making. And, I suppose, because I did
not trouble them, and knew a little about the
sea, they offered me the Port Inspectorship here.
There's no money in it—if I were a poor man.
Marseilles will never be a port again. Narbo
has ruined her for good.'

'But Marseilles is far from under-Lebanon,'
Baeticus suggested.

'The further the better. I lost my boy three
years ago in Foul Bay, off Berenice, with the
Eastern Fleet. He was rather like you about the
eyes, too. You and your circumcised apes!'

'But—honoured one! My master! Admiral!
—Father mine—how *could* I have guessed?'

The young man leaned forward to the other's
knee in act to kiss it. Quabil made as though to
cuff him, but his hand came to rest lightly on the
bowed head.

' Nah ! Sit, lad ! Sit back. It's just the thing the Boy would have said himself. You didn't hear it, Sulinor ? '

' I guessed it had something to do with the likeness as soon as I set eyes on him. You don't so often go out of your way to help lame ducks.'

' You can see for yourself she needs under-girting, Mango ! '

' So did that Tyrian tub last month. And you told her she might bear up for Narbo or bilge for all of you ! But he shall have his work-ing-party to-morrow, Red.'

Baeticus renewed his thanks. The River man cut him short.

' Luck of the Gods,' he said. ' Five—four —years ago I might have been waiting for you anywhere in the Long Puddle with fifty River men—and no moon.'

Baeticus lifted a moist eye to the slip-hooks on his yardarm, that could hoist and drop weights at a sign.

' You might have had a pig or two of ballast through your benches coming alongside,' he said dreamily.

' And where would my overhead-nettings have been ? ' the other chuckled.

' Blazing—at fifty yards. What are fire-arrows for ? '

' To fizzle and stink on my wet sea-weed blindages. Try again.'

They were shooting their fingers at each other, like the little boys gambling for olive-stones on the quay beside them.

'Go on—go on, my son! Don't let that pirate board,' cried Quabil.

Baeticus twirled his right hand very loosely at the wrist.

'In that case,' he countered, 'I should have fallen back on my foster-kin—my father's island horsemen.'

Sulinor threw up an open palm.

'Take the nuts,' he said. 'Tell me, is it true that those infernal Balearic slingers of yours can turn a bull by hitting him on the horns?'

'On either horn you choose. My father farms near New Carthage. They come over to us for the summer to work. There are ten in my crew now.'

Sulinor hiccoughed and folded his hands magisterially over his stomach.

'Quite proper. Piracy *must* be put down! Rome says so. I do so,' said he.

'I see,' the younger man smiled. 'But tell me, why did you leave the slave—the Euxine trade, O Strategos?'

'That sea is too like a wine-skin. 'Only one neck. It made mine ache. So I went into the Egyptian run with Quabil here.'

'But why take service in the Fleet? Surely the Wheat pays better?'

'I intended to. But I had dysentery at Malta that winter, and Paul looked after me.'

'Too much muttering and laying-on of hands for *me*,' said Quabil; himself muttering about some Thessalian jugglery with a snake on the island.

'*You* weren't sick, Quabil. When I was getting better, and Paul was washing me off once, he asked if my citizenship were in order. He was a citizen himself. Well, it was and it was not. As second of a wheat-ship I was *ex officio* Roman citizen—for signing bills and so forth. But on the beach, my ship perished, he said I reverted to my original shtay—status—of an extra-provinshal Dacian by a Sich—Sish—Scythian—I think she was—mother. Awkward—what? All the Middle Sea echoes like a public bath if a man is wanted.'

Sulinor reached out again and filled. The wine had touched his huge bulk at last.

'But, as I was saying, once *in* the Fleet nowadays one is a Roman with authority—no waiting twenty years for your papers. And Paul said to me : " Serve Caesar. You are not canvas I can cut to advantage at present. But if you serve Caesar you will be obeying at least some sort of law." He talked as though I were a barbarian. Weak as I was, I could have snapped his back with my bare hands. I told him so. " I don't doubt it," he said. " But that is neither here nor there. If you take refuge under Caesar at sea, you may have time to think. Then I may meet you again, and we can go on with our talks. But that is as The God wills. What concerns you *now* is that, by taking service, you will be free from the fear that has ridden you all your life." '

'Was he right?' asked Baeticus after a silence.

'He was. I had never spoken to him of it,

but he knew it. *He* knew! Fire—sword—
the sea—torture even—one does not think of
them too often. But not the Beasts! Aie!
Not the Beasts! I fought two dog-wolves for
the life on a sand-bar when I was a youngster.
Look!'

Sulinor showed his neck and chest.

'They set the sheep-dogs on Paul at some
place or other once—because of his philosophy!
And he was going to see Caesar—going to see
Caesar! And he—he had washed me clean after
dysentery!'

'Mother of Carthage, you never told me that!'
said Quabil.

'Nor should I now, had the wine been
weaker.'

AT HIS EXECUTION

I am made all things to all men—
    Hebrew, Roman, and Greek—
    In each one's tongue I speak,
Suiting to each my word,
That some may be drawn to the Lord!

I am made all things to all men—
    In City or Wilderness
    Praising the crafts they profess
That some may be drawn to the Lord—
By any means to my Lord!

Since I was overcome
    By that great Light and Word,
I have forgot or forgone
The self men call their own
(Being made all things to all men)
    So that I might save some
    At such small price, to the Lord,
As being all things to all men.

I was made all things to all men,
But now my course is done—
And now is my reward—
Ah, Christ, when I stand at Thy Throne
With those I have drawn to the Lord,
Restore me my self again!

Unprofessional

Unprofessional

SINCE Astronomy is even less remunerative than
Architecture, it was well for Harries that an uncle
of his had once bought a desert in a far country,
which turned out to overlie oil. The result for
Harries, his only nephew, was over a million
pounds invested, plus annual royalties.

When the executors had arranged this, Harries,
who might have been called an almost-unpaid
attaché at Washe Observatory, gave a dinner to
three men, whom he had tried and proved beneath
glaring and hostile moons in No Man's Land.

Vaughan, Assistant Surgeon at St. Peggotty's,
was building himself a practice near Sloane Street.
Loftie, pathologist, with the beginnings of a reputation, was—for he had married the unstable
daughter of one of his earlier London landladies
—bacteriological advisor to a Public Department,
on five-hundred-and-seventy pounds per annum,
and a prospect of being graded for pension.
Ackerman, also a St. Peggotty's man, had been
left a few hundreds a year just after he had
qualified, and so had given up all serious work
except gastronomy and the allied arts.

Vaughan and Loftie knew of Harries' luck,

which Harries explained in detail at the dinner, and stated what, at the lowest count, his income would be.

'Now,' said he, '"Tacks" can tell you.'

Ackerman made himself small in his chair, as though it had been the shell-hole whence he had once engineered their retreat.

'We know each other fairly well,' he began. 'We've seen each other stripped to the Ultimate Atom pretty often? We needn't camouflage? Agreed? You're always saying what you'd do if you were independent. Have you changed your minds?'

'Not me,' said Vaughan, whose oft-told dream was a nursing-home of his own near Sloane Street. He had marked the very house for it.

'Do you think I'd keep on with this sewage job if it wasn't for the pension?' Loftie asked. He had followed research the more keenly since, at twenty-two, he had wrecked his own happiness.

'Be free, then,' said Ackerman. 'Take three thousand——'

'Hold on,' Harries broke in plaintively. 'I said "up to five."'

'Sorry, old man! I was trying for the commission. Take up to five thousand a year from Harries for as long as you choose—for life, if you like. Then research on your own lines, Loftie, and—and—let the Bull know if you stumble on anything. That's the idea, isn't it?'

'Not all.' Harries surged a little in his seat. 'A man's entitled to use a telescope as well as a microscope, isn't he? Well—I've got notions I want to test. They mean keeping one's eyes open and—logging the exact times that things happen.'

'That's what you said when you lectured our company about Astrology—that night under Arras. D'you mean " planetary influences ? " ' Loftie spoke with a scientist's scorn.

'This isn't my lecture.' Harries flushed. 'This is my gamble. We can't tell on what system this dam' dynamo of our universe is wound, but we know we're in the middle of every sort of wave, as we call 'em. They used to be "influences." '

'Like Venus, Cancer, and that lot?' Vaughan inquired.

'Yes—if you choose. Now I want Vaughan to start his clinic, and give me a chance to test my notions occasionally. No! Not faith-healing! Loftie can worry his cells and tissues with radium as much as he likes. But——'

'We're only on the threshold of radium,' Loftie snapped.

'Then get off it ! ' was the blasphemous retort. 'Radium's a *post hoc*, not a *propter*. I want you merely to watch some of your cell-growths all round the clock. Don't think ! *Watch*—and put down the times of any changes you see.'

'Or imagine? ' Loftie supplemented.

'You've got it. Imagination *is* what we want. This rigid " thinking " game is hanging up research. You told me yourself, the other night, it was becoming all technique and no advance,' Harries ended.

'That's going too far. We're on the edge of big developments.'

'All the better! Take the money and go ahead. Think of your lab., Lofter! Stoves, filters, sterilisers, frigidaria—everything you choose to indent for!'

'I've brought along Schermoltz's last catalogue. You might care to look at it, later.' Ackerman passed the pamphlet into Loftie's stretched hand.

'Five thousand a year,' Loftie muttered and turned the enthralling pages. 'God! What one could afford! . . . But I'm not worth the money, Bull. Besides, it's robbery. . . . You'll never arrive at anything by this astrology nonsense.'

'But *you* may, on your lines. What do you suppose is the good of Research?'

'God knows,' Loftie replied, devouring the illustrations. 'Only—only it looks—sometimes —as if He were going to tell.'

'That's all we want,' Harries coaxed. 'Keep your eye on Him, and if He seems inclined to split about anything, put it down.'

'I've had my eye on that house for the last half-year. You could build out a lift-shaft at the back.' Vaughan looked and spoke into the future.

Here the *padrone* came in to say that if more drinks were needed, they should be ordered.

Ackerman ordered; Harries stared at the fire; Loftie sank deeper into the catalogue; and Vaughan into his vision of the desirable house for his clinic. The *padrone* came back with a loaded tray.

'It's too much money to take—even from you, Bull.' Vaughan's voice was strained. 'If you'd lend me a few hundred for my clinic, I could . . .'

Loftie came out of the catalogue and babbled to the same effect, while he reckoned up for just how many pounds a week the horror that defiled his life and lodgings could be honourably removed from both till it drank itself dead.

Harries reared up over them like a walrus affronted.

'Do you remember the pill-box at Zillebeeke, and the skeleton in the door? Who pinched the bombs for us *then*?' he champed.

'Me and The Lofter,' said Vaughan, sullen as a schoolboy.

'What for?'

'Because we dam' well needed 'em.'

'We need 'em worse now! We're up against the beggar in the pill-box. He's called Death—if you've ever heard of him. This stuff of mine isn't money, you imbeciles! It's a service-issue—same as socks. We—we haven't kept on saving each other's silly lives for *this*! Oh, don't let me down! Can't you *see*?' The big voice quavered.

'Kamerad, Bull! I'll come in,' said Loftie. Vaughan's hands had gone up first, and he was the first to recover himself, saying: 'What about "Tacks?" He isn't let off, is he?'

'No. I'm going to make commission out of the lot of you,' said Ackerman. 'Meantime! Come on, me multi-millionaires! The Bald-

headed Beggar in the pill-box is old, but the
night is yet young.'

The effects of five thousand a year are
stimulating.

A mere Cabinet Minister, dependent on elec-
tions for his place, looking in on a Committee
where Loftie was giving technical evidence, asked
in too loud a whisper, if that all-but-graded Civil
Servant were ' one of my smell-and-tell tempor-
aries.' Loftie's resignation was in that evening.
Vaughan, assisted by an aunt, started a little nursing-home near Sloane Street, where his new household napery lift and drying-cupboards almost led
to his capture by ' just the kind of girl, my dear,
to make an ideal wife for a professional man.'

Harries continued to observe the heavens, and
commissioned Ackerman to find a common meet-
ing-place. This—Simson House was its name—
had been a small boys' school in a suburb without
too many trams. Ackerman put in floods of water,
light and power, an almost inspired kitchen-range,
a house-man and his cook-wife, and an ex-Navy
petty rating as valet-plumber, steward-engineer,
and butler-electrician ; set four cots in four little
bedrooms, and turned the classroom in the back
garden into a cement-floored hall of great possibilities, which Harries was the first to recognise.
He cut off a cubicle at one end of it, where he
stored books, clocks, and apparatus. Next, Loftie
clamoured for a laboratory and got it, dust and
air-tight, with lots of the Schermoltz toys laid out
among taps and sinks and glass shelves. Hither

he brought various numbered odds-and-ends which Vaughan and other specialists had sent him in the past, and on which, after examination, he had pronounced verdicts of importance to unknown men and women. Some of the samples— mere webs of cancerous tissue—he had, by arts of his own, kept alive in broths and salts after sentence had been executed on their sources of origin.

There were two specimens—Numbers 127 and 128—from a rarish sort of affliction in exactly the same stage of development and precisely the same position, in two women of the same age and physique, who had come up to Vaughan on the same afternoon, just after Vaughan had been appointed Assistant Surgeon at St. Peggotty's. And when the absurdly identical operations were over, a man, whose praise was worth having, but whose presence had made Vaughan sweat into his palms, had complimented him. So far as St. Peggotty's knew, both cases were doing well several months after. Harries found these samples specially interesting, and would pore over them long times on end, for he had always used the microscope very neatly.

' Suppose you watch what these do for a while,' he suggested to Loftie one day.

' *I* know what they'll do well enough,' the other returned. He was hunting a line of his own in respect to brain-cells.

' Then couldn't you put Frost on to watch 'em with a low-power lens? ' Harries went on. ' He's a trained observer in his own line. What? Of *course* he's at your disposition, old man. *You* could make anything of him. Oh, by the way, do you happen to remember what time of day you operated on One-twenty-Seven and Eight?'

'Afternoon, of course—at St. Peggotty's—between three and five. It's down somewhere.'

'It don't matter. I only wanted to get an idea. Then you'll turn on Frost to watch 'em? Thanks awfully.'

Frost, the valet-plumber, etc., was ex-captain of a turret, with the hard blue eye of the born gun-layer—a middle-aged, uncomely man, no mean mechanic, and used to instruments of precision. He liked sitting in a warm room, looking through a microscope at what he called ' muckings,' with instructions to ' watch 'em all round the clock and log all changes.' But no sooner did he begin than Loftie, jealous as two women, and knowing what beginner's luck may do, stood watch and watch with him. Loftie was in hard work on his brain-cells, and the monotony of this sentry-go made him fear that his mind might build theories on self-created evidence. So he told Frost, after a while, that the whole thing was absurd, as well as bad for the eyes. ' Isn't it?' he added.

' I don't know how it is with *you*, sir,' Frost replied. ' It sometimes makes *me* feel as if I were seeing a sort of ripple strike up along the edges of 'em. Like broken water, with the sun tipping it. Like Portland Race in open-and-shut weather.'

' That's eye-strain. But when does it come on —with you?'

' Sometimes through the middle watch—from

twelve to four a.m. Then, again, it will come on through the first and second dog-watches—four to eight p.m., sir.'

'No matter which—what sample—you are looking at?' Loftie asked keenly.

'I'd say it depended on the sample. Now, One - twenty - Eight — 'seems to me — plays up in the middle watch—from midnight on—and One-twenty-Seven in the afternoon. I've logged it all.'

Three months later, at Simson House, Loftie told the others that, while not in the least departing from his own theories, there was a phenomenon, which for the sake of brevity he would call 'tide,' in Samples 127 and 128. It occurred at certain hours, which had all been noted and passed on to Harries—'for what *that* may be worth.'

Harries smiled, and hired an expensive expert to photo the two samples and film them; which took several weeks and cost some hundreds of pounds. They all checked the magnified 'tides' by some curious tables which Harries had worked out—'for what *that's* worth,' as Loftie said.

Harries said it was worth the expense, and took to spending a good deal of his leisure at Simson House. Vaughan, too, reeking of ether, would put in for shelter there, as the hunt after him (which his aunt whipped) quickened with his successes. Loftie had been almost a fixture in his lab. from the first; and poor 'Tacks,' who could no more have made a dishonest penny than he could have saved an honest one, catered for them so lavishly that even the cook shied at the weekly bills, which Harries flatly refused to audit.

Three months after their first film's 'release,' Loftie read them a typed paper before dinner, asserting there was 'tide' in the normal cells of all tissues which he and his helper, Frost, had observed; but he could see no sign of 'tide' in the malignant areas. He detailed tests and observations till they yawned. Then Frost ran the latest film for them—in slow and quick time—and they sat round the fire.

' I'm not committing myself to anything,' said Loftie, speaking like a badly-shaken human being, ' but every dam' tissue up till now seems to have its own time for its own tides. Samples from the same source have the same tides in strength and time. But, as I showed you just now, there are minute constant variations—reactions to something or other—in each tide, as individual as finger-prints. I wouldn't stake my reputation on it except to you. But I *know* it's so.'

' What do you suppose it means? ' Vaughan half-whispered.

' As I read it,' Harries spoke quietly, ' the minor differences in those " tides " in the tissues are due to interferences with the main or external influence—whichever it may be—which sets up, or which *is*, the main tide in all matter. They both come from with*out*. Not with*in*.'

' How far out? ' Vaughan asked.

' 'Can't tell—yet—to a few light-years. I've been trying to disentangle the minor interferences or influences—which may be due to the nearer—

er—influences—from the main tide. In *my* opinion——'

'Stop!' Loftie cried shrilly. 'You swore us all not to theorise before a year.'

'Hear me out! I've verified some of my calculations at *my* end of the game, and they justify me in saying that . . . we are all justified in getting tight to-night.'

So, then, they did: being drunk with the ferment of their own speculations before they went to table. Loftie, whom Ackerman confined to strong beer as best for tired brain-cells, rose up above the savoury, and said that he was 'the Servant of the Infil-tresimally Minute, but not of that fat tape-worm, Tacks.' Harries described to them the vasts of the Ultimate Heavens fizzing in spirals 'with—or rather like—champagne,' but all one generating station of one Power drawn from the Absolute, and of one essence and substance with all things. Then he slept soundly. Vaughan—the professional man—merely wanted to telephone for a taxi that he might drive to discredit a hated West End rival by calling him to his bedroom window and there discussing 'dichotomy'—a hard word at 3 A.M.

Then they packed Loftie off for a month's holiday, with a cubic metre of seven-and-sixpenny detective novels, *plus* Vaughan's aunt to see that he ate and dressed properly. On his return, he began certain experiments with mice, which Frost took charge of in the boiler-room, because he remembered when their ancestors served in the earliest submarines. It seemed that 'tides' worked in their tissues also; but slipped a little round the clock according to the season of each litter's birth.

And there were born to them mice among mice with prodigious 'tides.' Some of these, inoculated at the flood, threw off the trouble, and were promoted by Frost to the rating of pets. Treated on their lowest ebbs, they perished less quickly than the average. Harries kept careful count of their times in all things and ways, and had Frost sling some of their cages on various compass-bearings or set them out in moonlight or thunderstorms.

This last was too much for Loftie, who returned once more to the legitimate drama of cultures and radium emanations, and the mysteries of malignant cells which never acknowledge any 'tide.' At the end of three weeks, he, and Frost, broke off the campaign.

He said to Harries one evening after watching their usual film: 'What do you suppose germs think of?'

'If you've got as far as that,' was the answer, 'you'll develop an imagination one day.'

Then Vaughan came in full of trouble. His matron had been immobilised by sciatica, and his household staff had taken base advantages. He needed at once, some table-napkins, some bath-towels, two jacketed water-jugs and a metal—not china—bedroom breakfast-set. Ackerman said he would speak to Frost and see what could be spared from the ship.

While they were laughing at Vaughan, St.

Peggotty's rang him up. He replied: 'Well, well! If it was coming, it was to be expected now. . . . One of *my* beds empty? . . . You can have it. . . . Send her over to me. . . . You *must*! . . . I'll warn my people to expect her? . . . Oh? *That's* all right. . . . I'll send the car. . . . Yes, and all other expenses. . . . Because I operated on her originally, of course. We'll expect her at nine, then. . . . Righto! . . . Not in the least. Thank *you*, old man.'

He then telephoned his home to prepare for a patient, and returned to the still circle by the fire.

'It's one of those twin cases of mine,' he explained. 'One of 'em's back again. Recurrence —in the scar—after eighteen months.'

'That means?' said Harries.

'With that particular kind of trouble—three— five months' reprieve—perhaps. Then final recurrence. The other one's all right, so far, they say.'

'She would be. This one is One-twenty-Eight,' said Loftie.

'How do you make that out?'

Frost had entered and was going through Vaughan's indent with Ackerman.

'Frost, what is One-twenty-Eight's timing?' Loftie interposed.

'One-two-Eight, sir? Flood from midnight till four a.m.—ebb from four to eight p.m. . . . Yes, sir, I can make the table-linen all right, *and* the jugs. But we're short on bath-towels just now.'

'Would it prove anything if she lasted out

nine months?' Harries picked up the thread of talk with Vaughan.

'No. There are rallies and reserves.'

'A full year?'

'*I* should accept that. But I know who wouldn't.' Vaughan gave a great name.

'Thanks for reminding me,' said Ackerman over his shoulder. 'Frost, the bathroom hot-water pipe has got arterial sclerosis, too. Operate on it.'

'When shall *you* operate, Taffy?' Harries held on.

'To-morrow at a quarter to ten. I always feel fittest then.'

'Think of the patient for a change. Suppose you stand-to at a few minutes to midnight to-morrow? I'll telephone you zero from here.'

Vaughan seemed a shade taken aback. 'Midnight? Oh, certainly,' he said. 'But I'll have to warn my anaesthetist.'

'And Ferrers 'll swear you've taken to drink or drugs,' said Ackerman. 'Besides, think of your poor matron and the nurse who's got to have her evening off? *Much* better let the woman conk out in Trades Union hours, Taffy.'

'Dry up, *padrone*,' said Loftie. 'No need to bring in Ferrers. I'll take his place—if you think I'm safe.'

Since this was as if Raeburn had volunteered to prime a canvas for Benjamin West, Vaughan accepted, and they sat down to eat.

When he and Loftie had refreshed their memories of One-two-Eight's construction and

arrangements, they asked Harries why he had
chosen that time for the operation. Harries said
that by his reckonings it should fall nearer the
woman's birthday. His guess at its actual date
he wrote down and was passing it to Vaughan,
when Vaughan's Nursing Home reported the ar-
rival of the patient, not unduly fatigued and most
anxious to thank ' Doctor ' Vaughan for the
amazing kindness which had rescued her from
the open ward.

The table listened to Vaughan's reply, soothing and sustaining, and, by tone, assuming the
happiest issue out of this annoying little set-back.
When he hung up, he said : ' She—wants it the
day after to-morrow, because that's her birthday.
She thinks it 'll be lucky.'

' Make it midnight, then, of the day after to-
morrow, and look at the date I wrote down. . . .
No ! The Devil has nothing to do with it. By
the way—if it won't cramp your style—could you
set the table on——' Harries gave a compass
bearing.

' Don't be shy,' said Ackerman. ' He'd stand
her on her head to operate now, if the Bull told
him. Are you off, Taffy? Frost 'll put all your
towels and pots in a taxi. 'Sorry if I've hurt your
feelings.'

Loftie's account of the operation did not
interest Frost so much as the samples he brought
back. It took both of them three or four days to
plant them out properly. In return, Frost told
Loftie that ' our end of the show,' with Major

Harries at the sidereal clock, waiting 'till the sights came on,' and Captain Ackerman at the telephone, waiting to pass the range to Captain Vaughan in Sloane Street, was 'just like Jutland.'

'Now, this lady of ours,' he said after a busy silence. ' How would she lie in her bed?'

Loftie gave a bearing which he had heard Harries give Vaughan.

'I expect Major Harries knows, if anyone,' was Frost's placid comment. 'It's the same as ships' compasses varying according as their heads lay when they were building.'

'It's crazy mad. That's all!'

'Which was what the Admiralty said at first about steam in the Navy,' Frost grinned.

He put away a set of sealed cover-glasses and reverently returned some lenses to their velvet shrines.

'Not to talk of that lady of ours—' he straightened up as he spoke—'some of my mice aren't behaving as I could wish.'

'Which?' said Loftie. There were several types of experiments under way.

'One or two of some that recovered after inoculation—since discharged and promoted to pets. But it looks as if they'd had a relapse. They're highly restless—always trying to escape out—as if they were wild, not white. I don't like it.'

'Clean up, then,' Loftie answered, ' and we'll go down to the boiler-room.'

In one of the cages there, a doe with a plum-coloured saddle was squeaking, as she strove desperately to work through the wires with semi-transparent hand-like forefeet. Frost set the cage on a table under an electric and handed her dossier to Loftie. This gave her birth, age, date and nature of inoculation, date also when her system seemed to have cleared itself of the dose; and, of course, the times and strengths of her 'tides.' It showed dead-ebb for her at that hour.

'What does she think she's doing?' Loftie whispered. 'It isn't her natural squeak, either.'

They watched. She laboured increasingly at the barrier; sat up as though most intently listening; leaped forward and tore into her task beneath the glare of the basement-bulb.

'Turn it out,' said Loftie. 'It's distressing her.'

Frost obeyed. In a few seconds the little noises changed to a flutter and ceased.

'I thought so! Now we'll look again,' said Loftie. 'Oh! Oh! God!'

'Too late,' Frost cried. 'She's broke her neck! Fair broken her pretty little neck between the wires! How did she do it?'

'In convulsion,' Loftie stammered. 'Convulsion at the last. She pushed and pushed with her head in the wires and that acted as a wedge . . . and . . . what do *you* think?'

'I expect I'm thinking pretty much the same as you are, sir.' Frost replaced the cage under the leads and fuses which he had painted man-o'-war fashion. 'It looks like two tides meeting,' he added. 'That always sets up a race, and a race is worst at ebb. She must have been caught on her ebb—an' knocked over! Pity! There ought to be some way of pulling 'em through it.'

'Let's see if there isn't,' said Loftie, and lifted out the tiny warm body with a needed droplet of blood on the end of the nose.

One-two-Eight (Mrs. Berners) made a good recovery, and since she seemed alone in the world, Vaughan said that, as payment, she must stay on in his home and complete it to his satisfaction. She was touchingly grateful. After a few months (her strength returning) she asked to do something for her benefactors. No one seemed to look after the linen at Mr. Vaughan's. Might she repair, count, store, and, even, give it out— for she had had experience in that line as a housekeeper. Her prayer was granted, and the work of getting at the things Vaughan had started the Home with; had bought, but had never entered; had raided from Ackerman, and thought—or worse, was quite sure—that he had sent back; or had lost by laundries and through servants, did her good. It also brought her over to Simson House to return things to Frost, where Harries and Ackerman complimented her on her appearance, and Loftie asked her to administer his chance-bought body-linen. She was delighted. She told them that, when she had nothing to do, she mostly felt in people's way, and as if she ought to go on elsewhere. Loftie asked her why. She answered that, when her troubles were on her, they kept her busy, if it was only at trying not to cry. But now that they had been removed—

and by *such* kind gentlemen—the busiest day was none too full for her. She had a trick of tossing her head sideways and upwards, sometimes in the midst of her overseeings, and would say: ' Well, well! I can't keep at this all the time. I must be off elsewhere where I'm wanted '—Loftie's Home or Simson House as the case might be.

They discussed her at long and at large, one evening, throughout a film which—Vaughan and Loftie collaborating—was based on her more recent productions.

Vaughan was well satisfied. ' You see! Nothing has struck back. I know that her strength —notice how the tides have steadied—and our new blankets weigh a bit, too—is above normal. She has covered seven months and twenty-three days, and—I tell *you*—her scar is simply beautiful.'

' We'll take your word,' said Harries. ' Now bring on your mouse-film, Loftie.'

And Loftie, while Frost slowed, speeded, or went back at command, spoke of mice that had recovered apparently from certain infections, but had fallen later into a characteristic unease, followed by nervous crises—as shown—culminating in what seemed to be attempts at suicide.

In every case where an attempt had succeeded, the vacuoles—the empty centres—which do not take stain—of the brain-cells over a minute area seemed to have blown out, apparently as— (' This'll interest you, I know. I hired it from the Dominion Weather Bureau last week.') as— a house explodes through its own windows under the vacuum set up by a tornado. They then beheld a three-storey, clapboarded hotel vomiting itself outwards, while the black hook of a tornado's tip writhed and fished above it.

Sometimes, Loftie went on, an affected mouse would recover, after nervous upheavals very like those of tetanus—as they had seen—followed by collapse and amazingly sub-normal temperatures, and then a swift resumption of normal life. They could draw their own conclusions.

Ackerman broke their stillness. 'Frost, go back, please, to that bit showing the movement of their heads when the attacks are coming on.' Frost began again.

'Who's *that* like?' Ackerman called out suddenly. 'Am I wrong?'

'No, sir,' Frost groaned out of the dark. Then they all saw.

' " Well, *I* can't stay here! I've got to move on elsewhere where I'm wanted," ' Ackerman quoted half-aloud. 'And her hands working! The forefeet—I mean her hands! Look! It's *her*!'

'That's exactly her listening attitude, too,' said Harries. 'I never noticed it before.'

'Why would you—with nothing to check it by?' said Loftie. 'What does it mean?'

'It means she's as likely as not to chuck herself under a lorry some day, between here and Sloane Street,' Frost interrupted, as though he had full knowledge and right.

'How do *you* know?' Vaughan began. 'She's absolutely normal.'

The flexes of the camera had not been disconnected, so they were still darkling.

'She's *not*! She's all astray. God knows where she's straying; but she's not here, more'n the dead.' Frost repacked the camera and went out. They gathered round Harries.

'As I read it,' he laid down, after some preliminaries, 'she has been carried—yes, tided—over the time that her trouble ought to have finished her. That is two or three months now, isn't it, Taffy? *But*, she wasn't saved by the knife. She was saved by the knife at the proper time of tide.'

'She has lasted seven months and twenty-three days. Most unusual, I grant, with that type of growth; but not conclusive,' was Vaughan's retort.

'Hear me out. *Qua* Death, as created or evolved, on this planet (He needn't exist elsewhere, you know), and especially *qua* the instrument of decay that was to kill her, she's some odd weeks owing to the grave. *But*, *qua* the influence—tide, if you like—external to this swab of culture which we call our world, she has been started on a new tide of life. The gamble is that, after crises, something like those we've seen in the mice, that tide may carry her beyond the—er—the demand of the grave. It's beginning to be pull-devil, pull-baker between 'em now, I should imagine.'

'I see your line, Bull,' said Loftie. 'When ought her crises to be due? Because—it's all as insane as the rest—but there may be an off-chance of——'

'The suicidal tendency comes first,' said Ackerman. 'Why not have her watched when she goes out? Taffy's nurses can keep an eye on her indoors.'

' You've been reading my sleuth-tales,' Loftie smiled.

' Make it so, then. Any decent inquiry-agency would undertake it, I suppose,' said Harries.

' I'll leave the choice to Frost. I'll only take the commission. We're in for a wildish time. She's a woman—not a white mouse!' Ackerman said, and added thoughtfully : ' *But* the champion ass, as distinguished from mere professional fool, of us all, is Taffy ! '

Vaughan had ordered her never to go afoot between Simson House and the Nursing Home, and, also, to take taxis to and from her little ' exercise walks ' in the parks, where she so often picked up the nice elderly lady's-maid with the pom, the sales-lady from the Stores, and other well-spoken lady strangers near her own class (at ever so many shillings an hour). Of Mr. Frost she saw but little that summer, owing to the pressure of his duties and some return, they told her, of rheumatism contracted in the defence of his country. The worst that came to her was a slight attack of stiff neck, caught from sitting in a draught. As to her health, she admitted that sometimes she felt a bit flustered in the head, but otherwise could not be better.

She was recounting her mercies, a little ful-somely as usual, to Loftie one afternoon in the common-room of Simson House, where she had brought him some new shirts marked. Frost

had taken them upstairs, and Loftie had hinted
that he must get back to his work. She flicked
her head sideways and said that she was busy, too.
In the same breath, but in a whisper, she ran on :
' I don't want to die, Mr. Loftie. But I've *got* to.
I've reelly *got* to get out of this. I'm wanted elsewhere, but '—she shivered—' I don't like going.'

Then she raced, with lowered head, straight
towards the wall. Loftie snatched at her dress,
turned her, so that she struck the wall with her
shoulder and fell—and Frost came down to find
him grappling with her, not inexpertly.

She broke away and skimmed across the room.
Frost ran and tripped her, and brought her down.
She would have beaten her head on the floor,
but he jerked it up, his palm beneath her chin, and
dragged her to her feet. Then he closed.

She was silent, absorbed in this one business
of driving to the nearest wall through whatever
stood between. Small and fragile though she
was, she flung the twelve-stone Frost clear of her
again and again ; and a side-pushing stroke of
her open palm spun Loftie half across the hall.
The struggle lasted without a break, but her
breath had not quickened, when like a string she
relaxed, repeating that she did not want to die.
As she cried to Loftie to hold her, she slipped
away between them, and they had to chase her
round the furniture.

They backed her down on the couch at last,
Loftie clinging to her knees, while Frost's full
strength and weight forced the thin arms over
her head. Again the body gave, and the low,

casual whisper began: 'After what you said outside Barker's in the wet, you don't think I *reelly* want to die. Mr. Frost? I don't—not a mite. But I've *got* to. I've got to go where I'm wanted.'

Frost had to kneel on her right arm then, holding her left down with both hands. Loftie, braced against the sofa, mastered her feet, till the outbreak passed in shudders that shook all three. Her eyes were shut. Frost raised an eyelid with his thumb and peered closely.

'Lor'!' said she, and flushed to the temples. The two shocked men leapt clear at once. She lifted a hand to her disordered hair. 'Who's done this?' she said. 'Why've I come all over like this? I ought to be busy dying.' Loftie was ready to throw himself on her again, but Frost held up a hand.

'You can suit yourself about that, Mrs. Berners,' he said. 'What I've been at you all this time to find out is, what you've done with our plated toast-rack, towels, etcetera.'

He shook her by the shoulders, and the rest of her pale hair descended.

'One plated toast-rack and two egg-cups, which went over to Mr. Vaughan's on indent last April twenty-eighth, together with four table-napkins and six sheets. I ask because I'm responsible for 'em at this end.'

'But I've got to die.'

'So we've all, Mrs. Berners. But before you do, I want to know what you did with. . . .' He repeated the list and the date. 'You know the routine between the houses as well as I do. I sent 'em by Mr. Ackerman's orders, on Mr. Vaughan's indent. When do you check your linen? Monthly or quarterly?'

'Quarterly. But I'm wanted elsewhere.'

'If you aren't a little more to the point, Mrs. Berners, I'll tell you where you *will* be wanted before long, and what for. I'm not going to lose my character on account of your carelessness— if no worse. An' here's Mr. Loftie. . . .'

'Don't drag me in,' Loftie whispered, with male horror.

'Leave us alone! I know me class, sir. . . . Mr. Loftie who has done everything for you.'

'It was Mr. Vaughan. *He* wouldn't let me die.' She tried to stand, fell back, and sat up on the couch.

'You won't get out of it that way. Cast back in your memory and see if you can clear yourself!' Frost began anew, scientifically as a female inquisitor; mingling details, inferences, dates, and innuendoes with reminders of housekeeping ritual: never overwhelming her, save when she tried to ride off on her one piteous side-issue, but never accepting an answer. Painfully, she drew out of her obsession, protesting, explaining, striving to pull her riven wits into service; but always hunted from one rambling defence to the next, till, with eyes like those of a stricken doe, she moaned: 'Oh, Fred! Fred! The only thing I've ever took—*you* said so outside Barker's— was your own 'ard 'eart.'

Frost's face worked, but his voice was the petty-officer's with the defaulter.

' No such names between us, Mrs. Berners, till this is settled.'

He crumpled his wet eyes, as though judging an immense range. Then observed deliberately:

' 'Ask *me*—I'd say you're a common thief.'

She stared at him for as long as a shell might take to travel to an horizon. Then came the explosion of natural human wrath—she would not stoop to denial, she said—till, choking on words of abuse, she hit him weakly over the mouth, and dropped between his feet.

' She's come back!' said Frost, his face transfigured. ' What next?'

' My room. Tell Cook to put her to bed. Fill every hot-water bottle we've got, and warm the blankets. I'll telephone the Home. Then we'll risk the injections.'

Frost slung her, limp as a towel, over his shoulder, and, turning, asked: ' This—all these symptoms don't need to be logged, sir—do they? We—we know something like 'em?'

Loftie nodded assent.

She came up shuddering out of the seven days' chill of the cheated grave, and Vaughan's nurses told her what a dreadful thing was this 'suppressed influenza' which had knocked her out, but that she might report for duty in a few weeks. Ackerman, who loved Vaughan more than the others put together, testified on their next film-night that Taffy was almost worthy to be called a medical man for his handling of the case.

' Tacks,' said Vaughan kindly, ' you are as

big a dam' fool about my job as I was about Frost.
I injected what the Lofter gave me, at the times
that Harries told me. The rest was old wives'
practice.'

'She always looked like a wet hen,' said
Harries. 'Now she goes about like a smiling
sheep. I wish I'd seen her crises. Did you or
Frost time 'em, Lofter?'

'It wasn't worth it,' was the light answer.
'Just hysteria. But she's covered her full year
now. D'you suppose we've held her?'

'I should say yes. I don't know how you feel,
but '—Vaughan beamed—'the more I see of her
scar, the more pleased I am. Ah! That was a
lovely bit of work, even if I *am* only a carpenter,
Tacks!'

'But, speaking with some relation to ordinary
life, what does all this lunacy of ours prove?'
Ackerman demanded.

'Not a dam' thing, except that it may give us
some data and inferences which may serve as some
sort of basis for some detail of someone else's work
in the future,' Harries pronounced. 'The main
point, as I read it, is that it makes one—not so
much think—Research is gummed up with
thinking—as imagine a bit.'

'That'll be possible, too—by the time Frost
and I have finished with this film,' said Loftie.

It included a sequence of cultures, from mice
who had overcome their suicidal fits, attenuated
through a human being who, very obligingly, in
the intervals of running the camera, described the
effects of certain injections on his own rugged

system. The earlier ones, he admitted, had ' fair
slung him round the deck.'

' It was chuck it and chance it,' Loftie apologised. ' You see, we couldn't tell, all this
summer, when Mrs. Berners might play up for
the grave. So I rather rushed the injections
through Frost. I haven't worked out my notes
yet. You'll get 'em later.'

He stayed to help Frost put back some of the
more delicate gear, while the others went to
change.

' Not to talk about that lady of ours,' Frost said
presently. ' My first—though, of course, her
mother never warned me—drank a bit. She
disgraced me all round Fratton pretty much the
whole of one commission. And she died in Lock
'Ospital. So, I've had *my* knock.'

' Some of us seem to catch it. I've had mine,
too,' Loftie answered.

' *I* never heard that. But '—the voice changed
—' I knew it—surer than if I'd been told.'

' Yes. God help us ! ' said Loftie, and shook
his hand. Frost, not letting go of it, continued :
' One thing more, sir. I didn't properly take it
in at the time—not being then concerned—but—
that first operation on that lady of mine, was it
of a nature that'll preclude—so to say—expectations of—of offspring ? '

' Absolutely, old man,' Loftie's free hand
dropped on Frost's shoulder.

' Pity ! There ought to be some way of pulling
'em through it—somehow—oughtn't there ? '

THE THRESHOLD

In their deepest caverns of limestone
    They pictured the Gods of Food—
The Horse, the Elk, and the Bison
    That the hunting might be good ;
With the Gods of Death and Terror—
    The Mammoth, Tiger, and Bear.
And the pictures moved in the torchlight
    To show that the Gods were there !
            But that was before Ionia—
            (Or the Seven Holy Islands of Ionia)
            Any of the Mountains of Ionia,
            Had bared their peaks to the air.

The close years packed behind them,
    As the glaciers bite and grind
Filling the new-gouged valleys,
    With Gods of every kind.
Gods of all-reaching power—
    Gods of all-searching eyes—
But each to be wooed by worship
    And won by sacrifice.
            Till, after many winters, rose Ionia—
            (Strange men brooding in Ionia)
            Crystal-eyed Sages of Ionia
            Who said, ' These tales are lies.

We dream one Breath in all things,
    ' That blows all things between.
We dream one Matter in all things—
    ' Eternal, changeless, unseen.

' 'That the heart of the Matter is single
 ' Till the Breath shall bid it bring forth—
' By choosing or losing its neighbour—
 ' All things made upon Earth.'
   But Earth was wiser than Ionia
   (Babylon and Egypt than Ionia)
   And they overlaid the teaching of Ionia
   And the Truth was choked at birth.

It died at the Gate of Knowledge—
 The Key to the Gate in its hand—
And the anxious priests and wizards
 Re-blinded the wakening land ;
For they showed, by answering echoes,
 And chasing clouds as they rose,
How shadows could stand for bulwarks
 Between mankind and its woes.
   It was then that men bethought them of Ionia
   (The few that had not allforgot Ionia)
   Or the Word that was whispered in Ionia ;
   And they turned from the shadows and the
    shows.

They found one Breath in all things,
 That blows all things between.
They proved one Matter in all things—
 Eternal, changeless, unseen ;
'That the heart of the Matter was single
 Till the Breath should bid it bring forth—
   Even as men whispered in Ionia,
   (Resolute unsatisfied Ionia)
   When the Word was stifled in Ionia—
All things known upon earth.

Beauty Spots

NEIGHBOURS

The man that is open of heart to his neighbour,
 And stops to consider his likes and dislikes,
His blood shall be wholesome whatever his labour,
 His luck shall be with him whatever he strikes.
The Splendour of Morning shall duly possess him,
 That he may not be sad at the falling of eve.
And, when he has done with mere living—God bless
  him !—
 A many shall sigh, and one Woman shall grieve !

But he that is costive of soul toward his fellow,
 Through the ways, and the works, and the woes of
  this life,
Him food shall not fatten, him drink shall not mellow ;
 And his innards shall brew him perpetual strife.
His eye shall be blind to God's Glory above him ;
 His ear shall be deaf to Earth's Laughter around ;
His Friends and his Club and his Dog shall not love
  him ;
 And his Widow shall skip when he goes under-
  ground !

Beauty Spots

MR. WALTER GRAVELL was, after forty years, a director of the Jannockshire and Chemical Manure Works. Chemicals and dyes were always needed, and certain gases, derived from them, had been specially in demand of late. Besides his money, which did not interest him greatly, he had his adored son, James, a long, saddish person with a dusky, mottled complexion and a pleuritic stitch which he had got during the War through a leaky gas-mask. Jemmy was in charge of the firm's research-work, for he had taken to the scientific side of things even more keenly than his father had to the administrative.

But Mr. Gravell, having made his fortune out of solid manures, now naturally wished to render them all unnecessary by breathing into the soil such gases as should wake its dormant powers. He believed that he had had successes with flower-pots on balconies, but he needed a larger field, and a nice country-house, where Jemmy could bring down friends for week-ends, and he could listen to them talking and watch how they deferred to his son.

On a spring day, then, Mr. Gravell drove

sixty miles by appointment to a largish, comfortable house, with a hundred acres of land. These included a ravishing little dell, planted with azaleas, and screened from the tarred road by a belt of evergreens—a windless hollow, where gas could lie undisturbedly to benefit vegetation.

Thereupon he bought the place, told Jemmy what he had done, and, as usual, asked him to attend to the rest. Jemmy overhauled drains and roofs ; imported the housekeeper and staff of their London house ; reserved a couple of rooms for his own week-ends, and settled in beside his father. There had been some talk lately, behind the latter's back, of increased blood-pressures, which would benefit by country life.

After a blissful honeymoon of months, Jemmy asked him whether he had met a Major Kniveat in the village, who expected his name to be pronounced ' Kniveed,' the *t* being soft in that very particular family.

' *Is* there a village here ? No-o, my dear. Who is he ? '

' One of the natives. You might have run across him.'

' No. I didn't come down here to run across people. I'm busy.' Mr. Gravell went off to the dell as usual, to help the vegetation.

Jem had asked because Mrs. Saul, their housekeeper and a born gossip, had told him that a Major Kniveat, retired, of the Regular Army, had told everyone at the Golf Club that Mr. Gravell had bought the house for the purpose of thrusting himself into local society, and that the Major was

eagerly awaiting any attempt in this direction, so
that the village might show how outsiders should
be treated. Jem had not dwelt on this till, at a
tennis-party, he had been cross-examined by the
Rector's very direct wife as to whether his father
meant to offer himself for the Bench of Justices
of the Peace, or the County, District, or Parish
Councils. She hinted that the Major was ambitious—in those directions. Putting two and
two together, as scientific men should, Jem made
the total four.

The house was burdened with a ' home farm,'
which sent up milk, butter, and eggs, at more
than London prices. That month they were making some hay. Jefferies, the working-foreman,
was carrying the last field, and, though it was
Saturday, when ' work ' in England stops at noon,
had cajoled his men to ' work ' till five, promising
he would pay them their wages and overtime in a
field near a public-house, and remote from wives.
While Mr. Gravell was busy in his dell, a woman
came upon him, crying: ' You ain't paid your
men ! '

' I don't,' said Mr. Gravell.

' But I've got to get into town for my week-end
shoppin's. Why ain't you paid 'em off at noon,
same as always?'

' I don't know.'

' Don't ye? Then I lay you don't know what
I'm goin' to do. I'm goin' right up to the Street
(village), an' I'm goin' to tell 'em there that this
'ouse don't pay its people. *That's* what I'm goin'
to say, and I'll lay they'll believe it.'

Mr. Gravell was so sure that this was one of the things Jemmy attended to that he forgot to mention her to him. But Mrs. Jefferies's tale ran, by way of tradesmen, gardeners, and errand-boys, through the village. After Major Kniveat had had his turn, it was common knowledge that ' them Gravellses ' (in the higher circles, ' those manure-dealers ') were undischarged bankrupts, who had made a practice of cheating their ' labour ' elsewhere, but who could not hope to work that trick here. Mrs. Saul told Jem, who asked Jefferies what it meant. Jefferies apologised for the temper of his wife, who had nerves above her station, and took tonic wines to steady them, and was sorry if there had been any ' misunderstanding.' Jemmy, survivor of an unfeudal generation which had had all the trouble it wanted, telephoned the county town auctioneer to offer all live and dead stock on the home farm at the first autumn sales. Next, he let the fields as accommodation-land to local butchers ; arranged for dairy produce to be delivered at the house by a real farm at much lower rates, and—for the North pays its debts—brought down from the main Jannockshire Works a retired foreman, who had married Jem's nurse, to sit rent-free in the farmhouse. But angry Mr. Jefferies joined the Public Services of his country, and worked on the roads for one-and-threepence an hour at Government stroke—till he became an overseer.

In six weeks nothing remained of the Gravells' agricultural past save one Angelique, an enormous white sow, for whom none would bid at the sales ;

she being stricken in years and a notorious gate-crasher. What did not yield to the judicial end of her carried away before the executive, and then she would wander far afield, where, though well-meaning as a hound-pup (for she had been the weakling of her litter and brought up in a Christian kitchen) her face and figure were against her with strangers. That was why she was indicted by a local body—on Major Kniveat's clamour—for obstructing a right-of-way by terrifying foot-passengers—three summer London Lady lodgers, to wit. They blocked her most-used gaps with barb-wire, which tickled her pleasantly, and she broke out again and again, till the local body, harried by the Major, indicted Mr. Gravell once more as proprietor of a public nuisance.

After this, she was kept in a solid brick sty at the home farm, where Mr. and Mrs. Enoch, the childless couple from the Jannockshire Works, made much of her. At intervals she would be let out to test stock-proof fencing or gates; when, often, Jemmy and his young friends would be judges, and her prize a cabbage.

Father and son passed a pleasant autumn to-gether, varied by visits to town, and visits from young men who never showed up at church. But the imported staff, headed by Mrs. Saul, went there regularly for the honour of the establishment and to catch neighbourly comments after divine service. They heard, for a fact, that Mr. Gravell had ' cohabitated ' with a person of colour, which explained his son's Asiatic complexion.

' All right,' said Jemmy to Mrs. Saul, who was

full of it. 'Don't let it get round to Dad, that's all.'

'And that Major Kniveat at their nasty little cat-parties he calls you " The 'Alf-Caste," ' Mrs. Saul insisted.

'Nigger, if you like. Dad isn't here for that sort of thing. He doesn't know there *is* a village. Tell your wenches to keep their mouths shut, or I'll sack 'em.'

On Saturday of the next week-end, when Mr. Gravell had gone to bed, Jemmy told the tale to Kit Birtle—all but his own brother. Kit was the son of Jem's godfather and brevet-uncle, Sir Harry Birtle, who was the Works' leading lawyer—and he ranked therefore as brevet-nephew to Mr. Gravell, and kept changes of raiment at his house. He had done time as an Army doctor, and now specialised in post-war afflictions visible and invisible. Jem's point was that his own dusky colour gave an interesting clue to the composition of some gas which he had inhaled near Arras a few years before. Said Kit: 'You *do* look rather a half-caste. Get yourself overhauled again by that man in France.'

'L'Espinasse, you mean? I will, but not just yet. It 'ud worry Dad. But talking about gas——'

Then they both talked, for they were interested in some new combinations which had produced interesting results.

'And you might use Angelique as a control for some of it,' Kit suggested. 'She hasn't any nerves.'

That brought out the tale of her doings, the footpaths that she was said to have blocked, and Major Kniveat's public-spirited activities in general.

' 'Can't make him out,' said Jem. ' We came down here to be quiet, but this sword-merchant seems to take it as a personal insult. What's the complex, Kit? '

' We've something like it in our hamlet—a retired officer bung-full of public-spirit and simian malignity. Idleness explains a lot, but I've a theory it's glands at bottom. 'Rather noisome for you, though.'

' Oh, Dad don't notice anything. He hands it all over to me, and *I* haven't time to fuss with the natives. What 'ud you care for to-morrow? The golf-course ain't fit yet, but I've got another patent stock-gate if you like——'

' Angelique every time! ' said Kit, who knew her of old, and often compared her to one Harry Tate, an artist in the stage-handling of deck-chairs and motor-cars.

Sunday forenoon, they loafed over to the farm, released the lady, and introduced her to the patent gate. Her preliminary search for weak points was side-splitting enough : but by the time she had tucked up, as it were, her skirts, had backed through the gate with the weight and amplitude of a docking liner, had reached her cabbage, and stood with the stalk of it, cigarette-wise, in her mouth, asking them what they thought of Auntie now, the two young men were beating on the grass with their hands. Getting her back to her sty was no small affair either, for she valued her Sunday outings, and they laughed too much to head her off quickly. As they rolled back across the fields, reviewing the show, Major Kniveat appeared on a footpath near by. It was, he had given out, part of his Sabbath works to see that public paths were not closed by newly-arrived parvenues. The two passed him, still guffawing over Angelique, and Monday morn brought by hand a letter, complaining that the Major had been publicly mocked and derided by his neighbours (there was some reference also to ' gentlemen ') till he had been practically hooted off a right-of-way. The car was due for town in half an hour, and Jemmy spent that while in written disclaimer of any intent to offend, and apology if offence had been taken. He did not want the thing to bother his father in his absence. Major Kniveat accepted the apology, and ran about quoting it to all above the rank of road-mender, as a sample of the spirit of half-castes when frontally tackled.

Then spring bulb-catalogues began to arrive, but, in spite of them, Mr. Gravell was worried by Jemmy's increasing duskiness; and he and Kit at last got him shipped off to L'Espinasse, the French specialist, who dealt in his kind of trouble. Mr. Gravell went with him to the South of France, where the specialist wintered, and saw him bedded down for the treatment. Thence he botanised along the heathy Italian foreshore, branched north to Nancy, where the best lilacs are bred, and so home by bulbous Holland.

Altogether five weeks' refreshing holiday. On return he found a good deal of accumulated correspondence for Jem to attend to; but, since the boy was away, he opened one letter all by himself. It was from the same local body as had written about Angelique and her misdeeds. It informed Mr. Gravell that certain trees on his property overhung the main road to an extent constituting a nuisance of which ratepayers had complained, and which he was called upon to abate within a given time. Failing this, the local body would themselves abate the said nuisance, charging him with the cost of the labour involved. It had been posted two days after he had left England.

Mr. Gravell went to look.

For twenty yards along the main road, the mangled and lopped timber laid the dell open to passing cars and charabancs. Nor was that all. Under the trees ran a low sandstone wall, which time had hidden beneath laurel and rhododendron. In dropping on to, hauling over, or stacking behind it, the limbs that were cut, the rhododendrons had been badly torn, and lengths of wall had collapsed. A raw track showed where people had already entered the dell to pick primroses. A gardener came up to him.

'They never told me,' the man said. 'If they'd said a word, I could have tipped back they few branches they fussed about, and 'twould have been done. But they said naught to nobody. They done it all in one day like, and that Major Kniveat 'e came down the road and told 'em what *was* to be done, like. They didn't know nothing.

So they did it as 'e told 'em. They've fair savaged it—them and Jefferies.'

'So I see,' said Mr. Gravell. Then he wrote to the Company's lawyer, Sir Harry Birtle, his lifelong friend.

The answer ran :

'DEAR WALTER,—I also live in Arcadia. My advice to you is not to make trouble with local authorities. They will regret that their employees have exceeded their instructions, and that will be all. This Major Kniveat of yours, not being on any public body, has no *locus standi*. I know the type. We have one with us. If you insist, of course, my firm will give you a losing run for your money ; but you had much better come up and dine with me, and I'll tell you pretty stories of this kind. Love to your Jem, who writes my Kit that he is bleaching out properly in France,

'Ever as ever, HARRY.'

This was, on the whole, a relief, for, after sending the letter, Mr. Gravell saw that the weight of the campaign would fall on his son when he came back and could attend to rebuilding the wall.

So he ordered his own meals, took his car when he wanted it, instead of waiting till Jemmy should be free, and went up to the London Office of the Works with the padded arm-rest down, which was never the case when his Jemmy came along.

On his return he would visit the head of the dell before people were about, and discharge the contents of carefully stoppered phials into the traps of some two-inch land-drains, which had been laid down to carry off surplus water. These followed the contours of the slopes, and all met at the bottom of the hollow. By April he began to think that the grasses there were responding to the stimulus of the liquids that purred off softly into heavy gas, as he freed them down the traps. It cheered him, for it showed that, despite lack of early training, he was in the way to become such a scientist as his own wonderful Jemmy.

By early summer, when azaleas and such are worth picking, motor-traffic had increased on all roads, and the high, commanding charabancs were much interested by the sight of Mr. Gravell's dell. Their drivers pulled up by the broken wall, which the publican at the White Hart, a little further up the road, recommended as a good pitch between drinks. So people used it more and more for picnics and pleasure, and after a Southern Counties Private Tour had removed as a trophy the pitiful little ' Trespassers will be Prosecuted,' which was Mr. Gravell's one protest, the gaps in the wall widened by feet in a week; the rhodo-dendron clumps shrank like water drops on a hot iron, and the dell became dotted with coloured streamers, burst balloons, tins, corks, food-bags, old paper, tyre-wrappers, bottles—intact or broken —rags of the foulest, cigarette-cartons, and copious filth. But Mr. Gravell's traps were on the upper levels, and, as has been said, he attended to them before rush hours. He very rarely went down into what had now become a rubbish-heap; for he was a fastidious man.

About that time, two children at the White

Hart, who sold little bunches of flowers to trippers, developed an eruption which puzzled Dr. Frole, the local practitioner. He had never before seen orange and greenish-copper blotches on the healthy young. But, as these faded entirely in a week or so, he wrote it down ' errors of diet,' and said there was no need to close the schools.

It was different when a private party of thirty-two gentlemen and ladies, mostly in the retail jewellery business, and all near enough neighbours in Shoreditch to use the same panel-doctor, poured into that man's consulting-room, comparing blotches as far as they dared, and wailing before an offended Deity. They were asked where they had been and what they had eaten. They had, it seemed, been in ever so many places, and by the way had eaten everything in Leviticus and out of it. Then a practitioner in Bermondsey, where they also make up select tours to the Beauty Spots of England, wrote to a local paper about an interesting variety of summer rash. This—so bound together is the English world—let loose a ' Welsh Mother,' who had trusted four of her brood to a local pastor on a Beauties-of-England tour. She complained in a popular journal of unprecedented circulation that they had returned looking ' like the Heathen.'

Some weeks of perfect touring weather followed, and, as the roads filled and stank with charabancs, Carlisle, Morecambe Bay, Frinton, Tavistock, the Isle of Man, Newquay, and Alnwick, among others, reported strange cases of ' blotching ' in all ages and sexes.

Entered, duly, in the journals of the democracy, ' specialists,' who, after blood-curdling forecasts, ' deprecated panic ' and variously ascribed the origin of the epidemic to different causes, but, supremely, to the *laissez-faire* attitude of the Government.

At the height of the discussion, Jemmy wrote that he was coming home on the Sunday boat, ready for anything.

Mr. Gravell, anxious to avoid an explosion *à deux*, had invited Sir Harry and Kit to help welcome and divert the prodigal, whose stitch and complexion had vastly improved. But Mrs. Saul waylaid Jem on the stairs with a summary of Major Kniveat's doings in the past three months, and his open exultation over Jefferies's work in the dell, which sent Jem down there before dinner. The trippers had gone, but he found Angelique busy among the remains of picnics. When he tried to chase her out, she lay down and refused to be moved. So he threw stones at her, sent word to the Enochs that she was loose again, and changed for dinner, not in the best temper, although he tried not to show it.

' It don't really matter,' his father said. ' Wait till you hear what your Uncle Harry tells us. Oh, but I'm glad you're back, Jemmy! I've wanted you desperate.'

' Me, too, Dad.' The hug was returned. ' You're quite right. We won't have a shindy about the wall. It ain't worth it.'

' Then, run along and get up the champagne. Your tie's crooked, my dear.' He put up his hand tenderly, as a widower may who has had to wash and dress a year-old baby.'

' Oh, Dad, I *am* sorry! You must have had a hellish time of it.' Jem hugged his parent again.

' Not a bit!' said Mr. Gravell, glad that the boy was taking it so well. ' It hasn't interfered with my experiments. I always finish before the trippers come. I'm on the track of a mixture now that *really* gingers up the bacteria. I'll tell you about it, dear. Didn't you notice how rich the grass was?'

' I didn't notice anything much except Angelique. I landed her one or two for herself with a rock, though.'

Dinner went delightfully. Sir Harry Birtle was full of tales of ' bad neighbours ' elsewhere, and the wisdom of leaving them alone, which, he said, annoyed them most. The present business was to rebuild the wall, and Jem was sketching it on a tablecloth for Kit, when the Sunday paper came in. Sir Harry picked it up.

' One thousand and thirty-seven cases up to date,' he read aloud.

' What of? ' asked Mr. Gravell. ' I don't read the papers.'

' They call it Bloody Measles, Uncle Wally,' said Kit, the doctor. ' It's all over the place. It's a sort of ten-days' rash—greenish-copper blotches on the face and body. Not catching. No temperature ; but no end of scratchin'. The papers have made rather a stunt of it.'

In time the young men went off to the billiard-room, while the elders sat over the wine, each disparaging his own offspring that he might better draw the other's rebuke and tribute.

Billiards ended with an inquiry into Jem's treatment, and L'Espinasse's views on gassing in general. ' I was right about the gas that knocked me out,' said Jem. 'L'Espinasse admitted that, on my symptoms, it *must* have been Adler's Mixture. That's one up for me and the Works.'

' But the Hun was only using straight mustard-gas round Arras then,' said Kit.

' Not altogether. 'Remember that purple-and-white-band big stuff that used to crack and whiffle? I got a dose in the cutting behind Fampoux waiting for the train. *That* was Adler's . . . But—never mind that. I've got to knock Hell's Bells out of the Major. He might have upset Dad a good deal. But he took that outrage on the dell like a lamb.'

' There's a reason for that, too,' said Kit, and explained how Mr. Gravell's blood-pressures had dropped satisfactorily.

' 'Glad to hear it,' said Jem. ' But it won't excuse Mister Field Officer when I'm abreast of my arrears.'

They talked till bed-time, went up to town together next morning, pursued their several businesses till Saturday, came down again, and that evening wandered round the home-made nine-hole course, and fetched up by Angelique's sty near the barn. It was empty.

' She's broken out again,' said Kit. ' Give her a shout.'

Jem hailed, and was answered by the lady, in a muffled key, from the house.

They went to look. Mr. and Mrs. Enoch received them, and complimented Jem on his improved appearance.

'Ah'm gradely,' Jem went back to the speech of the Works, in which he and Kit had almost been born. 'But what's ta doin' wi' t'owd la-ady in t'house, Liz?'

'She've gotten Bloody Measles—like what's in arl t'pa-apers. We've had her oop to t'wash-house,' Enoch explained.

He led along a back passage, and in the brick-floored wash-house, well strawed, lay Angelique, patterned all over with greenish orange-brown blotches, which she wore coquettishly.

'Good Lord!' said Kit. 'I didn't know Bloody Measles attacked animals! She looks like a turtle with dropsy.'

''Nowt to what she wor o' Thursdaa. She wor like daffadillies an' wall-flowers, Thursdaa.' Enoch spoke with pride.

'Ah, but she's hearty—she's rare an' hearty. Tha's none offen tha' feed, *is* tha, ma luv?' said Mrs. Enoch tenderly.

'She'll have to be killed,' said Kit.

'Kill nowt,' said Mrs. Enoch. 'She'll lie oop here till t'spots gan off again. They showed oop a' Tuesdaa neet, an' to-morra's Soondaa.'

'What's Sunday got to do with it?' Kit cried.

'T' Major, blast him!' said Enoch. Man and wife spoke together. Translated out of their dialect, which broadened as it flowed, the Major's

Sunday patrol of rights-of-way generally included the path round the barn beside Angelique's sty. If he should notice her now—what his powers for making trouble might be they knew not, but feared the worst. But they *did* know that an Englishman's house, even to his wash-house, is his castle. Thither, then, they had conveyed Angelique on Tuesday night, and there should she stay until her spots faded, as they had faded upon the publican's brats at the White Hart.

'She came out with 'em on Tuesday—did she?' said Jem thoughtfully. 'Well, we don't want the Major poking his nose into this just now.'

That released Mrs. Enoch again. Mrs. Saul had said much about Major Kniveat, but the gleanings of Mrs. Enoch's threshing-floor were richer than all the housekeeper's harvests. She said he was consumed with desire to take some step which the ' manure-makers ' should be compelled to notice. She reminded Jem of foremen and fore-women in the Works, who had given trouble on the same lines. Psychologically it was interesting, but Jem's concern was that neither she nor her husband should talk to his father about it.

'If this epidemic is going to attack live-stock, there'll be trouble,' said Kit, on the way home.

'I don't think it will,' said Jem, who had been silent for some while.

'What's the idea?' his all-but-brother asked suspiciously.

' My idea is that it's Dad, if you want to know. Dad—and his dell ! '

' The Devil ! Why ? '

' I asked our London Office (they were rather worried about it, too) what sort of stuff he'd been drawing from the Lab. while I was away, to ginger up his bacteria. Well, what he actually got was fairly hectic, but he tells me he's taken to mixin' 'em. *So*—Lord knows what they mayn't throw up ! Anyhow, the dell must be soaked with it. Wait a shake ! Angelique was picnickin' down there the Sunday night I got home. She came out with spots on Tuesday—call it forty-eight hours' incubation.'

' Stop ! Let me take this in properly,' said Kit. ' You mean your dad—is responsible for —one thousand and thirty-seven cases of Bloody Picnickers—up to date ? '

Jem nodded. ' 'Looks like it. He's transmitted his scientific twist of mind to me, but outside that he's a rank amateur, you know.'

Here Kit sat down. ' Amateur ! You aren't fit to have my own Uncle Wally for a father. An' he doesn't read the papers ! An'—an' the British Medical Association recommends treating Bloody Measles with *chawal-muggra* oil. And Sir Herbert Buskitt says it's due to atonic glands. The whole of my sacred profession's involved ! Don't you realise what your dad's done, you—you parricide ? '

' Dam-well I do. Here are the bases of the stuff he's been working on.' Jem passed over some chemical formula that sent Kit into fresh hysterics. 'You see, he's avoided lethal constituents so far, but he's strong on the colour-fixation bases. 'Spose he wants it for the gorze-blooms. —Get up, you idiot!—Well! I've short-circuited *that*. He'll have everything he writes for in future, as far as labels go. The muck don't show or smell or taste. He'll be just as happy.'

'But *I* shan't,' said Kit, as soon as he could stand and talk straight. 'I want more. Let's lure the Major into the dell, and—er—Angelique him! He'd look rather pretty, ma luv!'

'Not now. We'd be acting with guilty knowledge. The main thing is to get Angelique right before he spots her. She'll come round, won't she?'

''Question of temperament—and sex. After all, she's a lady. Wait and see. Oh, my Uncle Wally! *And* my dad! How are we to keep our faces straight with 'em?'

Since each of the Seven Ages of Man is separated from all the others by sound-and-X-ray-proof bulkheads, the parents only noticed that their young were in the spirits natural to their absurd thirty-odd years. Sunday passed, and the Major, too, on his rounds, in peace. They left Angelique in the wash-house Monday forenoon, visibly paling, but as interested and as interesting as ever. (Mrs. Enoch said she was company when one knitted.) On Saturday morning of that same week a wire from Enoch told Jem in town that she had cleared up. He showed it to Kit, who took him to lunch at a certain restaurant, before the drive down. There sat at the next table a globular female, with pendant mauve-washed cheeks, indigo eyelids, lips of orange vermilion, and locks of Titian red. She reminded Kit of Angelique in the height of her bloom, and . . . Here Jem and Kit together claimed the parentage of the Great Idea.

At any rate, in that hour, between them it was born. They went to a theatrical wigmaker and bought lavishly of grease-paints for Chinese, Red Indian, and Asiatic make-ups, as well as for clowns and corner-men.

They drove down, not a little to the public danger, and made a merry feast before their ancestors that summer evening. Next morning —Sunday at nine o'clock to be precise—Mrs. Enoch told them that her week in the wash-house had so filled Angelique with social aspirations, that ' after setting with t'owd lady and readin' t'pa-apers to her, ah hevn't heart to give her t' broomhead when she comes back again.'

' Ask her oop,' said Jem.

She came gratefully, and they told the Enochs what was in their minds.

' He'll say it's t'Bloody Measles, an' he'll turn all his blasted committees on us,' said Enoch. ' He's a tongue on 'im like a vi-iper, yon barstard.'

' That's what we're gambling on. But she's a bit too scurfy for the stuff to hold,' said Jem, looking into the wash-house copper.

' But tha winna mak' a fool o' t'poor dumb beast, will tha', lads ? ' Mrs. Enoch pleaded, as she dipped the broom in warm water and began on that enormous back.

Angelique lay down at command, sure that these things were but prelude to more admiration. They scrubbed her, till she was as white as a puff-ball. Then, area by area, she was painted with dazzle-patterns of greenish-yellow and purple-brown, till it was hard to say whether she moved to or from the beholder. Jem took her head, jowl, and neck, where the space was limited. So he was forced to use spots which, by divine ordering, suggested the foulest evidences of decomposition. Remembering the lady in the restaurant, he paid special attention to her eyes and brows.

'If t'Major niver had 'em before, she'll give 'em to him proper,' was Enoch's verdict.

'She lukes like nowt o' God's makin' already,' Mrs. Enoch agreed. 'But she's proud of hersen! —Sitha! She's tryin' to admire of her own belly! Wicked wumman! She'll niver be t'saam to me again.'

'It'll wash off. Now we'll go for a walk. Shove her into t'sty, Enoch, and pray the Major comes this morning.'

Their prayers were answered within the hour. They saw the Major, on his regular Sunday round, descend the slope to the home farm. Then they turned, on interior lines, which brought them face to face with him rounding the barn by Angelique's sty. At the sound of their well-known voices, she reared up ponderously, and hitched her elbows over the low door, much as Jezebel, after her head was tyred, looked out of the window. It was not the loathly brown and yellow-green blotches on bosom and shoulder that appalled most, but the smaller ones on face, jowl, and neck, for she had been rubbing her cheeks a little, and the pattern had drawn into wedges and smears, perfectly simulating a mask of unspeakable agony coupled with desperate appeal. Moreover, so wholly is hearing dominated by sight, that her jovial grunt of welcome seemed the too-human plaint of a beast against realised death.

When, with haggard, purple-bordered eyes, she looked for applause and cabbage, the horror of that slow-turning head made even the artists forget their well-thought-out lines.

' 'Mornin', old lady,' said Jem at last, and Kit echoed him.

But the Major's greeting was otherwise. He blenched. He held out one dramatic arm. He stammered: 'How—how long has that creature been like that?'

'Always, hasn't she, Jem?' said Kit sweetly. 'We're just taking her for a walk.'

'I—I forbid you to touch her. Look at her spots! Look at her spots!'

'Spots?' Kit seemed puzzled for a moment.

'Yes. Spots!' The voice shook.

'Spo-ots! Oh yes. Of course.' This was in Kit's best bedside-manner. 'Certainly we won't let her out if you feel *that* way.'

'Feel! Can't you *see*? She's infected to the marrow. She's rotting alive. Put her out of her misery at once!'

Here Enoch appeared with a broom, and the Major commanded him to kill and keep the body.

Enoch merely opened the sty door, and Angelique
came out. The Major backed several yards,
calling and threatening. But everyone except a
few female summer-visitors had always been kind
to her. This person—she argued—might be
good for an apple, or—she was not bigoted—
cigarette-ends. So she went towards him smiling,
and her smile, for reasons given, was like the rolling
back of the Gates of Golgotha.

Whether she would have rubbed herself against
his Sunday trousers, or fled when she had seen
his face, are " matters arguable to all eternity."
It is only agreed that the Major floated out of her
orbit by about a bow-shot in the direction of the
village, and thence onward earnestly.

'Well, that proves it ain't glands, at any rate,'
Kit pronounced. 'He'll stay away for a bit, but
we won't take chances. Come along, Angelique !
Washee-washee, ma luv ! '

Then and there they treated her in the wash-
house with petrol, which removes grease-paints,
and sacking soaked in warm water, which takes
off the sting of it, till she was fit to turn out into
the orchard and root a bit, lest she should be too
clean at any later inspection. By then it was
nearly lunch-time.

'Tha sees,' said Jem, slipping on his coat.
'Pe-wer as a lily ! There's nowt need come
'twix thee an' t'owd lady now, Liz—is there,
ma luv ? '

Upon which Mrs. Enoch very properly kissed
him, while Enoch sat helpless on a swill-bucket.

Mrs. Saul and the rest of the staff came back

from evening service fully informed, for the Major had spent every minute since his meeting with Angelique in talking about her to everyone. He said, among other things, that she had been wilfully hidden, that she was being taken out for secret exercise when he discovered her condition, and that he was going to attend to the matter himself.

Thus Mrs. Saul on the landing as the two young men went up to change.

'Very good,' said Jem. 'Don't go to Dad about it, though.'

'But we—but I've been down to Enoch's to look at her. She's as clean as me. Isn't it shocking to be that way—on a Sunday morning? He took the bag round, too! You can never tell what these old bachelors are really like . . .'

They had finished dessert—the State-aided summer sunlight was still on the table—and the boys had gone to the billiard-room, when the Major was announced on an urgent matter.

'Better have him in here, Wally,' Sir Harry mildly suggested. 'I believe he's a bit of a bore.'

So he entered, and told his story, summarising the steps he would take, out of pure public spirit, to deal with this plague, and this menace, and these evasions.

'*I* see! *You*'ve seen a spotted pig,' said Mr. Gravell at last. 'Well, that *couldn't* have been our Angelique. She's a Large White, you know, and—my son generally attends to this sort of thing.'

' *He* saw her, too. As I've been telling you, your son saw her! He was perfectly cognisant of her condition. So was yours.'

The Major wheeled on Sir Harry, who was not a Company lawyer for nothing.

' We won't dispute that. Better call the boys in, Wally,' said he.

They entered, without interest, as the young do when dragged from private conferences.

' So far as I understand you, Major Kniveat,' Sir Harry resumed, ' you saw a pig—spotted yellow and green and purple, wasn't it?—this morning?'

' I did. I'm prepared to swear to it.'

' I accept your word without question. There's nothing to prevent anyone seeing spotted pigs on Sunday mornings, of course; but there are lots of things—on Saturday nights, for example— that may lead up to it. Can you recall any of them for us?'

The Major wished to know what Sir Harry might infer.

' Oh, he saw them all right,' Kit put in.

' You did, too. You agreed with me at the time,' the Major panted.

' Naturally. Any medical man would—in the state you were then. Now, can you remember, sir, whether the spots were fixed or floating? *Merely* green and yellow, *or* iridescent with unstable black cores—oily and, perhaps, vermicular?'

The Major rose to his feet.

' It's all right—all right,' Kit spoke soothingly. ' It won't come here! We won't let the nasty pig come in here. And now, if you'll put out your tongue, we'll see if the tip trembles.'

' Jem, what *is* it all about ? ' Mr. Gravell wailed against the torrent of the Major's speech.

' Angelique,' Jem answered, wearily. ' He thinks she's spotted green and purple and Lord knows what all.'

' Then why doesn't he go down to Enoch's and look at her ? There's plenty of light still,' the father answered. ' Take him down and let him *see* her.'

' I suppose we must. Come on, Kit, and help. . . . Oh, hush ! Hush ! Yes ! Yes ! You shall have your dam' pig ! '

The Major, among other things, said he wished for impartial witnesses and no evasions.

' About half the village have been down there already,' said Kit. ' You'll have witnesses enough. Come along ! '

' That's right. That's all right, then,' said Mr. Gravell, and dropped further interest in the matter, for he was of a stock that attended to their own business and held their own liquor. But Sir Harry Birtle joined the house-party. He knew his Kit better than Mr. Gravell knew his Jemmy.

They went down through the long last lights of evening to the home farm. People were there already—a little group by Angelique's sty that melted as they neared, leaving only the local solicitor ; Dr. Frole, the general practitioner ; and a retired Navy Captain—a J.P. who did not much affect the Major. As the other folk of lower degree moved off, they halted for a few words with the Enochs at the farmhouse door. Thence they joined friends who were waiting for them in the lane.

'Do you want more witnesses?' Jem asked. The Major shook his head.

'Major Knivead — to see Angelique,' Jem announced to the local solicitor. 'The Major says he saw her this morning after divine service spotted green and yellow and purple. Look at her now, Major Knivead, please. She is the only pig we have. Would you like an affidavit? . . . We-ell, old lady.'

Angelique, once again hitched her elbows akimbo over her sty door, crossed her front feet, smiled, and — white almost as a puff-ball — said in effect to the company : 'Bless you, my children!'

'Wait a minute. You haven't seen all of her yet,' Kit opened the door. She came out and — it was a trick of infancy learned in the Christian kitchen — sat on her haunches like a dog, leering at the Major, Dr. Frole, the solicitor, and the Navy J.P. This latter sniffed dryly but very audibly. Sir Harry Birtle said, in the tone that had swayed many juries : 'Yes. I think we all see.'

'Now,' said Jem. 'About your spots?'

The Major would have looked over his left shoulder, but Kit was there softly patting it. 'It's all right. It's all right.' said Kit. 'The ugly pig won't run after you this time. *I'll* attend to that. Look at her from here and tell me how many spots you count now.'

'None,' said Major Kniveat. 'They're all gone. My God! Everything's gone!'

'Quite right. Everything's gone now, and here's Dr. Frole, isn't it—yes, your own kind Dr. Frole—to see you safe home.'

The generation that tolerates but does not pity went away. They did not even turn round when they heard the first dry sob of one from whom all hope of office, influence, and authority was stripped for ever—drowned by the laughter in the lane.

THE EXPERT

Youth that trafficked long with Death,
    And to second life returns,
Squanders little time or breath
    On his fellow-man's concerns.
Earnèd peace is all he asks
To fulfil his broken tasks.

Yet, if he find war at home
    (Waspish and importunate),
He hath means to overcome
    Any warrior at his gate;
For the past he buried brings
Back unburiable things—

Nights that he lay out to spy
    Whence and when the raid might start;
Or prepared in secrecy
    Sudden Things to break its heart—
All the lore of No-Man's Land
Moves his soul and arms his hand.

So, if conflict vex his life
    Where he thought all conflict done,
He, resuming ancient strife,
    Springs his mine or trains his gun,
And, in mirth more dread than wrath,
Wipes the nuisance from his path!

The Miracle of Saint Jubanus

THE CURÉ

Long years ago, ere R—lls or R—ce
    Trebled the mileage man could cover;
When Sh—nks's Mare was H—bs—n's Choice,
    And Bl—r—ot had not flown to Dover:
When good hoteliers looked askance
    If any power save horse-flesh drew vans—
'Time was in easy, hand-made France,
    I met the Curé of Saint Juvans.

He was no babbler, but, at last,
    One learned from things he left unspoken
How in some fiery, far-off past,
    His, and a woman's, heart were broken.
He sought for death, but found it not,
    Yet, seeking, found his true vocation,
And fifty years, by all forgot,
    Toiled at a simple folks' salvation.

His pay was lower than our Dole;
    The piteous little church he tended
Had neither roof nor vestments whole
    Save what his own hard fingers mended:
While, any hour, at every need
    (As Conscience or La Grippe assailed 'em),
His parish bade him come with speed,
    And, foot or cart, he never failed 'em.

His speech—to suit his hearers—ran
  From pure Parisian to gross peasant,
With interludes North African
  If any Legionnaire were present:
And when some wine-ripe atheist mocked
  His office or the Faith he knelt in,
He left the sinner dumb and shocked
  By oaths his old Battalion dealt in. . . .

And he was learned in Death and Life;
  And he was Logic's self (as France is).
He knew his folk—man, maid, and wife—
  Their forebears, failings, and finances.
Spite, Avarice, Devotion, Lies—
  Passion ablaze or sick Obsession—
He dealt with each physician-wise;
  Stern or most tender, at Confession.

.   .   .   .   .

To-day?   God knows where he may lie—
  His Cross of weathered beads above him:
But one not worthy to untie
  His shoe-string, prays you read—and love him!

The Miracle of Saint Jubanus

THE visitor had been drawn twenty kilometres beyond the end of the communal road under construction, by a rumour of a small window of thirteenth-century glass, said to represent a haloed saint in a helmet—none other, indeed, than Saint Julian of Auvergne—and to be found in the village church of Saint Jubans, down the valley.

But there was a wedding in the church, followed by the usual collection for charity. After the bridal procession had passed into the sunshine, two small acolytes began fighting over an odd sou. In a stride the tall old priest was upon them, knocked their heads together, unshelled them from their red, white-laced robes of office, and they rolled—a pair of black-gabardined gamins locked in war—out over the threshold on to the steep hillside.

He stood at the church door and looked down into the village beneath, half buried among the candles of the horse-chestnuts. It climbed up, house by house, from a busy river, to sharp, turfed slopes that lapped against live rock, whence, dominating the red valley, rose enormous ruins of an old château with bastions, curtains, and keeps, and a flying bridge that spanned the dry moat.   Valerian and lilac in flower sprang wherever there was foothold.

'All acolytes are little devils,' said the priest benignly, and descended to the wedding-breakfast, which one could see in plan, set out by the stream in a courtyard of cut limes.   His bearing was less that of a *curé* than a soldier, for his soutane swung like a marching-overcoat, and he lacked that bend of the neck, 'the priest's stoop,' with which his Church stamps her sons when they are caught young.

The wedding-feast had ended, and the heat of the day was abated before he climbed up again, beneath an enormous umbrella, to find the visitor among the ruins beside the little church. . . .

'I make a rule not to smoke unless it is offered. A thousand thanks! . . . This ought to be Smyrna. . . .' He exhaled the smoke through his finely-cut nostrils. 'Yes, it *is* Smyrna. . . . Good! And Monsieur appreciates our "Marylands" also? Hmm. *I* remember the time when our Government tobaccos were a national infamy. . . . How long here am I? Close upon forty years. . . . No. Never much elsewhere.   It suffices me. . . .'

'A good people. Composed of a few old clans—Meilhac—Leclos—Falloux—Poivrain— Ballart. Monsieur may have observed their names upon our Monument.'   He pointed downward to the little cast-iron *poilu*, which seemed to be standard pattern for War memorials in that region. 'Neither rich nor poor.   When the

charabanc-road through the valley is made they
will be richer. . . . Postcards for the tourists, an
hotel, and an antiquity shop, for sure, here beside
the church.   A Syndicate of Initiative has, indeed, approached me to write on the attractions
of the district, as well as on the life of Saint Jubanus. . . . But *surely* he existed !   He was a Gaul
commanding a Gaulish legion at the time when
Christianity was spreading in the Roman Army.
We were—he was engaged against the Bo—the
Alemanni—and was on the eve of attack when
some of his officers chose that moment to throw
down their swords and embrace the Cross.
Knowing that he had been baptized, they assumed
his sympathy ; but he charged them to wait till
the battle was finished.   He said, in effect :
" Render unto Caesar the things that are Caesar's,
and to God the things that are God's."   Some
obeyed.   Some did not.   But even with defaitist
and demoralised forces he won the day.   They
would then have given him a triumph, but he
put aside the laurel wreath, and from his own
chariot publicly renounced his profession and the
old deities.   So—I expect it was necessary for
discipline to be kept—he was beheaded on the
field he had won.   That is the legend. . . .

‘ His miracles ?   But one only on record.   He
called a dying man back to life by whispering in
his ear, and the man sat up and laughed.   (I wish
I knew that joke.)   That is why we have a pro-
verb in our valley : " It would take Saint Jubans
himself to make you smile."   I imagine him as an
old soldier, strict in his duty, but also something

of a *farceur*. Every year I deliver on his Day a discourse in his honour. And you will perceive that when the War came his life applied with singular force to the situation. . . .

'They called up the priests? Assuredly! I went. . . . It is droll to re-enter the old life in a double capacity. You see, one can sometimes— er—replace a casualty if—if—one has been—had experience. In that event, one naturally speaks secularly on secular subjects. A moment later one gives them Absolution as they advance. But they were good—good boys. And *so* wastefully used! . . . That is why I am of all matchmakers in our village the least scrupulous. Ask the old women! . . . Yes, monsieur . . . and I returned without a scar. . . . The good God spared me also the darkness of soul which covered, and which covers still, so many—the doubt—the defiance— the living damnation. I had thought—may He pardon me!—that it was hard to reach the hearts of my people here. I saw them, after the War, split open! Some entered hells of whose exist- ence they had not dreamed—of whose terrors they lacked words to tell. So they—men distraught— needed more care in the years that followed the War than even at Chemin des Dames. . . . Yes, I was there, also, when it seemed that hope had quitted France. I know now how a man can lay hands upon himself out of pure fear!

'And there were those, untouched, whom the War had immobilised from the soul outwards. In special, there was Martin Ballart, the only one of his family who returned—the son of a good

woman who died at his birth. Him, frankly, I
loved from the beginning, and, I think, he loved
me. Yes, even when I took him for one of my
acolytes—you saw the type at the wedding?—
and I had very often to correct him. He was not
clever nor handsome, but he had the eyes of a
joyous faithful dog, and the laugh of Pan himself.
And he came back at the last—blasted, withered,
dumb—a ghost that gnawed itself. There had
been his girl, too. . . . When they met again he
did not know her. She said : " No matter. I
will wait." But he remained as he was. He
lived, at first, with his aunt down there. Oh, he
worked—it was no time for idleness—but the
work did not restore. And he would hide himself for an hour or two and come back visibly
replunged in his torments. I watched him, of
course. It was a little photograph—one of those
accursed Kodak pictures, of a young man in a
trench, dancing languorously with a skeleton. It
was the nail of his obsession. . . . I left it with him.
Had I taken it, there might have been a crisis.
Short of that, I tried every expedient, even to
exorcism. . . . But why not? You call them
mick-robs. We call them Devils. . . . One thing
only gave me hope. He took pleasure in my
company. He looked at me with the eyes of a
dog in pain, and followed me always. It came
about in effect that he lived up here. He would
sit still while I played piquet with our schoolmaster, Falloux. . . .

' Ah, *that* was a type upon whom our War had
done bad work ! No, he had not served. He

had some internal trouble, which I told him always was a mere constipation of Atheism. Oh yes— he was enormously a freethinker! A man with a thick black beard, and an intellect (he carried it in front of him like his stomach) never happy unless it was dirtily rude to the Bon Dieu and His Saints. Little unclean stories and epigrams, you understand. He called Saint Jubanus a militarist and an impostor—this defaitist of a Zeppelinistic belly! But he could play piquet, and he was safer at my house than infecting our estaminet with his witticisms. I told him always that he would be saved on account of "invincible ignorance." Then he would thunder:

'"But if your God has any logic, I shall be damned!"'

'"Be content," I would reply. "The Bon Dieu will never hear your name. You will be certified, together with the Cartel, by some totally inferior specialist of a demon as incapable of receiving even rudimentary instruction."

'Then he would clutch at his beard and throw down the cards, which poor Martin picked up for us. But apart from his rudeness to God and the Hierarchy, he was of exemplary life. Pardi, he had to be! *She* charged herself with that. Not believing in God, he had naturally married a devil before whom he trembled. *She* took him to Mass. That was why he was always most extravagant at my house on Monday evenings. His atheism, Monsieur, was, after all, but the *panache* without which a good little Frenchman cannot exist. *A fond*, there are few

atheists in France. But, I concede, there are
several *arrivistes*. Knowing this (and *her*), I
hardly troubled to pray for him.

' It was for poor Martin that I prayed always ;
but not with full passion until his aunt told me
she would take him to Lourdes. . . . Every man,
besides being all the other base characters in
Scripture, is a Naaman at heart. You have
seen Lourdes, Monsieur ? A-ah ! . . .

' So I exposed this new trouble and my own
mean little soul to the Bon Dieu. It was He—
I remember the very night—Who put it into my
heart to pray seriously to Saint Jubanus. I had
prayed to him, oh, many times before ; but it
occurred to me at that hour that my past demands
had not, in view of his secular career, been
sufficiently precised or underlined. The idea
kept me awake. I got up. I went to the church,
which is, as you see, not three steps. There—
it is—it was—an old duty of my life in the world
—I kept my—I walked up and down in the dark.
At last I found myself constating my case, not
formally to a Saint, but officially as to my commanding officer. I said—substantially :

' " Mon General, the time has come for action.
You gave your single life to uphold the honour
of your military obligation. There are some
two million Gauls who have given up theirs
for much the same object, as well as twenty-
three out of your very own village here. Surely
some of these must by now have appeared before
you ! I address you simply, then, as an old
moustache who is trying to beat off an attack of

the Devil on the soul of Martin Ballart, Corporal, 743rd of the Line, Two Citations. (One must be precise always with the Hierarchy.) I am at the end of my resources. God has ordered that I should report to you. I ask no obvious miracles, because, between ourselves, I do not in the least desire this pleasant retreat of ours to develop into a Lourdes. I beg only your help as my officer in the case of a good boy who, by fortune of war, is descending alive into Hell." I concluded, textually: " Mon General, many reputations rest upon a single action. That also is the fortune of war. But I submit, with respect, after your sixteen-hundred years in retreat, it is not too much that an old and very tired combatant of your own race should signal for a small rein-forcement from his Commandant. . . ."

' I think—I *know*, indeed, from what happened afterwards—he was moved by this last thrust. It was as though all God's good night had chuckled above me. I went to my bed again and slept in confidence. . . .

' Did I look for a sign ? Did Gouraud give any when he took our revenge for Chemin des Dames—when he let the enemy fall into the trap by their own momentum ? No ! I con-tinued my work, and always I prayed for Martin. Then there came down the valley—as he does yearly—the itinerant mender of umbrellas, for whom my housekeeper stores up her repairs. She had acquired a piece of material to re-cover my umbrella, which, as you can see, is somewhat formidable in point of size, and of a certain antiquity. Indeed, I do not know whether there still exists another effective machine of its type, constructed, see you, from the authentic bone of the whale. Look! Vast as it is, it was still more vast when that artist arrived. My Mathilde's piece of material was found to be inadequate in extent. But the man said that, with a small cutting down of the tips of the ribs, he could accommodate the area to the fabric. The result you behold. A fraction smaller, but essentially the same. And equally strong. Mon Dieu, *that* was needed! . . . Yes, sometimes I dare to think that that crapulous vagrant might have been Saint Jubanus himself! . . .

'This was in the interval—while the good Saint prepared his second line—just like our Gouraud. During that time I listened to poor Martin's aunt making her arrangements to take him to Lourdes, of which officially I had to approve. For, what miracle had *we* to offer? Further, I endured the attacks of that Falloux. Something that I may have said in respect to The Almighty diverted his dirtinesses from that quarter, and he fell back on Saint Jubanus. My own vanity — the Syndicate of Initiative having approached me, as I have told you, to write his life for prospective tourists—drew *that* on my head. I fear that, once or twice, I may have lost my dignity with him as a priest. He asserts that I swore like a Foot Chausseur, which had been his service. (Poor little rats of the Line!) . . .

'And our Saint's Day that year was wet, so I knew all the world would attend. I had been

summoned out of the village before the discourse
—a couple of kilometres down the road. On my
return, because it dripped water by rivers, I set
my repaired umbrella to dry. . . . But we will go
over to the church. It is not three steps, and I
will show you the place. Also, it will be cooler
in there. . . . It is true we are in horrible neglect,
but, as you say, that window is a jewel. It
represents beyond doubt Saint Jubanus. . . .

'My umbrella? I deposited that behind this
pillar here, outside the sacristy. And by the side
of the pillar, as you see, is as much as we have of
a vestiary—this press, with its shelves. Remark
that I laid my umbrella, always open, in this spot,
on its side. Thus! For myself, when I preach,
though I am not an orator, I prefer the naked
soutane—it hampers action less; but—out of
respect for our Saint—I put on the cotta. At
the same time I tell my two acolytes—who are
of precisely the type you saw after the wedding;
it is fixed by the Devil—to prepare me the vestments for the Service of the Benediction which
would succeed my discourse. It was to them to
extract these vestments with some decency from
that press there. In this there was a little delay.
I stepped aside to look, for—an acolyte is capable
of anything—it seemed to me that they had chosen
that hour to amuse themselves with my umbrella.
I demanded why they did not leave it alone.
One replied that he could not; and the other
opened that terrible giggle of the nervous small
boy. Heaven pardon me, but I am of limited
patience! I signified that I had means of enfor-

cing my orders. There is a reverberation in this place effective for the voice at dramatic moments.

' But it was my umbrella which at that moment began to take the stage. It receded from me with those two young attached to different points of its circumference. At the same time it gyrated painfully in that shadow there. I followed, stupefied, and demanded some explanation of the outrage. It replied in two voices of an equal regret that it was attached and could not free itself. I hastened to aid. They said afterwards they misconstrued my motives. All I know is that my umbrella, open always, but tortured by unequal compressions, descended indescribably those three steps here into the body of the church, where the congregation awaited my discourse. On one side of its large circle, which you see, was an acolyte, facing inwards, clawing at the laces on his bosom and his elbow. On another was his companion, inextricably caught high up under the armpit, which he could not reach with the other hand, because he was facing outwards, pinned there by his vestments. The central effect, Monsieur, was that of an undevout pagoda conducting a *pas de trois* in a sacred edifice, to the accompaniment of increasing whimpers. This was before they collapsed, those young. Whether by accident or design, the child facing inwards snatched at the back of the head of the other. We shave our boys' heads in France, fortunately; but he had nails, that one, and the other protested. . . .

' I ? I followed, men said, step by step, slowly, with my mouth open. Some instinct doubtless

warned me not to approach lest I should be—er—
caught up by that chariot. Also, which often
happens to me inopportunely, the incident struck
me as humorous. I desired to see the end. . . .
But this was but the beginning. My people
gasped. My umbrella pursued its career, unde-
cidedly but continuously. Then one of the little
Juggernauts—if that be the word—began to
weep. The other followed. . . . And then? Then,
Monsieur, that Falloux—that practical and logical
atheist, who believes reason is the source of all—
leapt into the breach, crying: "But they are
attached! Stand still, and I will detach you."
But that they would not do. My perambulating
mosque of an umbrella resumed command. Its
handle, see, tripped and slid over the stone floor
like the pointed foot of a danseuse. This, with
the natural elasticity of the ribs, furnished all the
motifs of the ballet. As Falloux stooped to the
rim of its circumference—being short-sighted in
all respects—one side elevated itself, and the point
of a rib caught him in the beard beneath the chin.
It appeared then that he could not disengage. He
made several gestures. Then he cried: "But it
is _I_ who am also attached! Stand still, you mis-
begotten little brats, till I detach myself!" And
he laboured with his hands in the thickets of his
beard like a suicide who has no time to lose. But
he remained—he rested there—conforming with
yelps of agony to the agonies of the rival circus,
into whose orbit had now projected itself, at their
own level, the head of their abominated preceptor,
distorted and menacing. . . . And then? . . .

'There are occasions, Monsieur, when one must lead or oneself mount the tumbril. I exploded a fraction of a second before my people, saving, doubtless, some a ruptured blood-vessel. We did not—see you—laugh greatly. We were beyond that point when we began. Soon—very soon—we could no more. We could but ache aloud, which I assure you is most painful—while my insolent umbrella promenaded its three adherents through pagan undulations and genuflexions. It was Salome's basin, you understand, dancing by itself with every appearance of enjoyment, and offering to all quarters the head of the Apostle *and* of two of the Innocents. But not the Holy Ones!

'Then *she* rose in her place, and said : " Imbecile! But stand still. I will bring the scissors."

'And she went out. It was cruel of the Saint to force us to recommence. We could do nothing except continue to ache and hiccough and implore Falloux to stand still. He would not—he could not—on account of those young, who, weeping with shame, continued to endeavour to extricate themselves individually. Falloux followed their movements in every particular. You see, he was attached to his troupe by hairs, which it hurts to pull—oh, exquisitely! But he did his best. I have never conceived such motions, even in dreams. You will comprehend, Monsieur, that there are certain physical phenomena inseparable from the contortions of a globose man labouring through unaccustomed exercises. These also were vouchsafed to us! . . .

' It is said that I was on my knees beating my forehead against the back of a *prie-Dieu*, when we heard, above all, the laugh of Faunus himself—the dear, natural voice of my Martin, rich with innocent delight, crying: " But, do it again! If you love me, Uncle Falloux, do it all again! "

' We turned as one, and Martin's girl, who sits always where she can see him, took him in her arms. The miracle had happened! . . . Yes, from that moment Falloux lost the centre of his stage. Then *she* returned—like Atropos. She cut him free; she threw down the shears; she led him out. . . . I? I picked them up and I conducted my autopsy on my acolytes with more of circumspection. Beards renew themselves, but not our poor little church vestments when they are torn. . . .

' The explanation? Modern and scientific, Monsieur. Saint Jubanus—the repairer of umbrellas—had, as I have told you, shortened the ribs of my umbrella. Look! He had then capped the point of each rib with a large, stamped, tin tip, which you perceive locks down. It bears some likeness to the old snap-hook on the pole of an Artillery waggon, and is perfectly calculated to catch in any fabric—or hair. But, to make sure, that inspired scoundrel had, in pushing on his labour-saving capsules—which are marked S.G.D.G. (that ought to be " A.M.D.G.")—bent back the terminal laminae—fibres—what do you call them?—of the whale's bone. You can see them protruding hungrily from the neck of each rib-cap, and also from the slits at the side of it. . . .

Have you forgotten those heads of grass with which one used to entangle and wind up the silky hairs in the nape of a girl's neck? Just that, Monsieur; but in a sufficiently gross beard, inextricable, and causing supreme torture at every twitch. . . .

'Yes. We were all stilled after Martin had laughed, except Martin and his girl. They wept together—the tears from the soul. I said to them:

'"Go out, my children. All the world is for you to-day Paradise. Enter there!"

'I had reason. They would never have listened to my beautiful discourse. Ah! It was necessary to reconstruct *that* while we regained our gravity, because at that moment (it is true, Monsieur, that the Devil's favourite lair is beneath the Altar), at that moment came my temptation! Falloux had been delivered into my hands by Saint Jubanus. He who had mocked and thrust out his chin against God and the Saints had, logically, by that very chin been caught and shaken in the face of the *souk*, as I myself—as I have seen a man handled at Sidi bel Abbas! Never should he survive it! With my single tongue I would unstick him from his office, his civilisation, and his self-respect. But I recalled that he was a Gaul who had been shamed in public, and was, therefore, now insane. One did—one should—not mock afresh a man who has thus suffered. For so I have seen many good soldiers lost to France. Also, he was a soul in my charge. . . .

'Yet, you will concede, the volteface demanded skill. At that moment Saint Jubanus came to my aid. It was as though he himself had signalled:

" To the next objective—charge! Martin is saved! Save now by any means the man whom I have used as his saviour. If necessary, old comrade, lie! Lie for the Honour of the Legion! " ('Pristi! What a Commander he must have been in his prime!) I took at once for my text our saying : " It would need Saint Jubans himself to make you laugh."

' I made plain to them first, of course, that his merits were wide enough to cover the sin of laughing in church. I demonstrated what that laughter had effected for our poor Martin, whose agonies they knew all. I told them—and it is true—that the Bon Dieu demands nothing better from honest people than honest laughter, and that he who awakens it is a benefactor. Then I extolled the instrument by which the miracle had been wrought. That is to say, I extolled Falloux, who had lent himself so willingly and with such self-sacrifice to this happy accident. (After all, he had sworn creditably enough—for a Foot Chasseur!) I said that we two had often discussed Martin together. (My orders were to lie, and I interpreted them liberally.) I made clear how a smaller-minded man than he would have broken loose (which he could not have done except by *her* scissors) before the experiment had terminated ; but that he, Falloux, was of a moral stature sufficient to advance under a *mitraille* of derision to the complete awakening of Martin's soul. I said that though a freethinker, Falloux—this same animal Falloux —realised the value of moral therapeuthy. (They were enormously delighted at this. They thought

it was a new vice from Paris.) For Falloux himself, who—*she* told me later—was biting his nails
in the hen-house convulsed with shame, I extem-
porised a special citation. No. Our village does
not read Rabelais, but *he* did. So I compared—
Heaven forgive me!—that unhappy costive soul
with all its belly to Gargantua. Oh, only by im-
plication, Monsieur! I stated that the grandeur of
his moral gesture of self-effacement was Gargantuan in its abandon. That phrase impressed them
also. They realised now that it was not a comedy
at which they had assisted, but a Miracle. . . .

'And thus I laboured with my people. Mon
Dieu, but I sweated like an ox! At last they
swung in the furrow, and I claimed their homage
for him. And I succeeded! I led them down the
hill to offer it *en masse*! He came out upon us
like a wild beast. But when I had explained our
objective, he—this enormity Falloux—was convinced that he had scientifically lent himself to
a Gargantuan jest of abandoned self-abnegation
because he was an expert in moral therapeutics!
. . . That, setting aside my discourse, which
was manifestly inspired, was the second miracle,
Monsieur—the abasement of Falloux on—my
faith!—his tenderest point. *And* his redemption!
For it is *she* who is more the unbeliever of the two
these days. She is a woman. She knows that I
can be, on occasion, a liar almost as formidable. . . .

'But this has been an orgy of the most excellent cigarettes, and, for me, a debauch of conversation. It demands at least that I offer a cup of
coffee which may not be too detestable. Let us

go. . . . But my little house is here—under the hand, see you—not three steps. . . . But think of the pleasure you give *me*, Monsieur! . . . What? What? What is it that thou singest to me there? . . . A thousand pardons for the phrase! But Saint Julian of Auvergne has no affinity whatever with Saint Jubanus. They are uniquely different. I *implore* you to abandon that heresy! Auvergne! Auvergne! "Famous for its colleges and kettles," as I once read somewhere in the world. Impossible a million times! Saint Julian was a Roman officer—doubtless of unimpeachable sanctity—but a Latin; whereas our General was a Gaul—as Gallic as——'

He beckoned to a young man of the large-boned, well-fleshed, post-war type, who was ascending the hill from the fields behind a yoke of gold and silver oxen with sheepskin wigs. He moved up slowly, smiling.

'As Gallic as he,' the priest went on. 'Look at him! He was that one who was pinned to my umbrella by his back on that day and—tell Monsieur what they call you in the village now.'

The youth's smile widened to a heavenly grin. 'Parapluie, Monsieur,' said he, and climbed on.

The priest stopped at his own door. 'Mathilde,' he cried, 'the larger bottle—er—from Martinique; thy gingerbread; and my African coffee for two. Pardi, Monsieur, forty years ago there would have been two pistols also, had I known or cared anything about the Saints in those days! . . . Saint Julian of Auvergne, indeed! But I will explain.'

SONG OF SEVENTY HORSES

Once again the Steamer at Calais—the tackles
Easing the car-trays on to the quay.   Release her !
Sign—refill, and let me away with my horses
(Seventy Thundering Horses !)
Slow through the traffic, my horses !   It is enough
    —it is France !

Whether the throat-closing brick-fields by Lille, or her
    pavées
Endlessly ending in rain between beet and tobacco ;
Or that wind we shave by—the brutal North-Easter,
Rasping the newly dunged Somme.
(Into your collars, my horses !)   It is enough—it is
    France !

Whether the dappled Argonne, the cloud-shadows
    packing
Either horizon with ghosts ; or exquisite, carven
Villages hewn from the cliff, the torrents behind them
Feeding their never-quenched lights.
(Look to your footing, my horses !)   It is enough—it is
    France !

Whether that gale where Biscay jammed in the corner
Herds and heads her seas at the Landes, but defeated

Bellowing smokes along Spain, till the uttermost head-
*   lands*
Make themselves dance in the mist.
(Breathe—breathe deeply, my horses!)   It is enough
*   —it is France!*

Whether the broken, honey-hued, honey-combed lime-
*   stone*
Cream under white-hot sun; the rosemary bee-bloom
Sleepily noisy at noon and, somewhere to Southward,
Sleepily noisy, the Sea.
(Yes, it is warm here, my horses!)   It is enough—it is
*   France!*

Whether the Massif in Spring, the multiplied lacets
Hampered by slips or drifts; the gentians, under
Turbaned snow, pushing up the heaven of Summer
Though the stark moors lie black.
(Neigh through the icicled tunnels;) ' It is enough—it
*   is France!'*

The Tender Achilles

HYMN TO PHYSICAL PAIN

(Mr. C. R. Wilkett's version)

Dread Mother of Forgetfulness
    Who, when Thy reign begins,
Wipest away the Soul's distress,
    And memory of her sins.

The trusty Worm that dieth not—
    The steadfast Fire also,
By Thy contrivance are forgot
    In a completer woe.

Thine are the lidless eyes of night
    That stare upon our tears,
Through certain hours which in our sight
    Exceed a thousand years :

Thine is the thickness of the Dark
    That presses in our pain,
As Thine the Dawn that bids us mark
    Life's grinning face again.

Thine is the weariness outworn
    No promise shall relieve
That says at eve, ' Would God 't were morn ! '
    At morn, ' Would God 't were eve ! '

And when Thy tender mercies cease
  And life unvexed is due,
Instant upon the false release
  The Worm and Fire renew.

Wherefore we praise Thee in the deep,
  And on our beds we pray
For Thy return that Thou may'st keep
  The Pains of Hell at bay!

The Tender Achilles

St. Peggotty's annual 'Senior' dinner drew Keede from his south-eastern suburbs to listen to the Head of his old Hospital reviewing work and casualties for the past year.

Barring a few guests—I was one of Keede's—the company represented, as the Press said, all branches of the healing art, from authoritative specialists to rural G.P.'s, whose faces told that they worked their practices in light cars. But they all cheered Sir James Belton's speech as though they were students again. Its opening dealt guardedly with the Great Search on which the Hospital teams were engaged in the newly endowed and extended biological laboratories; and he was sure that all who had the Search at heart would be glad to know that since their Mr. C. R. Wilkett had resumed his old post of bacteriologist, a certain amount of exploration of promising avenues had been initiated.

He then spoke of St. Peggotty's more domestic concerns. There were esoteric allusions here; professional similes, anecdotes, nicknames, and reminiscences which set some of the whiter heads shouting. But he was not wholly inaudible till he expounded his well-known views on the Pharmacopoeia Britannica, and, incidentally, the 'Galenical Physician,' or General Practitioner. Then his hearers overbore him with yells of applause or dissent according to their specialities, and called upon him by the honoured name of Howlieglass, which he had borne when they walked the hospitals, till, at last, they all went home, merry and made young again by good wine and memories renewed.

Keede had discovered in an eminent guest, a friend and a colleague of the War,—a dryish, clean-looking man, who kindly included me in his invitation to come and smoke a pipe with him at his diggings. These proved to be a large, well-administered house in Wimpole Street. He took us to a room at the back of things, where we found the tray set and the fire in order. Keede formally introduced him once as Sir Thomas Horringe, who, he said, specialised in 'tripe.' Otherwise and always he called him 'Scree.'

'He's all right,' Keede explained. 'He doesn't know anything *really*, except how to climb Matterhorns. I only ask him in to please the heirs. He's as ignorant as the rest of these knife-*wallahs*.'

Sir Thomas said that the darkness of the surgeon was as electric light beside the mediaeval murk of the 'medicine-man,' or General Practitioner, and was beginning to tell me what Keede really did and prescribed when he was a sixpenny doctor at Lambeth; but broke off to tell him that, even if they were not too old to fight with siphons, the wife would notice the mess on the rugs next morning, and he would catch it.

Keede then advised me that all surgeon-specialists look on every case as a surgical—' that is to say, a carpenter's '—job, whereas the G.P., who represents ' the Galenical integrity of medicine—before these dam' barbers wriggled into it '—considers each patient as a human being.

' In other words,' he concluded, ' medicine and surgery is the difference between the Priest and the pew-opener.'

Again the other dissented, and the two carried on some discussion they had begun at dinner about the Great Search, and whether Mr. C. R. Wilkett, whom they called ' Wilkie ' or ' Wilks,' had hit on the right line. The only flaw in this person's perfection, according to Sir Thomas, was that he had once inclined to ' Maldoni's theory of the causation of indeterminate growths,' which heresy he had now abandoned.

' But he has got imagination,' Sir Thomas pointed out. ' That's what his coming back to St. Peggotty's will give the whole team. Howlie-glass never lost sight of him. He wanted to get him back to the bug-run; and he did.'

' He's the only man who'd have had the nerve to do it. He's worthy to be a G.P.'

' In the name of the College of Surgeons, ever so many thanks for the compliment, Robin,' Sir Thomas laughed. ' Never mind. We've got him again. Howlieglass wants his head, not his feet.'

' Or, for that matter, his hands. 'Rummy

thing! You never find a man of his type who
really loves a neat job.' Keede made a suggestive
motion of the right hand above the left.

'Who is Wilkett?' I demanded, for these two
were taking him very seriously.

'Just now? The best man in his line at St.
Peggotty's. What he'll be in ten years' time, the
Lord only knows; but Howlieglass is betting
on it.'

Keede interrupted the other for my benefit.

'He's bugs—agar-agar—guinea-pigs—slides
—slices. The microbe-game.'

'The *Lancet's* right,' Sir Thomas meditated
aloud. 'You G.P.'s ought to learn to read sometimes, and try to catch up with what's being done.'

'And leave you knife-*wallahs* to kill our
patients? *We* daren't gut 'em and tell the widows
they died of shock.'

Sir Thomas turned to me.

'If you've had dealings with him, you'll know
what an impostor Keede is. He's as good with
the knife as——'

'Any other post-War assassin. But *I* don't
cut old ladies into bits because it didn't kill
youngsters in the pink of condition. *I* don't
pose as an expert because I had to take chances
in the War. *I* don't lecture and publish on
insuff——'

'You're right, Robin.' Scree dropped a hand
on his shoulder. 'There has been a deal too
much cut-and-thrust since the War. Specially
among the youngsters.'

''Glad *some* of you know that, at any rate. It's

the same between Doctor and Patient as it is between Man and Woman. Do you want to prove things to her, or do you want to keep her?'

'There's a middle way, though,' Scree observed. 'Howlieglass wanted to keep Wilkie, but he had to prove a few things to him first.'

'Why on earth was Wilks sent to the Front at all? 'Sheer waste!' said Keede angrily.

'We knew it. Howlieglass did his best to have him kept back, but Wilkie thought it was his duty.'

'Lummy! As if any of *us* could get out of *that!*' Keede snorted.

'The "duty" notion was part of the imaginative equipment, of course,' said Scree. 'They used him at the base for a while. He was all right there, because he had time to think.'

'That's the research-temperament. But there's a time for all things.' Keede spoke severely.

'I don't say he was even second-class in his surgery,' Scree went on, 'but what did that matter under the circumstances? Only, as you say, Robin, that type of mind wants absolute results, one way or the other; *or* else absolute accuracy. You don't get either at a Clearing Station. You've got to acknowledge the facts of life and your own limitations. Ambitious men won't do that till they are broke—like Wilkie was.'

'What was his trouble?' I demanded.

Scree hesitated for a definition. Keede supplied it.

'Bleedin' vanity,' said he.

Scree nodded.

'Lambeth has spoken. The way Howlie-glass would put it is a shade more refined.'

'Let's have it!' Keede cried; then, to me: 'Scree's splendid as Howlieglass. Listen!'

Here Sir Thomas Horringe, whom few would suspect of parlour-tricks, gave a perfect rendering of the Head of St. Peggotty's thus:

'Gen-tel-men. In our Pro-fession we are none of us Jee-ho-vahs. Strange as it may seem, not an-y of us are Jee-ho-vahs.'

In the few precisely articulated words, one could see Sir James himself—his likeness in face and carriage to the hawk-headed Egyptian god, the mobile pursed lips, and the stillness of the wonderful hands at his sides.

'*I* ought to know,' said Scree, after our compliments. 'I was his dresser. . . . Yes, Wilkie was sent up to the dog-fight, and it was too much for him.'

'Why?' I said, foolishly enough.

'Robin'll tell,' was the reply. 'He had it.'

I waited on Keede, who delivered himself at some length; his half-shut eyes on the past.

'When you are at the Front, you are either doing nothing or trying to do ten times more than you can. When you *are*, you store up impressions for future use. When you *aren't*, they develop. Either way, God help you! A C.C.S. has to be near railhead, hasn't it?—to evacuate 'em. That means troops and dumps. That means bombing, don't it? . . . The actual setting? . . . Oh! They take a couple of E.P. tents and join 'em together, and floor 'em with tarpaulins that have—

been in use. Then they rig up a big acetylene over each operating table; your anaesthetist gets his dope and the pads ready; your nurses and orderlies stand by with the cutlery and odds and ends, and you're ready for visitors. They've been tagged and labelled by some poor devil up under fire — I've been him, too! — and the Receiving Officer sends in the ones that look as if they had the best chance. About that time, Jerry drops an egg or so to steady your hand, and someone vomits.'

' He does,' said Scree.

' Then your job begins. You've got to make up your mind what you are going to do, as soon as your man is on the table, because the others are waiting. Often, you lead off with a long break of identical gun-shot wounds in the head—shrapnel on tin-hats, advancing. Then the five-point-nines find 'em, and it's abdominals. You have to explore and act on your own judgment—one down, t'other come on—till you drop.

' The longest single stretch I ever put in was three and a half days, four hours' sleep each night, after Second Vermuizendaal in '16. The last thing I remember, before I rolled over behind the stores, was old " Duck " Ruthven sluicing off his fat arms in our tea-bucket, and quacking, "Fifteen minutes ! My God ! Fifteen minutes *per capita* !" He was the final London word in trephining, and he'd come out to show the young 'uns how to do it. In his own theatre with his own troupe, he considered an hour and a quarter good going for one case; but Berkeley's team, at the next table, had been polishing 'em off four to the hour for five hours. Talking of Ruthven, did you hear what he said when the Aussies broke into the milliner's shop at Amiens, just before Villers Bretonneux, and dressed 'emselves lady-fashion all through? He had to cut three of 'em out of their undies afterwards.'

It was no language that Mr. Ruthven would use to a Harley Street patient; but it made us laugh. Keede took on again:

'I've given you a rough notion of things. Six or seven teams working like sin ; the stink of the carbide from the acetylene ; and the dope ; and the stink of your anaesthetist's pipe—*my* man ought to have been hung !—mixed up with an occasional egg from Jerry.

'And when you've dropped in your boots, not dead, but dead *and* buried, someone begins waggling your foot (the Inquisition invented that trick !) and whisperin' to you to wake up and have a stab at some poor devil who has been warmed and slept off some of his shock, and there's just a chance for him. Then you dig yourself up and carry on if you can. But God is great, as they say in Mespot. Sometimes you get a card from the base saying you didn't stitch his diaphragm to his larynx, and he's doing well. There was a machine-gunner (I remember his eyes) and he had twenty-three perforations of the intestines. I was pretty well all in by then, and my hands hadn't belonged to me for two days. I *must* have left the bloke his stomach, but I fancy I made a clean sweep of everything below the duodenum. And now he's a head-gardener near Plaxtol.

'Pinches his employer's celery and sends it to me in sugar-boxes.'

This reminded Scree of a man one-third of whose brain he had personally removed, who on recovery wished to show his gratitude by becoming his town chauffeur. As the two talked, the old Army oaths blossomed on their happy tongues, and coloured the rest of their speech for the night.

' This Hell's hoop-la was too much for Wilkie,' said Keede, when, at last, I recalled him. ' He hadn't the time he needed to think things out; and he was afraid of injuring his own reputation (God knows he was no surgeon!) by doing the wrong thing. But *I* think what really coopered him, was being in charge of an S.I.W. show just before Armistice.'

' What is an S.I.W.? ' I said.

' A hospital for self-inflicted wounds. He had to look after a crowd who had blown off their big toes, and so on, and were due for court-martial as soon as they could stand. Enough to send a tank up the pole, ain't it? And a week before the Eleventh, a Gotha going home had unloaded one on an outhouse, and a bit of tin or something had caught him through the boot and lodged near ——' Keede gave the bones their proper names and showed the position of the wound on his own plump little instep. ' It wasn't anything that mattered. He picked it out with the forceps, cleaned it, and it healed. I got that from his colleague when I was sitting on a court of inquiry into missing medical comforts in that sector. (I was a Major then, by God!—so I was.) And that's where I met Wilkie again. He hung on to himself till proceedings were over; and then he wrung his hands. 'Don't often see a man do that.'

' They do it oftener than women,' said Scree, which puzzled me till he gave a reason.

' He said there was blood on everything that he ate. He said he'd been guilty of the murder of a certain number of men because he hadn't operated on 'em properly. He had their names down in a pocket-book. He said he might have saved 'em if he hadn't knocked off for a cigarette or a doss. He said he had kept himself going on rum sometimes, and was woozy when the pinch came; and he hadn't waked up and carried on when the orderlies waggled his foot and asked him to take a long shot with a dog's-chancer. He didn't know *that* lot by name; but he had 'em numbered and dated. He wanted me to go through all his vellum cards, from the C.C.S., so he could prove it. *And*, of course, he was eternally damned. Liquor? Not enough to have flustered a louse! Besides—he couldn't stand it. 'Hair-trigger stomach. I've seen him. My worrd! He had 'em bad. Everything that a man's brain automatically shoves into the background was out before the footlights, and dancing Hell's fox-trot, with drums and horns.'

The simile seemed to convey something to Scree.

' I didn't know that,' he said lazily. ' Were there noises, then, from the first? '

' Yes. That's what made me take notice. Of course, I argued with him, but *you* know how much good that is against fixed notions! I told him we were all alike, and the conditions of our job hadn't been human. I said there were limits to the machine. We'd been forced to go beyond 'em, and we ought to be thankful we'd been able to do as much as we had. Then he wrung his hands and said, "To whom much has been given, from the same much shall be required." That annoyed me. I hate bookkeeping with God! It's dam' insolence, anyhow. Who was he to know how much had been given to the other fellow? *He* wasn't the Almighty. I told him so. Oh, I know I was a fool. . . .

'The only thing that kept him at all anchored was his silly foot. That wound I told you about had broken out and was discharging. He dressed it himself twice a day. I reported on him, which I had no right to do, and his Colonel shipped him off to one of those nice "nervous" hospitals where they wore brown gloves and saluted their C.O.'s in case they should forget there had been a war. But I was so busy getting demobbed and trying to pick up what my locum-tenens had left of my practice, that I lost sight of him. He went off to live with his mother.' Keede gave way to Scree at this point.

'Yes, his mother kidnapped him. *She* didn't know there had been a war, either. She was afraid neighbours might think he was insane, and there hadn't been any insanity in her family, and she didn't want the tradespeople to talk. So she hid him in the country and suppressed all letters. There were lots like her. I was trying to get back my practice, too. Do you suppose that mattered to Howlieglass? He had his new bug-runs built and endowed, but he hadn't got his Wilkie to manage 'em, and he chose to damn my eyes for not producing him. He gave me the telling-off of my life the day I went up for my Knighthood. I told him I wasn't a gynecologist, and he'd better make touch with the old lady and tackle her himself. No! He said that was my job, because I'd worked with Wilkie on some of the earlier research details. So I had to trace him.'

' Is—er—Sir James that kind of person?' I ventured.

' 'Don't know what you mean by " person," ' said Scree. ' But when Howlie begins to dissect his words, you generally attend to him. Luckily, I found a woman who had kept her eye on Wilkie's whereabouts—mother or no mother. I gave Howlieglass the address, and he kindly let me go on with my practice.'

' He didn't *me*! ' said Keede. ' He wrote me to report to him after consulting hours, and I went. He told me to look up Wilkie at once. It was only two hundred miles, and one night out. It was lodgings by the seaside, and his mother did social small-talk without daring to stop, and Wilkie played up to her. She said he was all right, and he swore he was.

' *And* it rained. I got him let out for a walk on the beach with me. He went to bits behind a bathing-machine. It was the trephining work that had stuck on his mental retina. (Odd! It used to be abdominals with *me*, the first few months after.) He saw perspectives of heads—gunshot wounds—seen from above and a little behind, as they'd lie on the tables ; with the pad over their mouths, but still they all accused him of murder. On off nights he had orderlies whispering to him to wake up and give some poor beggar a chance to live. Then they'd waggle his foot, and he'd wake up grateful for the pain, and change the dressings. His foot was in a filthy state. The thing had formed a sinus. 'Acted as a safety valve, perhaps.'

'None of your mediaeval speculations here, Robin,' said Scree. 'Facts are all that the ex-am-in-ers reequire, gen-tel-men.'

'He was quite rational, apart from being damned, and walking down those perspectives, and hearing shouts of "Murder !" We had high tea, with a kerosene lamp and crossword puzzles after. She talked about the pretty walks in the neighbourhood. Great thing—mother-love, ain't it? . . . I turned in my notes to Howlieglass, and he asked me to dinner. My worrd ! ' Keede patted his round little pot. ' And where *does* he get his champagne ? '

' From grateful appendices—same as your bloody 'umble,' said Scree. ' G.P.'s are only entitled to birds and *foie gras*.'

' Get out ! I had a whole tin of salmon once from a kosher butcher. . . . We-ell ! Howlie took me through Wilkie's case for half an hour, on my notes. I can't imitate him, but he said that none of us were Jee-ho-vahs, and if, in my con-sidered judgment, Wilkie's foot *was* tuberculous, the best thing would be to give him a bed in his old hospital, and have Scree operate. *I* hadn't said a word about tubercle. I'd been working out mental symptoms. . . . Where in Hell does hysteria shade into mania?' Keede broke off.

'Not on these premises, old man. I'm a knife-*wallah*,' said Scree. 'Carry on.'

'Howlieglass told me that the best of us make mistakes; but a mistake made by a G.P. of my standing and antecedents would only be natural, and would not shake the faith of my flat-u-lent old ladies. Just *that*! He was prepared to abide by my verdict because I knew Wilkie's constitutional needs; and if I recommended homeopathic treatment, he would bow to that, too.'

'But you tumbled to it?' said Sir Thomas Horringe, K.C.B., with a grin.

'Not that very minute, because it was my third glass. But I noticed he was beginning to dissect his words, so I agreed at once. Then he said it might amuse Wilkie to conduct his own tubercle tests with guinea-pigs and culture in his own fetid atmosphere. That wasn't *my* affair. I was to go back and tell the mother that the foot needed attention. He left the rest to my bedside-manner. You needn't laugh, Scree. He said that you'd come in later as the " bungling amateur," and— you dam' well did.

'Then I went back to the " British Riviera," and convinced the old lady. She said the change might do him good. But Wilkie became the bacteriologist at once. He disputed the notion of tubercle; but when I told him he could put the question to the guinea-pigs, and examine the slides himself, he was willing to come up and show me what a fool I was. I say, Scree, was Wilkie *always* as offensive as he is?'

'Pretty nearly. It's his sniffle does it. But he's a genius.'

'I don't care for geniuses. He came up with me, and I gave him a bed for the night. He began to see his heads when he was turning in; and, not having his mother to play up to, he let go aloud.'

'Was he playing up to *you*?' Scree demanded.

'How can one tell with a patient? I 'phoned to Howlieglass to come and look. He stayed till nearly daylight, watching. Wilkie talked about being damned and having much required of him. Howlieglass never said a word till just as he was going. Then he told me he couldn't afford to lose Wilkie's intellect for the sake of his bleedin' vanity. No, old man! That wasn't Lambeth. It was Howlieglass said it.'

'I apologise to Lambeth.'

'And then, on the doorstep—he'd sent his car home, and my man waited for him—just as he was getting in, he saw a star (you know how keen he is on astronomy) and he stared at Tweed for about half a minute, and then he said: "Oh, Lord! What *do* You expect for the money?" He was only questioning the general scheme of things, the way he does sometimes; but my man thinks he's the Devil. He's more afraid of him than I am. . . . Oh, well, and then we put Wilkie into one of the new paying-rooms at the Hospital, and we hurried up the tests, and they showed unmistakable tubercle. Wilkie saw it for himself. He was fairly winded. What annoyed him more than anything was that it would have to be a Syme operation.'

'Who is Syme?' I asked.

'He's dead,' said Scree, 'but he begat rather a pretty operation on the foot.' Bob Sawyer-like, he illustrated it with a folded sandwich. 'Then you turn the flap under like this,' he concluded, 'and it makes a false heel that a man can walk about on very comfily.'

'Then, why was Wilkie annoyed?' I inquired. Keede answered the question.

'Because he'd done a good few of 'em in the S.I.W. on chaps who had fired into their own insteps. He said it was a judgment on him for shirking. He was seeing his heads every night while he waited. Howlieglass never noticed 'em. He'd drop in and talk bugs with him however looney he was.'

'I never knew Wilkie more brilliant than he was in his lucid intervals, then. He used to talk bugs to me, too,' said Scree. 'I operated, of course. Howlieglass came to look (he never thinks it makes a man nervous) and—I couldn't help laughing—just as Wilks was going under—Howlie turned to one of the nurses and said: " Yes, my de-ar. The best of us can make mis-takes. We are none of us Je-ho-vahs—not even Mr. Wilkett." All the same, I made rather a neat job of that Syme.'

'*You* hadn't to stand being kicked for it,' said Keede. 'We gave Wilks a week to pull round in.

Then I called and told him that, if he'd been a patient, I should have held my tongue : but, as he was one of us—No, I said, as he *had* been one of us, and that made him wince—I had to confess that his foot was no more tuberculous than mine. I took full responsibility for the error. . . . Do you want me to tell you what he really said to me?'

I did indeed.

'He said : " *You*! What on earth do *you* matter? You're only a G.P. The tests were scientific. They *can't* lie. I'll go into that later ; but I'll attend to you first." He did. He ended up by annoying me a little, though I'm the meekest medico on the register. He said : " How could even *you* make such a ghastly blunder? You had all the *time* there was. You had whatever *judgment* you possess under your control. You weren't *hurried*. Were you *drunk*? "

'I said I wasn't, but I didn't say it with too much conviction. As I told you, he annoyed me. I said that his infernal heads' nonsense and his hysteria must have biased me, but, if he *was* eternally damned, the mistake wasn't worth fussing about. If he wasn't, he knew as well as I did that errors of this kind happened under the most careful system ; and he'd be hopping about on his Syme heel in no time ; and at any rate he ought to be grateful I hadn't diagnosed his trouble as something scandalous.'

'Not bad, for the meekest medico on the register,' said Scree approvingly.

'I was annoyed,' Keede confessed, ' but I wasn't as annoyed as Wilkie. When he'd polished me off, he wanted the slides and test records. *I* don't know what hanky-panky they had worked; but a youth turned up from the bug-run and said there had been a mistake in the samples or the filing of the guinea-pigs, and they were tracing the responsibility in the basement. Meantime, here were the genuine articles.

'Then Wilks began again on *him*: " But you had all the *time* you wanted! You had no reason to *hurry*! You were under no *strain*! You had only to label and number." *That* showed what he had been suffering from, at the back of his mind, at the Front. But he went too far. He asked the pup how long he thought he would be allowed to hold his job after this disgraceful exposure.

'I had to remind him that he was one blooming civil case in one blooming bed, and he would get his bill, and he could bring his civil action when he pleased, but he did *not* command the Hospital staff. The youth got out. I took the rest of the barrage. No mistake about it—it was a desperately important affair to Wilkie, damned or saved. Then that " bungling amateur," Scree, came in.'

'Was this all a put-up job?' I asked.

'Not in the least. It was Scree's regular round. Wilkie wasn't as offensive to him as he'd been to me. More professionally pained and shocked, you know. That put Scree on his high horse at once. He said he was an operative mason, not a speculative one.'

'You infernal old liar,' Scree broke in, passing over the siphon.

'That was the sense of it, at any rate. Scree

said he'd been told to operate on a foot reported as tuberculous, and it wasn't his job to question me. Then he mentioned the figures that the crowned heads of Europe always paid him for cutting their corns, and he implied that being operated on by him was equivalent to a K.C.B. You ought to hear Scree's top-note. It cowed the bacteriologist. And *then* he sat down by the old boy's bed and began to talk Research with him, giving the impression that he was sitting at the feet of Gamaliel. It was—shut up, Scree! This *is* true!—the prettiest and kindest bit of work I've ever known even that hardened ruffian do. It had Wilkie steadied in five minutes, and in another five he was sailing away about Research, with his brain working like treacle.'

The tiny muscle that twitches when we feel certain sorts of shame showed itself beneath Scree's lower eyelid.

' In the middle of it Howlie came in, and Scree put up his hand to stop him speaking till Wilkie had finished.'

' Wilkie was giving his reasons for having chucked Maldoni's theory,' said Scree in extenuation.

' Then Howlieglass slid into the conference, and there they sat, with me playing bad boy in the corner, while they talked about taming spirochetes. Didn't you, Scree?'

' We talked, if you want to know, about the general administration of St. Peggotty's New Biological Laboratories Extension,' said Scree.

' Did you? Then you can carry on,' said

Keede; and Sir James Belton was heard speaking through Scree's lips: ' " I am ver-ree sor-ree to say that there has been a mis-take, Mis-ter Wilkett, about your foot. It was due to an err-on-eous di-ag-nosis on the part of Mis-ter Keede, who is onlee a sub-urban Gen-eral Prac-titioner. We must not judge him too hard-ly." '

'And then,' Keede supplemented, 'Scree, who might have had the decency to have kept out of it, said it was an infernal and grotesque blunder on my part.'

'Sorry,' said Scree, returning to his natural voice, 'I thought you only wanted to know what Howlieglass said. Yes, of course I went for Keede for compromising my professional career that way. We all went for Keede.

'*I* haven't forgotten.' Keede turned to me again. 'I'm rather an exponent of the bedside manner, though you mightn't think it; but for sheer bluff and tying a poor devil into knots I never heard anything within miles of that show round Wilkie's bed. They had him apologising at last for owning a foot at all, and hoping he hadn't given too much trouble.'

'But how about the mix-up of the slides? Did they saddle you with it?' said I.

'Worse! Much worse! Wilkie was drawing up to the subject—he'd have apologised for that, too—but Howlieglass got in first, and——'

Keede nodded towards the obedient Scree. Once more we heard the voice of the head of St. Peggotty's, preciser than ever.

' " If you had been at your post here after the

War, Mis-ter Wil-kett, in-stead of relaxing your mind in rest-cures, this lit-tle af-fair, which we have ag-reed to for-get, would never have ta-ken place. I trust you will not al-low it to oc-cur again." And, damn it all!'—Scree's operating hand smacked on my knee—'poor Wilk's mouth went down at the corners like a child's, and he said, " I see that now, sir. I'm so sorry, sir." '

'Did it cure him?' I asked later as we moved towards the taxi-cup.

'Ab-so-bally-lutely,' said Keede. 'Not a head or a hoot since.'

'And was the foot tuberculous?' I persisted.

'Anything with a sinus of long-standing may turn into anything. It's always best to be on the safe side,' was the response. 'We were playing for the man's reason—not his carcass.'

'One more,' I ventured. 'How was the mix-up in the slides managed? It's rather a grave matter to play with samples, isn't it?'

'By the same woman who knew where his mother had taken him. It wasn't a job to trust to a man. A man would have said that he had a reputation or something to lose.'

'Arising out of the reply to the previous question, does Mr. Wilkett realise about the lady? . . .'

'No,' said Sir Thomas Horringe very gravely to me; 'that's where he has made a mistake.'

'Mistake! Poor devil! He *has*!' said Keede with equal solemnity.

THE PENALTY

Once in life I watched a Star;
  But I whistled, 'Let her go!
There are others, fairer far,
  Which my favouring skies shall show.'
Here I lied, and herein I
Stood to pay the penalty.

Marvellous the Planets shone
  As I ranged from coast to coast;
But beyond comparison
  Rode the Star that I had lost.
I had lied, and only I
Did not guess the penalty!

When my Heavens were turned to blood,
  When the dark had filled my day,
Furthest, but most faithful, stood
  That lone Star I cast away.
I had loved myself, and I
Have not lived and dare not die!

Uncovenanted Mercies

Uncovenanted Mercies

If the Order Above be but the reflection of the Order Below, as that Ancient affirms who has had experience of the Orders,[1] it follows that in the Administration of the Universe all Departments must work together.

This explains why Azrael, Angel of Death, and Gabriel, Adam's First Servant and Courier of the Thrones, were talking with the Prince of Darkness in the office of the Archangel of the English, who—Heaven knows—is more English than his people.

Two Guardian Spirits had been reported to the Archangel for allowing their respective charges to meet against Orders. The affair involved Gabriel, as official head of all Guardian Spirits, and also Satan, since Guardian Spirits are ex-human souls, reconditioned for re-issue by the Lower Hierarchy. There was a doubt, too, whether the Orders which the couple had disobeyed were absolute or conditional. And, further, Ruya'il, the female spirit, had refused to tell the Archangel of the English what the woman in her charge had said or thought when she met

[1] See ' On the Gate,' *Debits and Credits.*

the man, for whom Kalka'il, the male Guardian Spirit, was responsible. Kalka'il had been equally obstinate ; both Spirits sheltering themselves behind the old Ruling :—' Who knoweth the spirit of man that goeth upward, and the spirit of the beast that goeth downward to the earth ? ' The Archangel of the English, ever anxious to be just, had therefore invited Azrael, who separates the Spirit from the Flesh, to assist at the inquiry.

The four Powers were going over the case in detail.

' I am afraid,' said Gabriel at last, 'no Guardian Spirit is obliged to—er—give away, as your people say, his or her charge. But '—he turned towards the Angel of Death—' what's your view of the Ruling ? '

' " Ecclesiastes, Three, Twenty-one," ' Satan prompted.

' Thank you *so* much. I should say that it depends on the interpretation of " Who," ' Azrael answered. ' And it is certainly laid down that Whoever Who may be '—his halo paled as he bowed his head—' it is *not* any member of either Hierarchy.'

' So I have always understood,' said Satan.

' To my mind '—the Archangel of the English spoke fretfully—' this lack of—er—loyalty in the rank and file of the G.S. comes from our pernicious system of employing reconditioned souls on such delicate duties.'

The shaft was to Satan's address, who smiled in acknowledgment.

' They have some human weaknesses, of

course,' he returned. 'By the way, where on earth were that man and the woman allowed to meet?'

'Under the Clock at —— Terminus, I understand.'

'How interesting! 'By appointment?'

'Not at all. Ruya'il says that her woman stopped to look for her ticket in her bag. Kalka'il says that his man bumped into her. Pure accident, *but* a breach of Orders—trivial, in my judgment, for——'

'Was it a breach of Orders for Life?' Azrael asked.

He referred to that sentence, written on the frontal sutures of the skull of every three-year-old child, which is supposed, by the less progressive Departments, to foreshadow his or her destiny.

'As a matter of detail,' said the Archangel, 'there *were* Orders for Life—identical in both cases. Here's the copy. But nowadays we rely on training and environment to counteract this sort of auto-suggestion.'

'Let's make sure,' Satan picked up the typed slip, and read aloud:—' " *If So-and-so shall meet So-and-So, their state at the last shall be such as even Evil itself shall pity.*" H'm! That's not absolutely prohibitive. It's conditional—isn't it? 'There's great virtue in your " if," and '—he muttered to himself—' it will all come back to me.'

'Nonsense!' the Archangel replied. 'I intend that man and that woman for far better things. Orders for Life nowadays are no more than Oriental flourishes—aren't they?'

But the level-browed Gabriel, in whose department these trifles lie, was not to be drawn.

'I hope you're right,' Satan said after a pause. 'So you intend that couple for better things?'

'Yes!' the Archangel of the English cleared his throat ominously. 'Rightly *or* wrongly, I'm an optimist. I *do* believe in the general upward trend of life. It connotes, of course, a certain restlessness among my people—the English, you know.'

'The English I know,' said Satan.

'But in my humble judgment, they are developing on new planes. They must be met and guided by new methods. Surely in your dealings with the—er—more temperamental among them, you must have noticed this new sense of a larger outlook.'

'In a measure—ye-es,' Satan replied. 'But I remember much the same sort of thing after printing was invented. Your people used to come down to me then, reeking—positively Caxtonised —with words. Some of 'em were convinced they had invented new sins. We-ell! Boiled and peeled (we had to do a little of *that*, of course) their novelties were only variations on the Imperfect Octave—Pride, Envy, Anger, Sloth, Gluttony, Covetousness, Lust. Technique, I grant you. Originality, *nil*. You may find it so with this new *Zeitgeist* of theirs.'

'Ah, but you're *such* a pessimist,' the Archangel retorted, smiling. 'I *do* wish you could meet these two I have in my eye. Charmin' people. Cultured, capable, devout, of the happiest influences on their respective entourages; practical, earnest, and—er—so forth—they will each, in their spheres, supply just that touch which My People need at the present moment for their development. Therefore, I am giving them each full advantages for self-expression and realisation. These will include impeccable surroundings, wealth, culture, health, felicity (unhappy people can't make other people happy, can they?), and—everything else commensurate with the greatness of the destiny for which I—er—destine them.'

The Archangel of the English rubbed his soft hands and beamed on his colleagues.

' I hope you're justified,' said Satan. ' But are you quite sure that your method of—may I call it cosseting people, gets the best out of them?'

' 'Rather what I was thinking,' said Azrael. ' I've seen wonderful work done—with My Sword practically at people's throats—even when I've had to haggle a bit. They're a hard lot sometimes.'

' Let's take Job's case.' Satan continued. ' *He* didn't reach the top of his form, as your people say, till I had handled him a little—did he?'

' Possibly not—by the standards of his age. But nowadays *we* don't give very high marks to the Man of Uz. *Qua* Literature, rhetorical, *Qua* Theology, anthropomorphic and unobserved. No-o, you can't get away from the fact that new standards demand new methods, new outlooks, and above all, enlarged acceptances—yes, enlarged acceptances. That reminds me '—the Archangel of the English addressed himself to Azrael— ' I've sent in—perhaps it hasn't come up to you yet—a Demi-Official asking if you can't see your way towards mitigating some of your Departmental methods, so far as those affect your—er—final despatch-work. My people's standards of comfort have risen, you know ; and they're complaining of the—the crudity of certain vital phenomena which lie within your provenance.'

For one instant Azrael lifted his eyes full on the hopeful countenance of the Archangel of the English, but no muscle twitched round his mouth as he replied:—' Death *is* a little crude. For that matter, so's Birth ; but the two seem, somehow, to hang together. What would you say to an Inter-Departmental Committee——'

'*Or* Commission—that gives ampler powers— to explore all possible avenues with a view to practical co-ordination? The very thing,' the Archangel ran on. ' As a matter of fact, I've had the terms of reference for such a conference drafted in the Office. I'll run through 'em with you—if you can spare a few minutes.'

' 'Nothing I should like better,' Satan cried whole-heartedly. ' Unluckily, I'm not always master of my time.' He rose. The others followed his example and, due leave taken, launched into the Void that lay flush with the Office windows.

.   .   .   .

' Now, *that*,' Satan observed after an interval

which had sunk three Universes behind them, ' is a perfect example of the dyer's hand being subdued to what it works in. " *We* don't give high marks to the Man of Uz." Don't we? I'm glad I've always dealt faithfully with all schoolmasters.'

' And he objects to my methods!' Azrael muttered. ' If he weren't immortal—unfortunately—I—I could show him something.'

The notion set them laughing so much that the Ruler of an Unconditioned Galaxy hailed them from his throne; and to Satan's half-barked ' No! —No!'—sign that they were Powers in flight and not halting—returned a courteous ' On You be the Blessing.'

' He has left out " and the Peace," ' said Azrael critically.

' There is no need. They've never conceived of Your existence in these parts,' Gabriel explained, as one free of all the Creations.

' Really?' Azreal seemed a little dashed. ' Our young English friend ought to apply for a transfer here. I fancy I should have to follow him before long.'

' Oh no,' Gabriel chuckled. ' He'd eliminate *you* by training and environment. You're only an Oriental flourish—like Orders for Life to a soul. D'you suppose there's no one in his Office who knows what Kismet means?'

' I should say not—from the quality of the stuff he sends down to us,' Satan complained. ' Did you notice his dig at me about " our pernicious system " of Guardian Spirits? I do my best to recondition his damned souls for re-issue, but——'

'You do it very thoroughly indeed,' said Gabriel. 'I've said as much in my last Report on Our Personnel.'

'Thank you. It's heavier work than you'd imagine. If you're free for a little, I'd like to show you how heavy——'

'You're sure it wouldn't——?' Gabriel began politely.

'Not in the least. Come along, then! . . . Take Space! Drop Time! Forgive my going first. . . . Now!'

The Three nose-dived at that point where Infinity returns upon itself, till they folded their wings beneath the foundations of Time and Space, whose double weight bore down on them through the absolute Zeroes of Night and Silence.

Gabriel breathed uneasily; for, the greater the glory, the more present the imperfections.

'It's the pressures,' Satan reassured him. 'We came down too quickly. Swallow a little and they'll go off. Meantime, we'll have some light on our subjects.'

The glare of the halo he wore in His Own Place fought against the Horror of Great Darkness.

'Have we gone beyond The Mercy?' Azrael whispered, appalled at the little light it won.

'They're delivered into *My* hands now,' Satan answered.

'Usen't there to be a notice hereabouts, requesting visitors to leave all their hopes behind them?' Gabriel peered into the Gulf as he spoke.

'We've taken it down. We work on hope deferred now,' Satan answered. 'It acts more certainly.'

'But I'm not conscious of anything going on,' Azrael remarked.

'The processes are largely mental. But now and again . . . For example!' There was a minute sound, hardly louder than the parting of fever-gummed lips in delirium, but the Silence multiplied it like thunders in a nightmare. 'That is one reconditioning now,' Satan explained.

'A hard lot. They frighten me sometimes,' said Azrael.

'And me always,' Gabriel added. 'I suppose that is because We are their servants.'

'Of whom I am the hardest-worked,' Satan insisted.

'Oh, but you've every sort of labour-saving device, these days, haven't you?' Gabriel said vaguely.

'None that eliminate responsibility. Take the case of that man and that woman we were talking about just now. What conclusion did you draw from the evidence of their Guardian Spirits?'

'There was only one conclusion possible—if they should meet,' Gabriel replied. 'You yourself read the copy of their Orders for Life.'

'And what did our young friend do? 'Rode off on glittering generalities about uplift and idealism and his precious scheme for debauching them both with all the luxuries, because "unhappy people can't make others happy." You heard him say it? He's hopeless.' Satan spoke indignantly.

'Oh, I wouldn't go as far as that. He's English.' Gabriel smiled.

'And then,' Satan held on, 'did you see him look at me when I read out " *Evil itself shall pity* ?" That means, if and when the worst comes to the worst *I* shall have to put it straight again. *I* shall be expected to do the whole of his dirty work—unofficially—and shoulder the unpopularity—officially. *I* shall have to give that couple Hell—and our young friend will take the credit of my success.'

'The attitude is not unknown elsewhere,' said Azrael. 'Ve-ry little would persuade our worthy Michael, for instance, that his Sword is as effective as mine.'

'I'll prove my contention now,' Satan turned to Gabriel, 'if you'll permit—we don't need both of 'em—the woman's guardian, Ruya'il, to report here for a moment. It's night in England now. I can jam " all ill dreams " while she's off duty. We shall have to manage the interview like one of their own cinemas, but you'll overlook that, I hope.'

Gabriel gave the permission without which no Guardian Spirit may quit station, even for a breath, and on the instant, monstrously enlarged upon Space, her eyes shut against the glare that revealed her, stood Ruya'il in her last human shape as a woman upon earth.

Azrael moved forward.

'One instant,' said he. 'I think I have had the pleasure of meeting you, Mrs. ——' (he gave her her name, address, and the date of her death). 'You called for me at the time. You seemed glad to meet me. Why?'

'Because I wanted to meet Gregory,' came the answer, in the flat tones of the held.

'There's our trouble in a nutshell,' said Satan, and took over the inquiry, saying:—' You were under Our Hand for recondition and re-issue, Mrs. ——. For what cause?'

'Because of Gregory.'

'Who was re-issued as Kalka'il. And he because of you?'

'Yes.'

'On what terms were you issued as Guardian Spirits, please?'

'There were no terms. Gregory and I were free to meet in the course of our duties, if we could. So we did. It wasn't *his* fault.'

'Those, by the way, were the last words Eve ever spoke to me,' Azrael whispered to Gabriel.

'Indeed!' Satan resumed. 'So you met and, incidentally, your charges met, too. I think that will be all—oh, one minute more. You know ——?' he named a railway terminus.

'Yes.' The eyelids quivered.

'In London and—Ours here?'

'Oh, *please*, don't! Yes!' A tear forced its way out, and glittered horribly on the cheek.

'I beg your pardon! Thank you so much. I needn't detain you any longer.'

'Now you see my position,' said Satan to the others. 'Our young friend should have had all this information on his blotter before his inquiry began. When he called me in, he should have communicated it to me. Then I should have known where I stood. But he didn't. He makes my job ten times more difficult than it need be by burking the essentials of it—stabs me in the back with his crazy schemes of betterment—and expects me to carry on!'

'I'm afraid my Department must be responsible for the original error of detailing those two particular Guardian Spirits to those two particular people,' said Gabriel. 'At any rate, I accept the responsibility, and apologise.'

Satan laughed frankly. 'No need. We've been opposite numbers since Adam. Mistakes *will* happen. I merely wished to show you something of our young friend's loyal and helpful nature.'

'Meantime, what steps are you taking with that man and that woman?' Azrael asked.

'Tentative, only. Listen!'

He lifted his hand for silence. A broken whisper that seemed one with all Space fought itself into their hearing:

'*My God! My God! Why hast Thou forsaken me?*'

'Was that an echo?' said Gabriel presently. 'Or was it in duplicate?'

'In duplicate. But we don't attach too much value to that class of expression. Very often it's only hysteria—or vanity. One can't be sure till much later.'

'What were those curious metallic clicks after the message?' Azrael asked.

'In the woman's case,' Satan explained, 'it was one of her rings against her tiara as she was putting it on to go to Court. In the second, it was the Star of some Order that the man was being invested with by his Sovereign. That proves how happy they are!'

A certain amount of human time passed.

'Surely there's music, too,' Gabriel went on. 'And words?'

Both were most faint, but quite clear:

> 'I have a song to sing, oh!
> Sing me your song, oh!'

A break, a patter of verse, and then—on an almost unendurable movement that seemed to brush the heart-strings:

> 'Misery me! Lackaday-dee!
> He died for the love of a lady!'

Last, the fall of a body.

'Oh, that's on a stage somewhere,' said Satan. 'They must be enjoying themselves now at a theatre. Everything's coming their way. "Unhappy people can't make people happy, y'know." Well! Now you've heard them, I suggest that, if it doesn't bore you too much, you meet me here on—Azrael must know the dates—they are due for filing and we'll watch the result.'

After a glance into the future, Azrael gave a date in time as earth reckons it, and they parted.

As Death returned to his own sphere, by way of that Galaxy which had been denied knowledge

of his existence, its Ruler heard a voice under
the stars framing words, to him meaningless, such
as these :

> ' His speech is a burning fire,
>   With his lips he travaileth.
> At his heart is a blind desire,
>   In his eye foreknowledge of Death.'

.   .   .   .   .   .

The Archangel of the English, to whom, as to
his people, the years had brought higher education, was more optimistic than ever.   This time,
he confided to the Three Archangels that, since
Mass-Action was the Note of the Age, he had
discovered and was training an entire battalion of
hand-picked souls, whose collective efforts towards
the world's well-being he would aid with improved
sanitary appliances and gratuitous sterilised public
transport.

' What grasp and vision you have ! ' said Satan.
' By the way, do you remember a man and a
woman you were rather interested in, some time
ago ? " Male and female created He them "—
didn't He ? Ruya'il, I think, was the woman's
Guardian Spirit.'

' Perfectly,' said the Archangel of the English.
' They had a certain—not *quite* so large, perhaps,
as they thought, but a certain—share in paving
the way towards these present developments,
which I have the honour to direct a little, perhaps,
from my inconspicuous post in the background.'

' Good !   I remember you spoke rather highly
of them.'

' None the less '—the Archangel joined his

hands across a stomach that insisted a little—
' none the less I should ha-ardly mark those two
definitely as among the Saviours of Society.   We
say in the Department that social service can
be divided into two categories—Saviours and
Paviours.   Ha ! Ha ! '

' How *very* neat ! ' and Satan laughed, too.

' You see it?   As a matter of fact, it arose
out of one of my own marginal notes on an
Hierarchical docket.   No-o !   I think I should
be constrained to mark that couple as first-class
among second-class Paviours of Society.'

' And what has happened to them? ' Satan
pursued.

The Archangel of the English glanced towards Azrael, who replied : ' Both filed.'

' 'Sorry for that—'sorry for that,' the Archangel chirped briskly.   ' But of course I was
only concerned to get the best work out of them
which their limitations permitted.   And I think,
without unduly vaunting my methods, I have
succeeded.   By the way, I have just drafted a
little bit of propaganda on the Interdependence of
True Happiness and Vital Effort.   It won't take
ten minutes to——'

But once again it appeared that his hearers had
business elsewhere.   And indeed they met, soon
after, on the Edge of the Abyss.

' If I had nerves,' said Satan, ' my young friend
would arride them, as he'd say.   What was he
telling *you* when we left? '

' Oh,' said Azrael, ' our Interdepartmental
Commission hadn't come up to his expectations.

We couldn't agree on a form of words for a *modus moriendi*.'

'And then,' Gabriel added, ' he said Azrael hadn't the judicial mind.'

'How can I have?' said Azrael simply. ' I'm strictly executive. My instructions are to dismiss to the Mercy. *Apropos*—what has happened to that couple you were talking over with him, just now?'

'I'll show you in a minute.' Satan looked about him. The light from his halo was answered by a throb of increased productivity through all the Hells. He shaped some wordless questions across Space, and nodded. ' It's all right,' he said. ' She's been in one of our shops, on test for Breaking Strain. *He's* due for final test too. We '—Satan parodied the manner of the Archangel of the English—' took the liberty of thinking that there was a little more work to be got out of him in the Paviour line, after our young friend above had dropped him. So we made him do it—rather as Job did—on an annuity bought by his friends, in what they call a Rowton lodging-house, with an incurable disease on him. In *our* humble judgment, his last five years' realisation-output was worth all his constructive efforts.'

'Does—did he know it?' Gabriel asked.

'Hardly. He was down and out, as the English say. I'll show them both to you in a little. They met first at —— Terminus; didn't they? . . . Good! . . . Follow me till you see me check!—So! . . . And here we are!'

'But this *is* the Terminus! Line for line

and '—Gabriel pointed to the newspaper posters —' letter for letter ! '

' Of course it is. We don't babble about Progress. We keep up with it.'

' Then why '—Gabriel coughed as a locomotive belched smoke to the roof—' why don't you electrify your system? I never smelt such fuel.'

' I have,' said Azrael, expert in operations. ' It's ether '—he sniffed again—' it's nitrous oxide—it's—it's every sort of anaesthetic.'

' It is. Smells wake memory,' said Satan.

' But what's the idea? ' Gabriel demanded.

' Quite simple. A large number of persons in Time have weaknesses for making engagements—on oath, I regret to say—to meet other persons for all Eternity. Most of these appointments are forgotten or overlaid by later activities which have first claim on our attention. But the residue—say two per cent—comes here. Naturally, it represents a high level of character, passion, and tenacity which, *ipso facto*, reacts generously to our treatments. At first we used to put 'em into pillories and chaff 'em. When coaches came in, we accommodated them in replicas of roadside inns. With the advance of transportation, we duplicated all the leading London stations. (You ought to see some of 'em on a Saturday night!) But that's a detail. The essence of our idea is that every soul here is waiting for a train, which may or may not bring the person with whom they have contracted to spend Eternity. And, as the English say, they don't half have to wait either.'

Satan smiled on Hell's own —— Terminus
as that would appear to men and women at the
end of a hot, stale, sticky, petrol-scented summer
afternoon under summer-time—twenty past six
o'clock standing for twenty past seven.

A train came in.   Porters cried the number of
its platform ; many of the crowd grouped by the
barriers, but some stood fast under the Clock,
men straightening their ties and women tweaking
their hats.   An elderly female with a string-bag
observed to a stranger : ' *I* always think it's best
to stay where you promised you would. 'Less
chance o' missing 'im that way.'   ' Oh, quite,'
the other answered.   ' That's what *I* always do ' ;
and then both moved towards the barrier as
though drawn by cords.

The passengers filed out—they and the waiting crowd devouring each other with their eyes.
Some, misled by a likeness or a half-heard voice,
hurried forward crying a name or even stretch-
ing out their arms.   To cover their error, they
would pretend they had made no sign and bury
themselves among their uninterested neighbours.
As the last passenger came away, a little moan
rose from the assembly.

A fat Jew suddenly turned and butted his
way back to the ticket-collector, who was leaving
for another platform.

' Every living soul's out, sir,' the man began,
' but—thank ye, sir—you can make sure if you
like.'

The Jew was already searching beneath each
seat and opening each shut door, till, at last, he

pulled up in tears at the emptied luggage-van. He was followed on the same errand by a loose-knit person in golfing-kit, seeking, he said, a bag of clubs, who swore bitterly when a featureless woman behind him asked : ' *Was* you looking for a sweetheart, ducky ? '

Another train was called. The crowd moved over—some hopeful in step and bearing ; others upheld only by desperate will. Several ostentatiously absorbed themselves in newspapers and magazines round the bookstalls ; but their attention would not hold and when people brushed against them they jumped.

' They are all under moderately high tension,' Satan said. ' Come into the Hotel—it's less public there—in case any of them come unstuck.'

The Archangels moved slowly till they were blocked by a seedy-looking person button-holing the Stationmaster between two barrows of un-labelled luggage. He talked thickly. The official disengaged himself with practised skill. ' That's all right, Sir. *I* understand,' he said. ' Now, if I was you I'd slip over to the Hotel and sit down and wait a bit. You can be quite sure, Sir, that the instant your friend arrives I'll slip over and advise you.'

The man, muttering and staring, drifted on.

' That's him,' said Satan. ' " And behold he *was* in My hand "—with a vengeance. Did you hear him giving his titles to impress the Stationmaster ? '

' What will happen to him ? ' said Gabriel.

' One can't be certain. My Departmental

Heads are independent in their own spheres. They arrange all sorts of effects. There's one, yonder, for instance, that 'ud never be allowed in the other station up above.'

A woman with a concertina and a tin cup took her stand on the kerb of the road by Number One platform, where a crowd was awaiting a train. After a pitiful flourish she began to sing :—

> 'The Sun stands still in Heaven—
> Dusk and the stars delay.
> There is no order given
> To cut the throat of the day.
> My Glory is gone with my Power,
> Only my torments remain.
> Hear me! Oh, hear me!
> All things wait on the hour
> That sets me my doom again.'

But the song seemed unpopular, and few coins fell into the cup.

' They used to pay anything you please to hear her—once,' Satan said, and gave her name. ' She's saving up her pennies now to escape.'

' Do they ever? ' Gabriel asked.

' Oh, yes—often. They get clear away till— the very last. Then they're brought back again. It's an old Inquisition effect, but they never fail to react to it. You'll see them in the Reading-Rooms making their plans and looking up Continental Bradshaws. By the way, we've taken some liberties with the decorations of the Hotel itself. I hope you'll approve.'

He ushered them into an enormously enlarged Terminus Hotel with passages and suites of public rooms, giving on to a further confusion of corridors and saloons. Through this maze men and women wandered and whispered, opening doors into hushed halls whence polite attendants reconducted them to continue their cycle of hopeless search elsewhere. Others, at little writing-tables in the suites of overheated rooms, made notes for honeymoons, as Satan had said, from the Bradshaws and steamer-folders, or wrote long letters which they posted furtively. Often, one of them would hurry out into the yard, with some idea of stopping a taxi which seemed to be carrying away a known face. And there were women who fished frayed correspondence out of their vanity-bags and read it with moist eyes close up to the windows.

'Everything is provided for—" according to their own imaginations," ' said Satan with some pride. 'Now I wonder what sort of test our man will——'

The seedy-looking person was writing busily when a page handed him a telegram. He turned, his face transfigured with joy, read, stared deeply at the messenger, and collapsed in a fit. Satan picked up the paper which ran :—' *Reconsidered. Forgive. Forget.*'

'Tck!' said Satan. 'That isn't quite cricket. But we'll see how he takes it.'

Well-trained attendants bore the snorting, inert body out, into a little side-room, and laid it on a couch. When Satan and the others entered they found a competent-looking doctor in charge.

' " He that sinneth—let him fall into the hands

of the Physician," ' said Satan. ' I wonder what choice he'll make? '

' Has he any? ' said Gabriel.

' Always. This is his last test. I can't say I exactly approve of the means, but if one interferes with one's subordinates it weakens initiative.'

' Do you mean to say, then, that that telegram was forged? ' cried Gabriel hotly.

' " There are lying spirits also," ' was the smooth answer. ' Wait and see.'

The man had been brought to with brandy and salvolatile. As he recovered consciousness he groaned.

' I remember now,' said he.

' You needn't ;' the doctor spoke slowly. ' We can take away your memory——'

' If—if,' said Satan, as one prompting a discourteous child.

' If you please,' the doctor went on, looking Satan full in the face, and adding under his breath:—' Am I in charge here or are You? " Who knoweth——" '

' If I please? ' the man stammered.

' Yes. If you authorise me,' the doctor went on.

' Then what becomes of *me*? '

' You'll be free from that pain at any rate. Do you authorise me? '

' I do not. I'll see you damned first.'

The doctor's face lit, but his answer was not cheering.

' Then you'd better go.'

' Go? Where in Hell to? '

' That's not my business. This room's needed for other patients.'

' Well, if that's the case, I suppose I'd better.' He rebuttoned his loosed flannel shirt all awry, rolled off the couch, and fumbled towards the door, where he turned and said thickly :—' Look here— I've got something to say—I think . . . 'I—I charge you at the Judgment—make it plain. Make it plain, y'know . . . I charge you——'

But whatever the charge may have been, it ended in indistinct mutterings as he went out, and the doctor followed him with the bottle of spirits that had clogged his tongue.

' There! ' said Satan. ' You've seen a full test for Ultimate Breaking Strain.'

' But now? ' Gabriel demanded.

' Why do you ask? '

' Because it was written : " *Even Evil itself shall pity*." '

' I told you long ago it would all be laid on me at last,' said Satan bitterly.

Here Azrael interposed, icy and resplendent. ' My orders,' said he, ' are to dismiss to the Mercy. Where is it? '

Satan put out his hand, but did not speak.

The Three waited in that casualty room, with its porcelain washstand beneath the glass shelf of bottles, its oxygen cylinders tucked under the leatherette couch, and its heart-lowering smell of spent anaesthetics—waited till the agony of waiting that shuffled and mumbled outside crept in and laid hold ; dimming, first, the lustre of their pinions ; bowing, next, their shoulders as the motes in the never-shifted sunbeam filtered through it and settled on them, masking, finally, the radiance of Robe, Sword, and very Halo, till only their eyes had light.

The groan broke first from Azrael's lips. 'How long?' he muttered. 'How long?' But Satan sat dumb and hooded under cover of his wings.

There was a flurry of hysterics at the opening door. An uniformed nurse half supported, half led a woman to the couch.

'But I can't! I mustn't!' the woman protested, striving to push away the hands. 'I— I've got an appointment. I've got to meet the 7.12. I have really. It's rather—you don't *know* how important it is. Won't you let me go? *Please*, let me go! If you'll let me go, I'll give you all my diamonds.'

'Just a little lay-down and a nice cup o' tea. I'll fetch it in a minute,' the nurse cooed.

'Tea? How do I know it won't be poisoned. It *will* be poisoned—I know it will. Let me go! I'll tell the police if you don't let me go! I'll tell—I'll tell! Oh God!—who can I tell? . . . Dick! Dick! They're trying to drug me! Come and help me! Oh, help me! It's *me*, Dickie!'

Presently the unbridled screams exhausted themselves and turned into choking, confidential, sobbing whispers: 'Nursie! I'm *so* sorry I made an exhibition of myself just now. I won't do it again—on my honour I won't—if you'll just let me—just let me slip out to meet the 7.12.

I'll be back the minute it's in, and then I'll be good. *Please*, take your arm away ! '

But it was round her already. The nurse's head bent down as she blew softly on the woman's forehead till the grey hair parted and the Three could see the Order for Life, where it had been first written. The body began to relax for sleep.

' Don't—don't be so silly,' she murmured. ' Well, only for a minute, then. You mustn't make me late for the 7.12, because—because . . . Oh ! Don't forget . . . " I charge you at the Judgment make it plain—I charge you——" ' She ceased. The nurse looked as Kalka'il had done, straight into Satan's eyes, and :—' Go ! ' she commanded.

Satan bowed his head.

There was a knock, a scrabbling at the door, and the seedy-looking man shambled in.

' Sorry ! ' he began, ' but I think I left my hat here.'

The woman on the couch waked and, turning, chin in hand, chuckled deliciously :—' What *does* it matter now, dear ? '

.   .   .   .   .   .

The Three found themselves whirled into the Void—two of them a little ruffled, the third somewhat apologetic.

' How did it happen ? ' Gabriel smoothed his plumes.

' Well—as a matter of fact, we were rather ordered away,' said Satan.

' Ordered away ? *I* ? ' Azrael cried.

' Not to mention your senior in the Service,'

Satan answered. ' I don't know whether you noticed that that nurse happened to be Ruya'il——'

' Then I shall take official action.' But Azrael's face belied his speech.

' I think you'll find she is protected by that ruling you have so lucidly explained to our young friend. It *all* turns upon the interpretation of " Who," you know.'

' Even so,' said Gabriel, ' that does not excuse the neck-and-crop abruptness—the cinema-like trick—of our—our expulsion.'

' I'm afraid, as the little girl said about her spitting at her nurse, that that was *my* invention. But, my Brothers '—the Prince of Darkness smiled—' did you *really* think that we were needed there much longer? '

AZRAEL'S COUNT

Lo! the Wild Cow of the Desert, her yeanling
    estrayed from her—
Lost in the wind-plaited sand-dunes—athirst in the
    maze of them.
Hot-foot she follows those foot-prints—the thrice-
    tangled ways of them.
Her soul is shut save to one thing—the love-quest
    consuming her.
Fearless she lows past the camp, men's fires affright
    her not.
Ranges she close to the tethered ones—the mares by
    the lances held.
Noses she softly apart the veil in the women's tent.
Next—withdrawn under moonlight, a shadow afar
    off—
Fades. Ere men cry, 'Hold her fast!' darkness
    recovers her.
She the love-crazed and forlorn, when the dogs
    threaten her
Only a side-tossed horn, as though a fly troubled her,
Shows she hath heard, till a lance in the heart of her
    quivereth.
—Lo, from that carcass aheap—where speeds the
    soul of it?
Where is the tryst it must keep? Who is her
    pandar? Death!

Men I dismiss to the Mercy greet me not willingly ;

*Crying, ' Why seekest Thou me first?   Are not my
    kin unslain? '*

*Shrinking aside from the Sword-edge, blinking the
    glare of it,*

*Sinking the chin in the neck-bone.   How shall that
    profit them?*

*Yet, among men a ten thousand, few meet me other-
    wise.*

*Yet, among women a thousand, one comes to me
    mistress-wise.*

*Arms open, breasts open, mouth open—hot is her
    need on her.*

*Crying, ' Ho Servant, acquit me, the bound by Love's
    promises!*

*Haste Thou!   He waits!   I would go!   Handle me
    lustily!'*

*Lo! her eyes stare past my wings, as things unbeheld
    by her,*

*Lo! her lips summonsing part.   I am not whom she
    calls.*

*Lo! My sword sinks and returns.   At no time she
    heedeth it*

*More than the dust of a journey, her garments brushed
    clear of it.*

*Lo! Ere the blood-rush has ceased, forward her soul
    rushes.*

*She is away to her tryst.   Who is her pandar?
    Death!*